"WE'RE GOING TOO FAST, NEIL...."

He blinked dazedly, then smiled with tender concern. "Whatever you say, darling. I've waited a long time for you. I can wait a little longer."

Gratefully Terry settled her head on his shoulder. His fingers combed through her hair, sending delicious tremors coursing through her. Shifting slightly, again he brushed his hand over the silver blond strands, smoothing them to form a veil over her breasts.

"You know who you look like?" He chuckled with pleasure. "Alice in Wonderland, who's just taken a bite of the magic mushroom."

Terry went icy with apprehension. Her ex-husband's exact words.... She grabbed Neil's wrists to force his hands from her breasts. "You seem to expect me to fall straight into your arms like an untried schoolgirl—when I merely gave in to a passing impulse!"

WELCOME TO...

SUPERROMANCES

A sensational series of modern love stories
from Worldwide Library.

Written by masters of the genre, these longer,
sensual and dramatic novels are truly in keeping
with today's changing life-styles. Full of intriguing
conflicts, the heartaches and delights of true love,
SUPERROMANCES are absorbing stories—
satisfying and sophisticated reading that lovers
of romance fiction have long been waiting for.

SUPERROMANCES

Contemporary love stories for the woman of today!

LOVE IN EXILE

VIVIAN CONNOLLY

A SUPERROMANCE FROM
WORLDWIDE

TORONTO · NEW YORK · LOS ANGELES · LONDON

Published May 1983

First printing March 1983

ISBN 0-373-70063-6

CHAPTER ONE

THE BELL on the street door jangled. Terry heard footsteps enter the outer office, then pause uncertainly as though someone were wondering whether to knock. She carefully laid her T square on the table beside the unfinished architect's drawing, suppressing the urge to slam the instrument down in irritation. She really did need a secretary out there. But of course that was out of the question. Next year. Maybe next year.

A lock of silver blond hair had slipped out of her broad barrette with its beaded Indian pattern. It tickled her nose, making her feel like sneezing. Impatiently she pushed it back into place and sidled out from behind the drafting table, pulling open the door to the outer office. "Yes?" she said. "Can I help you?"

The tall dark-haired man looked a little startled. He stared at her with a small half frown, as though she presented some kind of puzzle. Terry suddenly felt very conscious of the faded look of her old blue Levi's, the badly scuffed toes of her tooled leather boots. She looked defiantly up at the silent stranger, trying to remember where she might have seen him. His face looked vaguely familiar, with its high, slightly slanted cheekbones, its deep-set hazel eyes beneath jet-black winged eyebrows. He was wearing the standard Taos combination of jeans and plaid flannel shirt. But something told Terry it wasn't his usual costume. There was something too new about it, too neat—almost unlived in.

"Yes?" she said again. Her voice held a hint of challenge. "You look as though you have some kind of problem. Perhaps I can help you to solve it?"

"I sincerely hope you can." The stranger's puzzled frown deepened into a look of determined grimness. "I want to talk to your boss. My name's Neil Brewster. Please tell Mr. Morrison I want to see him."

A tiny smile tugged at the corner of Terry's lips. So that's what the puzzled look had been all about. Then he must be a stranger in town, probably a tourist. And yet, she could have sworn she'd seen him before. She felt an instant of panic. Perhaps she had seen him. Perhaps he was one of those hundreds of interchangeable faces that had glittered and shimmered around her in that other life, the life with Paul, the life she thought she had finally succeeded in putting behind her.

She banished the disturbing thought, forcing herself to speak briskly. "You're looking for Terry Morrison? You don't have to look any further. You're speaking to her."

The hazel eyes flickered a little, the only indication that he was surprised. The square, sharply angled jaw jutted a little more grimly. "I'm sorry. Nobody told me. I suppose your contractor was playing a little joke on a greenhorn.'' He didn't look sorry. He looked angry, almost outraged. "He was the person who told me where to find you. He said he could only quit working if you gave him instructions.''

Terry stared at him in amazement. "Quit working? Why should Gus Pickett quit working? You mean the Martinez house up on the mesa? Why, he's just about ready to pour the foundation.''

"I'm well aware of that. I've been watching him from my back window for the past few days. Thank God I went over this morning to take a closer look, or I wouldn't have realized what he was up to.''

Oh, dear, Terry thought. *Cecilia was right. She had a hunch there was going to be trouble. Why didn't I listen to her, sound out this man before we started building?* She tried to smile, but her lips felt stiff and lifeless. "You must be Leo's and Sandra's neighbor—the man who bought the old Martinez place. I've been meaning to come and see you. I gather you've done a good bit of renovation.''

"I've spent fifty thousand on the place above and beyond the purchase price, which was pretty outrageous for a house in such poor condition.''

"It was a little run-down." Terry wondered why she sounded so apologetic. If this obviously well-heeled stranger wanted to throw away his money, it really wasn't any of her business. "It's a gem of a house, all the same. Those first two rooms must date back to the 1840s, and every generation since then has built on at least one addition. I love these old rambling adobes—and you have that beautiful view out over the valley.''

She broke off abruptly, aware that her voice sounded nervous and breathless. Her praise of his house only seemed to be enraging the stranger further. Now he was positively glowering. "You're absolutely right. It has a beautiful view—in all directions. I spent a long time searching for it, that house and that view. And I don't intend to let anyone spoil it."

Terry felt the telltale pulse as it began to beat along her left temple. *Terry, you lily-livered milksop! Just because he's a man, and angry, that doesn't mean you have to start quivering with terror. . . .* She drew a deep breath, willing herself to keep her voice steady. "The people I'm building the new house for are Sandra and Leo Martinez. Leo's a grandson of old Eloy Martinez. When Eloy died and the rest of the family decided to sell the house, Leo chose to take his portion in land instead of money." She raised her eyes to the stranger's, absorbing his angry gaze without flinching. "But I'm sure you know all this. Bill Taylor, the real-estate agent, must have told you. You knew when you bought the house that you were going to have neighbors."

"Of course I knew I was going to have neighbors. I accepted that. I didn't particularly like it, but I had to accept it. I knew that the old man's grandson planned to build a house on it someday. But I didn't expect him to do it so soon. And naturally, seeing the old family house, I assumed he'd build something pretty much like it: traditional Spanish colonial, blending into the landscape—not this freakish monstrosity you're about to inflict on me."

Terry felt herself go very still inside. The blood began to burn in her veins. She welcomed the surge of anger. It gave her strength, the strength to fight for the things she believed in. "How do you know what that house is going to look like?" Her voice resounded with challenge. "I bet you haven't even looked at the blueprints."

"I don't have to see your blueprints. I've already seen a lot of your finished products. Bill Taylor pointed them out when he drove me around to look at some other old houses. That one down near Ranchos that looks like a cross between a barn and an airplane hangar. And the other one up near Llano Quemado, the one like a broken-down silo. 'Crimes against the landscape,' that's what he called them. He told me about the crazy things they were built with, refuse out of the dump like old tires and beer cans. That's the Morrison trademark, I gather—building blocks made of beer cans. The moment I saw them stacked up by the site this morning, I knew I had to stop this particular crime from being committed."

Terry glared back at him fiercely. "How long have you lived here in Taos? Only about two months—not even that long. And you dare to lay down the law to people like Leo Martinez, whose people have been here for more than three hundred years? I'm sure Leo loves that old house. But he knows he can't build one like it. He can't afford it. Nobody named Martinez can afford it. The only kind of person who can afford it is some rich Johnny-come-lately who thinks money can buy him the kind of history that old

Eloy's ancestors suffered and fought and died for."

She was pleased to see him look startled. "Oh, come now, aren't you exaggerating? A new adobe house can't be all that expensive. Not a big one like mine, of course, but a two-bedroom, maybe—just enough to start with. In that simple flat-roofed style, they could easily add on more rooms later."

"Do you happen to know the current price of adobe bricks? They're sixty cents apiece now. Which means a simple two-bedroom house would cost about fifty-five thousand. The house I'm doing for Leo and Sandra will work out at about twenty thousand less than that."

He looked sincerely astonished. "I had no idea adobes cost that much. No wonder my builder was so careful to save the bricks he took out when he enlarged my windows. But why is it so expensive? There's adobe mud all around us." His tense angry face relaxed in a rueful smile. "I ought to know, after all those times I got stuck in my driveway until I had the good sense to trade in my Continental for something with four-wheel drive."

His whole face changed when he smiled. The austere bleak look vanished. He looked almost boyish. Terry felt herself relaxing, found her own lips curving into an answering smile.

"It's not the raw material that costs so much. Like everything else these days, it's the time and labor. The adobes we use around here come from Ralph Mondragon's place down in Ranchos. You should go there sometime and see all the work and skill that goes into the process."

The puzzled look was back in his eyes again. "But all these new houses I see going up south of town. . . . Those people can't all be—what did you call them—rich Johnny-come-latelies?" He grinned at her a little sheepishly, making a joke of accepting her angry label.

Terry felt a surge of new enthusiasm. This man wasn't really the hidebound intransigent monster he'd seemed at first. If she really tried to explain her work to him, she was sure he'd respond with compassion and understanding. Eagerly she plunged into her explanation. "You know what those houses are made of? Cheap lumber and chicken wire covered with plaster. Sure, Leo and Sandra could afford one of those. I've built some of them myself, for people who like the old style and want a cheap copy. But Leo and Sandra aren't satisfied with a copy. They want the real thing, don't you see—the real thing or nothing. They don't have the money to buy the real thing from the past, so they're reaching toward the real thing of the future. Okay, so you don't like the beer cans. But you won't see the beer cans. They'll be heavily camouflaged with cement and plaster. Look, let me show you the blueprints. I've got another set right here in my office. Wait till you see the soft round curves I've designed, curves that repeat the lines of the hills behind them. And just try to imagine the gleam of the solar collector, like a frozen lake in the mountains in winter."

She came to a sudden halt, seeing his face grow rigid, knowing she had lost him. She knew just when it had happened—the second she'd said those fatal words, "solar collector."

"I'm afraid I'm just wasting your time, Miss Morrison," he said stiffly. "It's clear neither one of us is going to convince the other. I'll have to talk to this Leo Martinez himself. Perhaps, on a man-to-man basis, I can make him see reason."

Terry felt herself flushing. "I'm afraid that won't work, Mr. Brewster. Both Leo and Sandra have their hearts set on my design. I've incorporated a lot of their own ideas. They won't agree to settle for fake adobe."

"I'm not so sure of that. Anyway, I'm going to try to persuade them. Where can I contact this Leo Martinez? I think Bill said he was living in Albuquerque?"

"Yes, he works there during the week. He and Sandra come up here every weekend. I can give you his telephone number—" Terry's voice was reluctant "—but he travels a lot for his company. He may be away on a business trip."

"I'll check that out for myself. The number, please." Neil Brewster's smile was grim and polite. No trace now of the wistful boyish look she'd glimpsed for that fleeting moment.

Terry knew Leo's number by heart. She'd dialed it often enough during the weeks she'd been working on plans for the house. She scribbled it quickly on a piece of scrap paper, then checked her address file for his business number.

"Thank you," Neil said brusquely. "I'll see if I can talk to him this morning. Meanwhile, please tell your contractor to cease operations."

Terry stared at him, wide-eyed. "I'll do no such thing! Are you crazy? Gus Pickett has got the work all planned out for his men. They've postponed two other jobs to do this one for Sandra and Leo. It's got to be livable by the first of July, when they both start their summer vacations."

The grim determined look returned to Neil Brewster's chin. The deep-set hazel eyes seemed to turn a few shades darker. "Miss Morrison, you don't seem to understand me. I will not let you build that house next to mine. If necessary, I'll have to take legal action. I've already asked one of my lawyers to check the local building regulations."

Terry compressed her lips firmly, fighting the impulse to order him out of her office. "Mr. Brewster, I'm a qualified architect. All my designs are fully up to code—no matter how much they offend your archaic aesthetic standards."

Brewster started to make an angry retort, then seemed to think better of it. "If I can get hold of Martinez," he said in a calm level voice, "we can settle all this without dragging in any lawyers. I'll ask him to phone you and let you know his decision. Meanwhile, as they say around here, *hasta luego*."

He turned abruptly and opened the door to the street. Terry saw him cross in front of her big picture window and climb into a mud-spattered red Blazer that was parked by the dusty curb in front of her battered Ford pickup. Still fuming with irritation, she watched him drive off. The arrogance of the man! Just because he was rich, he thought he owned the whole landscape! And the people in it, too. A snap of his fingers would make them all dance to his tune.

Impulsively she stepped out the front door of the office and stood there under the wooden *portal* that shaded the sidewalk from the hot direct rays of the bright June sun. To her left, up at the end of North Pueblo Road, the blue purple peaks of the Sangre de Cristo mountains emerged in soaring splendor above a lush green mass of tall cottonwood trees. A string of flat-roofed shops and office buildings marched toward her down both sides of the town's main street, their softly rounded walls running the gamut of earth tones, from palest cream through deep rosy tan to chocolate brown. Across the street to her right, the terra-cotta bulk of a new bank building sparkled in the sunlight, its second-story terrace looming over its low-lying neighbors like the well-buttressed fort of a Spanish colonial governor. The familiar beloved sight of her favorite village strengthened Terry's resolve. *Here's one girl who won't dance, Mr. Brewster.* That house would be built, just the way she'd designed it. Leo and Sandra would stand just as firm as she had. As for that threat of the law—just let him try it. "I've already asked one of my lawyers...." Did he think he could frighten her, dangling the boast of having his own private legal stable?

No doubt he thought she couldn't afford her own lawyer. She remembered the hazel eyes assessing the shabby front office, noting the telltale lack of an office secretary. She felt a sudden qualm in the pit of her stomach as she remembered the tiny balance in last month's bank statement.

He was certainly right in thinking she didn't have

money. But that didn't mean she was helpless. She looked at the sun again, making a quick calculation. It must be almost noon. David Quayle would have finished his morning stint of painting. It was time to go down and see him, talk to him and Cecilia. If worse came to worst, he could help teach Neil Brewster a lesson about how little one's bank account mattered here in Taos.

CHAPTER TWO

TERRY PARKED the old blue pickup beside the three-foot adobe wall that surrounded the Janus Gallery. She jumped out of the truck and paused for a moment, surveying the long low adobe building with its shady *portal* supported by hand-carved corbels and weathered wooden pillars. She felt a small thrill of pride as she noted how naturally the new extension flowed from the end of one wing of the eighty-year-old house. It could have passed for part of the original building, except for the big six-foot windows, set at an in-tilting angle in the thick red brown walls, inviting the art-buying public to come and inspect the treasures within.

So you see, Mr. Brewster, I'm pretty good at Spanish colonial, too. You wouldn't call this a crime against the landscape. She bit her lip in chagrin, surprised that his scornful words should have such power to hurt her. What did she care for that arrogant stranger's opinion about her work?

She walked up the flagstone path that wound between the waist-high piñons and junipers and peered in the window that formed the top third of the heavy hand-carved door. Without pausing to use the wrought-iron knocker, she pushed the door open and stepped inside, standing still for a moment to let her eyes adjust to the change from brilliant sunshine to the shadowy entrance hall of the gallery.

"Cecilia?" she called, and heard an answering shout from outside in the courtyard. She made her way past the roomful of paintings and into the long narrow kitchen-cum-dining room that linked the gallery wing with the Quayles' living quarters. A pair of glass-paned doors opened into the courtyard. Cecilia Quayle was standing outside by an oilcloth-covered table, gingerly stripping the tough outer skins from a panful of roasted green chilies. Glints of sunlight flashed from her long black hair, which she always wore loose to her waist, instead of piling it up on her head in a style like Terry's. As usual, she was dressed in a bright cotton ankle-length skirt and wide-sleeved tunic, made to her own design from remnants of drapery material. A stranger might have supposed the style had come in with the hippie invasion back in the sixties, but Terry knew it dated back further than that—to Cecilia's childhood in one of the artistic households so typical of Taos.

Cecilia's grandfather, Conrad Rampion, had come to the town in the 1890s. He had been one of a circle that had formed around the original nucleus of artists who had laid the foundations for the little town's fame as an artist's colony. The local legend said that Bert Phillips's wagon, bound for Denver, had broken a wheel just outside Taos. In the process of getting it mended, Phillips had fallen in love with the sleepy old Spanish village and settled down there. The artistic influx he started continued all through the

1920s and 1930s, drawing painters like Léon Gaspard and Nicolai Fechin, musicians like Stokowski, writers like D.H. Lawrence and Robinson Jeffers— giving the town the aura of creative endeavor that now enabled it to support more than eighty art galleries.

Conrad Rampion, though not as well known as other Taos School artists, had managed to establish an excellent reputation as a painter. His shrewd business sense, plus helpful advice from some stock-broker friends he'd left behind in New York, had enabled him to live sumptuously by Taos standards. He had supervised the building of the Rampion compound, where he'd reigned as paterfamilias in a big rambling adobe, surrounded by smaller houses inhabited by six of his seven children and their families.

The seventh child, Joseph Rampion, had struck out for himself, declaring that all this family closeness was smothering his own painterly talents. Old Conrad, beaming approvingly at this demonstration of independence, had provided him with a house far beyond what was then the outskirts of Taos and waited with pleasure for Joseph to add new luster to the name of Rampion.

Unfortunately, young Joseph had inherited neither his father's knack as an artist nor his business acumen. Still, by dint of hard work in the studio and the efforts of his wife, Carla, in the vegetable garden, he had managed to raise a family of four lively children, consoling himself with the thought of how privileged his offspring were to grow up amid such a wealth of natural beauty, in spite of material hardships.

The offspring, predictably, did not share his enthusiasm. All of them—three boys and one girl—had left the small town as soon as they'd finished high school and struck out for the big city, winding up in Dallas, New York and Denver. Joseph and Carla had glided into tranquil old age, the Rampion name anointing them with the status of Taos landmarks. They had died two years before, within a week of each other.

That was when their daughter Cecilia had come back to Taos, bringing with her a husband, David Quayle, and a three-year-old son, Jamie—a name quickly transformed by their Spanish-speaking neighbors to Diegito. Most Taoseños, observing the run-down state of the old Rampion adobe, assumed the young family would sell it and go back to New York, where David had just begun his career as a lawyer. But the Quayles, it seemed, had other ideas. Within a matter of weeks the crumbling old house had become the Janus Gallery, and Cecilia had settled back into the local artistic ambience as if she had never left it.

Now she was shoving aside the pan of chilies, wiping her hands on her skirt and throwing her arms around Terry in an affectionate hug. "Sweetie!" she cried. "It seems like months since you've been here. Why don't you come by more often? We've really missed you."

"I've missed you, too, Cecilia. You know you and David are two of my favorite people. But I've been really busy the past few weeks. Besides, I didn't want to interrupt David's painting. How is it going these days? Has he finished that gorgeous one of the mountain lion?''

Cecilia looked startled. ''Oh, yes, of course. He finished that ages ago—finished and sold it. He's off on a new kick now—really fantastic.'' Her tanned oval face glowed with a proud possessive smile. ''Really, Terry, that husband of mine is turning into a dynamite painter. He's into the Navaho legends— terrific juicy ideas—but I really can't describe them; you've got to see for yourself.'' Not giving her time to protest, Cecilia seized Terry's hand and pulled her across the courtyard and down to the former stable that was now David's studio.

David turned away from his easel when he heard the door open, an abstracted look in his eyes; he was still absorbed in the canvas before him. When he caught sight of Terry, his concentration relaxed. A delighted smile spread over his round rosy face, just saved from being cherubic by its sharp planes.

''Well, look who's here! It's great to see you, Terry.'' He plunged his brush into a jar of turpentine, then stood back from the easel, assessing the giant canvas through narrowed eyes. ''I know I can count on you for a candid opinion. How does this thing strike you? Is it any good?''

''Of course it's good. It's terrific!'' Cecilia sounded indignant at his disparaging tone. ''Look, Terry, isn't it great?''

''Quiet, woman. I asked for a candid opinion.'' David's nose wrinkled up in a teasing smile as he

slipped a fond arm around Cecilia's waist. Terry felt
a tiny ripple of envy. What a warm close marriage
Cecilia and David had. The wordless communication
between them seemed to grow deeper with every passing year. If only things could have been that way with
Paul. Perhaps if she'd been less self-centered, abandoned her own career, as Cecilia had, and devoted
herself to her husband.... A sudden image assailed
her: Paul, excited and laughing, sketching his plans
for the next ambitious film, surrounded by a circle of
admiring faces—and herself, ignored in a corner,
fighting down a tide of growing resentment....

She was appalled at the power the memory still had
to hurt her. What was she doing, raking up all those
dead coals? It seemed to have something to do with
meeting Neil Brewster. But why on earth should that
be? He and Paul looked nothing like each other.

And yet, there was a likeness. They both had that
air of tremendous self-assurance, expecting everyone
else to fall in with their plans without question—

"You see what I'm driving at, don't you?"
David's anxious voice cut into her ruminations. "It's
called *Mother Earth and Father Sky*—you know, the
Navaho myth of creation. But maybe I made it too
simple, not subtle enough?"

"Oh, no, David. I really like it—on my first impression at least. Give me a minute or two to really
absorb it." Feeling guilty for her lapse of attention,
Terry forced herself to concentrate on the painting.
At first sight it did seem simple—a spare, almost
abstract landscape, using the rich earthy colors of the
Southwestern palette—burnt umber, burnt sienna,

yellow ocher. A wide vista of valleys and mountains stretched out toward a distant horizon. Then slowly, other shapes began to emerge. The mountains became a woman's breast, belly and thighs. The lowering desert sky pressed down on her in a cosmic embrace of lovers. The sense of vast creative forces flowing together set a tiny prickle of warmth stirring somewhere deep in Terry's body. She turned to the painter, her eyes alive with wonder.

"Oh, yes, now I see it, David. I think it's magnificent. The way those bodies are buried in the painting, then slowly become visible and almost overwhelming! It's really great. I had no idea you were—" She stopped abruptly, afraid of hurting his feelings.

"Go ahead and say it, Terry!" Cecilia was grinning at her triumphantly. "Nobody did. I know what they say here in Taos—that he's only a rank beginner, hasn't had enough training. What do they know about it? I've had years of training myself, but I can't paint one-tenth as well as he can. And this breakthrough is just the beginning. David's got lots of other ideas. He's already done a great sketch of *Changing Woman*. Where is that one, David? Show it to Terry."

"Oh, yes," Terry said. "Please let me see it."

David grinned at them both, obviously pleased by the two women's admiration. "Maybe after lunch. One masterpiece is enough for this morning. Right now I'm so hungry I could eat a Gila monster. You're staying for lunch, aren't you, Terry?"

"Of course you are," Cecilia said briskly. "You know you can never resist my *chiles rellenos*. I'm sure that's the reason you finally decided to favor us with your presence. Your ESP must have told you what I was making.''

Terry felt guilty, as though she was here under false pretenses. ''I'd love to stay for lunch. But I really came here on business. I'd better tell you right now what it's all about. I hate to ask you, David, especially when you're so absorbed in your painting. . . .''

David flashed her a knowing grin. ''Come on, Terry, don't feel so guilty. I can already guess what you came for. You want some more legal advice?''

''I know it's an imposition, but I really don't know anyone else here to turn to. There's always Steve Galliard, of course, but I still owe him most of his fee for that case last year.''

''And how much do *we* owe you for the new addition?'' Cecilia's dark eyes flashed with determination. ''David would love the chance to pay off some of that debt. Wouldn't you, David? Besides, it's not just a matter of dollars and cents. Friends look out for each other, here in Taos. That's the only way that most of us can survive.''

''But one of the reasons David came to Taos was because he'd decided that practicing law was boring. You've worked so hard to get away from that life. Why am I always dragging you back into it?''

David made a dismissive gesture. ''We knew when we came here I'd have to take a few cases now and again. That's why I went to the trouble of passing the bar exam in Santa Fe. Besides, I don't think being a lawyer is all that awful. The stuff I did in New York did get pretty boring, but I never passed up the chance to defend a good-looking woman.'' He leered at her genially. Then his expression turned serious. ''Come on, Terry, spit it out. What sort of monkey business are you up to this time?''

Terry heaved a sigh of resignation. ''You know the house I'm building for Leo and Sandra Martinez up on the mesa? Well, it seems they've got a new neighbor who's trying to stop me.''

''I knew it!'' Cecilia exclaimed. ''Didn't I tell you? Bill Taylor told me about that big-city dude. He said the deal almost fell through because of that one strip of land that the family hung on to.''

''I remember your telling me that. I suppose I really should have sounded him out.''

David stirred restlessly, cocking a quizzical eyebrow at Cecilia. ''Come on, squaw. Why don't you get back to your kitchen and let Terry tell me her story without all these interruptions?'' The fondness in David's eyes took the sting from his words. Cecilia shot him a glance of mock irritation, then put her arm around Terry's shoulders and started pulling her out the studio door.

''Come on out with me, both of you, and watch me stuff the chilies. That way I can hear all about it and still feed this ravenous beast before he goes completely berserk.''

As they made their way over to the courtyard, David looked around as though searching for something. ''Where's Gito?'' he asked. ''Has he already had his lunch?''

''Gito's off on a picnic.'' Cecilia spoke hurriedly, skimming over an apparently unwelcome subject.

"He and Pedro are toasting hot dogs down by the
Rio Grande."

The barest trace of a frown ruffled David's forehead. "He's off with El Zopilote again? Do you really think that's such a terrific idea?"

"Look, David, we've already been through this.
Why don't you trust my judgment? Pedro Lopez is
harmless. And he's awfully fond of Gito. Surely you
can see that, just looking at them together."

"I can see Pedro's fond of Gito's hot dogs. They
must add a luxurious touch to his usual diet."

Terry felt a twinge of alarm as the sudden half
quarrel broke the usual serenity between the couple.
She knew Pedro Lopez by sight—a small gnarled old
man in an ancient ragged black suit who spend most
of his time sunning himself in the plaza. The natives
seemed to regard him with a mixture of contempt and
awe. He was usually referred to by one of his several
nicknames—El Loco, the Crazy One, or El Zopilote,
the Buzzard. He seemed a strange companion for
five-year-old Gito. But Cecilia, of course, must have
known him from childhood. It was strange that
David contested her opinion. He was usually so
proud of his wife's close involvement with the Spanish side of Taos life—a side from which most Anglos
were politely excluded.

And that grudging remark about Pedro's fondness
for hot dogs. It wasn't like David to balk at the sharing of food. But perhaps the gallery's slender income
couldn't keep up with galloping grocery prices. Why
hadn't she thought to ask how things were going?
Was she so wrapped up in her own troubles that she

couldn't take time to find out how her friends were
doing?

She tried to frame a question that would tell her
what she wanted to know without prying too deeply
into the Quayles' private finances. But David didn't
give her the chance to ask it. As Cecilia deftly stuffed
the green chilies with cheddar cheese, then dipped
them in an egg-and-flour batter to prepare them for
the pan of deep fat, he shot his own questions at
Terry, coaxing out all the details of Neil Brewster's
visit that morning—his angry rejection of her architectural designs, his plan to call Leo Martinez, his
ominous threat of some kind of legal action.

"Of course, this may all come to nothing," she
concluded. "But I hate the thought of his launching
the same kind of attack on Leo and Sandra. Of
course, I know they'll stand firm—"

"Are you really sure of that?" Cecilia asked.

Terry turned to her in surprise. "Why, of course
they will. They love the house I've designed. They've
put as much of themselves into it as I have." Her surprise turned into alarm as she saw the brooding look
on Cecilia's face. "You don't really think he'll get
them to change their minds?"

"I know they like the house, Terry." Cecilia kept
her eyes fixed on the chilies, as though reluctant to let
Terry read her thoughts. "But part of the reason they
like it is because they don't have very much money
for building. This Brewster, from what Bill said, is
stinking rich. He was offering all sorts of bait for
that last strip of land—even offered to trade an expensive lot down in Talpa, where land costs twice as

much as it does up there on the mesa. If he renewed that offer—maybe threw in some extra money to sweeten the deal—"

"Leo would never agree. He wants to live on the land that has always belonged to his family." But Terry felt a tiny quiver of doubt. "Still, I suppose if the money were really attractive...."

Cecilia sighed softly, looking across at David with a rueful half smile. "Money is pretty important to a young couple just getting started. Of course, for some of us, ideals are worth more than money. But I couldn't blame Leo and Sandra if they felt different. That might really be the solution after all. They could still have your house but have it built down in Talpa."

"But that house was planned for this site, that very spot up on the mesa. That's the whole point of it; don't you see?"

"I think I know what's bugging you, Terry." David's eyes were warm and approving. "You don't like this Brewster person calling the shots. I really don't like it, either. I hate being pushed around by people with money." He paused for a moment, his forehead creased in thought. "That name rings some kind of bell—oh, yes, I remember. I ran across a guy named Neil Brewster back in New York. But this couldn't be the same one. That guy was a kind of crusader, a real Ralph Nader type, taking big firms to court on behalf of consumers. He was challenging some of the real heavyweights—Olympia Tires, for instance. He filed a big lawsuit against them just about the time Cecilia and I left the city."

"That couldn't be this Neil Brewster," Terry said quickly. "This man doesn't give a damn for the rights of consumers. All he's concerned about is his own comfort. Besides, he's obviously loaded down with money. Consumer crusaders aren't usually very wealthy."

"Strangely enough, this one was. He inherited a hunk of the Brewster railroad millions. Maybe the guy had some kind of guilty conscience—trying to make amends for the crimes of the Brewster robber barons." The thoughtful frown faded as David dismissed the idea. "Still, it's not very likely that this could be the same Brewster. Like you say, he wouldn't be into harassing a poor young couple."

"Or a poor young architect, either." Cecilia grinned companionably at Terry. "Come on, people, let's eat. The chilies are ready."

David pulled up some chairs. They sat down at the patio table and started eating, washing down the spicy food with some frosty iced tea. Just as Terry was cutting into her second chili, she heard the ring of the phone inside the house. Her fork froze in midair as Cecilia jumped up and ran quickly into the kitchen. She laid down the chili untasted, disturbed by the uneasy hammering of her heart. "I'm sure that call is for me," she said to David. "I told my answering service I'd be down here. Maybe it's Leo Martinez. Maybe Brewster's managed to contact him."

Her hunch was confirmed by the worried look on Cecilia's face. "It's Gus Pickett for you, Terry. I'm afraid it sounds like trouble."

David followed her into the house and watched intently as she picked up the receiver. A puzzled look spread over her face as she listened. "Mr. Brewster's attorney? He did *what*? I'm sorry, Gus. Can you talk a little louder? We must have a bad connection."

She listened a minute longer, then turned to David with horror-filled eyes. "It's Gus Pickett, my contractor. He's up near the building site. He says Neil Brewster's lawyer is there with some kind of injunction."

"Here, let me have that phone. Hi, Gus, this is David Quayle. Will you read that injunction to me?" He listened for several minutes, then heaved a sigh of disgusted resignation. "I guess you'll have to obey it. No more work on the house today. I'll go right down to the courthouse and see what I can do about getting it lifted. With any luck, we can get a court hearing tomorrow. Tell me again the name of the judge who issued the order." He looked up at Cecilia, who had followed them into the house and was watching them both with questioning eyes. "Cordova? Which Cordova? Vicente or Charlie? Oh, yeah? You're sure of that?

"The judge is Charlie Cordova," he told Cecilia. "What do you think? How are the prospects?"

"The prospects are perfect." Cecilia's anxious look gave way to a mischievous smile. She held two fingers up in a jubilant V sign.

David nodded at her and returned to his phone conversation. "Don't worry about a thing, Gus. By tomorrow noon you're going to be back in business."

He put the phone down and looked at Cecilia and Terry. "Your new friend doesn't waste any time. Too bad Gus has to lose a day's work. We'd better get Leo or Sandra to come up from Albuquerque. Why don't you try to call them while I do my stuff at the courthouse?"

"Will it really be all right, David? You're not just saying this to make me feel good? It's really pretty scary, being challenged by Mr. Brewster's high-priced lawyers."

David looked at her blankly. "What's all this, Terry? Don't you trust me? I know I'm only a low-priced lawyer, but—"

"Oh, David, you know I don't mean it that way. I'm sure you're as good as anyone this awful Brewster could hire. It's just— Well, you've said it yourself a lot of times. Money talks in the courtroom."

David's face turned grim. "I'm sure Mr. Brewster thinks that's what's going to happen. What he doesn't know is that we've got a secret weapon." An impish gleam twinkled deep in his eyes. "He doesn't know about Taos-style EFP."

"ESP?" said Terry blankly. "What has that got to do—"

"No, Terry," interrupted Cecilia, "this is EFP. That stands for Extended Family Protection. Come on, now, let's try to call Leo and Sandra. And don't look so worried, sweetie. Things will work out just fine when we get to that courtroom tomorrow."

CHAPTER THREE

TERRY CAST A QUICK GLANCE at her watch as she swung her pickup into the parking lot behind the county courthouse. Five minutes past nine already! David had said to be there at 8:45. She should have guessed her decrepit alarm clock would choose this important morning to finally abandon its painful efforts.

She jumped quickly out of the truck, her long slim legs carrying her swiftly toward the entrance. Her coil of silver blond hair gleamed bright in the sunlight, enhancing the classical lines of her oval face, sharpened this morning by tension. Running up the courthouse steps, she pulled open the big wooden door and hurried across the lobby, her clear blue eyes anxiously searching for David. He was probably inside the courtroom, annoyed by her lateness—and Leo, too, and the county building inspector—

When she saw the tall broad-shouldered figure looming before her, she tried, too late, to check her headlong pace. If he hadn't reached out and caught her by the shoulders, she would have careered straight into Neil Brewster.

"Good morning, Miss Morrison." The self-assured voice was deeper than she remembered.

"You seem to be very eager to see our little argument decided."

He was still holding her by the shoulders, examining her at arm's length as though trying to gauge her feelings. He looked more citified today in a charcoal-gray suit of some silky material.

"It may be little to you. It isn't to me." She jerked away quickly, not wanting him to know how much more complex those feelings were than simple anger. The anger was certainly there, but the strength of his grip had aroused some other quite different feelings—a sudden warmth in her veins, a sense of unwilling pleasure in being held.

She reached out blindly, and seized the handle of the door to the courtroom, then turned back to him, stirred by a tardy tremor of compunction. "I apologize," she said primly, "for almost knocking you down a moment ago. I was afraid I was going to be late." Her strangely muddled thoughts regained their accustomed clearness. She looked up at him in surprise. "But you're not in the courtroom, either. Does that mean the hearing hasn't begun yet?"

He was looking down at her with a little half smile. A part of her mind observed the interesting fact that there were dark brown flecks in the hazel eyes this morning. Another part of her mind brushed away the observation as irrelevant nonsense.

"Nothing is happening yet. Anyway, your presence isn't really required. I'm sure David Quayle can say everything there is to be said on your side of the question."

His offhand manner made Terry bristle. Did he

mean to imply that there wasn't much to be said on her side of the question? "You've met Mr. Quayle, then?" she asked.

"Yes, I talked to him earlier this morning. A pleasant surprise, finding an old acquaintance so far from New York—even when he turns out to be my opponent."

"You knew David in New York?" A kaleidoscope of questions tumbled through Terry's mind. Was this really the ardent crusader David had mentioned? Then why was he here in Taos? And why was he fighting against her when they should be working together for the beleaguered consumers? "Are you really *that* Neil Brewster?" She tried to sound calm, but the words came out in a harsh accusing tone that surprised her. The tanned, sharply planed face looked a little puzzled. But before he could answer, Terry felt David's hand on her shoulder, tugging her urgently into the courtroom.

Terry looked down from the top of the tiers of spectator seats banked along two sides of the big square courtroom. The judge, apparently, had just taken his place on the dais. Leo Martinez, wearing jeans, boots and a western-style shirt with a bolo tie, was already seated at the long narrow table below the judge's rostrum. A man in a dark gray pin-striped suit was sharing the table. Terry knew he must be Neil Brewster's lawyer.

A handful of people watched from those seats above the legal arena. One of them was Cecilia. She turned and beckoned to Terry. David gave her a little push in his wife's direction, then went over to the long wooden table to take his place beside Leo.

Terry sank into the seat beside Cecilia. Her friend, wearing a long flowered skirt today, pressed her hand in welcome. Her eyes were bright with excitement. "Did David tell you?" she whispered. "Your neighbor turned out to be the real Neil Brewster." She stared at the gray-suited man who had just joined his lawyer at the table below them. "You didn't tell us he was so good-looking. After all this is over we'll have to invite him to dinner. Now that we're out of the rat race, it's kind of fun to talk about New York."

Watching Cecilia gaze admiringly toward Neil Brewster, Terry felt a little tug of resentment. This man was her enemy. How could Cecilia forget that? Her praise of Neil Brewster's good looks seemed like a kind of betrayal.

And yet, she thought, still following Cecilia's gaze, she had to admit the man really was handsome. Even in his citified clothes, he exuded an aura of rugged power. She found herself wondering what he would look like on horseback. Her imagination flashed a sudden image: herself riding beside him over the mesa, the wind streaming through their hair, his strong muscular thighs gripping a plunging stallion....

As if she had sent him a signal, he turned around and scanned the spectators' faces. His gaze met hers. Their eyes interlocked for a moment. His blank bored face lighted up with a smile of amused recognition.

Terry dropped her eyes quickly. That supercilious man with that smug triumphant smile all over his face! He clearly regarded her as a helpless lamb about to be led to the slaughter.

She resolutely ignored him and kept her thoughts fixed on the courtroom proceedings. David was questioning the county building inspector, eliciting the assurance that he'd examined the plans Terry had drawn up for Leo and Sandra and had found that they fully conformed to county standards. Then Gus Pickett, taking his place on the stand, gave his own testimonial to Terry's unusual designs and complained about his work being interrupted by the injunction, pointing out that in this high-altitude climate, only four months of the year were good for building.

Terry looked at Judge Cordova, hoping Gus's words about local unemployment were meeting with a sympathetic reception. But the judge's face was impassive. His shrewd dark eyes showed he was listening intently but gave no sign of his personal reaction.

Now Gus was dismissed, giving way to Leo Martinez. Under David's skillful questioning, he launched into a panegyric of some of the special features of Terry's design—the solar-heating collector, designed to cut fuel bills by fifty to sixty percent, the building blocks made of beer cans, providing inexpensive walls as thick and strong as adobe.

Terry found herself glowing with pleasure as Leo stepped down from the stand. She cast a swift glance at Neil Brewster. Surely he must be impressed, hearing from Leo's mouth all the technical points he'd refused to let her explain the day before in her office. But he was staring straight ahead, giving as little indication of what he was thinking as the judge up on his bench, now deeply absorbed in examining some legal papers.

She was surprised and chagrined at how disappointed she felt at his lack of response. Really, this was too stupid. What did it matter what the man thought of her work? The only opinion that mattered now was the judge's. She turned to Cecilia abruptly, not wanting her friend to see her staring at Brewster. "Wasn't that marvelous, the things Leo said about how much he loved the house? They really do care so much, he and Sandra. They'll be terribly disappointed if that awful man down there wins a judgment against them."

Cecilia was smiling broadly. "That's not going to happen, Terry. That awful man doesn't know what he's got himself into. Whether he likes it or not, he's going to be seeing a lot of you this summer."

"Not if I can help it," Terry said grimly. "The less I see of that self-centered boor, the better."

"He may turn out to be very nice once you get to know him." An impish gleam appeared in Cecilia's eyes. The look was familiar to Terry—all too familiar. She'd seen it often before, each time she'd been invited to meet "this new man in town who's just dying to know you." She'd brushed off the invitations without going into the reasons for her lack of interest. Even now, after five years, the failure with Paul still had the power to hurt her. She saw now how blindly she'd stumbled into that marriage, not understanding Paul's motives, thinking he was as much in love with her as she was with him. A fantastic future had seemed to stretch before them: Paul Fontaine, the brilliant new film director; Teresa Morrison, the rising young architect. Paul's sudden indifference, coming so quickly after the wedding, had shocked and depressed her. But the thing that had shaken her even more deeply was the obsessive way she had continued to love him—despite all his coldness, his other women, his openly flaunted contempt for her looks and talent.

When he had finally asked for a divorce, she had been utterly crushed, had fled from Los Angeles in heartbroken anguish like a wounded animal seeking a place to hide, a place as different as possible from the glittering Hollywood world of the man she was still so shamefully in love with. She had found some peace from that torment in Taos—Taos and work, hard work. Work was her anodyne, her salvation, her defense against all those painful memories. She clung to it blindly as she'd once clung to Paul, shying away from any intrusion that threatened the precarious peace it represented.

She shook her head brusquely, intent on stemming the rising tide of memory. To her relief, she saw Neil Brewster's lawyer rise and approach the bench. She signaled to Cecilia for silence, thankful she had once more escaped that particular conversation, and forced herself to listen intently while the man in the pin-striped suit spoke eloquently of his client's financial interests, the affront to local tradition, the likelihood of rapid deterioration, constituting a threat to both aesthetic values and public safety. Though she knew he was wrong in condemning her unorthodox building materials, she had a sinking feeling in her stomach. The lawyer seemed so sure of his case, reeling off precedents and quotations. Surely he must be right in assuming the weight of the law would come down on his side.

Sick with trepidation, she watched Neil Brewster step up on the stand, adding his calm support to the lawyer's allegations. When the pinstripe-suited man had finished his string of questions, the judge leaned over to speak to Neil Brewster himself. For one panicky moment Terry was sure he was about to congratulate him on winning the case. She told herself sternly not to be foolish and strained her ears to hear Judge Cordova's voice, its low musical tone tinged with a slight Spanish accent.

"And what is your occupation, Mr. Brewster?"

The dark-haired man hesitated a moment. Finally he murmured, "Currently, I'm a writer."

"Could you explain that more fully, Mr. Brewster? What kind of material do you write? Fiction? Nonfiction?"

Brewster looked startled. "Nonfiction, of course—mostly newspaper articles. However, I've just begun work on a book."

The judge's eyes sparked with interest. "An historical work, Mr. Brewster? A book about Taos? That's why you chose to take up residence here?"

"No, nothing like that." The words seemed to come out slowly, as though the man on the stand was reluctant to reveal some kind of secret. "Actually, it's a book on the power of big corporations—the way they manipulate and endanger the consumer."

"I see." The judge nodded. "Does this book have something to do with architecture?"

"Architecture?" Brewster stared at him blankly. "No. I don't plan to include any material on that subject."

"You are not, then, a student of architecture?"

"Of course not." Brewster's startled tone had turned to irritation. "I've never claimed to know anything about architecture."

Judge Cordova nodded again, his eyes still bright with what seemed like sympathetic interest. "And yet you dispute Miss Morrison's qualifications? You've heard Mr. Quayle describe them—a master's degree, five years of successful practice?"

Brewster drew a deep breath. When he spoke again, his voice was calm and respectful. "Your honor, I'm speaking only as a layman. I'm not disputing Miss Morrison's competence. Some of her designs seem to be highly ingenious. I believe they might fit in very well out where she came from. California is full of unorthodox architecture. But this isn't California; this is Taos, a place with its own long and distinguished architectural tradition. That's one of the things that attracts newcomers to Taos— the sense of history they find here, embodied in its gracious old houses."

The judge lifted a questioning eyebrow. "You're a scholar, then, Mr. Brewster? An expert on our New Mexico traditions?"

This time there was no mistaking the ironic note in that musical voice. Terry found herself bristling a little. Was it fair to bait him this way? She caught

herself up, surprised that she should be feeling so
sympathetic. Surely she should be delighted with the
judge's subtle challenge?

She saw Neil Brewster's chin stiffen in defiance,
then relax again as he answered the judge's question.
It was obviously taking considerable effort for him to
maintain his careful dispassionate tone. "I'm not a
scholar, your honor. But I have done a lot of
reading. I've been particularly interested in the colonial period in Taos. I've read quite a lot about the
sixteenth-century Spanish settlers—the soldiers who
came here with Alvorado and Onate, the Franciscan
fathers who founded the pueblo mission. I'm fasci-
nated by their persistence and courage—particularly
the way DeVargas came back in the 1690s after the
settlers had been expelled by the Indians."

Terry was surprised at the extent of Neil Brewster's
knowledge. Here only two months, and he seemed to
know as much about the town's history as she did.
But it wasn't only the knowledge that impressed her.
It was the feeling as well, the deep admiration in his
voice as he spoke of those early settlers. If that was
what the Martinez house meant to him, perhaps he
was right in resenting her modern impingement.

Hey, wait a minute, she told herself brusquely.
*This Neil Brewster is awfully persuasive. He's almost
conned you into agreeing with his hidebound ideas.
If he has that effect on the judge, you'll really be in
hot water.*

She looked anxiously at Judge Cordova. He had
dismissed Neil Brewster now and turned back to the
waiting lawyers. "Gentlemen," said the musical

voice, "do either of you have anything further to say?"

Terry caught her breath, her eyes on David. *Say something brilliant,* she prayed. *Something to counterbalance that eloquent speech of Neil Brewster's.* But David was shaking his head. So was the other lawyer. The judge took a minute to check the documents on the desk before him. Then he looked out at the courtroom.

"Very well. The court is ready to rule." The light tap of his gavel echoed through the emptiness of the courtroom. "The injunction is dissolved. Mr. Pickett will be allowed to go on with the building. Next case, please, Mr. Williams."

Cecilia's hand clasped Terry's and squeezed it. "I told you we'd win, didn't I, Terry? Come on, let's congratulate David—out in the hall, where our victory war dance won't disturb the courtroom."

Terry walked up the aisle in a kind of daze. Things seemed to be moving too quickly. Could the case really be all finished? She caught a brief glimpse of Neil Brewster, his head bent close to his lawyer's, his chin set grimly. She found the look strangely disturbing, felt a sudden pang of remorse for all the distress she'd caused him. Then she scolded herself for not feeling more triumphant. Surely that self-assured man didn't need her pity?

Out in the lobby, surrounded by beaming faces, she began to feel more elated. "Wasn't David terrific!" Leo Martinez cried, thumping him on the back jubilantly.

"You were pretty great, too," said Terry warmly.

"I really appreciated your testimonial." Her elation swelled into euphoria. It *was* a great victory. Leo and Sandra would have their house after all, just where they'd planned it. The forces of darkness were routed. Young love had triumphed. She put an arm around Leo's shoulders and hugged him. "Let's all go off to El Patio for a victory celebration. Lunch is on me. Terry Morrison, Inc. can write it off against taxes."

"Terrific!" Leo said. "But I'm the one doing the paying. With two such fantastic guests, the best lawyer and architect in all Taos County—"

David waved a hand in protest. "Thanks, Leo, but Cecilia and I have to take a raincheck. We've got to be back at the gallery before that art tour group gets here from Dallas."

Leo looked disappointed for an instant. Then his face brightened again. "Okay, okay," he said. "Go do your thing for those rich Dallas people. Terry and I will toast our victory for you." He turned to Terry, grinning broadly. "Come along, Terry. I know *you* won't turn me down. Let's go celebrate how us poor little Taoseños whupped the almighty stuffing out of that big, bold, bad Neil Brewster."

CHAPTER FOUR

TERRY TOOK ANOTHER SIP of her margarita, savoring the tang of salt on the frosted rim. She let her eyes stray contentedly around the patio leading from the indoor restaurant, relishing its many-colored contrasts—the bright explosion of flowers in the big cedar planters, the strings of dried red chilies clustered around the columns of the wooden *portal*, the vivid paintings by local artists arranged on the whitewashed walls. The noonday sun was bathing the open courtyard with golden warmth, giving her a sense of intense well-being.

She smiled across the table at Leo Martinez. "I really love this restaurant of Helen's—a perfect place for our victory celebration." A sudden question clouded her eyes for a moment. "But I still don't know why Cecilia was so certain we were going to win. It seemed to have something to do with Judge Cordova. She kept hinting mysteriously—"

"It's not really all that mysterious—" Leo was grinning broadly "—especially to someone who grew up here in Taos. You know Urban Montoya, up at the Texaco station?"

"Of course I know Urban. That's where I buy my gas."

"Urban Montoya is my mother's second cousin. And Charlie Cordova is Urban's *compadre*. You know how it is around here. Godparents become an important part of the family. Sometimes they're even closer than blood relations."

Terry felt a pang of vague disquiet. "You mean he was already prejudiced in your favor? Well, that certainly explains those mysterious hints, but it makes me feel a little uncomfortable. Isn't there some kind of rule that a judge should disqualify himself from a case involving a family member?"

Leo's grin grew even broader. "That wouldn't work here in Taos. Families here have so many links to each other that a rule like that would disqualify all our judges." He reached over and patted her hand. "Don't look so guilty, Terry. Don't you really believe the judge made the right decision?"

"Of course I do." The glow of victory rekindled in Terry's veins, dissolving the little knot of discomfort. "Neil Brewster has no right to dictate to us. I'm sure any judge would have made the same decision. We can't have these arrogant strangers walking in here and telling us how to live our lives—"

She paused in mid-sentence, her startled eyes looking past Leo's shoulder. Neil Brewster was standing there, framed by the weathered wood of the patio doorway. The hazel eyes blinked several times, adjusting themselves to the sunlight after the shadowy darkness of the indoor dining room. Suddenly they sharpened with recognition, and the tall gray-suited man began to weave his way through the tables directly toward Terry.

She felt an instant of panic. Then she reminded herself that Neil Brewster was no longer any danger to her. She smiled brightly at him, the magnanimous winner welcoming the vanquished opponent. "Good afternoon, Mr. Brewster. Why don't you join us for lunch? You can pull up a chair from one of the other tables...."

Her voice faded away. The tall dark-haired man was ignoring her completely, staring intently at the man who shared her table. "Mr. Martinez!" he said. "I'm glad I caught you before you went back to the city. Could we talk for a minute or two? It might be very much to your advantage."

Leo's smiling face turned bland and impassive. "I very much doubt that, Mr. Brewster. But since Miss Morrison has already asked you to join us, I guess it won't hurt to hear what you have to say."

Neil looked a little apologetic at that. He nodded briefly to Terry, then pulled up a chair and sat down, leaning earnestly toward Leo. "I'm not sure your wife understood what I said on the phone. I'd like to repeat my offer to you in person."

"That's not necessary, Mr. Brewster. Sandra had no trouble understanding your offer. You want to give us a parcel of land down in Talpa in exchange for our lot, part of the farm Mr. Hartnett bought from Elvira Sanchez—much richer land than ours, with plenty of irrigation. It even covers part of an apple orchard."

Neil nodded eagerly. "You know the place, then? You agree it's an excellent bargain?"

"Financially, you mean? Oh, yes, it's an excellent

bargain. Couldn't be better." Leo's dark eyes turned even more opaque. "The price of any land down in Talpa is twice as much as it is in our part of the county."

"Then you're going to accept my offer? That's really great." A delighted smile spread over Neil's face.

Leo raised a hand in warning. "Not quite so fast, Mr. Brewster. I didn't say I was going to accept it."

"But you just agreed the exchange was really a bargain. The land is worth a lot more—"

"Worth more to whom, Mr. Brewster? To a real-estate dealer, maybe. To an Anglo like you, who's just come into the county. It's certainly very nice land. Sandra would probably like it. We'd have a lot easier time with our vegetable garden. But the trouble is, it has just one big drawback. That land is Sanchez land, and I'm a Martinez."

Neil's eager smile gave way to a puzzled frown. "Still harping on that point, are you? The rest of your family didn't feel that way. They were very pleased to take the money I gave them."

A little smile quirked the edges of Leo's mouth. A stranger might have seen it as a smile of amusement, but Terry knew better. Beneath that impassive mask, Leo was seething with anger. "You are talking to me, Mr. Brewster, not the rest of my family."

The other man shook his head, apparently bewildered. "I really don't understand you, Mr. Martinez. Why is your grandfather's land so special to you? From what your aunt told me, you didn't even grow up there."

"That's right, Mr. Brewster, I didn't. We moved to Albuquerque when I was a baby. I've lived there most of my life, in rented houses. Always moving around, never really belonging in any one place. Now, thanks to my grandfather's will, I have a place that really belongs to me. I guess you could say I've finally found my roots."

Neil's eyes brightened with sympathetic interest. "I'm beginning to get the picture. Lots of young people today are searching for roots. But roots can be a danger as well as a comfort. They can bind you too closely sometimes, keep you from making your own decisions." The hazel eyes darkened. He seemed to turn inward, addressing his words more to himself than to Leo. "It's not good to live too much in our ancestors' shadows. When roots grow too strong, they can make you a prisoner."

"So you want to set me free, Mr. Brewster?" Leo's smoldering anger burst into open flame. "That's really great of you—really noble. But of course, you and your kind have always been noble. Like that noble war of yours, to free us from Mexico. That was really fine, Mr. Brewster, to give us our freedom. But you didn't stop there, did you, you noble Anglos? You saw we still carried that terrible heavy burden, all that land the Spanish king had granted to us. You knew we could never be free with that land weighing us down. So you kindly relieved us of it, took on the burden yourself, leaving us poor but happy with only a few scattered farmers still chained to their land. And now, Mr. Brewster, you're here to finish the job, strike off a few more

chains, bestow on another poor peon your kind of
freedom. Well, it won't work, Mr. Brewster. You're
not going to do it. I'm going to hang on to my land.''
He sprang up from his place at the table, his voice
growing shrill with challenge. "You're very rich, Mr.
Brewster. You think all those dollars will buy you
whatever you want. But Leo Martinez is not for sale.
So don't come around with any more of your of-
fers.''

Terry saw the heads of the other diners turning
toward them, realized their table had become the
center of attention. "Please, Leo—" she reached out
to touch his arm "—I'm sure Mr. Brewster didn't
mean to offend you.''

Leo looked down at her with a bitter smile. "So
you're taking his side now, Terry? I thought you
knew better.'' He quickly turned on his heel and
disappeared into the shadowy dining room. Terry's
first impulse was to run after him and catch him, try
to effect a reconciliation. But she knew at once that
was useless. She'd have to wait till Leo cooled down a
little.

She turned back to Neil and found him regarding
her with guilty chagrin. "I'm sorry," he said. "I really made a mess of that conversation. I hope I haven't
made trouble between you and your client.''

Terry was startled by his sudden change of manner. A minute ago, he'd have been the one in com-
mand—arrogant, sure of himself, controlling the
situation. Now he seemed hurt and bewildered, apparently deeply disturbed by Leo's outburst.

She had meant to answer him with an angry retort,

even ask him to leave if necessary. Now she found herself softening, sharing his hurt, wanting to ease the sting of that bitter encounter. "I'm not worried about my relationship with Leo." She chose her words carefully, keeping her voice low and neutral. "But I do resent your spoiling our victory luncheon."

"Good Lord, what a clod I am. I should have known better than to barge in right at that moment." His voice was alive with concern; his eyes abjectly apologetic. "I really could kick myself for being so stupid."

"That might be quite entertaining," said Terry crisply, "but it wouldn't solve the problem of my ruined lunch." Over his shoulder, she saw a waitress hovering, a heavily laden plate in each hand. Both she and Leo had ordered a *chalupa*. The waitress was obviously wondering what to do with Leo's.

"Look," she said, gripped by a sudden impulse, "Maria is here with the lunch Leo ordered. How about staying and eating it for him? That way, at least it won't be wasted."

His eyes widened in surprise. Then his face relaxed in a warm boyish smile. "So you want to make me eat crow, do you? Well, I guess I deserve it." He turned to the waitress, beckoning her to set the plate before him. He stared at the food for a moment as the waitress set the other plate down in front of Terry. "This looks a good deal more tasty than crow. What is it, anyway? One of the local dishes?"

"No, it's not really local, but people around here have adopted Mexican food. This dish is called a *chalupa*. Its base is a flour tortilla. Then come the beans, the ground beef, the cheese, the onions, the lettuce. The crowning touch is the sour cream and guacamole.''

"Terrific." Neil picked up his fork. "Especially the guacamole. That's my favorite way to eat avocado.''

He began a vigorous attack on the mound of food. Terry quickly followed his example. The lack of breakfast had made her enormously hungry. For several minutes they ate in silence, and Terry found herself drifting along on an airy cloud of well-being. The sun, the flowers, the food all seemed to blend into one euphoric experience, an experience strangely heightened by her unexpected choice of table companion.

Finally Neil looked up from his plate at her, raising a quizzical eyebrow. "Is this how you treat all your opponents? Fill them full of delicious food?''

His words jolted Terry out of her mood of contentment. He was right; he was her opponent. How could she have forgotten that so quickly?

"Only my defeated opponents," she said with a brief brittle smile. "I figure it helps to soothe their wounded egos.''

"Is that how you see my objections to your design? Simply a matter of overpowering ego?''

Terry gave a little sigh of frustration. She shouldn't have brought them back to that prickly subject—especially now, on this marvelous sunny day, with the flowers all around her. "Mr. Brewster," she said, "you're really a puzzle to me."

The eyebrow quirked again. "A puzzle? What kind of puzzle? I've always seen myself as being pretty straightforward."

"Really? That's surprising." Terry carefully maintained her bright social smile. "To me, you appear to be full of contradictions. You seem to have such a sensitive feeling for tradition—and yet, look how you treated Leo, completely ignoring the deepest of all his traditions, his love of the land. And then that consumer business. In New York, you defend them. When you come out here, you try to run over them roughshod."

Her companion's eyes sharpened. His expression was guarded, almost hostile. "I suppose David Quayle mentioned that—what you call the consumer business? What did he tell you?"

"Not very much. Just that you did a lot of consumer advocacy. He mentioned your case against Olympia Tires. How did that come out, by the way? Has it been decided?"

"They won. We lost." His jaw was set grimly.

"That's really surprising. David said your cases were usually so well prepared—"

Neil cut her off with an angry gesture. "Please," he said sharply, "I'd rather not talk about that fiasco!"

Terry bristled at his peremptory tone. So he was reverting to form, the real Neil Brewster. The apology, the abjectness, had been a mere interlude. She stared down at her plate, resolving to keep her own temper under control. Really, this lunch was hopeless. Why had she been so crazy as to ask him to join her?

She raised her eyes, rehearsing some formal phrases to smooth her departure. *I'm afraid I really must go now. I'll probably see you around, up at the site.*

The look of raw pain in his eyes startled and chilled her. What on earth had she said to provoke it? The Olympia Tires thing? But why should losing a case make him look like this, so lost and shaken?

She was certainly right about one thing: the man was a puzzle. Her curiosity flared, and with it, she sensed danger. It wouldn't be easy to probe Neil Brewster's depths, but it suddenly seemed to Terry supremely important.

Cautiously she tried an oblique approach. "You mentioned the book you're writing. How is that coming along?"

He gave her a startled look, as though she'd interrupted some absorbing inner thought process. Then the tense hurt look was replaced by a rueful smile. "Not very well, I'm afraid. Actually, I've only done a few pages. I guess I use it as a sort of phony excuse, something to say when I'm asked why I came to Taos."

"Don't feel bad about that," Terry heard herself saying warmly. "Plenty of people in Taos are in the same boat. If every would-be writer in this little town actually finished the book he's supposed to be writing, the shelves at the Harwood Library couldn't hold them."

She checked herself abruptly. Why did she feel

such a need to reassure him?. That look of pain, of course. It had really got to her. But it wasn't her job to soothe it. All she was interested in was solving a puzzle.

"So the book is a cover-up," she said more crisply. "All right, what's your real reason for leaving the great big city and coming to tiny Taos?"

Neil was silent a minute. His gaze moved over her face, studying it intently. When he spoke again, his voice was guarded and cautious. "Do I really have to explain that? You come from a big city, too. You left it for Taos. I presume your reasons weren't very different from mine."

Terry felt a spurt of angry frustration. "Why are you being so cagey?" she demanded. "Fencing with me as if we were still opponents? I thought that was all behind us. I thought there was a chance we might even be friends. But it seems you refuse to meet me on equal terms. You're so used to hiding behind all that money and power that you forget how to act like a mere human being."

She stopped abruptly, aghast at her outburst. What on earth was she doing? Where had it sprung from, that impassioned plea for friendship? Surely she wasn't so hungry for human contact as to search for it in this highly unlikely quarter?

She looked guiltily over at Neil, groping for a way to recall the passionate words. He was looking at her in puzzled surprise. "Is that how it seems to you? As though I'm trying to hide behind my money?"

Terry fumbled for a phrase to soften her stinging words, but she found there was no way to do that and still be honest. "Yes, it is." She raised her chin in defiance, expecting some arrogant comment.

It didn't come. The hazel eyes remained soft and puzzled. "I'm sorry if I gave that impression. Old habits die hard, I guess. I know I grew up depending too much on my money. I've been making an effort to change, these past few years. That was one of my reasons for getting away from New York. There's a falseness about most relationships in the city—not just New York, I think—any city. Out here, I hoped to find something truer, more honest."

"I know what you mean," Terry said impulsively. "That's just how I felt about life in Los Angeles."

"I gather you had a pretty successful practice there."

Terry felt herself flushing. "I did well enough, especially for a beginner. The firm I worked for had a lot of prestige."

Neil gave her an appraising look. "L.A. is a pretty rich town. I'd be willing to bet you earned twice as much there as you do around here. How come you decided to leave all that behind you?"

Terry's face stiffened. An all too familiar pain flared deep inside her. "That's a personal matter," she muttered. "I'd rather not talk about it, if you don't mind."

The probing eyes turned warm and sympathetic. "Sorry if I hit a sore spot. I have enough of my own to know what that feels like. Okay, your reasons for leaving the city are out of bounds. Let's try another question: of all the small towns in this country, why did you settle on this particular one?"

She flashed him a constrained smile, hoping it conveyed her thanks for respecting her privacy. "Why Taos? That's hard to say. It was one of those mysterious cases of instant attraction. I came here first with my husband, who was making a movie—"

"Your husband?" Something flickered in his eyes. Surprise? Disappointment? It was hard to say.

It was even harder to say why it made Terry feel such a surge of excitement. "My former husband," she assured him hastily, annoyed by the ease with which that reference to her past life had slipped out. "Paul Fontaine, the director. You may have heard of him."

Neil exclaimed in pleased recognition, and Terry felt herself wincing. She knew what was coming next—those inevitable comments about Paul's brilliant direction, the new look of interest directed at her, as though being a genius's wife—even ex-wife—gave her a heightened value. She braced herself, intent on not betraying the absurd resentment such responses always aroused.

She was startled to hear him saying something quite different. "What a strange coincidence. Don't tell me the movie was *Bless Me, Ultima*?"

"As a matter of fact, it was." She blinked at him in surprise. "But what do you mean about a coincidence?"

He scanned her face with a puzzled wondering look. "You asked me about my reasons for coming to Taos. That movie was one of the most important reasons."

Terry's eyes widened. "You came here just because you saw a movie?"

"Not just because. It was one of many reasons. I was already getting fed up with life in New York. I knew I wanted out, but I had no real idea where I wanted to go. Then some movie-buff friends took me to see that picture." He shook his head, a rueful smile on his lips. "It's hard to describe the effect it had on me. It seemed to cast some kind of spell, offer some special promise. The world it showed me seemed so utterly different from anything I'd ever known before."

"Of course, Paul was pretty selective," Terry said dryly. "The crumbling adobe village you saw in that film was a lot more idyllic than modern tourist-trap Taos."

Neil grinned in agreement. "I realized that, of course, the moment I saw the McDonald's signs on the highway."

"McDonald's, Kentucky Fried Chicken, Holiday Inn—not exactly the magical world you saw in the movie."

He waved his hand dismissively. "All that is superficial. The basic things haven't changed from *Ultima*'s time: that terrific sky, those brooding mountains, the way people live close to the land, the way human beings are dwarfed by the vast lonely landscape—and yet somehow manage to mark it with their imprint."

His words were compelling. They seemed to be pulling her into the vision he was describing. A warning signal sounded in Terry's brain. This man had the same forceful aura as Paul had. If she didn't watch out, it would happen all over again. She'd find herself being sucked into his orbit, drawn helplessly by the force of his magnetism. . . .

She made a determined effort to wrench herself free. "All this sounds like a very familiar story." She was pleased to hear how offhand and casual she sounded. She flicked her hand toward the other diners around them. "Probably everyone here has had similar feelings. This town is a sort of camp for refugees—people tired of big-city life and looking for something different."

The bright hazel eyes turned dull and opaque. His face closed up as if she had slapped him. "You're right," he said. "I suppose I'm just like a thousand others, following a well-worn path away from the city. Well, Miss Morrison—" his left eyebrow quirked in a quizzical challenge "—as a fellow refugee, can you give me any hints about life in the camp?"

Terry was suddenly overwhelmed with compunction. Why had she cut him down with that disparaging comment? Maybe because his reasons for loving Taos were uncomfortably close to her own?

"I'm really not being quite fair," she said impulsively. "I don't feel like a refugee. The word sounds too negative for what I've found here."

He brightened visibly. "That's what I want to know. What have you found here, Terry?"

His use of her Christian name sent a little shiver lancing along her spine. *Good Lord,* thought Terry, *what's going on here? I'm reacting like a girl in a romantic novel.* She drew a deep breath, trying to concentrate on what she wanted to tell him because she did want to answer his question, without being flip or casual. This man deserved better than that. He had opened himself up to her in that spellbound moment. She owed it to him to reveal her own feelings.

"What have I found here? Let's see if I can describe it. You mentioned a sense of living close to the land. I think that's at the core of what drew me to Taos. Life is more natural here, more in touch with the seasons. There's less of that man-made concrete and noise and schedules. It's easier to hear myself thinking." She flashed him a shy self-deprecating smile. "I'm really not much of a mystic, but somehow—out here—I feel like a part of the earth. It's as though I can feel the earth's rhythms in my own body—"

She broke off abruptly, flinching from the dangerous sound of the word. "I told you it was hard to describe, but I'm sure these feelings have shaped my architecture. My designs have become more fluid, more organic."

"I'd hardly call all those beer cans and tires organic." The words could have been sarcastic, but the smile that went with them was companionable, teasing.

"You just won't forgive those beer cans, will you, Neil?" She smiled back at him, marveling at her sudden feeling of ease. "But can't you see, they're all part of the Taos environment, too. It's no use fighting against them. The thing to do is find out how to make them fit in. Building them into houses is as good a way as any.''

His expression became serious. ''If you keep on talking like this, you may convert me. I'm beginning to see how well *you* fit into Taos. Tell me....'' He paused, evidently not sure he wanted to ask the next question. ''As an old hand here, give me your honest opinion. What about me? Do you think I'll ever fit in here?''

The hazel eyes were boring into hers. Once more she felt that inward flutter of danger. She sensed this was more than a superficial question, social chitchat over a casual luncheon. He was asking for some kind of verdict, a personal verdict she wasn't prepared to give yet.

Nervously she reached out and lifted her glass, evading his gaze, and swallowed the watery dregs of the margarita. ''That depends,'' she said. ''I think to become part of Taos, you have to make a commitment. That's sometimes hard for a city person to do. Take David Quayle, for instance. There are times he's been pretty fed up with life here in the backwoods. But he's never lost faith in the Janus Gallery.'' She went rattling on, explaining about the use of the Janus symbol—the god facing two ways, combining the best of the past with new approaches. He was listening to her politely, but deep in his eyes was a faint look of disappointment. They both understood that she was avoiding his question.

She went on for a few more minutes, talking about the Quayles, about Ivan Winter who had started the music festival, about the poet, Jim Franklin, who ran

the Black Bear bookstore. Neil kept listening, like a
dutiful student attending a boring lecture. Finally she
ran out of words and lapsed into nervous silence, trying to think of some way of changing the subject.

She felt acutely aware of the way he was studying
her face, as though looking there for the answer to
his question. The silence between them became a
palpable object, a band of pulsing energy binding
them to each other, humming with power, ready to
shoot out sparks at any moment.

In the end, it was he who broke the silence. "I envy
people like you." The words seemed to come out
slowly, as though it hurt him to make the admission.
"You and David and all those others. You've found
what you want to do with your life. It reminds me a
bit of those old desert fathers, the early Christian
monks who left the cities and went out to the wilder-
ness in search of some clear direction. I guess that's
essentially what I'm after, too."

Something wistful about his expression touched
Terry deeply. All her nervousness dropped away.
"'Some clear direction,'" she echoed. "Do you
think you're beginning to find it?"

He smiled at her, that rueful half smile she found
so appealing. "I've had a few glimpses. I find it helps
to really get up into the mountains. I've been taking
some backpacking trips in the Cimarron range, up
beyond Questa." His smile grew warm with remembered pleasure. "I found this terrific old ghost town,
the mining camp they called Midnight. But I guess an
old-timer like you knows all about that."

"Midnight?" Terry was puzzled. "That's funny.

I've never even heard it mentioned. Of course, I've been to Elizabethtown—"

"This is the same sort of thing on a smaller scale. Ruined cabins, a store, a small hotel—only it's not on the highway. It's up a dirt road in the middle of nowhere." His face was aglow with enthusiasm. "There's a tremendous view. You feel like you're standing on top of the world."

"It sounds exciting. I'll have to take a look at it one of these weekends. Where did you say it was? Up above Questa?"

He laughed, a surprised little chuckle. "You really haven't seen it? An old Taoseña like you?" His eyes turned intent as a new idea struck him. "Look, I tell you what. Why don't we drive up to see it right now?"

Terry stiffened with shock, all her defenses newly alerted. "Oh, no, I couldn't do that. There's a lot of work back at the office—and I ought to go look at the greenhouse addition I'm building for Vivian Hartnett."

"Oh, come on, Terry, your work can wait for a while." His voice, teasing and gentle, awakened an uneasy clamor deep inside her. "Don't tell me you're falling back into that nine-to-five trap. Isn't that what you came to Taos to get away from?"

The clamor inside Terry's body became more demanding. She found herself torn between two sets of inner voices—the stern voice of duty, calling her back to her work, and another, more frivolous voice, urging her up to the mountains. She remembered the pleasure she'd had, when she first came to Taos, hiking and camping alone on those brooding heights. It had been an intense experience, almost religious. Why hadn't she kept it up? She realized with a shock that it had been almost two years since she'd done any backpacking. Maybe Neil was right. Maybe she had let her work turn into a trap.

Quickly she made her decision. "All right, Neil. You've convinced me." Her voice sounded strange in her ears, high-pitched and breathless. "We're going to spend this afternoon at Midnight."

CHAPTER FIVE

"YOU'RE ABSOLUTELY RIGHT, NEIL. The view is fantastic!" Terry shaded her eyes with her hand as she looked out from the edge of the grassy plateau. Behind her lay the scattered ruins of ten or eleven tiny log cabins and the starker skeletons of two larger buildings, the weathered wood gleaming like silver in the vivid afternoon sunshine. Around the abandoned settlement a ring of cone-shaped peaks stood like guardians, their dark green pine-clad slopes shading to a hazy deep blue. In front of them, range after range of blue green hills rippled away into the distance. The air seemed unusually still, with only an infrequent breeze to break the silence as it sent sighs through the circling pines. The only other sign of life in the spellbound landscape came from the rushing stream far over to Terry's right, which scattered gleaming splinters of deflected sunlight as it tumbled headlong down the side of the mountain.

"It's beautiful, but also a little frightening." Terry turned to Neil, suppressing a little shiver. "All that space out there without any sign of human habitation!"

"I see it another way." Neil gestured toward the

ruined cabins. "There's your human imprint. Even now, it dominates the landscape."

Terry shook her head, a brooding look in her clear blue eyes. "Those hollow shells? They feel more like a warning to me. The land didn't want man here. Human strength gave way pretty quickly to all this wildness."

"A month ago, I would have felt that way, too." Neil's voice was meditative, his eyes fixed once more on the distant horizon. "When I first came out to New Mexico, those vast stretches of land and sky seemed forbidding and alien. Now they feel like a part of myself. That's what I love about being up in these mountains. All the petty everyday hassles drop away, and I feel as though I'm merging with all this vastness."

His words struck a responsive chord. Terry had gone through the same experience when she had first arrived in Taos, learning to come to terms with the awesome sweep of the southwestern landscape. She followed his gaze out over the sea of mountain crests. How good it was to know Neil shared her feelings! She reveled in the exhilaration that had been steadily building inside her all through their journey up here. At first she had tried to rationalize it away, attributing it to the break in her work routine, the unaccustomed feeling of playing truant. Now she was letting herself accept its true basis: Neil Brewster's electrifying presence.

The trip in the Blazer had taken about an hour—twenty miles along the main highway to Questa, then the bumpier slower stretch up the well-worn dirt road through Cabresto Canyon. At first she'd sat stiffly beside him, compulsively careful to avoid any random touch of their bodies. She had begun to realize then the unprecedented attraction of his wiry body. She had a panicky feeling of losing control. The more careful she was to avoid any contact with him, the more aware her own body became of his nearness.

The turning point came on that bumpy dirt road through the mountains. As they left the village behind and headed into the vast uninhabited mountains, all her defenses started to melt away. She stopped fighting to keep her distance and let the bucking car throw her body against his lean hard strength, welcoming the initial shock of contact, the warm insidious glow that rippled through her veins and nerves. By the time they reached the little ghost town, her blood was singing with pleasure.

She felt a sense of rebirth. How could she have let herself be trapped so long in that cold gray waste of unfeeling? Why had she allowed Paul's defection to cripple her so completely? That episode seemed far back in the past now. She found it difficult even to remember what he looked like. Up here, standing on top of the world with Neil, she could hardly believe that Paul had ever existed.

She drew in a deep luxurious breath of the clear mountain air. A teasing scrap of a song danced through her head. Impulsively she turned to the man beside her. "There's a tune that keeps nagging at me—an old pop song that came out when I was in college. The first few words are all I remember—

something about being on top of the world." She looked up at him hopefully. "Maybe you know it?"

His forehead furrowed in concentration. "I'm afraid I don't. I wish I could help you. I know how maddening it is, trying to seize those words that hover just out of your grasp." He let his eyes travel around the circle of landscape. Then he turned back to her, grinning with pleasure. " 'On top of the world' certainly fits this situation, but it's hard to believe any song could do it justice."

Their eyes locked and held. Terry could feel her heart pounding. *Do justice to what,* she longed to ask. *The magnificent sky and mountains? Or the joy of the two of us being here together?*

She was overcome by a sudden fit of shyness, but there was no panic in it this time. She was still completely at ease with her newly awakened feelings. She welcomed the powerful attraction flowing between them, but felt a need to maintain some control—not to be swept away by the surging tide within her.

Wrenching her eyes away from his probing gaze, she looked around at the scattered cabins. "All right, Professor Brewster," she said lightly, "it's time for my lesson in local history. When would you say those cabins were built? During that first big gold rush in the 1860s?"

He shook his head. "No, these date from much later. The library book I found says 1895. There were five or six big claims around here within walking distance. They did well for a while, mining both gold and silver. But apparently their luck gave out pretty quickly. By 1900 the place was deserted."

Even with her eyes carefully averted from him, she sensed him beside her, too close for comfort. Feeling the need to put some distance between them, she walked away to examine the shell of the old hotel, running her fingers across the smooth satiny wood. "These marvelous weathered timbers. I'm always looking for old wood like this to use in my houses. I don't suppose anyone owns this. I'll have to have a talk with the local ranger."

Stepping carefully over the crumbling threshold, she picked her way between the exposed floor joists. She could hear him following her, the sound of his shoes on the crumbling debris. The nerves in her back began to tingle unbearably. "Look at these hand-made nails," she murmured breathlessly. Across the room, a dark object beckoned to her from a half-shattered doorpost. "And that marvelous cast-iron door hinge! Or is it wrought iron, forged by the Midnight blacksmith?"

She started moving toward it, more intent on keeping her distance than on reaching the rusty old artifact. Her toe caught on the top of a joist, and as she stumbled and started to fall, a searing pain shot through her ankle. Then she felt Neil's arms around her, checking her plunge toward the splintery threat of the floor joists, pulling her upright, holding her close against his muscular body.

The surging tide of excitement crashed through its barrier. Her body had a will of its own; she pressed her length against him, turning her face yearningly up to his. Then his lips came down on hers, searching, demanding.

Joyously Terry abandoned all thought of control.
Her lips were as avid as his—seeking, finding,
devouring. Their leaping pulses seemed to throb together. His hands were moving over her back caressingly, cupping her buttocks, pulling her closer to
him. Terry shivered with pleasure, feeling her nipples
growing taut with response, the flaming void within
her eager for even more closeness, chafing against the
annoying barrier of clothes that bristled between
them. Her body felt light and weightless, like a shaft
of sparkling sunlight. She floated in breathless
delight, buoyed up by an uncanny sense of recognition, of finding a long-lost home after years of
exile.

Then, suddenly, everything changed. She couldn't
believe it at first when she felt his body stiffen and
pull away. Her arms instinctively tightened around
him, trying in vain to restore that marvelous closeness. But his arms were stronger than hers; they
pushed her firmly away, widening and widening the
intolerable distance between them, forcing her down
from the cloud of splendid abandon on which she'd
been floating.

Terry went weak with a mixture of loss and outrage. Incredulously she raised her eyes to Neil's face.
She found him staring at her as though she'd suddenly turned into some kind of unpleasant insect.

Shifting his gaze away toward the horizon, he
dropped his hands abruptly from her shoulders.
Terry stood frozen in numb incomprehension. What
on earth could have happened to change that ardent
embrace into this sudden brutal rejection?

"Sorry." He spoke with his back turned toward her. His voice was gruff, almost hostile. "I don't know why I did that. It must be the altitude. People tell me it plays strange tricks with one's judgment."

Stunned by the feeling of loss, the sudden wrenching away of the warmth of his body, Terry groped for some kind of casual comment. "It wasn't your fault," she managed to murmur. "Just me being clumsy."

She looked up at him, hoping to catch some trace of the fire that had flared so briefly between them. The hazel eyes were blank and opaque. "Did you hurt yourself? That joist gave you a nasty crack across your ankle." The words were solicitous, but his tone was that of a reluctant bystander, eager to leave the scene of an accident.

Terry walked a few steps, gingerly testing her ankle. "No," she said. "It seems to be all right." But disappointment overcame her. Where had it gone, all that joyous exhilaration? All she felt now was painful self-consciousness at having exposed all those shamefully turbulent feelings. She wanted to run and hide, to get away from Neil Brewster, blot out that searing memory forever. But she knew she couldn't do that. She was trapped on this mountaintop with the man who had seemed as close as her skin suddenly changed into a casual stranger.

Desperately she started making historical small talk, dredging up anecdotes she'd almost forgotten. "There must have been a bar here in this hotel. Can't you just imagine some of the scenes here? Like that story they tell about Elizabethtown—how eight men died of gunshot wounds within twenty-four hours. Or that famous bully, Red Hendricks, and his gun with the sixteen notches. Or that old Virginia colonel who became their first justice of the peace. There's that well-known yarn about how he used to marry couples—but of course, you've probably heard it.''

His face was a mask of cold politeness. "No, I haven't heard it. Why don't you tell me?"

All she heard in his words was an icy lack of interest. She knew she must sound like an idiot, rattling on in this stupid way, but she had to say something to break the embarrassing silence. "He made up his own little ritual. How did it go? Oh, yes, now I remember." She threw back her shoulders and puffed out her cheeks, acting the part of the bluff Confederate soldier.

"Underneath this roof in stormy weathah
This buck and squaw now come togethah.
Let none but Him who rules the thundah
Set this buck and squaw asundah.

"Then he'd pull out his sword, tap them each on the shoulder and shout, 'Now you're married, by God! Let's all have a drink.'"

She looked up at him, hoping for some kind of comment. He gave her a frosty smile. She plunged ahead, hardly knowing what she was saying. "I wonder sometimes what could have possessed those women, coming out to the wild frontier as the wives of miners. It must have taken tremendous courage."

Neil raised a sardonic eyebrow. "Tremendous greed is more like it. A man with gold always attracts a lot of camp followers."

His contemptuous tone set her teeth on edge. "What a chauvinistic remark! Surely there must have been other motivations—the chance for a new free life, the thrill of helping the men they loved make their fortunes—"

He cut her off with a dry sarcastic chuckle. "You think I'm chauvinistic? I assure you, I speak from experience. There's no such thing as an idealistic female. Women are very adept at throwing up idealistic smoke screens—devotion and love and all that. But when push comes to shove, they opt for their own self-interest."

Terry stared at him in open-mouthed amazement. "How can you make such a blanket statement? You're lumping all women together."

The look he gave her was harsh and unfriendly. "The minute I hear a woman start spouting idealistic nonsense, I start to distrust her. I usually turn out to be right. Look at yourself, for example, coming on with those high-flown phrases about helping poor young couples and fluid, organic beer cans—combining the best of the old and the new."

Terry felt as though he'd just dealt her a blow to the solar plexus. "What *about* me?" she gasped. "You're not going to say I don't really believe in those things?"

"You may think you do." His voice had a bitter edge. "But basically, you're concerned with enhancing your image. This unorthodox stance of yours has earned you a lot of free advertising—national TV coverage, articles in *Vogue* and *House and Garden*." He paused a moment, looking at her through narrowed eyes. "Why do you look so surprised? You must have known my lawyer would give me a rundown on your career."

Terry was silent for a moment, paralyzed by the force of his unexpected attack. She felt the sting of tears behind her eyelids, furiously blinked them back. What on earth could have triggered this change in his manner?

"How dare you judge me like that!" Deliberately she goaded herself into anger, the sure antidote for her shock and disappointment. "What you ought to do is take a good look at yourself. You threw up a pretty good smoke screen—all that stuff about finding yourself, following in the steps of the desert fathers. I admit you almost fooled me. You had me believing we really had something in common. But now I see I was right in my first impression. You're just an arrogant boor, entrenched in the power of your money. You'll never fit in here in Taos—not in a hundred years. That big-city mind of yours can never adapt to simple honest feelings."

She stared up at him in defiance and saw that none of her tirade had even touched him. "Is that your last word on the subject?" he drawled in a bored toneless voice.

"I'm sorry," Terry said stiffly, making sure he understood she didn't mean it. "I'm not being very polite, especially since you were so kind as to bring me up here."

"Don't let it bother you." His voice matched hers in frosty politeness. "I was only doing my bit as an expert in local history."

"Okay, you've done your duty. Now I really do have to get back to my office."

He nodded silently and led the way back to the Blazer. The trip down out of the mountains was conducted in total silence—Neil intent on his driving, Terry absorbed in a miserable bout of self-examination. She had been so sure that he, too, had experienced the powerful attraction between them. She couldn't be wrong about that. The tone of his voice, the look in his eyes—above all, that passionate moment of coming together.

Then why had he changed so abruptly? What had she said or done to make him lash out so fiercely? Carefully she retraced the conversation: Elizabethtown, the miners, the miners' wives. . . .

A sudden illumination set her cheeks burning. Marriage! That fatal subject! Why on earth had she started rattling on about marriage? "I speak from experience"—the bitter edge to those words. With the fabulous Brewster millions, he must have met more than his share of greedy women. Many of them, no doubt, had tried to parlay a casual kiss into a marriage proposal. To him she was simply one in a long procession.

But no, that couldn't be the sole explanation. The change had come earlier, while she was still deep in that mesmerizing kiss. . . .

Sunk in her ruminations, she hardly realized that the car had come to a stop in front of her office.

She came to herself with a start, hopped down out of the Blazer, stammered a few more words of ritual thanks.

"My pleasure." His tone belied the words.

Huddled over her drawing board minutes later, she tried vainly to concentrate on lines and angles. The ring of the phone brought an upsurge of sudden hope. Surely this would be Neil, apologizing. She could already hear the words: I behaved very badly, Terry. I hope you'll forgive me.

The call was an apology, but it wasn't the one she longed for. "Hello there, Terry. This is Leo Martinez. I've been trying to reach you all afternoon. Listen, I'm sorry about that scene in El Patio. I shouldn't have lumped you in with that Brewster bastard. I want to make up for it now. I'll pick you up and take you out to the Quayles'. Cecilia is cooking us a victory dinner. I told her I'd bring the champagne. How about it, Terry? Is it a deal?"

Terry stared at the black receiver, wondering why Leo's words meant so little to her. She ought to be feeling great—the significant triumph that morning, the prospect of a gala meal with loving friends.

"Sorry, Leo. It sounds like it's going to be a terrific evening, but I'm too exhausted tonight. I just can't make it."

She put down the phone, feeling the burden of failure like a weight on her shoulders. Exhausted. Yes, she was exhausted. But that wasn't really the reason she'd turned down the invitation. Cecilia, David and Leo—they were three of her closest friends. But it wasn't their faces she wanted to see across the table. The only face that could have revived her was the face of that baffling man who had brought her to life again, and then turned her newfound joy to humiliation.

CHAPTER SIX

TERRY SNATCHED UP the half-finished sketch from her drafting table, crumpled it into a ball and aimed a vicious throw at the wastebasket in the corner. The sketch just wouldn't come out right. Might as well stop trying. The idea, so clear in her mind, eluded her when she tried to put it on paper.

She bit her lip in chagrin. It was only too clear why her architect's skills weren't functioning this morning. She'd been awake most of the night, going over and over that scene with Neil, reliving again and again the feel of his arms around her, his body's warmth against her—then that moment of shocked surprise before the plunge into the lonely void. Just before dawn she'd managed to snatch an hour or two of sleep. Wide awake again at seven, she'd fled from her too-empty house to her little office, hoping that work would provide its soothing magic. But even that refuge had failed her. Neil's face kept appearing, blotting out the design she was trying to transmit to paper.

Come on, Terry. You can't let this man obsess you! You've spent one whole night wallowing in emotion. Now daylight is here, it's time to do some straight thinking. She leaned back in her chair, rais-

ing her eyes to the small, square back window. She
watched the long blue shape of the mountains, growing more solid each minute as the sun burned away
their misty night shrouds. They seemed to give
her new strength to face up to the painful assessment.

All right, she'd met an attractive man, had come
on too strong—so strong that he'd backed away.
That really wasn't such a tragic event. A very common mistake; she'd made it herself, more than once,
in the days before she met Paul.

Where had it come from, this sudden overwhelming need she felt for Neil Brewster? The man was attractive, yes, but not all that special. She knew very
little about him, and a lot of what she did know
didn't do him much credit. Arrogant, insensitive,
selfish—that was the basic Neil. The wistful searching mood she'd found so intriguing was merely an
aberration.

No, that fierce compulsion she'd felt had little to
do with any qualities in him. It owed its strength to
her own turbulent feelings, feelings she'd tried for so
long to dam up and ignore. Yesterday, for some unknown reason, the dam had broken—and Neil had
simply been there, a convenient object, a blank
screen on which to project the fantasies from her sub-
conscious.

Really, she ought to be glad he'd backed away.
He'd kept her from making a bigger fool of herself.
To him, the whole thing had been just a casual encounter. He would never know, thank God, how her
stupid emotions had tricked her, had invested that

trivial kiss with all the power of high romantic
drama.

Painful as it had been, there was a positive side to
this whole debacle. At least she'd experienced the
strength of those buried emotions. That sense of
opening herself to life had been no illusion; she'd cut
herself off for too long from the world of feeling.
Opening up was fine, was exciting and healthy. Next
time she'd know enough to go more slowly. Instead
of throwing herself at the nearest available male,
she'd take time to choose someone who valued her as
a person, instead of a second Paul, self-centered,
petty, domineering.

Paul. . . . That was it; he was just like Paul. That
must have been part of the sudden irrational attraction. She had thought the divorce had at least taught
her *that* lesson. Apparently Miss Morrison was a very
slow learner. Well, thanks to fate and Neil Brewster,
she'd been given a second chance to learn it.

*So much for the man. Just write him off as a
valuable learning experience.* The sense of reaching a
useful decision made Terry feel a good bit more
cheerful. The drab little office suddenly seemed confining. She'd been hiding out here too long, nursing
her wounds. It was time to face the big buzzing
world, talk to some interesting people, feel life surging around her.

She shrugged on her old denim jacket and headed
for Michael's Kitchen, a half block away along North
Pueblo Road. This thriving coffee shop was the Taos
morning hangout. Michael Ninneman's coffee and
freshly baked pastries provided the fuel to stoke up

the fires of art and commerce: shop and gallery owners, awaiting ten o'clock and the start of business; sculptors, writers and painters, revving up for a day of creative endeavor; while a sprinkling of that uniquely skilled genus, the Taos idler, perfected its craft in the midst of the genial hubbub.

Terry paused in the paneled passage that linked the dining-room area with the bakery, enjoying the backwoods look of the roughly hewn booths and tables, the Victorian ceiling fans. Waves of heat from the big iron wood stove with its shiny chrome trimmings brought pleasant relaxation to muscles tensed against the chill of the morning.

The room was crowded with people, eating, smoking and talking. Terry looked toward the far side of the room, knowing there wasn't much chance that her favorite seat would be empty.

She was right. The corner booth beside the big front window was already occupied. Neil Brewster was sitting there, leaning over the brightly varnished plank table in earnest conversation with a dark-haired young woman. Terry's first reaction was panic; despite her new resolution, she wasn't quite ready to face him again. To her relief, she saw that she wouldn't have to. He was too deeply engrossed in talking to his companion to take any notice of what went on around him.

Terry's gaze rested curiously on the woman. She had never seen her before. She must be new to Taos. Very attractive, really, with that thick braid of jet-black hair, intertwined with Indian beads, tossed casually in front of one shoulder. Despite the western

style of her honey-beige suede jacket and jeans, she
had a citified look about her. Perhaps it came from
her make-up—unobtrusive, yet clearly involving
more time and effort than the usual Taos female
cared to devote to that task. Or perhaps it was something elegant in her posture, a sense of conscious control, like a *Vogue* photographer's model posing on
the fence of a cowboy corral.

As Terry stared at her, she felt the slow burn of insidious anger. How dare this stranger usurp Neil's
attention—attention Terry longed for and needed?
And what about Neil? How dare he be so absorbed in
this slickly veneered, artificial-looking woman when
he'd shown such disdain for her own honest burst of
feeling?

Then the woman reached out and placed her hand
on top of his. A tightness seized Terry's chest, as
though a giant fist were squeezing her rib cage. She
turned blindly away, scarcely knowing where she was
heading, knowing only that she couldn't stand to see
Neil's response to that intimate gesture.

A familiar voice interrupted her headlong exit.
"Terry! Terry Morrison! Trot on over here, girl.
There's some big things happening."

Skeeter Phillips was waving to her from the back
of the crowded room. Ordinarily she would have
been pleased to see him. The star reporter of the little
town's weekly newspaper was one of her favorites
among the people she'd described to Neil as refugees
from the city. Christopher Atherton Phillips had
followed in his father's footsteps through Groton
and Harvard, then decided the stock exchange was

not "where it's at," and cut loose on a wandering path that eventually brought him to Taos. Most of the time he affected a cowboy drawl, which combined with his drooping blond mustache and shaggy shoulder-length hair to give him a frontier gunfighter image. This morning, though, his speech had an Ivy League crispness about it, a sure sign that he was intensely excited.

Terry hesitated. She didn't feel like talking to anyone until her feelings were back under her control. But she couldn't ignore the shouted invitation.

Reluctantly she made her way to the back of the room, where Skeeter, in his fringed deerskin jacket, was sitting at a table below the wood mosaic mural of sunrise over Wheeler Peak. She nodded to the stocky older man sitting beside him, Paco Reyes, who owned Frank's Hardware. His square olive-skinned face looked unusually somber.

"Hi, Paco. Hi, Skeeter." She slid into the chair on the other side of the table, while Skeeter signaled the waitress for another coffee. "What's the latest flash from the *Taos News*? Don't tell me the town's about to buy a new snowplow?"

Skeeter frowned with irritation. He was obviously not in the mood for their usual joking. "This thing is serious, Terry, a real blockbuster. So far it's only a rumor—but take it from me, it's really a hot one."

"Could turn out too damn hot for a lot of people." Paco Reyes's eyes were dark with foreboding. Terry looked at him sharply. Paco wasn't much of a talker. His usual style was to look wise and keep his own counsel. When he did choose to make a comment, it was generally worthy of serious attention.

"How does this grab you, Terry?" Skeeter's voice was tense with suppressed excitement. "This little mud village of ours is going big time. We're about to sprout a high rise, a fifteen-story supercondominium."

Terry stared at him in shocked disbelief. "Come on, Skeeter. It's way past April Fool's Day."

The straight black lines of Paco's heavy eyebrows merged in a frown of disgust. "For some kind of fools, it's always open season."

The bitterness in his voice sent a little chill chasing along Terry's spine. "Skeeter!" she said, her own voice sharpening with tension, "for heaven's sake, tell me what's going on."

"It's some big outfit from Dallas—Southwestern Towers. They've just submitted a proposal to the town council: an apartment house with one- and two-bedroom units, fifteen stories, forty-five apartments. The plan is to sell them as time-sharing condominiums."

"Forty-five new apartments! Won't that put an awful dent in the water table?" She understood now why Paco was looking so gloomy. He was the volunteer fire marshal, responsible for the little town's fire protection. For the past few days he'd been conducting a campaign of protest, along with some local farmers, against the rash of new wells that were tapping the southwest's scarcest resource.

"Yeah, ain't it the pits?" Skeeter's indignation gave his mustached face the look of a frontier desperado. "It was bad enough when they brought in the Holiday Inn a few years ago. But that was just thirty units for overnight sleepers. These apartments will all have full kitchens and a washing machine for every family."

"Those stupid Dallas high rollers," Paco put in. "Do they really expect the town to supply all that water? I keep telling the guys on the council we already have too low a pressure to fight a good-sized fire once it got going."

She looked at Paco uncomprehendingly. "You mean they're planning to build this thing here in town—not out on the Ski Valley Road with those other new buildings?"

Skeeter looked grimmer than ever. "I told you it was the pits. Now we come to the real humdinger. You know where they want to put it? Smack dab in the middle of Kit Carson Park."

Shock kept Terry speechless for a moment. When she found her voice, it was shrill with indignation. "But that's crazy, completely crazy." She pictured the gracious expanse of tree-shaded grass where Taos families came for their Sunday picnics, the memorial grove honoring the Taos School artists, the little cemetery where soldiers from five of their country's wars shared their last resting place with the frontier scout, Kit Carson.

Skeeter stroked his drooping mustache, smiling sardonically. "The rumor is that the state has already agreed to sell them the land—the whole southeastern corner of the park. The cemetery is part of the big attraction when they're peddling these pads to the suckers in the city. All the comforts of modern living, plus an Indian fighter's headstone for your dog to use as a sanitary convenience.''

Terry scarcely heard the sarcastic comment. She was too absorbed in a horrifying vision: a raw, bleak concrete tower thrusting its way toward the sky, screaming its blatant challenge to the modest earth-hugging buildings around it, casting a chilling shadow over the picnic tables, dwarfing the giant cottonwood trees—assuming they left any trees. They'd probably cut most of them down to make room for their heavy construction machinery.

"That's awful," she said in a small stunned voice. "If this thing goes through, it will change the whole look of Taos."

"I guess it's the wave of the future," Skeeter said glumly. "Pretty soon the whole country's going to look like Dallas."

"But can't we do something to stop it? Does the state have the legal right to sell that land?"

Skeeter gave a gloomy shake of his head. "Those guys down in Santa Fe have a lot of power. The sale was arranged in a very hush-hush manner, but apparently it's perfectly legal. There *is* one small ray of hope, though. The sale won't become final until the Taos town council gives its approval and waives the current zoning regulations."

Terry tossed her head back sharply, her eyes alive with grim determination. "Thank goodness for that small favor! They may be able to sell this crazy pipe dream in Dallas, but that doesn't mean they can get away with it here. The council will never approve it.

They know why all the tourists come to Taos—to see something different, a quaint little Spanish village. They're not going to let some Texas sharpies turn the place into a modern high-rise city. That's what the tourists are trying to get away from.''

"I dunno," Skeeter murmured. "This outfit seems to pack a lot of clout. They've already built a similar complex in Scotsdale, and I hear they've got the permits to build one in Prescott.''

"In Prescott?'' Terry was shocked. She knew the sleepy old cow town had a strong preservationist movement. If Southwestern Towers had managed to circumvent it— "Wait just a minute. Aren't we forgetting something? That land is part of the Taos Historical Zone. They'll need more than the town's permission to let them build there. They'll have to comply with federal regulations.''

Skeeter shook his head gloomily. "The scuttlebutt says they've already got a federal waiver. I tell you, Terry, these are big-time operators. With all the support they've lined up in Santa Fe—''

"The fat cats in Santa Fe don't have to live here. It's up to us Taoseños. The council wouldn't dare let this thing go through. They know it would turn the local voters against them.''

"The council has made some pretty strange decisions.'' Paco's forehead was furrowed with deep concern. "Remember the Holiday Inn fight? They'll be trotting out the same old arguments. More jobs, more tourists, a few choice plums for the local building contractors.''

An icy hand was squeezing Terry's heart. "You

really think they might approve it? Then we've got to work fast, build up a protest campaign, get people aroused against what they're doing in Taos.''

Paco's somber face relaxed in a smile. ''You're with us, then, Terry? You'll help us fight this project?'' His tone conveyed a sense of surprise and relief.

''Of course I'm with you. Did you think there was any chance I wouldn't support you?''

Paco looked a little embarrassed. ''I wasn't quite sure. Some of your houses are kind of, well, modernistic. I thought you might like this Dallas-style architecture.''

Terry shook her head decisively. ''Some of my houses may look a little far-out, but I wouldn't build one of those in downtown Taos. I love the old traditions, the way all the separate buildings blend into one big design. Southwestern Towers may think its buildings are modern. Personally, I think they're barbaric.''

Skeeter's approving grin firmed into a look of brisk resolution. ''I'm afraid the bad hombres have got a big head start on us. We'll have to work fast if we're going to overtake them.'' He started outlining some plans: meetings, a phone campaign, posters, a citizens' rally.

Terry listened intently, beginning to comprehend the task she'd embarked on. It would mean a lot of hard work, the sort of work she'd never been good at—dealing with people. She felt a pang of dismay, remembering her days at Fairfield & Warner. How she'd hated those dismal committee meetings, the

eternal demand for diplomacy and caution, the strain
of coaxing a lot of high-powered egos to work together. It had been a relief to put all that talk behind
her, run her own show from her own little office.
Now she was being thrust back into the public arena.
She had to do it, of course. She couldn't stand on the
sidelines and watch Taos be ruined. Besides, hadn't
she just decided it was time to stop hiding out in that
cozy office?

She plunged into the planning with Skeeter, putting forth some of her own suggestions. She would
line up the other architects, form her own committee.
She'd call some of the gallery owners, enlist the support of the Taos Society of Artists. . . .

Skeeter had pulled out his notebook and was jot-
ting down names of the people they thought would
support them. He handed the list to Paco to get his
comments. The stocky man shook his head. "It's
good as far as it goes. But most of these people are
Anglos. We've got to get more of the Spanish-
speaking leaders."

"I know that," Skeeter said. "That's why I want
your suggestions." He scribbled another list and gave
it to Paco. "I know who the leaders are, but Terry
and I aren't the right people to approach them—not
only because we're Anglos, but both of us are too
new to Taos. It'll take someone they have a lot of
respect for to get them to join us."

Paco chuckled dryly. "That means Paco Reyes, I
guess. Okay, I'll do what I can. But remember, I've
only been here for one generation. Some of these real
old-timers—they still look at me as a fly-by-night

Mexican peddler.'' His eyes grew cloudy with thought, and a new idea seemed to strike him. He looked intently at Terry. ''You know who might be a big help? Cecilia Rampion, or what's her name now—Mrs. Quayle? Even though she's an Anglo, she's got a lot of friends among the old Spanish families.''

Terry's spirits lifted. ''Of course! Cecilia's just right for the job. She's so good at working with people—much better than I am. And I know she'll be glad to do it. She'll be just as shocked as we are when I tell her about this awful proposal.''

Terry saw Skeeter's gaze flick upward, then come back to her with a puzzled expression. Raising her own eyes, she found that Neil was standing beside the table. He smiled when he saw that he'd finally got her attention. ''Good morning, Terry,'' he said. ''Looks like a perfect day for pouring that house foundation.''

The self-confident tone of his voice grated on Terry's nerves. Who did he think he was, this smug Neil Brewster? Yesterday he'd been cold and rejecting. Now he was coming on so cheerful and friendly, as if that scene in the mountains had never happened.

''Good morning, Mr. Brewster.'' Her eyes were as cold as his had been up at Midnight. The cheerful grin faded abruptly. Without another word he left the table and headed toward the cashier's desk near the front door, where the black-haired woman was waiting with obvious impatience.

Skeeter gave a low whistle. ''What's all this,

Terry? Doesn't the famous Neil Brewster rate something more than that bitchy brush-off?''

Terry frowned with irritation. ''What do you mean, the famous Neil Brewster? I wasn't aware he'd done anything to make himself famous.''

''Tsk, tsk, aren't we touchy this morning. You act as though millionaires are a dime a dozen. They're not, even here in Taos. Besides, I checked out the guy when I heard he'd come to live here. He's not just your standard rich playboy. He did some good work in New York, financing a lot of suits for irate consumers. I guess the last one was more than he could handle. He really tackled a big one—Olympia Tires. Looked for a while as if he was going to win, but then he suddenly folded, withdrew the suit and faded into the night. Since then, he's supposed to have turned into a recluse, a Howard Hughes type, not telling anyone where he was going. The rumors said he'd gone off to build a hotel in Tahiti. Then he was supposed to be looking for gold in Alaska.'' He scanned her face curiously. ''Apparently you two have got to know one another. Has he dropped any hints on how long he intends to stay here?''

''I really don't know him at all.'' Terry's voice was controlled and icy. ''We did have one brief conversation. He says he's tired of the big-city rat race. And he's spent several thousand dollars on fixing up the old Martinez house.''

''That doesn't mean much.'' Skeeter looked meditative. ''Rich people buy and sell houses as if they were popcorn. I'd give him about a year before he gets bored with all the peace and quiet. Besides, that girl friend of his is definitely too high-powered for a place like Taos."

She felt herself wincing as a stab of loss and pain shot through her. "She's a very attractive woman," Terry said in a voice that she tried to keep casual. "I suppose you've checked her out, too? I haven't seen her around before this morning."

"She's some kind of mystery woman, very stand-offish. I tried to pump her last night when she was alone at the Sagebrush bar. She did condescend to tell me that her name is Lenore Hitchcock, that she comes from New York and that she's only been here for the past three days. But she really clammed up when I tried to find out what had brought her to Taos."

Paco flashed him a knowing grin. "You're usually better than that at interviewing. Maybe your interest wasn't strictly professional?"

Skeeter looked vaguely sheepish. "Okay, so I may have come on a little too strong. I didn't know she already had a boyfriend. They look pretty chummy this morning. My guess is she probably followed him here from New York."

"Why this sudden excess of prurient interest?" Terry's voice was sharp. "Is the *Taos News* going to start a gossip column?"

Skeeter looked at her in surprise. "What's eating you, Terry? You're not your usual sunny self this morning."

"I'm sorry, Skeeter," she said, suddenly contrite. "It's just that I'm pretty annoyed with Mr. Brewster. He's already cost me a lot of time and trouble." She went on to tell the two men about the injunction and described the scene in Judge Cordova's courtroom. Skeeter listened with eager interest and flashed a broad smile when she came to the judge's verdict.

"That's showing them, Terry! Those millions of dollars don't always tip the scales. Let's hope we can teach Southwestern Towers the same lesson." He plunged once more into plans for the protest campaign. Terry tried to follow his lead, to produce her own list of names and committees, but her mind felt muddled and fuzzy. All her previous indignation seemed to have drained away, leaving her feeling spent and lifeless.

Finally Skeeter noticed her lack of attention. He stopped in mid-sentence and gazed at her curiously. "What on earth is the matter, girl? You look like your mind is a thousand miles away."

No, not a thousand, Terry thought. *Is it four miles or five to the old Martinez house? I wonder what she'll think of the fancy new improvements. I suppose she'll move in with him—or, for all I know, she may be living there already....*

She shook her head, dismissing the painful vision. "Sorry," she said. "I guess I was thinking of some of my work in the office."

Skeeter's boyish face crinkled into a frown of concern. "I suppose you *are* pretty busy. Maybe all this campaign work is too much for you to handle?"

"Oh, no, I didn't mean that," Terry declared on a new upsurge of resolution. "The campaign is just what I need. Work can get pretty boring, day after day. It's good to have a cause to throw myself into."

Skeeter seemed reassured and rattled happily on with his list of committees. Terry listened intently and gradually felt her enthusiasm returning. The thought of phone calls and meetings turned from a burden into something exciting. It *was* the perfect way to emerge from her hideout. But more important than that, it might even help her stop thinking about Neil Brewster.

CHAPTER SEVEN

"OF COURSE WE'LL HELP." Cecilia's eyes were bright with determination. "I'll start making phone calls this morning. That's a great idea of Paco's, having that *cabrito* roast this Sunday. I'm sure I can turn out a lot of the Spanish contingent for a feast of young goat."

"And I'll start rounding up the other lawyers." David was pacing nervously up and down the long, low-ceilinged living room behind the Janus Gallery. "There must be a lot of legal objections to this kind of project. We'll have to be well prepared to give chapter and verse if we intend to prove that to the council."

Terry set down her coffee cup on the richly carved wood of the Spanish-style coffee table. "I was sure I could count on you both. But I do feel a little guilty. It's going to get in the way of David's painting and all your efforts to build up a clientele for the gallery."

David poked moodily at the small piñon-wood fire in the beehive-shaped corner fireplace. "The gallery won't have much chance if we sit back and let these idiots ruin Taos. We've got to get into this fight. Our whole reason for coming back here is being threatened."

There was something forced, almost desperate, about his manner that triggered a small alarm bell in Terry's mind. "Incidentally," she said in a cautious tone, "how are things going with the gallery? Did you have a pretty good show at Fred Dernahan's opening?"

A shadow of worry dimmed Cecilia's cheerful expression. "Oh, yes, there were plenty of people. But most of them were the local freeloaders. We still don't attract much serious business. We sold only two of Fred's paintings. He's talking now about going to another gallery."

"Oh, Cecilia, that's so unfair! After all the publicity you managed to get him—that piece in *Southwestern Art*, that full-page spread in the Santa Fe paper—"

Cecilia waved a hand in weary protest. "You really can't blame him. Publicity doesn't mean much to a hungry family. It's okay, though; we can make it without him. We're planning to have a show of my father's paintings. They're not really all that good, but the Taos School is a kind of fad now. People will buy them just for the historical interest. At least we'll raise enough for the next mortgage payment."

Terry went cold with dismay. She knew how Cecilia loved the paintings her father had left her. Selling them was like selling a part of her childhood. Was the gallery really in that much danger?

She chose her words carefully, not wanting to make her friend feel worse than she already did. "I didn't realize your house was mortgaged. I suppose your parents needed the money to live on?"

"*They* didn't take out the mortgage." Cecilia's defiant tone showed how deeply her pride was wounded. "The house came to us free and clear. We were the ones who brought the bank into the picture. I wish now we hadn't done it. We should have gone more slowly, not spent all that money on renovations. But we didn't know the price of gas was about to double. Our heating bill was a whole lot more than we planned on, plus Gito's hospital bill for that bout of asthma. That put another awfully big dent in our savings."

Terry was appalled at Cecilia's revelations. She'd known the Quayles were struggling but hadn't guessed they were on the brink of disaster. Why hadn't she asked before? Had she really been so self-centered that she'd missed the ominous signs of financial trouble? Or had she made herself deliberately blind to their problems, knowing her own finances were still so shaky that she couldn't offer the loan that might have helped them?

She groped for comforting words but couldn't find them, then grasped with relief at the chance to change the subject. "How *is* Gito these days? The asthma hasn't been giving him any more trouble?"

Cecilia smiled, a fond maternal smile. "No, that's all under control. Gito is fine, growing like a weed and getting into all kinds of five-year-old mischief." She jumped up and went to the doorway that led to the bedroom wing. "Gito," she called, "come and say hello to Auntie Terry."

"Auntie Terry! Auntie Terry! Are we going to ride on the camel?" Gito entered the living room like a

miniature whirlwind and threw himself at Terry's
lap. She gave him a welcoming hug, then held him
away from her, assessing the changes in him since the
last time she'd seen him. He did look a lot more
healthy. The alarming pallor was gone, and the dark
brown eyes, so like his mother's, were sparkling instead of listless. "You're getting to be a big boy
now," she told him admiringly. "You must have
grown two or three inches since the last time I saw
you."

"The camel! The camel, Auntie Terry!" Gito
wriggled out of her grasp, seething with impatience.

"No, Gito, the camel's gone. He won't come back
till July, when it's time for fiesta. That's a long time
from now, a whole six long weeks."

The little boy's face clouded over with disappointment. Casting around for something to distract him,
Terry noticed the carved wooden toy he held in one
hand. "You've got a nice toy there, Gito. Will you let
me see it?"

Beaming with instant pleasure, Gito thrust the object into her hands. "It's a nice horse!" he shouted.
"Uncle Pedro made it."

Terry turned the toy around in her hands. Despite
the rough primitive carving, there was something
supremely horselike about it. The strong back legs
seemed to be just about to break into a gallop,
while the arch of the neck and shape of the head proclaimed the proud lineage of an Arab stallion.

"It *is* a nice horse," she said. "You must have lots
of fun pretending to ride it."

"I don't ride this horse." The boy's soft full lips

pursed in stubborn denial. "This horse is just for Sam Geromino. Uncle Pedro made him for Sam Geromino to ride on."

"You mean Geronimo, don't you?" David looked at his son with fond indulgence. "Is that what you and old Pedro do down by the river? He tells you stories about Indians and cowboys?"

"Not Ger-on-i-mo." Gito sounded each syllable distinctly. "Sam Geromino. He's a friend of Uncle Pedro. And Mrs. Geromino, she's the mommie. And all the little boys that get the spankings." He stared earnestly up at his father as though it was very important to make him understand that this was something quite different from cowboys and Indians.

"What's that?" David barked. He looked angrily over at Cecilia. "I thought my son had never even heard the word spanking. What has that crazy old coot been up to? I swear, if he's dared to lay a finger on Gito—"

"For heaven's sake, David, don't jump to conclusions. I keep telling you, Pedro loves Gito. I'm sure he would never do anything to hurt him. He's probably been telling him some old Spanish folktales." She turned appealing eyes toward the dark-haired boy. "Tell daddy that's all it is, sweetie. That stuff about the spankings—isn't it just a story?"

"No!" Gito insisted, exasperated. "It's not just a story. Sam Geromino lives there. Sam Geromino lives with Uncle Pedro—and Mrs. Geromino, too, and all the boys. They live with Uncle Pedro. He's their daddy."

David looked questioningly at Cecilia. "What the

hell is all this? You never told me old Pedro had a family."

Cecilia looked flustered and a little uncertain. "Oh, no, I'm sure he doesn't. I've known him since I was a child. He was always a loner. He lives by himself in a little old shack down near the old Taos bridge."

"How do you know? Have you ever seen it?" David's voice was unusually harsh. "Don't you think it might be a good idea if we checked out the place where our son spends so much of his time?"

Cecilia's chin lifted defiantly. "I know Pedro better than you do. He's a proud intelligent man, despite the fact that he looks like a tramp. I can't just barge into his house unless he invites me. Oh, come on, David." Her voice softened into a tone of affectionate coaxing. "It's nothing to make such a fuss over. Kids Gito's age have lots of imaginary playmates. You should be pleased he has this rich fantasy life— shows he's inherited some of his father's talent."

Ignoring David's frown of disagreement, she turned briskly to Gito. "Run along now and play with your horse. Aunt Terry and mommie and daddy have to do some grown-up talking."

"Okay, mommie, I'm going." Gito seemed as relieved as Terry to disengage himself from the sudden flurry of conflict. He ran toward the door, then turned to look anxiously at Terry. "When the camel comes back, can we go ride him? Promise, Auntie Terry?"

"Absolutely," Terry laughed. "When fiesta time comes, we'll go for a ride on the camel."

A beatific grin spread over the little boy's face. He disappeared into the hallway, heading back to his playroom.

"Now, you guys, let's get back to business," Cecilia said crisply. "David, I've thought of another job for your legal committee. It can start doing some research on Southwestern Towers, find out about all their financial connections."

"Do we really need any research?" Terry asked. "Skeeter seemed to know a lot about them. He says they're a Dallas-based outfit and they've already built a number of similar projects."

"I'd be willing to bet it's not quite as simple as that." David's expression was alert and calculating. "They're sinking a lot of money into these projects. Where does the money come from? They're probably part of some big conglomerate that can afford to take a loss in one of its ventures to offset its excess profits in another."

"Things are sounding worse and worse by the minute," Terry groaned. "Dallas money was bad enough. Now we're talking about a nation-wide combination."

"Or worse than that," Cecilia corrected somberly. "A lot of these outfits are multinational. I know it sounds pretty daunting, but we've got to know the extent of the power we're fighting. Besides, we may unearth some useful surprises. If some of the money turns out to be Japanese, for instance, we could play on that in stirring up opposition. People here wouldn't feel very friendly toward the guys who are giving American factories so much competition."

"Exactly," David said. "Let's hope Southwestern Towers turns out to be linked to some unpopular product—like high-priced feed or antibiotics for cattle. Okay, that's number one on our agenda. Steve Galliard handles a lot of corporate cases. He should be able to tell us where to start digging."

"You know who else might help?" Cecilia's eyes lighted up with sudden excitement. "Your newfound neighbor, Neil Brewster. He's had lots of practice in this kind of research."

"That's a great idea!" David seemed to catch fire from Cecilia's enthusiasm. "From all I've heard about him, he really hates these big conglomerates— thinks they have too much power over the consumer. Besides, this campaign is going to be expensive. If we can line Brewster up on our side, he may be willing to donate some of his money."

Terry felt as though a lead weight were pressing down on her. She'd hoped this campaign would help her forget Neil Brewster. Now it seemed to be leading her straight back to him. "What makes you think he'd be willing to help us?" she exclaimed in what she recognized as a shrill hostile tone. "The man is a stranger to Taos. He has no real idea of what's at stake here. Anyway, Skeeter says he's become a complete recluse. He's put all that crusader stuff behind him."

"Oh, Terry, he *does* care a lot about Taos traditions. Wasn't that the reason he asked for that injunction? And you heard what he said in court about the way he admires the early settlers' courage. Well, now's his chance to show the same kind of courage, helping us fight Southwestern Towers.''

Terry heaved a sigh of exasperation. ''You're misreading him completely. The man is absolutely self-centered. He has no concern at all beyond his own comfort. We'd simply be wasting our time to even suggest he should help us with this campaign.''

But her frantic attack failed to dent Cecilia's faith in her new idea. ''So what if we do waste our time? I think it's worth trying. Let's phone him right now—or better yet, let's go see him in person.'' She jumped up eagerly from the couch. ''Yes, that's what we'll do. That way we can make him see how strongly we feel about it. We'll all go up there right now. David, go get your jacket. We can drop Gito off at his usual baby-sitter's, so we can spend as much time as we need to convince Neil Brewster.''

A wave of panic swept over Terry. ''No!'' she cried. ''I won't go along with you. Neil Brewster has already caused me too much trouble. I won't lay myself open for any more insults.''

Cecilia stared at her in shocked amazement. ''Wow, Terry, that's quite an outburst. Don't you think you're taking this whole thing too personally? Just because you and this guy had a small disagreement, now that you've won, can't you let bygones be bygones?''

Embarrassed by the concern in Cecilia's eyes, Terry groped for the words to explain her dislike of Neil. If Cecilia only knew the reason behind it—the facile charm that had undermined her defenses, the pretense of friendship, the humiliating rejection.

But, of course, those were just the things she could never tell her—never. No one must ever know what a fool she'd been.

"Oh, come on, Terry," David said. "You don't have to like the man, but he might be a lot of help in saving Taos. Don't let your personal feelings stand in the way."

Terry realized she was trapped. There was no way now to escape this unpleasant visit. "All right. I suppose we should try it." She rose wearily to her feet, picked up her denim jacket and pulled it on over her drooping shoulders. "But I still think we're wasting our time. A self-centered boor like Neil Brewster will never understand how we feel about Taos."

CHAPTER EIGHT

THE OLD MARTINEZ HOUSE was a U-shaped building perched on the edge of a high plateau that fell away steeply to the wide fertile valley surrounding the small town of Taos. As the Quayles' truck and Terry's pickup rattled along the curving driveway that wound between the front of the house and the edge of the mesa, Terry inspected the improvements that Neil had made to the old adobe building.

The principal change was a huge picture window set into the wall that looked out over the valley. He'd also replaced some of the old wooden pillars in the *portal* that shaded the front of the house. Some local craftsmen had done a good job of carving new corbels to match the old ones, though the additions still had a raw naked look, contrasting with the silvery weathered wood of the original structure.

She noticed he'd done a lot of new planting. A scattering of young piñons now softened the rocky edge of the mesa, providing a brighter green accent among the soft gray green of the ubiquitous sagebrush. The new lilac bushes along the side of the house were flourishing their white and purple blossoms as confidently as if they'd been there forever.

Cecilia, more single-minded, didn't pause to examine the additions. She ran quickly up onto the *portal* and started beating a heavy tattoo with the horseshoe-shaped knocker. Terry reluctantly followed her up to the house, almost sick with suspense. This is stupid, she told herself. The man wasn't a monster. Why was she feeling this overwhelming panic, this fear that she wouldn't be able to cope with the situation?

It was really very simple. He would come to the door in a moment. She would say, "Hello, Neil," and introduce Cecilia and David. Then he'd invite them in, they'd make their big pitch for his help, he'd give them his refusal—polite but firm—and then her brief ordeal would be behind her.

It wasn't until she saw his face in the doorway that she realized the deeper source of her panic. She'd been expecting to see Lenore there, and for some crazy unexplained reason, that would have been much more unpleasant than any encounter she could imagine with Neil himself.

The hazel eyes flicked over the little group, then came to rest on Terry. His first look of blank surprise gave way to a smile that seemed to blend incredulity with amusement. Terry felt a hot rush of humiliation wash over her. She had certainly given him plenty of cause for amusement—snubbing him coldly this morning, and now turning up abjectly on his doorstep. No doubt he thought she'd come crawling back, completely subdued by the Brewster magnetism.

Come on, Terry, speak up. Let's get this charade over and done with. "Hello, Neil," she said lightly, marveling at the casual sound of her voice. "Could we come in for a minute? My friends and I have something we'd like to ask you."

The charm clicked on as though she'd pressed a button. He turned a beaming smile toward her companions. "David, it's good to see you. And this must be Cecilia. Come in, come in. You arrived at the perfect moment. I've been trying my hand at mixing margaritas. I could use some advice from some local experts."

He beckoned them through the doorway and led the way down the narrow hall into a room of unexpectedly large proportions. Terry saw at once what Neil had done. He'd ripped out two of the original walls, turning three smaller rooms into one big one. One of them had evidently been the old *sala*, the room dedicated to formal family gatherings. Neil had preserved the original *bancos*—the seating ledges built out from the walls—covering them with cushions in a brown-and-white batik fabric. The beehive-shaped fireplace in one corner looked old enough to be part of the house's most ancient section. The big picture window that filled the rest of the room's north end was obviously an addition, providing a view of the mountains to complement the front window's view out over the Taos Valley.

Cecilia breathed a little sigh of pleasure as she looked around at the way the room was furnished, noting the trim modern lines of the L-shaped sofa upholstered in brown-and-white cowhide, the rust-colored velvet covering the comfortable armchairs clustered around the fireplace, the brazier-type cof-

fee table with its copper receptacle in the center for
charcoal, the kachina dancer perched on the mantel,
the painting by Tàpies covering the whole back wall
with its abstract shimmer of glowing colors. "You've
done a lovely job here, Neil. It's a beautiful mix of
antique and modern."

Neil looked sincerely pleased at the compliment.
"Thank you. I'm glad you like it. Please make yourself comfortable now while I go take care of those
margaritas."

"That's really not necessary." Terry's voice
sounded tinny in her ears. "This isn't a social visit.
We're here on business." She saw him frown in apparent displeasure, and flushed as she realized what
he must be thinking. After her big spiel yesterday
about the Janus Gallery's struggles, he would suppose she'd brought her friends here to sell him something.

"Not personal business," she hurried on breathlessly. "Civic business—something very important.
It concerns the survival of Taos."

His eyebrows went up in a questioning look. "The
survival of Taos. That sounds pretty portentous. But
it doesn't need to rule out the margaritas. I'm a great
believer in combining business with pleasure."

"So am I," Cecilia chirped, plopping herself onto
the cowhide sofa. "I'd love one, and so would
David."

Terry felt as though she wanted to hit her. Why
was Cecilia getting them all bogged down in this
social nonsense? They should get right down to brass
tacks, present their case and hear his refusal. Then

she could escape from this man's unnerving presence.

"Terry, it seems you're outvoted. Will you yield to majority rule and have one, too?" Again that smile of barely concealed amusement, a smile that told her he was sure his charm had completely enthralled her.

"No thanks," she said firmly. "It's still a bit early for drinking." She caught Cecilia's astonished glance and hoped Neil hadn't seen it. In the schedule-free world of Taos, no time of day was considered too early for drinking.

Neil made no further attempt to persuade her. He nodded and headed out of the room, presumably toward the kitchen. As she saw the door close behind him, Terry could feel her tensed-up muscles relaxing. No longer feeling the need to brace herself against her host's attraction, she let herself sink into a comfortable armchair and take further notice of the room around her.

He did have a feel for the old Spanish tradition. That old wooden chest, for instance, with its primitive red-and-green paintings of lions and rabbits; and the graceful secretary-style trastero, its door panels carved with the familiar design of rosettes and pomegranates.

"He's got some really great stuff here." Cecilia's comment echoed what she'd been thinking. She grinned insinuatingly at Terry. "Now that you've seen this room, do you still think Neil Brewster doesn't understand Taos?"

All Terry's defenses snapped back into place. "What makes you think he knows anything about the treasures he's got here? They were probably chosen for him by some designer.''

"Terry, sweetie, what on earth has got into you?" Cecilia peered at her worriedly, as if she feared that Terry was coming down with a fever. "You don't usually make such a quick judgment on a stranger."

But that's just it. Neil isn't a stranger. He's much too good at getting under my skin. I have to fight like the devil to keep a safe distance between us. "I'm sorry," she muttered. "I know I'm in a bad mood. I guess I'm bracing myself against the inevitable moment when he rejects us."

"Rejects *us*?" Cecilia's eyes grew bright with speculation. "That's a strange way of putting it. Suppose he does turn down our request to join the campaign. It's not us he'd be rejecting—just a lot of work and bother." Her wide full lips curved in a little cat smile. "But somehow I have a feeling that's not going to happen."

Just at that moment Neil came back into the room, sparing Terry the need for further protest. He handed the drinks he was carrying to David and Cecilia, took one himself, then seated himself in a thronelike armchair, lavishly decorated with Mexican carving.

As she heard her friends echo Neil's murmured toast of *"Salud,"* Terry felt an irrational spurt of resentment, like a child being turned away from the grown-ups' party. After a few silent moments of appreciative sipping, Cecilia pronounced her verdict. "They're very good, Neil—just the right tartness. You could hold your own with any bartender in Taos."

"That's right," David agreed. "You may have found yourself a new vocation."

Neil inclined his head graciously. "Thank you for those kind words." He took another sip of the salt-frosted glass, then set it down on the table beside him and said to them briskly, "Okay, let's get down to business. Exactly what is this threat to Taos's survival?"

As if his words had been a starter's signal, Cecilia and David launched into a passionate explanation of the project Southwestern Towers was planning to foist on Taos, the need for resistance, what had been done thus far in organizing their campaign of protest. Terry, feeling awkward and out of things, watched from the sidelines, trying to assess the dark-haired man's reactions. He was listening intently, but his face was devoid of emotion.

It was David who finally asked the crucial question. "So that's how things stand, Neil. Now it's your turn to make a decision. Are you willing to help us fight Southwestern Towers?"

A veil descended over the hazel eyes. He sat for a moment in silence, seeming to consult some inner voice. When he finally spoke his tone was deeply troubled. "It looks as if you're up against really big money. Are you sure you know what you're getting into?"

"Of course we do." Cecilia's eyes flashed. "It will take hours and hours of hard work and a lot of money. We wouldn't have started this fight if we weren't prepared to pay that price."

Neil turned to her with a searching look. "Time

and money, yes. But that's only the beginning. These big outfits play by their own set of rules. If you set yourself up as a target, they can be pretty ruthless. You may find yourself in all sorts of personal danger."

David looked puzzled. "That sounds pretty melodramatic. Fighting this outfit may lose us a few Dallas customers, but outside of that, they can't do much to hurt us."

Neil's lips firmed into a thin grim line. "Don't be too sure of that. Remember, I speak from experience. I don't want to bore you with all the lurid details. Let's just say they hurt me enough that I'm pretty reluctant to stick my neck out again."

A rejection. Just what she'd predicted. Terry was startled at the strength of her disappointment. Wasn't this what she had hoped for, that the protest campaign would be free of Neil's distracting presence? Then why was she suddenly yearning for him to reverse his decision?

"That's quite understandable, Neil," she heard herself saying. "After all, you came here to get away from the rat race. Why should you risk disturbing your peaceful existence?"

Neil gave her a long level look. "That makes me sound pretty selfish. Is it fair to judge me without really knowing my motives?"

"Your motives seem to change from moment to moment." Terry was appalled by the acid tone in her voice, but some demon within her seemed to be driving her on to provoke him further. "One day you're proclaiming your deep love of Taos traditions. The next day you're saying it's not worth your while to help save them.''

Neil's chin came up in a gesture of angry defiance. "Speaking of changeable motives, you don't do too badly yourself. After all those splendid paeans to the Taos beer can, you're suddenly all gung-ho for tradition!''

"Whoa, there, you guys." Cecilia's voice cut through the heated exchange. "It makes me feel good to see your adrenaline flowing, but I think you've both got the wrong script for this here movie. We're supposed to fight Southwestern Towers, not each other.''

Terry was gripped by a sudden spasm of guilt. What on earth had she been doing, lashing out at him in that bitter attack? "I'm awfully sorry," she said in a quieter voice. "I really didn't intend to be so bitchy. I just got carried away. You remember how we were talking about commitment? I guess that's what I've found in this campaign—a way of making a real commitment to Taos." She laughed a little shakily. "And like any true believer, I overreact when I run into opposition.''

Something stirred deep in the shuttered hazel eyes. "Commitment," Neil said softly. "Does such a thing really exist? I thought it did, once. But the word meant something different to other people. In the end, it all turned out to be an illusion.''

"But it doesn't have to be that way. Commitment is what *you* make it. It doesn't depend on other people's reactions. Look, Neil—" Terry's voice was alive with enthusiasm "—you asked me yesterday if you'd ever fit in here. If you really want to, here's your chance to make some real friends in Taos. Once you join us in this campaign, no one will think of you as a mere outsider.''

His face relaxed in a rueful smile. ''You're an eloquent spokesman, Terry.'' His eyes searched her face questioningly, almost wistfully. Then he sat up straight in the regal chair, his eyes no longer veiled but full of excitement. ''All right, my friends, I'm in this all the way. Watch out, Southwestern Towers, we're coming to get you!''

''That's great, Neil,'' David said.

''Super!'' Cecilia exclaimed.

Terry smiled but couldn't manage a comment. She was still too astonished at her own peculiar behavior. Talk about commitment! It seemed she'd committed herself to spending a lot of time with the man she had just resolved to forget completely. Still, she could handle him now. And after all, he could really be a big help in their campaign.

The campaign, that was what was important—to forget all this personal garbage, just think about saving Taos.

''A toast!'' she heard someone saying. ''Let's have a toast to Southwestern's coming defeat.''

Neil was on his feet, heading for the door to the kitchen. He turned and cocked a quizzical eyebrow at Terry. ''You'll join us in this round, won't you? Or is it still too early?''

Terry nodded primly. ''Yes, I'll have one, thank you—if it's not too much trouble, that is.''

Neil's quizzical look deepened into amusement.

"No trouble at all, I assure you. Back in a moment."

When he returned a few minutes later, he was carrying a well-stocked tray—four salt-frosted drinks, a bowl of tortilla chips and a dish of *salsa*. The defeat of Southwestern Towers was duly toasted, and the four campaigners relaxed in companionable silence, sipping their lime-flavored drinks and dunking the crunchy chips in the piquant tomato-and-pepper sauce.

Over the rim of her glass, Cecilia grinned at Terry. "You realize the significance of this moment? Neil's offered you bread and salt—" she raised a chip in one hand and her glass in the other "—and you've accepted. According to the old Arab custom, that means you can't be enemies any longer."

Neil looked surprised and a little disconcerted. "Were we really enemies, Terry? I thought we'd merely had a small disagreement." His gaze was fixed appealingly on her, willing her to agree that it hadn't been that important. She tried to resist that appeal.

"You came on pretty strong that day in my office. And challenging me in court—that seemed like something more than a small disagreement."

She was pleased to see him look distinctly embarrassed. "Perhaps I reacted too quickly. Now I've had time to reflect, I realize the house isn't really so awful. I asked Gus Pickett to show me the plans this morning, and some features about it really impressed me. I understand now what you meant about your design fitting in with the line of the mountains."

Terry felt a flicker of pleasure. So he was finally

admitting her work had some merit. Perhaps they did have something in common, after all. . . .

Watch it, Terry. There goes that charm again. She felt herself stiffen with caution. Why should those half-hearted words of praise make her feel so absurdly happy?

"I'm glad you're becoming a little more reasonable," she said coolly, "but we didn't come here to talk about my houses. Shouldn't we be discussing the protest campaign? I'm sure you can give us a lot of good suggestions."

David picked up his cue and raised the question of research into the Dallas outfit's financial backing. Soon he and Neil were deep in earnest discussion about all the places to look for the relevant data. Neil seemed to grow more and more enthusiastic, pacing restlessly up and down as he threw out a string of suggestions.

As she watched his lithe muscled physique striding past her, Terry felt her body awaken to glowing awareness. This time she didn't try to damp down the warmth. The man was extremely attractive, no doubt about it. Safe on the sidelines like this, with no risk of involvement, she was free to relax and admire him for what he was—a magnificent animal, very much at home in his body.

She became abruptly aware that Cecilia's eyes were on her, and she checked her wandering thoughts, hoping they hadn't shown on her face.

"Well, sweetie, what about it?" Cecilia murmured under her breath. "Have you changed your mind about the big bad Neil Brewster? It seems he's not so self-centered as you made out.'' Her eyes, watching Terry, were shrewdly appraising. The matchmaker's gleam hovered just below the surface.

Terry flushed a little, gripped once again by an upsurge of caution. ''He talks a good game, I'll admit. But I'm going to wait till I see how he follows through.''

Cecilia rolled her eyes in mock exasperation. ''Ye gods, you're a tough nut to crack. You still dislike him, don't you?'' She hesitated a minute, looking speculatively at Terry. ''Or maybe it's not dislike. Maybe the trouble is you like him too much.''

Terry's cheeks positively flamed then. Just at that moment the men turned back toward them, evidently having finished their discussion. Cecilia's words seemed to trumpet into the silence. Terry stared at the floor, praying that Neil hadn't heard them, or if he had, that he wouldn't divine their meaning.

''It's getting pretty late,'' David said. ''We'd better make tracks for home. We can meet tomorrow and get our plans down on paper.''

''Please don't rush away like this. I feel I'm just getting to know you. Why don't you stay for supper? I can mix up a pan of something vaguely Chinese—nothing gourmet, but enough to sustain life for a while. Then after supper we can go on with our planning.''

David looked pleased. ''That sounds like a great idea—''

''Wait, David. What about Gito?'' Cecilia's voice cut into his unfinished sentence. ''It's awfully nice of you, Neil—'' her smile was bland ''—but being par-

ents, we'll have to take a rain check." She turned to
Terry, her expression decidedly mischievous. "Terry,
you don't have to go. Why don't we deputize you?
We'll put you in charge of getting all this down on
paper. I'm sure you don't mind, do you? Then you
bring your notes down to me tomorrow morning,
and I'll type them up for David and his committee."

All kinds of alarm bells were jangling in Terry's
head. She couldn't stay here with Neil. She just
wasn't ready for that kind of exposure. Desperately
she groped for some excuse. *I'm sorry, I have an appointment.... Thank you a lot, but I'm meeting
someone for dinner.... I promised to stop at
Skeeter's and give him a briefing....*

But none of the words would come out. Some trick
of her muscles was keeping them stuck in her throat.
Meanwhile Neil was smiling at her, that tentative
wistful smile she found so irresistible. "Yes, please
do stay, Terry. I'm getting kind of fed up with my
peace and quiet. I'd really enjoy some company for
supper."

"Of course she'll stay. That's already settled.
She's got her own pickup outside, so transportation
won't be any problem." As she headed out of the
room and down the hallway, propelling a bewildered
David in front of her, Cecilia kept up a nonstop line
of chatter, making it hopeless for Terry to get a word
in. "Bye-bye, Neil," she called out, dashing across
the *portal* toward their truck. "Awfully glad to meet
you. See you at the *cabrito* roast on Sunday."

As the truck rattled off into the gathering twilight,
Terry became abruptly aware that she and her host

were sharing the doorway. She felt a compelling need to escape from the narrow hall and retreat to the big living room, where she could deal with him at a comfortable distance.

Neil was still gazing after Cecilia and David, watching the truck make its way down the bumpy road past Leo's and Sandra's house site. Terry slipped quietly down the hallway, feeling oddly like a prisoner trying to escape her captor.

By the time he joined her, she was back in her armchair, nervously dunking a chip in the dish of *salsa*. She expected him to go back to the thronelike chair. Instead he moved over to stand beside her, looking down at her with an indecipherable smile. "How about helping me finish the margaritas? I've still got two in the pitcher. Then I'll get down to work on our Chinese dinner."

She didn't want a second margarita, but she couldn't think of a way to refuse it without making things even more awkward. He took her silence for assent and went out to the kitchen, carrying both empty glasses.

She sat there stiffly, waiting for his return. Her body ached with what seemed intolerable tension. The room around her seemed to throb with emptiness. In the deepening twilight, without Cecilia's and David's comforting presence, it seemed a forbidding place, full of shadowy dangers. She felt an overwhelming urge to cut and run, leave this provoking man in the solitude he claimed to crave, jump in her pickup and race down to her safe little house in Talpa.

He came back so quietly that she hardly heard him. She accepted the salt-rimmed glass, carefully avoiding any physical contact. For a moment she thought he was going to sit on the nearby sofa. Then, mercifully, he moved back to the thronelike chair. He smiled at her across the shadowy distance.

"I like this time of day. The house feels full of mysterious presences—all the souls of departed Martinez owners."

Oh, no, she thought, *no more of this mystical stuff. That was part of what made me so foolish at Midnight.* She stared at the floor in silence, trying to find the words to put things back on a businesslike basis. "Look," she blurted out abruptly, "you don't have to do this, you know. You're not obliged to provide dinner for anyone who turns up on your doorstep."

His eyes widened in surprise. Then he grinned a little. "Actually, this is the first invitation I've issued. I assure you, I wouldn't have asked you unless I meant it. You're not just anyone, Terry. I've been thinking about you a lot since yesterday, hoping for a chance to apologize for some of the things I said up there at Midnight. But you didn't give me a chance today at the coffee shop."

Terry felt her chest constrict, her breathing grow shallow. Here it was, the apology she'd been hoping for so desperately last night. But now she felt strangely reluctant to hear it. It seemed to threaten her painfully achieved equilibrium.

"There's no need for apologies," she said stiffly. "As a matter of fact, I'd rather not talk about it."

"But I want to talk about it." Neil was leaning toward her, his eyes full of earnest entreaty. "I said some very harsh things on the spur of the moment—accusing you of not being sincere in your work, of merely wanting to enhance your image. That was really out of line, completely unjustified. How can I judge your motives? I hardly know you."

The weight of disappointment seemed to pervade her entire body. This wasn't the apology she had longed for. What she wanted to hear were different words altogether: "Terry, I'm sorry I said all those things about heartless women. You're not heartless, I know. I realized that the moment I kissed you. . . ."

Grow up, Terry, she told herself harshly. *It's time you left this fairy-tale nonsense behind you.* She forced herself to give him a brief frosty smile. "That *was* a bit hard to take, Neil, especially since, as you say, you hardly know me. Okay, you've apologized. Now let's let bygones be bygones."

He made a little grimace of dissatisfaction. "You say that so glibly. I don't believe you really mean it."

Terry breathed a sigh of exasperation. "Really, Neil, you're pretty provoking. You just apologized for presuming to read my thoughts. Now you're at it again, telling me I don't really mean what I'm saying."

Neil's lips were set in a line of stubborn resistance. "You tell me in words you forgive me, but your body language is sending a different message. Look at you now, perched on the edge of your chair, all your muscles tensed, ready for fight or flight. How can I help believing that you're still nursing a grudge against me?''

Terry started to protest, then realized he'd been speaking the obvious truth. She made a conscious effort to relax her muscles. But even as she leaned back into the armchair, she felt the tension tighten along her jawline. "What do I have to do to show you I mean it?" She tried to make her voice sound light and casual. "Flop around the place like a Raggedy Ann doll?" A sudden unwanted vision assailed her: Lenore Hitchcock this morning, gently placing her hand on top of his. *I bet you don't lecture her on her body language.*

The hazel eyes lighted up with quick amusement. "I'm obviously not doing a very good job of apologizing. What I'd like to do is start again from the beginning—that lunch at El Patio. I felt we were starting to move toward a solid friendship. Can't we go back to that moment and take it from there? I'd really like to have you as a friend."

His voice was soft, almost pleading. His earnest eyes were watching her intently. Terry knew she should have been feeling triumphant. Here was the great Neil Brewster, formerly so scornful, now almost begging for the gift of her friendship.

But with a sinking heart, she realized friendship wasn't enough—not since that moment at Midnight. Friendship was a thin pale substitute for the feeling she really wanted from this man.

She had to be sensible. He wasn't here to assuage her pent-up emotions. She had to rid her mind of all that romantic nonsense, start treating him as a friend, imagine he was someone pleasant but unexciting—a brotherly type like Skeeter, for instance. Yes, that was the way to get this thing under control. Whenever the Brewster charm started to overwhelm her, she'd just blank him out and pretend she was talking to Skeeter.

The thought made her face relax into a genuine smile. "Okay, Neil. We've just made a bargain. We'll wipe all the bad stuff out and start again on the basis of friendship. So now that we've both finished our margaritas, why don't I give you some friendly help in the kitchen?"

After that, things started going very much better. Her awkwardness dropped away as they chopped up a mound of onions, mushrooms and peppers. The "vaguely Chinese" dish turned out to be delicious. They brought it into the living room and ate it in front of the fireplace, where Neil had started a pile of piñon logs blazing. Soft music drifted around them from hidden speakers, an unobtrusive accompaniment that enhanced the cozy feeling of the shadowy room, lighted only by firelight and candles.

There were one or two moments when Terry felt herself slipping into a yearning mood. She tried the ploy of thinking of him as Skeeter, and it worked surprisingly well, filling her with increasing self-confidence. She did have this thing licked, by golly. Those stupid emotions were well under her control now. Pretty soon Neil Brewster would no longer be a problem.

After they finished eating, they settled down to putting their plans on paper. As she took notes on his carefully marshaled scheme for research, Terry felt her admiration growing. She sensed the depth of experience from which he drew his battery of suggestions. Skeeter was right; he wasn't the standard rich playboy. There was something deeper here, a sense of real dedication.

Secure in her new-found control, she let herself relax completely—which, she decided later, was why the song had affected her so powerfully. She didn't recognize the first few bars, only knew it was something teasingly familiar: the Carpenters, one of her favorite groups. Idly she let herself follow the softly crooned words.

> Such a feelin's comin' over me,
> There is wonder in most ev'rything I see,
> Not a cloud in the sky, got the sun in my eyes....

Suddenly she tensed. She knew what was coming next. She couldn't bear to hear those words at this moment.

"All right, Neil," she said briskly, raising her voice to drown out the insinuating lyrics, "that about wraps it up. You can add any further details when you talk to David."

He looked up at her in surprise. "There are still a few more points we ought to cover." The words of the song seemed to sweep up around them. To Terry's ears, the lyrics sounded horribly obvious.

> And the reason is clear,
> It's because you are here....

"Sorry, Neil," she said loudly. "I've got to go now. I've got a lot of things to do tomorrow."

The Carpenters had just launched into the chorus. Neil turned his head, smiling in pleased surprise. "Listen," he said. "That song. Isn't that the one you were trying to think of at Midnight?" He listened intently, humming along with the words.

> I'm on top of the world lookin' down on creation
> And the only explanation I can find. . . .

"Is it? I don't remember." Terry snatched up her jacket and started toward the hallway. She knew only too well how that chorus went on from there. She couldn't stand to be there when Neil heard it.

She stepped out into the hallway. The Carpenters followed her, their voices pouring out from another hidden speaker. . . .

> The love that I've found
> Ever since you've been around
> Your love's put me at the top of the world.

Neil had followed her into the hallway and now stood with his back against the heavy front door, barring her exit. "What the hell is all this rush, Terry? It's not all that late—only eight-thirty. If you're fed up with all this planning, let's relax with a little nightcap." He reached out and placed a comradely hand on her shoulder. His touch seemed to burn through her denim jacket, and it triggered a memory of another, more intimate touch:

Lenore's hand on his this morning at Michael's.

Terry jerked herself out of range, aware that she was acting irrationally, but unable to stop. "No thanks," she said. "I've got to be going. I'm sure you can find someone else to share that nightcap."

He let his hand drop to his side. "Someone else?" he said blankly. Then his eyes narrowed in sudden understanding. "The woman you saw me with at Michael's? Is that what's bothering you? Is that why you keep that chip on your shoulder?"

Terry's cheeks flamed with humiliation. She thought she had put this morning's jealousy behind her. But apparently it still seethed under the surface, awaiting this off-guard moment to erupt in shameful self-revelation. Desperately she fought to regain her composure. "I don't know what you mean by a chip on my shoulder." Her voice rang in her ears, fraught with telltale tension. "All I care about is this campaign. Your busy social life really doesn't concern me." She stopped abruptly, aware that she was only exposing herself more clearly. Neil stared at her with a thoughtful frown.

"But it does concern you, Terry. That woman you saw in Michael's—she's very much involved in our...misunderstanding. I think I ought to explain—"

"Please don't. I don't want to hear it. If you'll just get away from that door and let me go now—"

"Not till you hear me out. Listen, Terry, we've been skirting around the real issue. What really upset you at Midnight was the confused state of my emotions—the way I switched from a kiss to a brutal attack. I've been wanting so much to explain that, but I kept shying away—I suppose because it's such a painful subject. That woman at Michael's this morning—she's a very important part of the explanation.''

Terry's whirling emotions coalesced into a burst of illumination. ''A very important part. . . .'' Why, of course she was! She was the woman Neil was really in love with. But like any man, he had his moments of aberration when his senses trapped him into a passing adventure. That's what had happened at Midnight. Alone in that lovely setting, with a new unknown female who was obviously only too willing. . . .

Of course. That explained the sudden coolness. A moment of unguarded passion—and then the guilt of remembering his real commitment. No wonder he'd lashed out at her as if he loathed her. It was really himself he hated for being unfaithful.

She felt the tears pricking behind her eyelids. Resolutely blinking them back, she raised her chin and stared at him unflinchingly. ''You really don't need to explain, Neil. I've already got the picture. We all have these little moments of weakness, especially up in the mountains. The altitude does crazy things to your psyche. I was obviously feeling a little unbalanced myself—''

''Terry, please don't talk nonsense. You don't understand at all. Come on back and sit down now and let me explain what really happened.''

The soft concerned tone of his voice went straight to her marrow. *I've got to get out of here,* she thought wildly. *Another few seconds and I'll really start crying.* She summoned her last ounce of

strength, willing her voice to sound brisk and friendly.

"Look, Neil, this is all very silly. You told me a
while ago that you'd like to start over. I'd like to start
over, too. But the only way we can really develop our
friendship is by erasing what happened at Midnight
from both our memories."

Neil's face closed up and turned impassive. He
stood looking at her for a moment as though weighing her words one by one, testing how seriously she
meant them. Then he shrugged lightly and moved
away from the door. "All right—if that's the way
you want it."

"Yes, Neil. That's how I want it." She reached for
the doorknob and pulled the big door open. "Good
night," she said in a bright social voice. "Thank you
so much for the lovely dinner."

She flung herself out the door and dashed toward
her pickup. Resisting the urge to look back at the
doorway, she gunned the truck into motion and set
off down the little rise in a spray of gravel.

A thousand feet down the dirt road, Leo's and
Sandra's foundation was a pale gleaming mass under
the moonlight. She pulled off the road and cut the
motor. Feeling completely drained, she collapsed on
the steering wheel, burying her face in her outstretched arms.

Thank God, she thought. *I got out of there before
I made an utter fool of myself.* She shivered a little,
realizing once more the strength of those buried emotions. Still she hadn't done too badly, all things considered. She'd kept her feelings in check through

most of the evening. And most important of all, she'd solved the nagging puzzle of Neil's strange behavior at Midnight.

She raised her head and stared into the darkness above her. The starry night sky—diamonds against black velvet—made her sigh with wonder. Yes, all things considered, she'd handled things very well. Then why did she feel this unbearable sense of loss, just because a ghost town named Midnight was no longer part of her personal history?

CHAPTER NINE

"Wow! Look at that mob scene! That's a whole lot more people than I expected." Skeeter nosed his battered VW bus onto the graveled space beside the old stable that now served as Paco's workshop. Terry jumped out of the van and stared down at the rambling farmhouse nestling in the hollow behind them. Under the gnarled apple trees that surrounded it, more than a hundred people were milling and talking, coming together in little groups, then moving apart to form new combinations.

On a patch of bare ground between the two beds of portulacas that framed the big front door, a mound of coals glowed brightly. The little goat's carcass was stretched on a spit above it. One of Paco's teenage sons was busy turning the browned side upward, giving the paler portions their chance at the searing heat. A tall gray-haired woman, her portly body bulging above her tight denim jeans, was ladling a marinade over the *cabrito*. Drops of oil-and-wine mixture sizzled and flared as they rained down on the fiery layer of coals beneath it.

"I'm not surprised," Terry said. "Cecilia's phone committee is really efficient. She's got it down to a science—ten people phone ten people, then each of those has another ten people to call. In the past three days they must have contacted half the people in Taos.''

"And of course food is always a great incentive. Paco was right; this makes a good campaign kickoff. Now if even half these people can be persuaded to donate some of their time—''

"They will. I'm sure they will.'' Terry's voice rang with confident pleasure. "Now why don't you go start mingling and spreading the gospel? I'll take this potato salad in to Maria and see if she can use my help in the kitchen.''

She slid open the van's side door and lifted out a huge foil-covered bowl. Making her way through the crowd in the grassy yard, she stopped from time to time to exchange a few words with a friend or acquaintance. She was surprised and pleased to find so many strange faces among them—most of them dark haired and dark eyed, evidently the modern descendants of those pioneers who had arrived in the time of DeVargas.

The front door of the flat-roofed adobe farmhouse led directly into the big country kitchen. Terry saw at a glance that her services wouldn't be needed. The big room was already filled with chattering women, busily cutting up salad or taking turns at stirring the two big pots of *pozole* that were filling the air with the smell of spicy meat broth.

Paco's wife, Maria, greeted her with a beaming smile and carried the bowl of potato salad off to join the rows of other donations. It was understood at affairs like this one that the host's sole duty was to provide the *cabrito*. His guests could be counted on to fill in the rest of the meal—casseroles, salads, a dazzling array of pies, cakes and other confections.

"So good to see you, Terry. Isn't it great that we've got this big a turnout? I've met so many new people—here's one of them now. Let me introduce you. This is Mr. Brewster. He's a new Taoseño, only here for a couple of months."

As Neil's tall figure loomed up behind her hostess, Terry felt an electric shock lance through her. It startled her to see him in these surroundings. These past few days she'd been so busy campaigning that she'd almost forgotten he would be at the party.

"I've already met Mr. Brewster." She gave Neil a cool brittle smile. "I'm glad you were able to make it tonight. It's really a special privilege to share in this old tradition."

Maria grinned up at Neil with obvious approval. "Thank you for all that wine, Mr. Brewster. I'm sure it will be appreciated." She looked over Terry's head and sighted her husband, just coming in the door with the empty marinade bowl. "What do you think of that, Paco? A dozen bottles of real Italian Chianti. How's that for class? It certainly beats our usual bargain jug wine."

Paco nodded in approbation. "Neil may be a New York Anglo, but he's already picked up a lot of the Taos spirit. Thanks a lot, Neil, for that truckload of piñon. With the price of firewood these days, that's really a help. Now after the goat is finished, we can build a big bonfire to keep the party going."

Terry felt a twinge of vague disquiet. She was glad

Neil had chosen such thoughtful contributions, but the fact that he'd made them without asking her advice somehow detracted from her own importance. Unconsciously she'd cast herself in the role of his guide and mentor. Now it seemed he was doing quite well in gaining acceptance without any help from her.

She quickly damped down the tiny flare of resentment. "We're really lucky to have Mr. Brewster with us. Now how about you, Maria? Can I do anything to help you?"

"You sure can, Terry. The goat will be done in another few minutes. The boys have already set up the trestle tables. Maybe you could take out this oilcloth and spread it on them. And you, Mr. Brewster—see all those bags in the corner? They're full of paper plates and plastic utensils. Let's get them out on the tables, so these hungry hordes will have something to put their food on."

As Terry made her way with him toward the trestle tables, which the boys had set up under the apple trees, she groped awkwardly for a topic of conversation. The thought of her ignominious exit that other evening returned to plague her, especially the way she'd exposed her jealousy of Lenore Hitchcock. At least she could make amends for that particular blunder, show him she understood the claims of that prior commitment.

"Is Miss Hitchcock with you tonight? I was hoping to meet her. But perhaps she doesn't care for our rustic amusements?"

Neil stopped in his tracks, staring down at her with a questioning look. "What's all this about Miss

Hitchcock? This is the third time today someone has asked me about her. I didn't realize she was so well known in Taos.''

Terry felt herself flushing. ''Are you finding out what it means to live in a town as small as this one? It's pretty hard to keep one's relationships private.''

''I'm beginning to realize that. My fellow townsmen seem to have an absolute genius for leaping instantly to the wrong conclusions. But I didn't expect you to go along with the gossips.''

The accusing note in his voice made her temper flare. ''Is it really so awful for a friend to be concerned about you? To tell you the truth, I'm delighted that you have someone to help you to be less of a hermit.''

''Thank you so very much, Terry—'' Neil's voice had gone heavily sarcastic ''—but I'm afraid your delight is distinctly premature. Lenore isn't planning to stay in Taos. As a matter of fact, she's left for Albuquerque. I've just been bidding her Godspeed over a farewell drink in La Cocina.''

Suddenly Terry felt a rush of elation coursing through her. *Calm down,* she told herself. *This doesn't change things. Just because she's left town, that doesn't mean the relationship is over.* Lenore might easily change her mind and come back tomorrow. Or Neil might decide to follow her back to New York. And anyway, why should her absence be making Terry so happy? Did she still have some silly idea of taking her place? Neil had already made it clear he was not in the market. And besides, he was too much like Paul. Getting involved with him would only mean trouble.

She became aware that Neil was looking at her strangely. She'd been so absorbed in her own reactions that she'd forgotten all about the bundle she was carrying. She came to herself with a start. "For heaven's sake, why am I standing here daydreaming? Give me a hand with this oilcloth, won't you?"

As he helped her spread the bright orange covering over the tables, Terry kept her eyes averted from his. She felt absurdly transparent. Could he see right through her to all that adolescent-type turmoil inside? She was trying to think of a graceful way to escape his unnerving presence when she heard Paco's voice ring out over the hubbub.

"The *cabrito*'s ready, folks. We're going to carve it. Line up with your plates and grab yourself some good eating."

Terry was caught in a sudden inundation of people. When, plate in hand, she took her place at the end of the serving line, she saw Neil up ahead, some twenty guests between them. She breathed a sigh of relief and turned to the friendly middle-aged woman behind her, who she quickly found out was a local high-school teacher. By the time they had claimed their portions of the *cabrito*, Terry had enlisted her help in designing a campaign flyer.

As she paused to pick up some salad from one of the tables, a beaming Cecilia appeared beside her. "Hi, sweetie. I almost missed you in all this crowd. It's turning out to be a terrific party."

"Thanks to you and all your hard work on the

phone. Where are David and Gito? Aren't they with you?''

"David's around here somewhere. Gito's off on one of his jaunts with Pedro. I tried to get the old man to come to the party, but I guess he's too much of a hermit. I promised to bring him back a hunk of *cabrito*." She cast an appraising glance over the crowd. People were standing in clusters, attacking their piled up plates with evident relish. "Speaking of hermits, your friend Neil Brewster seems to be really coming out of his shell. Look at him, over there with Eloy Hernandez. I hope he can talk him into supporting us. His little Spanish weekly reaches a lot of influential people.''

Terry followed her gaze and saw Neil standing over near Paco's workshop, talking intently to a heavyset fortyish man with a dark goatee and mustache. Beside him stood a voluptuous teenage girl, her smile a brilliant contrast of flashing white teeth against her olive complexion.

"Looks like he's charming Eloy's daughter, too. You really can't blame her. The guy is so good looking, and it must be a big surprise, finding an Anglo who speaks such fluent Spanish.''

"Neil speaks Spanish?" Again that flare of irrational resentment. She was supposed to be the Taos old-timer. But he, the newcomer, was already making friends in circles where she had only a nodding acquaintance.

"He speaks it better than I do. Seems he was working with some Puerto Rican neighborhood organizations.''

Terry felt a twinge of disquiet. The more she learned about Neil, the more she admired him. Perhaps she'd been really off base in her first assessment. Perhaps he wasn't as arrogant as he'd seemed. For a man with all that money to throw himself into all these unpopular causes—

"Hi, Terry. *¿Qué tal?*" She heard Leo's voice behind her and turned to greet him.

Sandra was standing beside him, grinning at Terry in impish delight. "Hi, Terry. It's good to see you. I hear this husband of mine has been forgetting his manners. I've told him he has to apologize in person."

Terry felt a quick stab of pain. She didn't want to remember that scene in El Patio, but Sandra's words were forcing her to relive it. "Don't be silly, Sandra. He's already apologized. Besides, that neighbor of yours really provoked him. I hear he's been nosing around out at the house site. I hope he hasn't been giving you any more trouble."

"No trouble at all." Leo grinned broadly. "In fact, he seems to have done some kind of flip-flop. He's still not too crazy about your design for the house, but he seems to be trying to find things to like about it. And he's turned surprisingly cordial. Yesterday he asked Gus and me in for a beer."

Terry started to answer, but her words were cut short by a loud electronic shriek. She turned and saw Paco Reyes climbing up on an improvised platform, while one of his sons rearranged the PA system.

"Fellow Taoseños, you all know I'm not much of a speaker. I wouldn't be up here at all, except that

I'm plain damn scared—scared and angry—about what this big corporation is trying to do to Taos.''

He paused for a moment, scanning his listeners' faces. "I'm glad to see you all here tonight. If you haven't done it yet, I'm asking you now to write your name down for one of our committees." He waved his hand toward the farmhouse. "Maria and some of her friends are waiting inside to sign you up. I warn you, folks, this will be a long hard fight. But with people like you behind us, I'm sure we're going to win this battle.''

He paused again, and his face took on a somber look. "You all know that sometimes, *aquí en Taos*, we don't do such a good job of working together. We split up into little factions—Anglos against Hispanos, rich against poor, newcomers against old-timers. That's what these Southwestern people are counting on. They'll do their best to split us, turn us against each other.''

His face relaxed in a beaming smile. "But the people I see here tonight aren't going to fall for those tired old tactics. We're going to stick together, all us Taoseños, and show them they can't destroy the town we love!''

A chorus of cheers erupted into the twilight. Paco stepped down from the platform into a crowd of enthusiastic well-wishers. As the cheers died away, Terry felt a rush of warm feeling flood her body. Paco was right. They were all in this together. The cold hard forces of money would have to yield before this vibrant outpouring of human spirit.

She turned toward Leo and Sandra, her face alight

with emotion. "He's right, you know. We *are* going to win."

"I hope so, Terry." The voice sent a shock running through her. Leo and Sandra had disappeared. In their place stood Neil, looking wary and troubled. Alone among all the crowd, he seemed untouched by Paco's enthusiasm. "Don't forget, the campaign is only beginning. It will take more than eloquent speeches to make Southwestern Towers abandon their project."

Terry felt as though she'd been splashed with a pail of cold water. Her first reaction was a spurt of resentment. How could he stand there so calmly, so immune to the crowd's excitement? A second later she realized he was right. Too much false confidence could be a drawback. It might keep them from seeing the true situation.

She nodded. "You're right, of course. We've had a lovely party, but now it's over. Starting tomorrow we've got to get down to hard work."

His gloomy look was replaced by a teasing smile. "The party's not over yet. There's still plenty of wine left, and the boys are getting the bonfire started. How about joining me in a glass of Chianti?"

All Terry's high spirits suddenly drained away, leaving her feeling inert and bone-weary. "No, I don't think so, Neil. I've run out of energy. I guess I'm not used to being with so many people."

"I know what you mean. I'm kind of talked out myself, with all this politicking. All the same, I don't feel like going home yet. You know what I'd like to do?" His eyes searched her face for a moment, alert and questioning. "Is there some quiet bar with an outdoor garden where we could sit and watch that magnificent sunset?"

"There's a place called Que Sera. Have you ever been up there?" Her wary desire to keep her distance gave way to a generous impulse to share with him one of her favorite haunts. "It's up in Valdez, just off the Ski Valley Road—makes you feel you could almost reach out and touch the mountains."

"Sounds great. Let's go. The Blazer is over there behind that old stable." He stepped aside to let her move ahead of him through the crowd. Halfway to the stable, she caught sight of Skeeter, deep in conversation with R.C. Gorman, the flamboyant Navaho artist, resplendent tonight in a red-and-purple beaded headband.

"Wait just a minute, Neil. I've got to go talk to Skeeter. He drove me here this evening. I'd better go tell him I've got a ride home."

"Okay. I'll meet you there by the car."

The grassy space under the apple trees was still crowded with people. A few were drifting away toward the parking area, but the mob didn't seem to be appreciably smaller. It took her several minutes to work her way over to Skeeter and Gorman.

Skeeter saw her coming and greeted her with a Navaho shout of welcome. "*Ya ta he*, Terry. Had enough of the party? Gorman was just suggesting we adjourn to the Sagebrush. How about it?"

"Thanks, Skeeter, but I'm kind of tired. I think I'll skip it. I just came to tell you I've got a ride home with Neil Brewster."

Skeeter's face stiffened into an icy mask. "Oh, you have, have you? Well, isn't that just peachy. Okay, run along, Terry. Far be it for a lowly reporter to stand in the way of the heir to the Brewster millions."

Terry stared at him in surprise. "For heaven's sake, Skeeter, don't be silly. Neil's only making a friendly gesture."

Skeeter glowered at her over his drooping mustache. "Sorry, Terry. It's really none of my business, but you already know I'm a pretty silly person."

Terry, nonplussed by his strange reaction, groped for some soothing phrase to smooth things over. She started to say, "See you tomorrow in Michael's," but Skeeter had ostentatiously turned his back and resumed his earnest conversation with Gorman.

As she made her way toward Neil's four-wheel drive, Terry tried to make sense of Skeeter's sarcastic comment. Why should this pleasant young man, whom she'd always thought of as a kind of younger brother, suddenly start to sound so hurt and jealous? Was it really impossible for a man and a woman to have a plain old uncomplicated friendship?

When she reached the Blazer, Neil was already sitting behind the wheel. As she climbed into the seat beside him, she could feel a knot of excitement warming the pit of her stomach. She smiled ruefully into the gathering shadows. She could hardly describe her friendship with Neil as uncomplicated, but maybe this unexpected invitation would help her get things back on an even keel. At least it would give her more practice in reining in her own unruly emotions.

THERE WAS ONLY ONE other couple on Que Sera's flagstoned terrace, cantilevered from one of the hillsides that formed the southern rim of the Valdez Valley. Neil and Terry chose a table facing due west, where the sun, a bright orange ball in the mauve-and-crimson sky, was about to dip below some distant mountain ranges that looked like dark blue clouds—or perhaps they were dark blue clouds that looked like mountains. The jutting peaks directly behind them looked much more solid, a wall of gray-and-green rock closing in the end of the valley, marking the limits of human habitation.

Neil raised his glass of Fundador brandy. "*Salud*, Terry. Thank you for bringing me here. You're doing an excellent job of introducing a rank outsider to Taos."

Terry smiled at him over the rim of her glass. "You don't really need a guide, Neil. You were doing well on your own tonight. You seem to have made a lot of new friends."

Neil waved his hand in a deprecatory gesture. "It takes more than one conversation to make a friendship, but at least I gave people the chance to look me over. I was pretty impressed with Eloy Hernandez. He was filling me in on the younger Chicano writers. And then there's a shrewd old guy named Ben Montoya—"

"You met Ben Montoya?" Terry was startled. "I didn't even know he was at the party. He's supposed to be the real power behind the local political scene."

"He's Leo Martinez's uncle. Leo made a point of getting me to meet him."

Terry felt another jolt of obscure disquiet. In all the time she'd known Leo, he'd never mentioned the fact that Montoya was one of his uncles. "That's quite a switch," she said dryly. "I guess you've been making some special efforts to be a good neighbor."

He flashed her a rueful smile. "I've been doing my best to mend my fences. I hope I can make everyone forget that bad first impression. That's one of the reasons I'm glad you came up here with me."

Terry felt all her muscles tightening. That intimate smile of his seemed to be signaling something warmer than friendship. She groped for a way of defusing the conversation, putting it on a more impersonal basis.

"I always like to bring newcomers up here. It's so different from modern-day Taos—more like it must have been fifty years before. You feel you're someplace a hundred miles into the mountains."

"You come here pretty often?"

Terry wrinkled her nose in a little grimace. "I really don't go any place much these days. My work has been keeping me tied down to my office. But when Paul was making the film, we practically lived here. He shot a lot of scenes down there in Valdez. We'd come up here for lunch every day and stay here most of the evening after he finished shooting." She gazed meditatively down into the darkening valley. The distant houses looked like a little toy village. Lights were beginning to appear in some of the windows. "It's expanded a lot since then—mostly newcomers building summer houses."

"What year was that? It must have been about '79."

"The summer of '78. He finished the film in September, just a couple of months before the end of our marriage."

"You split up that long ago? That's a little surprising."

"How do you mean, surprising?" Terry found herself in the grip of two conflicting emotions. She still found it painful even to mention her marriage, but for some undiagnosed reason, she felt an urgent need to tell Neil just what had happened.

He looked at her cautiously, obviously trying to guess the strength of her feelings. "It's really none of my business, but somehow I get the impression that you're still very much involved with your former husband."

"No, not really." Terry knew she wasn't being entirely truthful, but she didn't want him to see her as the poor wounded victim. "I guess it did take a long time for the scars to heal. For a while it turned me into a kind of hermit. But these past few months, I've started coming out of my shell. I think my spell of hibernation is almost over."

His face lighted up in a brilliant smile. "It's good to hear that, Terry." His eyes turned thoughtful. He seemed to be taking stock of some inner reaction. "I suppose all it takes is time. After a while, a person gains some perspective. One eventually gets to the place where one even stops feeling that sickening sense of betrayal."

Betrayal. Yes, that was the worst part about it. How does he know that's the way I felt about Paul? She probed gingerly at some of her personal sore spots. The scars were still there, all right, only partly healed over, the most painful one being Paul's duplicity—the way he'd pretended to be so concerned about all her plans and ambitions—and then turned around and treated them with disdain. Worse than that, he'd made her feel guilty for having some goals of her own instead of prostrating herself before Paul Fontaine's genius.

She was just on the verge of telling Neil all about it but stopped abruptly, warned by an inner voice. *Whoa, Terry. He'll think you're wallowing in self-pity. Is that the way you want Neil to see you?* "Don't you think we're getting into a pretty personal area? If we're really going to be friends, we ought to respect each other's territory. I'm sure you wouldn't like it if I started asking you about Miss Hitchcock."

"I have no objections to talking about Lenore Hitchcock." He was looking directly into her eyes now, intent on convincing her. "I tried to tell you about her the other night."

Terry felt her breath catch in her throat. She realized she was longing to hear his explanation. Why had Lenore left Taos? Had their relationship really ended, or was this just one phase in a long-term commitment?

She hesitated a moment, alarmed by the very intensity of her feelings. Why was she so concerned about Lenore Hitchcock? If all she wanted was friendship, she'd have to get rid of this stupid jealousy. "Really, Neil, I'd rather not hear it." She tried to make the words casual, but tension gave her voice a contradictory edge of protest.

Neil's eyebrows lifted in quizzical amusement. "Don't look now, Terry, but I think that chip is back on your shoulder."

Damn. Why were her feelings always so transparent? Really, she was being as silly as Skeeter. Why couldn't she simply accept the friendship Neil offered without dragging in all these irrational feelings?

"I'm sorry," she said. "It really has nothing to do with you as a person. I've been hiding out for so long in my little cave that I tend to put up barriers against everybody."

Again he seemed to test her words against some inner reaction. "I know," he said softly. "Once you've been hurt, it's hard to trust anyone. But you have to keep taking the risk. It's pretty lonely, this business of hibernation. Taking risks is part of the price of friendship."

Terry felt a quick leap of sympathy for the brooding man beside her. It was comforting to have someone share her feelings. Why did she keep trying to typecast him in Paul's image? He did have a lot of Paul's characteristics—self-confidence, magnetism, the kind of charisma that made him the center of attention. But in other ways he was very different. This offer of friendship, for instance. Paul would have scorned so pallid a feeling as friendship.

Pallid, that inner voice scolded. *Is that how you feel about friendship? Sounds like an echo of Paul. Has he still got you brainwashed?* The memories came flooding back, all the heady excitement of Paul's extravagant courtship: the rooms full of flowers, the insistent phone calls from all over the globe, the time she'd refused to see him and he'd camped in a tent on her doorstep.

She was twenty-two when she met him at a charity cocktail party during the final year of her architectural studies at U.C.L.A. From the first she had found him immensely attractive. After her quiet childhood in the middle-class Los Angeles suburb where she'd spent the summers working in her father's drugstore, she found it exhilarating—and a little frightening—to be pursued by this man from so different a background, the glittering world of Hollywood and Beverly Hills. Fearful of being overwhelmed by Paul's powerful ego, she'd tried with determined resistance to ward him off. But her impulse for self-protection had acted on Paul like a challenge. He was piqued and surprised when she didn't fall instantly into his arms like all the other women who kept buzzing around him.

It had been his proposal of marriage that finally broke through her resistance. The great Paul Fontaine, who'd proclaimed himself an eternal bachelor, caring so much for her that he wanted to live with her for the rest of his life! To a woman already dazzled by his attraction, that offer had been a heady inducement. She'd abandoned any attempt to control her headstrong emotions and leaped confidently into what seemed to be a rapturous future.

And then, the sickening sequel. She realized now that he'd never had any intention of following through on the partnership he'd promised. To him, she'd been merely a trophy, a prize to file away in his collection while he went blithely on to newer, more glamorous conquests.

The memories kept coming, filling her with the same old unbearable pain: that studio party just two days after their wedding—Paul paying obvious court to the chic Italian reporter while Terry sipped her drink, bewildered, in a corner; the nights, growing more and more frequent, when he came home at two in the morning; those other nights when he didn't come home at all. . . .

Stop this, Terry, she told herself firmly. She remembered Neil's surprise at learning five years had passed since the end of her marriage. He was right; she should have got over it long ago. Why did she keep rehashing these painful memories? It was time she put them behind her and refused to think of anything but the present.

She remembered a sentence from one of the endless series of self-help books to which she'd become addicted just after the breakup: *There is only one way to get rid of old habits: replace them with new ones.*

Wasn't it time to put that advice into action? She could start right here, with the way she behaved toward Neil. Thus far she'd been waiting for him to make all the moves—the invitation to Midnight, the cozy dinner, this excursion to Que Sera. Obviously she was following the same old pattern, the pattern that had led her straight to disaster. She'd been so concerned with her role as reluctant virgin that she hadn't bothered to really get to know Paul. Perhaps it was time to try a new kind of behavior—break out of her passive role, play an active part in defining this newfound friendship.

She felt her heart start to race. This new approach was a little scary. New habits, she told herself, gritting her teeth. The phrase seemed to ring in her mind like a battle slogan.

She smiled at Neil, bolstered by the sudden resolution. "Could you come to my house for dinner tomorrow night? I think you know Talpa, don't you—that little village ten miles south of Taos? I can't promise you anything festive like Paco's *cabrito*, but it would mean another chance to get out of your cave."

He looked a little surprised, then smiled at her in evident pleasure. "I'd like that, Terry. I'd like that very much. Now how about one more glass of this excellent brandy? Let's drink to the end of our mutual hibernation."

CHAPTER TEN

TERRY SLID THE ROASTING PAN halfway out of the oven and poked a long fork at the cinnamon-coated chicken that lay on its bed of fresh green chilies and onions, simmering in a bath of diluted sherry. Good, it was almost done. Right on schedule. The antique schoolhouse clock on the kitchen wall was just about to strike seven. That meant her dinner guest would be here any moment.

Nervously she checked over the last-minute details: places laid on the old refectory table, cooked rice keeping hot in the other side of the oven, a pan of freshly picked snow peas ready for steaming, a pitcher of margaritas keeping cool in the refrigerator.

What else, she thought. *I know I'm forgetting something.* She felt a knot of tension forming in her stomach. She must be suffering from hostess's jitters. How long had it been since she'd had someone here for dinner? Thanksgiving Day, six long months before. She'd cooked the pheasant Ivan Winter had shot. The realization shocked her. She really had been turning into a hermit. She hadn't seen Ivan for months—or Meg and Jim Watson, either, the other guests who had spent the holiday with her.

She made a mental note to telephone the three of

them tomorrow. The protest campaign would give her a good excuse for getting in touch after all these months of silence.

She was really glad now that she'd decided to join the campaign. Even those organizational meetings she'd dreaded were proving less awful than she had anticipated. She felt a little glow of satisfaction, remembering her first committee meeting. It had been an impressive turnout—six of the seven architects in Taos. And they'd been surprisingly willing to work together, once she'd eased them away from their speculations about George Anhiser's motives for shunning the protest. She still found it hard to believe that George had accepted a contract from Southwestern Towers. True, he seemed to like building condominiums, but thus far they'd all been well outside the town boundaries. Surely he realized that a high-rise building would destroy the special flavor of downtown Taos. . . .

She brushed the thought from her mind, telling herself to concentrate on the dinner. What was it she'd forgotten? Something important— Oh, yes, the Parker House rolls!

She snatched the tube of chilled dough from the little refrigerator. Just as she broke it open, she heard the buzz of the door bell. As she stared at the sticky dough ballooning out of its cardboard casing, she felt an instant of panic. She'd been looking forward all day to being the perfect hostess, poised and gracious. Now Neil would see how completely inept she was, maybe sneer, as Paul used to do, at what he called her utter disorganization. . . .

She drew a deep breath and managed to pull herself together. Shoving the rolls back on the shelf from which she'd plucked them, she wiped her doughy hands and assumed a welcoming smile as she hurried to answer the second buzz of the door bell.

She'd given a lot of thought to how she should greet him. Something warm but not too warm, friendly but not too friendly. She'd decided to use the old Spanish phrase, *Mi casa, su casa*, the traditional way of saying a guest should consider the house he was entering as his own home.

When she saw him standing there, almost filling the low narrow doorway, she felt her bones dissolving into some jellylike substance. Her head seemed to buzz with confusion; the well-rehearsed phrase went straight out of her mind. The best she could do was to gasp out a hasty hello and wave her hand in an invitation to enter.

He didn't seem to notice her flustered manner. He stepped into the low-ceilinged living room and handed her a square, flat gift-wrapped package. "I brought you a little present. I just happened to see it downtown and remembered it was one of your favorite records."

Terry's heart gave a sickening jolt. Even before she got the package unwrapped, she was virtually sure what it would turn out to be. She stared blankly down at the Carpenters' album, trying hard to manage a smile of pleasure. She forced herself to scan through the list of titles. Yes, there it was—"Top of the World."

Instantly she saw herself up at Midnight, standing

beside him as they gazed out over the endless vista of
mountains, her whole body aroused and aching with
awareness. She brushed the vision away and looked
at him through a fog of pain and confusion. "Thank
you so much, Neil. How nice of you to remember."
She thrust the album into her record rack, gripped by
a feeling of helpless anger. Why did he keep remind-
ing her of that fiasco? She was working so hard at
uncomplicating their friendship. He should keep his
side of the bargain, forget it completely, help her pretend it had never happened.

She glanced up at him, tempted to take back her
words, tell him it wasn't really nice of him to remember. But recalling her role as hostess, she stifled
the impulse. "I won't play it now, though—maybe
later, after we've finished dinner."

He grinned down at her with a maddening lack of
comprehension. "Personally, I like the record you're
playing much better. Julian Bream, isn't it?" He
looked around the room appreciatively, noting the
beehive fireplace, the roughly peeled *vigas*, big pine
logs, that formed the ceiling beams, the little aspen
twigs, known as *latillas*, arranged in a herringbone
pattern between them. "His style of guitar fits in so
well with this architecture." A teasing note crept into
his voice. "You have a lovely place here but not quite
what I expected. There seems to be a surprising
absence of beer cans. And your roof is completely
devoid of solar collectors."

She grinned back at him, relieved that the conversation had moved to this joking level. "The beer cans
are there. You just can't see them under all the

adobe. And I've got great plans to turn the house solar. Whenever I manage to find the time and money, I'll put in a layer of rocks under my living-room floor to absorb the heat blown down from my solar collectors—which, incidentally, I plan to make out of black-painted beer cans.''

Neil gave an appreciative chuckle. "Well, at least you're running true to form, though it's hard to believe you can stand to waste all that sunlight in the meantime."

"I don't entirely waste it." Terry looked up at him with a challenging smile. "Come along, let me show you the greenhouse. We can have some drinks out there while we watch the sunset."

She led the way through the candle-lighted study, doing double duty tonight as a dining room. He sniffed appreciatively as they entered the brightly lighted kitchen. "Something smells good. A local recipe?"

She nodded. "*Gallina borracha.* I picked it up at the Tres Muchachas in Santa Fe. It won't be done for another few minutes—plenty of time to enjoy our margaritas." She glanced at him nervously, overcome by another attack of hostess's jitters. "Unless you'd like something else? There's Scotch or red wine, or a little bourbon."

"No, thanks," said Neil, still grinning. "As you already know, I'm hooked on margaritas. All that lime juice is making me very healthy."

She took out the icy pitcher and filled two salt-frosted glasses, then led the way through the side door into the little greenhouse.

Though the sun was already low on the western horizon, the day's heat lingered, wrapping them in a tropical atmosphere. Her nervousness faded away as she pointed out each flat of thick green foliage—the tomato and bell-pepper plants, the lettuce, the perky green onions. Neil smiled down at her in evident admiration, "So you grow your own salads all through the winter? That's pretty impressive. I bet they taste a lot better than the stuff they sell at Safeway."

"You can judge for yourself tonight at dinner. But this setup does more than just provide me with salad. During the day, I leave the door to the kitchen open, and the heat from the greenhouse helps to warm the house."

"You're a pretty good saleswoman, Terry. You sold me on your campaign, and now you've almost convinced me I need a greenhouse." His eyes took on an intimate musing look. "I wonder what you'll convert me to next?"

Standing next to him in the narrow greenhouse aisle, Terry was fiercely aware of how tiny the space was between them. The warm moist air closed in around her, smothering her. Waves of heat seemed to radiate between their two bodies, pulling her inexorably into Neil's orbit. She had a sudden impulse to reach out and touch his arm, so close to her, so achingly familiar....

You've got to get out of here, Terry. You can't stand this. She groped for a way of escape and remembered the garden. "This is only part of my self-sufficiency program," she chirruped brightly. "Come on out here, and I'll show you the rest."

She stepped out the door at the other end of the greenhouse, beckoning him to follow. The cool evening air acted on her like a tonic, strengthening her wavering resolve. She realized she'd been perilously close to overstepping the bounds of mere friendship. Well, that wouldn't happen again. She'd learned her lesson. She couldn't do much to tame her treacherous body, but she could keep plenty of space between herself and this man who claimed he only wanted her friendship, but whose physical presence kept sending a different message.

She waved a hand toward the network of neatly plowed furrows. "It's still too early for most kinds of outdoor planting, but I've put in a few of the things that can stand cold weather—radishes, cabbages, and my all-time favorite, those Chinese snow peas."

Neil stooped down and snipped off one of the pale green pea pods. "Terrific," he said, looking down at her as if they were sharing some momentous secret. "Isn't it strange that we seem to have all the same tastes—margaritas, Julian Bream and now these snow peas." He nibbled on the edge of the tender pod, his eyes fixed on hers, his lips sensuous and caressing. Terry stood mesmerized. Anticipation rippled through her body. For a moment they both stood transfixed in the deepening twilight. Then Terry broke away, heading for the safety of the kitchen.

He followed her in and silently accepted a second margarita. His eyes were searching her face. He seemed to be asking himself some puzzling question.

"What's the matter, Neil?" she asked lightly.

"You look as though you've seen something you weren't expecting."

"I guess I didn't think you were so...well, domestic. The professional women I've known didn't go in much for things like gardening and cooking." He looked a little embarrassed then at making such a personal comment. "But of course, in the city it's harder to do things like this. Most people don't own enough land to grow their own produce."

"It doesn't take all that much land. The way real-estate prices have doubled and tripled since I came here, I think I'm lucky to have a whole acre. It's really all in the way you use it." She grasped at the chance to switch to a more neutral topic. "I've made a special study of Japanese gardening methods. They can grow stuff on land Americans would call useless—like some of the rocky hillsides we have around here. As a matter of fact, I've designed a low-cost housing project for some land in Llano Quemado, just a few miles from here—land that's going for only two thousand an acre."

His eyes were alive with interest and amusement. "A housing project? That sounds pretty ambitious. Where do you think you're going to find all the beer cans?"

She acknowledged his teasing smile with a humorous grimace. "I'm sorry, no beer cans in this one. They wouldn't fit in with the federal regulations. I'll have to go back to lumber covered with plaster." She looked up at him excitedly. "Would you like to see my design? It's nothing like the usual housing project."

"Knowing you, I'm sure it's not." He smiled indulgently at her, and she was briefly aware of how attractively his eyes crinkled at the corners. Then her troubling personal reactions dissolved in a rush of professional pride. "Come on and have a look at the plans. I've got a copy of them here in my study."

As she started to leave the kitchen, Neil laid a restraining hand on her arm. "Wait a minute, haven't you forgotten something? You didn't lock the outer door of the greenhouse."

Terry steeled herself against the shock of physical contact. "I never bother to lock my doors," she said stiffly. "I know all my neighbors are honest. Anyway, if someone wanted to rob me, it's the easiest thing in the world to force one of these windows."

Neil looked slightly abashed. "I'm afraid it will take me a little more time to shed my big-city suspicions." When he took his hand away, Terry felt as though it had left a scorched imprint.

She hurried on into the study and pulled a big, rolled-up drawing out of the weathered nail keg she used as a bin. She felt a moment's frustration at not being able to lay it out on the refectory table. Then she beckoned to Neil to take hold of the bottom edge while she unrolled it.

He peered intently at the drawing that stretched between them. After a minute or two of concentration, he raised astonished eyes to Terry. "This is fascinating, what you've done here. The houses look so unregimented. I guess it's because they're set at all sorts of angles instead of being lined up like an army barracks.''

"That's because of the way I've fitted them into the hillside. You can see it better in this cross-sectional drawing.'' She fished around in the bin and pulled out another long roll of paper. Eagerly Neil helped her unroll it. Terry felt herself flushing with pleasure at his reaction. She was sure he wasn't just being polite. He was genuinely impressed with her ideas. Well, the plans were good, damn it! Why did she always feel such a need for some man's approval?

Neil was tracing some lines on the drawing, trying to visualize the finished houses. "Each one of these has its own little greenhouse attached, but there doesn't seem to be much room for gardens.''

"Oh, yes, there is. Look here.'' She traced some crosshatched areas with her finger. "Each house has a series of eight terraced plots, each one of them ten feet square. On eight hundred square feet, you can raise a lot of produce. And the best thing about it is how much you save on water. The irrigation starts up here at the top and trickles down through all the rest of the garden. That's the Japanese way of insuring no water is wasted.''

Neil whistled in admiration. "Very ingenious. Very ingenious indeed. In fact, I think this is brilliant. When do you think you'll get a chance to build it?''

Terry gave him a rueful smile. "You know what I call this project? *El sueño imposible*—the impossible dream, especially now with all these federal cutbacks. Once it's built, it could be self-supporting.

But first I'd have to have the initial investment."

Neil's eyes turned meditative. "Don't give up too quickly. I'm sure there must be some way of solving that problem." He released the edge of the drawing, returning it to its rolled-up position. Then he pulled another smaller drawing out of the nail keg. He didn't wait for her to help him unroll it but pulled it open between his outstretched arms. "What's all this?" He sounded astonished. He flicked a glance at Terry, his eyes full of questions. "I thought you didn't go in for high-rise buildings."

"Oh, that old thing. You can just disregard that. It's something I designed while I was a student—a typical L.A. condominium complex. Even back then, I wasn't too crazy about it. But it did win first prize for me in a competition, and that's what got me my job with Fairfield and Warner."

Neil was still studying the drawing, pursing his lips in concentration. "Don't downgrade yourself, Terry. This isn't just a typical condominium. It's got some very nice features—the balconies, for instance, and that patio area up on the tenth floor. If I were ever forced to live in L.A., I wouldn't mind living in this particular building."

"That's nice of you, Neil, but I really don't have any interest in that kind of work." She seized the drawing almost brusquely, rolled it up and thrust it back into the bin. She knew why the sight of the drawing made her uneasy. It belonged to her life with Paul, the life she was trying so hard to leave behind her. That's why she'd never shown it to anyone here in Taos.

Don't think about that now, Terry. Just concentrate on the present moment. You're supposed to be serving the man a dinner, remember? So how about getting those rolls into the oven?

Doing her best to act the proper hostess, she settled him with another drink in front of the fireplace. Once she was out in the kitchen, away from Neil's disturbing presence, the dinner preparations proceeded smoothly. In a matter of minutes the food was all on the table, the claret uncorked and ready to pour.

By the time they had finished dinner, she was blessedly free of her adolescentlike turmoil. She suggested they drink their coffee in front of the fireplace and settled down beside him on the sofa, feeling completely at ease despite his nearness. Even the touch of his fingers as he passed her the sugar didn't trigger the usual unsettling tingle.

Good girl, Terry. You're learning. She leaned back, feeling a glow of pleasant relaxation. Somewhere outside, she heard the hoot of her resident owl, the one who lived in the big pin oak tree beside the garden. Farther off in the distance, a chorus of frogs was beginning its nightly performance.

"Listen to all the night sounds," Neil murmured softly. "That's one of the nicest things about living out here in the country: the birds, the frogs, the crickets—and all that silence. You feel like you're a million light years away from the city."

He gave an amused little chuckle. "It really hit me today, when David and I went down to the State Park Commission. You know how small Santa Fe is, compared to New York or L.A., but it seemed like a huge buzzing mass of noise and confusion. The city traffic was almost too heavy to cope with. I kept longing to get back here to peace and quiet.''

Terry looked up at him alertly. "I didn't realize you'd been down there. Did you learn anything from the commission?''

Neil shook his head glumly. "They're an accomplished bunch of stonewallers. When we mentioned the deal with Southwestern Towers, they clammed up completely—kept referring us to a couple of legislators. When we tried to track *those* gentlemen down, no one could find them. David and I think some commission staffer must have warned them.''

"It's too bad your trip was such a waste of time.''

Neil sighed resignedly. "You get used to that in this business. These big corporations know how to throw up smoke screens. Half your time is spent chasing down blind alleys.''

"I'm sure you must have found it pretty frustrating—the consumer-advocacy thing, I mean. How did you get into it in the first place?''

He raised a quizzical eyebrow. "You mean how did a rich man like me get involved with the poor folks? That's a long story, Terry. I never felt rich while I was growing up. Of course, I heard some vague talk about all the Brewster millions. But my parents only gave me a small allowance, and our family life wasn't especially luxurious. I guess they were determined not to spoil me.

"Then when I went to Harvard, I learned more about how my great-grandfather had built his empire. You've read about the age of the robber barons? Caleb Brewster was one of that breed's prime examples—a ruthless manipulator, bamboozling his trusting stockholders and ripping off the U.S. treasury.

"That was a shock to me. I didn't like the feeling of being linked with that old pirate. It seemed to tie me down, limit my freedom to be myself. I was very fond of my father, who spent a few hours a day in his Wall Street office and the rest of his time overseeing the work of his charitable foundation. Still, I couldn't shake off the shadow of that old rascal, Caleb, whose money had given his grandson the luxury of being altruistic.

"When my father died, I was twenty-four, just two years out of college and still not quite sure what to do with my life. He left a generous trust fund for my mother, but the bulk of the Brewster empire came to me. Even after all I'd read about its history, I found it hard to believe the extent of my holdings. It didn't feel right, one person inheriting all that money— money I felt was tainted by old Caleb's ruthless tactics.

"I gave a lot of it to good causes. But that all seemed so unreal, just shuffling around meaningless bits of paper. I had a nebulous feeling that I ought to be getting involved in some kind of action.

"Then this consumer group came to me with a protest petition. One of the Brewster companies was marketing a toy that was dangerous to children. Their evidence was very convincing, and I promised them I'd try to do something about it. Since I owned more than half the company's stock, I assumed it would be a breeze to get the toy off the market.

"That's when I started learning the facts of corporate life. The management of the company was very good at making excuses and camouflaging the problem. What they weren't very good at was obeying my orders. In the end, I had to bring my own suit against them. You can imagine the sensation that caused—Neil Brewster vs. Brewster Enterprises.

"Other consumer groups began to adopt me as their champion, and pretty soon I was up to my ears in the advocacy business. I liked it at first—I found it exhilarating. During most of the past seven years, it has given my life a sense of purpose. But finally I got carried away by my own self-importance. I took on an outfit that was too big for me to handle."

"Olympia Tires, you mean?"

Neil nodded curtly, his eyes brooding. But he'd revealed more about himself in the past few minutes than Terry had dared hope for. That encouraged her to probe further.

"David said you pulled out of that case before it was settled. What happened, Neil? Why did you get so discouraged?"

His face became rigid as he stared tensely into the fire. "I just told you what happened. I overestimated my own importance. I was used to fighting middle-sized corporations. But Olympia Tires was part of a huge conglomerate. I should have known they were too big for one man to tackle." He turned to her, his eyes dark now with sudden anguish. "I don't know much yet about Southwestern Towers, but I have this gut feeling about them. I think we're up against the same kind of power."

Terry felt a chill of apprehension. She knew Neil was speaking from painful experience. Was it really true that she and her friends could lose this battle? Then she remembered Paco's stirring words, the cheers of more than a hundred voices filling the old apple orchard. "They may have a lot of power, but we can beat them. This time you're not alone in your fight with the giant. As Paco said, we're all in this together."

Impulsively she laid a hand on his arm and looked deeply into his eyes, willing him to absorb some of her sureness. "Just put all those doubts aside, Neil. By the time this is over, you'll be very glad you joined us."

"I'm already very glad." His eyes looked almost black in the flickering firelight. His voice had turned softer, deeper. "It brought you back into my life. That's all that matters."

Terry sat there immobile, feeling the fireworks explode throughout her body. A familiar tension was starting to throb between them. She struggled to shift her gaze away from his, but some overwhelming force kept their eyes locked together.

Too fast. Things were moving too fast. Her heart started hammering in sudden panic. Desperately she groped for some way to break loose from the paralyzing web of attraction. The silent night closed in around them, making her feel that no one else existed but the two of them there in the firelight, poised on the brink of some fateful decision.

"The night is too quiet for me. Let's have some music." She forced out the words through her tightened throat. "I'll go put on another record."

"Don't go, Terry." He reached out and touched the back of her hand, then closed his own hand around hers and held it tightly. Her firm decision dissolved in a rush of unbearable longing.

He pulled her roughly into his arms. His lips searched hers with a desperate need for closeness. For a second, she found his intensity almost frightening. Then, her starved body arching against him, she exulted in his wiry muscular strength. Lost in his arms, she felt the solid world melting away around her, as though the two of them were rushing through a long dark tunnel, welded together, hurtling toward some unknown destination.

His hands pressed fiercely into her shoulder blades, drawing her even more intimately against him. Her arms closed around his broad shoulders, pulling his muscular torso down to crush her throbbing breasts. Her hands moved caressingly across his back, delighting in the feel of his hard taut flesh. Sensuously, she pressed her slim body against him, feeling new barriers disintegrating with every delicious second they clung together. Finally, after what seemed an aeon of golden closeness, his grip relaxed a little. He lifted his lips from hers and gazed down at her, his eyes filled with wonder. "Terry, Terry!" His voice was soft and husky. His breath was coming in short hard gasps.

A sparkling fountain of joy welled up inside her, filling her veins with tingling effervescence. The joy

was contagious; she saw the answer glow in his soft
hazel eyes. Reaching out, she traced the lines of his
face, stroking the winged black eyebrows, outlining
his sharply angled cheekbones, caressing the firm
edge of his jaw. Her eyes were luminous with pleasure, her parted lips softly inviting. She saw Neil's
face flush with a new upsurge of desire. Then he
cupped her head tenderly in his hands and began dot-
ting kisses along the side of her neck, dipping into the
hollow of her throat, then retreating back to her
earlobe—tender firefly kisses, each infinitesimal
touch sparking a tiny explosion of feeling. His lips
moved around to the sensitive skin at the back of her
ear. His tongue began circling inside it, teasing her
singing nerves. Every inch of her body was humming
with expectation. Parts of herself she'd almost forgotten existed came suddenly alive with a violent
clamoring hunger.

Her need was almost too much to be borne. Just
when she thought she couldn't stand it a moment
longer, she felt his hands close around her breasts,
filling her flesh with a soothing warmth. Deep inside
her, an answering warmth swelled to greet it, flooding through her body, filling her limbs with a languorous weakness. She clasped her own hands over
his, forcing him to grip her breasts more tightly, and
gasped as a jolt of powerful desire shot through her,
wiping out all conscious thought.

The warmth gave way to a scorching heat. Her cotton shirt felt harsh against her skin. Moving as
though in a dream, she reached up to unfasten her
top button, then took his hand and guided it under

her bra onto her naked flesh. His fingers closed convulsively, then relaxed in a cradling caress, stroking
her breast in feathery circles. Then he lifted it out of
her blouse, and she felt the warm sigh of his breath
wafting across the stiffened nipple. When his lips
came down and closed softly around it, they seemed
to draw out the last ounce of strength from her body.
She felt as though she were made of air, floating
effortlessly on some magic carpet. Gratefully she
abandoned all conscious thought, overwhelmed by a
bodily pleasure far beyond anything she'd ever experienced.

Then his hands were gently stripping the blouse
from her shoulders, his fingers trailing down the
sides of her rib cage, probing with teasing touches,
triggering new minefields of sensation. The caresses
became more demanding. His hands gripped her
shoulders, pulling her close against him. With a deep
groan, he reached out and lifted her legs, stretching
her out full length on the sofa.

Her body welcomed him as she felt his heavy
warmth covering her like a blanket. Her hips began
to move against his in a sinuous motion. She shifted
her slim legs, making room for his hard lean thigh to
slip between them, then closed them to grasp him
tightly. Every inch of her flesh rejoiced in the way
their bodies fitted together, gloried in the sense that
they were made for each other, like interlocking parts
of a jigsaw puzzle.

His lips were on hers again—hungry, demanding—
his hands moving restlessly over her narrow waist
and softly rounded hips. With each maddening

touch, she felt a sense of discovery, as though his caresses were creating a new, more perfect body, more adept at giving pleasure, more generous in surrender. She felt herself shudder as wave after wave of sensation lifted her higher and higher toward the center of a dazzling circle of light. She lost all sense of herself as a single being. There were no longer any such people as Neil and Terry—only one glowing, triumphant creature, soaring, soaring....

A coal burst in the fireplace, startling her back into the realm of reason. She felt dizzy, disoriented, as though she'd just stepped back from the brink of a dangerous cliff. She drew a little away from Neil, feeling a sudden need to put some space between them.

"We're going too fast, Neil," she murmured. "This is too important a thing to rush into blindly."

Neil blinked at her dazedly. Then he smiled with tender concern. "Whatever you say, my darling. I've waited a long time for you. I guess I can wait a little longer."

He eased his weight against the back of the sofa and lay quietly there beside her, his hand gently tracing her face's outline. Grateful for his undemanding nearness, she settled her head contentedly on his shoulder. "What a surprise." Her voice was soft and teasing. "Just when you had me convinced that all you wanted was friendship."

He gave a little groan and pulled her tightly to him. "I thought that was all I wanted. I thought years would have to go by before I could fall in love with any woman. But with you—how can I say it, Terry—

I feel such a sense of rightness. When I came through your door tonight, I felt as though I was coming home—finding my roots at last, after a long confusing journey.''

She felt his fingers combing through her hair, sending delicious tremors all the way from her scalp to her toe tips. Then he shifted slightly away, smiling down at her as he brushed his hand over the silver blond strands, pulling the hair out of its coil, stretching it down to form a veil over her breasts, patting it over them with delicate touches.

He chuckled with pleasure. "You know who you look like now? Alice in Wonderland. A wide-eyed Alice, half afraid, half elated, who's just taken a bite of the magic mushroom."

She stiffened in shock, feeling herself grow icy with apprehension.

Alice in Wonderland. That's what Paul had called her, taunting her with her lack of sophistication. "You're such an idiot, Terry. Did you really think I was going to be your White Rabbit? It's time you got over those adolescent daydreams."

She pulled away from Neil, grabbing his wrists to force his hands from her breasts. "This is all very pleasant, Neil, but you're still moving too fast. It's hard to keep up with all these sudden mood changes."

He stared at her, bewildered. "What's the matter, Terry? You're looking as if I'd said something to hurt you."

"It's nothing you said, Neil. It's just your whole attitude." She snatched up her shirt and pulled it back over her shoulders. Quickly she buttoned it up, obstinately confining her gaze to her busy fingers. "You seem to expect me to fall straight into your arms as if I were some sort of giddy schoolgirl."

A frown of perplexity creased Neil's forehead. "I wish I knew what you're really thinking. Are you punishing me for the way I behaved up at Midnight?"

Terry attempted a laugh, but all that came out was a tight little choking sound. "Why must you keep harping on that tired old theme? I'm fully aware of what happened up there in the mountains. You succumbed to a passing impulse—just as I did these past few minutes. Then when you came to your senses, you realized it wasn't all that important."

Small sparks of anger flashed in his eyes. "You've got it all wrong. I keep trying to tell you what really happened—"

"I've already told you, I don't want to hear it. I know all I need to know about your reactions. I thought you wanted my friendship, but it seems that was just a ploy to get me off guard. What you really want is another conquest to add to your string of trophies."

He stared at her in amazement. "For God's sake, Terry, who are you talking to? Not me, that's for sure. I don't treat women as trophies. You must have got me confused with somebody else." His eyes narrowed in sudden comprehension. "Is that what your husband did? Treated you like just another conquest?"

Terry felt limp and drained. Her mind was foggy,

uncertain. "Please, Neil," she said wearily, "I don't want to talk about it. Let's just write tonight off as another wrong turn. I really do want your friendship—"

"Friendship be damned." Neil's voice was harsh and intense. "What I feel for you is a whole lot stronger than friendship. I won't buy that nonsense about 'just a passing impulse.' You're beginning to fall in love with me, Terry. I know it. I could feel it tonight in every cell of your body. We've got something very good going between us. I'm not going to let you destroy it."

His voice, taut with determination, seemed to penetrate straight to Terry's marrow. She found herself suddenly aching with longing. How good it would feel, having his arms around her. She had only to reach out a hand, and they'd both be back in that golden world of warmth and closeness. . . .

But some perverse demon seemed to keep driving her on, impelling her on a self-destructive course. "I'm sorry, Neil." She made her voice sound casual. "I think it's time to adjourn tonight's meeting. Maybe once we've had a cooling-off period, we'll be able to get things back on an even keel."

Neil glared at her angrily for a few moments. Then gradually his anger faded, and he made a little gesture of resignation. "Is that what you really want, Terry? A cooling-off period? Okay, I'm willing to wait. Maybe we should take things a little slower. But I warn you, darling, I'm not going to wait forever. There's an empty spot in my life, and I want you to fill it."

He pulled himself up from the sofa in one lithe graceful motion and stood staring down at her, his eyes probing hers. "Terry, I'm not going to let you spoil this. I know you love me. Sooner or later you're going to admit it."

Without waiting for her to answer, he moved to the door and disappeared into the silent darkness. She heard the sound of his car driving off toward the highway. Then the silence closed in again, and she was alone by the dying fire.

CHAPTER ELEVEN

TERRY PAUSED in front of the door of the Janus Gallery, trying to decide whether or not to lift the knocker. Was it fair to take up Cecilia's precious time with what she knew in her heart was a phony mission? Ostensibly she was here to pick up the latest campaign news. What she was really doing was escaping from her office—and the intolerable strain of waiting for Neil to phone her.

Despite the way she'd dismissed him on Monday night, she'd expected to hear from him the very next morning. But now, well into Thursday afternoon, she was beginning to wonder if he'd ever call her again.

Serves you right, Terry. You must have really convinced him you didn't want him. But no, she corrected herself, *Neil wouldn't give up so quickly.* She remembered the look of steely insistence, the way his voice rang with determination when he'd said, "I'm not going to let you spoil this." He had meant that sincerely. There must be some other reason behind this strange silence of his.

"Sweetie! What on earth are you doing, dithering here on the doorstep?" Cecilia'a delighted voice broke into her ruminations. She let herself be shepherded into the house and provided with a cup of aromatic red tea made of hibiscus flowers. Cecilia beamed at her across the kitchen table. "I was just going to phone you. Something marvelous has just happened. The good news came through an hour ago."

"Well, come on, Cecilia, tell me!" Terry's heart started thumping with excitement. "Has Southwestern Towers agreed to abandon the project?"

Cecilia looked startled, then shook her head in amused comprehension. "I'm not talking about our campaign. That's still slogging along at its usual pace. This is personal stuff, a stroke of luck for the Janus Gallery. We just got a call from a big oil man out in Phoenix. A friend of his who came through here last weekend told him about David's Navaho-myth-type paintings. Now this big shot, a Mr. Clark Enderby, is talking about commissioning a mural. Seems he's building a library for the city and wants the artwork to reflect southwestern traditions. He asked me to send some slides of David's paintings, and hopes to get up here pretty soon in person."

"That's wonderful, Cecilia. You and David can certainly use the money. I hope he's offering a hefty advance?"

"We haven't discussed money yet. First he's got to decide if David is right for the project. But even apart from the money, it would mean a tremendous boost to David's reputation. I'm sure it would bring in a lot of other commissions."

Terry felt a glow of vicarious pleasure. "That's wonderful news, Cecilia. Where's David now? Out in the studio working? Do you think he'd mind if I went to congratulate him?''

Cecilia shook her head. "David's not home just now. He's off on some campaign business. He and a new volunteer named Lenore Hitchcock have gone to see Reuben Abeyta, the council chairman."

Terry felt as though a fist had pounded into her stomach. "Lenore Hitchcock?" she murmured weakly. "You mean that glamorous girl friend of Neil Brewster's?"

"Glamorous, I'll grant you. She's really quite a dish compared to the outdoor types around Taos. But I don't think she even knows Neil. In fact, I'm certain she doesn't. David and she were talking for hours about some of the work she's done back in New York. She's been in on a lot of consumer-protest projects. But I'm sure Neil's name was never mentioned."

Terry fought back a wave of desolation. What was Lenore doing back in Taos? Did this mean their relationship was not really over? Or—horrible thought— maybe she'd never left town in the first place. Maybe Neil had been lying about her departure.

The questions whirled through her mind, then slowed into a dismaying revelation. *This* was the reason Neil hadn't called her. That tantrum of hers Monday night had sent him straight back into the arms of that sophisticated stranger.

"Auntie Terry! Auntie Terry!" Gito's excited voice cut through the haze of disappointment. "Come and help me work my new backhoe!"

"*Ay! Caray!*" Cecilia slapped her forehead in

mock desperation. "I thought I had him tucked away in his playroom. Terry, would you be a superhoney and keep Gito out of my hair for about ten minutes? I was just about to make some important phone calls."

"Sure, Cecilia, I'll be glad to. But how come he isn't off on one of his trips with Pedro?"

Cecilia looked a little uneasy. "I'm afraid old Pedro is out of the picture. You know how David feels about him? Well, he finally put his foot down—said he didn't want Gito going down to his cabin until he knew more about this Sam Geromino and all those mysterious children."

"Surely he could have asked Pedro for some explanation?"

"That's just it. He did ask him. Ye gods, what a bad scene that was! Pedro clammed up completely, just wouldn't talk at all. He started flashing that wild-eyed grin of his, the one that makes people call him El Loco. Of course, that made David even more antsy. So he issued an ultimatum—no more Pedro."

Terry nodded thoughtfully. "I can understand why he might have been worried. It's too bad for Gito, though. He really seemed to adore the little old man."

"I know he misses Pedro, but maybe he's better off without him. He was getting too wrapped up in that fantasy world."

The phone shrilled sharply. Cecilia frowned in annoyance. "Oh, damn, there's the phone again." She cast a meaningful glance toward Gito. "Would you mind, Terry? Just for about ten minutes?"

Terry took Gito's hand and led him back to his playroom. Gito showed her how to work the toy backhoe, scooping up several handfuls of marbles. Then he pulled out a box full of old-fashioned wooden clothespins and started lining them up against the wall.

"Here's Sam Geromino," he crooned softly, "and here's the mommie, and here's all the little boys who get the spankings."

Terry's mind prickled with interest. Here was a chance to learn more about the mysterious goings-on in old Pedro's cabin. "Tell me about them, Gito. Does he talk to you, this Sam Geromino? What does he say? And who are all these boys who get the spankings?"

Gito stared at her for a moment, deciding whether to share his secret. "Sam doesn't talk to me. He only talks to Uncle Pedro," he said in a grudging tone.

"And the spankings, Gito? Who gives the boys the spankings?"

Gito's expression turned sullen. He shifted his eyes away, staring bleakly down at the line of clothespins. Then he reached out and knocked them into a jumbled heap. "Those aren't really boys," he muttered softly. "Those are only mommie's clo'sepins. They're no good! No good!" He struck at them savagely, scattering them all over the playroom floor. When he turned back to Terry, his eyes were brimming with tears. "Auntie Terry," he wailed, "can we go see Uncle Pedro? Can we go down to the river and see Sam and the mommie? The boys want me to come back. The boys get sad 'cause they can't see me."

The childish voice was shrill with hurt. Terry longed to snatch him up and take him immediately to Pedro's cabin. But she knew that was out of the question. "You'll have to be patient, Gito. We can't go down there today. Maybe after a while, at fiesta time—"

Before she could pledge herself to what she knew in her heart was an empty promise, Cecilia burst into the room, her eyes alight with mischievous excitement. "Phone call for you, Terry, sweetie—long distance from Albuquerque."

Terry jumped to her feet. "It must be Leo Martinez. I promised to call him this morning, but it slipped my mind."

She hurried into the living room and picked up the receiver. "Leo," she said, "I'm afraid I got sidetracked—"

"This is Neil, Terry. I'm here at the airport. I just got back from my trip to Dallas. It will take me another few hours to get back to Taos."

Terry's knees felt as though they'd give way in another minute. She groped for a chair, feeling a wave of elation surge through her body. "Hello, Neil." She was pleased to hear her voice sounding light and casual, giving no hint of the way her heart was pounding. "I didn't realize you were going to Dallas. Campaign research, I suppose?"

"Didn't David tell you? I went down to check out Southwestern's financial tie-ups."

David's not here. He's out gallivanting around with your Lenore Hitchcock. Terry bit back her impulse to fling the woman's name at Neil. "I haven't had a chance to talk to David,'' she said in a level voice. ''I hope you found some useful information?''

''You bet I did!'' His voice had a steely ring to it. ''I want to tell you about it—right away. How about dinner tonight at the Taos Inn? I'll pick you up at your house about seven-thirty.''

''Well, yes, I suppose....'' Terry faltered. The line went dead before she could finish her answer. She stared out the living room window with unseeing eyes. Instead of the neatly pruned shapes of lilac and piñon, she saw an endless succession of blue mountain ranges. Music seemed to be pulsing through her bloodstream. *"On top of the world, looking down on creation, and the only explanation I can find...."*

''What's that you're humming, Terry? It sounds familiar.''

Terry clamped her lips shut, very aware of Cecilia's shrewd eyes upon her. She hadn't realized she'd been humming. ''That was Neil Brewster,'' she said in a businesslike tone. ''He says he's got some interesting news from Dallas.''

''It must be pretty good news to send you off in a trance like that.'' Cecilia's generous mouth widened into a meaningful grin. ''Seems like I was right about that old bread and salt stuff. Come on, sweetie, tell me all about it. Are you finally going to break down and start acting human?''

A sudden commotion next door in the gallery saved Terry the need to contrive a suitable brush-off. A moment later David burst into the room, his arm tossed casually around Lenore Hitchcock's suede-jacketed shoulders.

"We did it, Cecilia," he shouted. "We got the old buzzard to come out into the open."

He stopped abruptly, noticing Terry. His face turned a little red. He dropped his arm away from Lenore in a self-conscious gesture. "Hi, Terry," he said. "Glad to see you. I don't think you've met our new volunteer yet." He turned to the woman beside him, her striking face a mask of soigné perfection. "Lenore, this is Terry Morrison, the well-known architect and civic crusader."

Terry's body felt stiff and unreal. She forced her face muscles into what she hoped was a reasonably pleasant expression. "Hello, Lenore. I've already heard a lot about you. You know how people talk in a small town like this."

Lenore tilted her head to one side, lifting a well-groomed eyebrow. "I'm beginning to learn all about that. One hears the most extraordinary rumors. Tell me; I'm curious. What sort of things have people told you about me?" Her eyes raked Terry's face in what seemed like a subtle challenge.

Terry, taken off guard, hesitated a moment. "Nothing all that important—mostly speculation about how long you were planning to stay here." She plucked up her courage and launched a dart straight at her target. "As a matter of fact, somebody told me you'd already left town."

Lenore's eyebrow rose a few notches higher. "Really?" she drawled. "I wonder who that could have been. I did take a shopping trip to Albuquerque, but I don't have any intention of leaving Taos.

I've fallen in love with the place. I intend to stay here a long, long time.''

Her large, beautifully made-up eyes stared straight into Terry's. Terry flinched away from the blatant challenge she saw there now, looking down in confusion. David stepped in to break the awkward silence.

"I'm glad to hear that, Lenore. We're really lucky you came here right at this moment." He turned to Cecilia, alive with enthusiasm. "You should have seen her, Cecilia. She handled old Reuben like a real professional. When we started to pump him about the Southwestern proposal, he claimed he wasn't allowed to make it public before the next council meeting. But Lenore started needling him, putting forth such outrageous assumptions about the project that he finally broke down and showed us the proposal, just to prove it wasn't as bad as she suggested.''

Lenore smiled complacently, accepting his praise with self-assured condescension. "I do have some expertise in handling these small-time politicians. I'm only too glad to be able to use it in such a good cause."

The phoniness in her voice grated on Terry's nerves. What was this woman up to? Whatever was keeping her here, it obviously wasn't her love for Taos. It must have something to do with Neil. Then why was she pretending not to know him?

David pulled a handful of notes out of his pocket and launched into a detailed account of Southwestern's plans. Terry sat listening silently, her mind numbed by confusion, trying to comprehend what he was saying. Lenore's vivid presence was making her more and more nervous. She felt an urgent need to make her escape before she said or did something really stupid.

"I'm sorry, I have to go now." The words came out more brusquely than she intended. Cecilia and David looked at her in surprise. "I just this moment remembered," she murmured lamely. "Something I promised to take out to Gus Pickett."

"Such a busy lady." Lenore's voice oozed with cloying sweetness. "As a matter of fact, I ought to be leaving, too. Unfortunately, my car's still in the repair shop. Maybe you could give me a lift to the plaza?"

Terry felt trapped and angry. The last thing in the world she wanted was another five minutes of Lenore Hitchcock's company. "Of course," she said. "I'd be glad to. So long as you don't mind my battered old pickup."

Lenore's white-toothed smile looked phonier than ever. "I'm getting accustomed to Taos-style transport. This rugged existence is doing great things for my constitution."

The Quayles saw them off in a flurry of fond good-byes and come back soons. Once the truck was in motion, Lenore underwent an abrupt change of manner. The overbright smile gave way to a guarded secretive look. "I can guess who it was who told you I had left Taos. It must have been our mutual friend, Neil Brewster."

Terry's heart gave a sudden lurch. So Lenore was dropping her smoke screen. Why was she bringing

Neil's name up now, when she'd concealed their connection from David and Cecilia?

She forced herself to keep her voice cool and level.
"I really don't remember who told me. It could have
been Neil, or it might have been someone else."

"Oh, come on now, Terry." The carefully made-
up lips curved into a suggestive smile. "You two are
very good friends—at least that's what Skeeter
Phillips tells me."

"Skeeter exaggerates things. We have spent some
time together, but only on campaign business."

Lenore shot her a skeptical glance. "Really? I
can't believe you haven't discussed me. No doubt he
told you I worked as his assistant?"

That was an unpleasant surprise. It was disturbing
enough to think of Lenore as Neil's girl friend. But
his assistant—that could mean she'd been an even
more important part of his life. She stared at the road
ahead in stubborn concentration. "He didn't mention that. But as I just told you, our only contacts
have been on campaign business."

Lenore sighed softly. It sounded to Terry more
theatrical than pathetic. "Isn't that just like Neil!
You knock yourself out for three long years, giving
him all your energy and enthusiasm. Then when you
dare to assert your own opinion, he promptly forgets
he ever knew you."

Terry compressed her lips firmly. "Look, Lenore,
let's drop the subject. Neil Brewster's past life is really none of my business."

Lenore's glance at her was amused and knowing.
"Whatever you say. I won't mention his name again,

if that's how you want to play it. But I would like to ask you one favor. Please don't drop any hints around town about my...connection with Neil in New York. There's already been a lot too much gossip about us.''

''If you don't want your name linked with his, you shouldn't have dates in Taos hangouts like Michael's.'' The words shot out before Terry could stop them. She felt the blood rush to her face, saw Lenore's gaze turn subtly triumphant.

''That morning still rankles, does it? Let me set your mind at rest. I have no intention of 'having dates' with Neil, as you put it. We've agreed to go our separate ways. But I don't intend to leave this marvelous town just to suit the almighty Lord Brewster's convenience.''

''You really sound bitter about him.'' Terry shot a quick sideways glance at her.

Lenore's mouth drooped in a rueful smile. ''I can see you've already guessed I was more to him than just an employee. All right; I admit there was... well...a thing between us. I really should have known better. I had plenty of warning about Neil's usual pattern. He tends to go through his women pretty quickly.''

In spite of her dismay at these words, Terry made a tremendous effort to sound indifferent. ''As you say, Lenore, all this is ancient history. Look, here we are at the plaza. Where would you like me to drop you?''

Lenore seemed to sense her relief at bringing an end to the awkward conversation. A mischievous little smile played over her lips. ''I'm meeting Skeeter

Phillips at La Cocina. Why don't we all have drinks and dinner together? I'm sure poor Skeeter would love that. He really adores you.''

Terry stifled the impulse to hotly deny Skeeter's alleged adoration. She braked to a stop in front of the restaurant. "No, thank you, Lenore. I already have plans for dinner.''

Lenore shrugged casually and slipped off the seat of the pickup onto the arcaded sidewalk that ringed the plaza. Terry jolted the truck into motion and turned right at the traffic light, heading for Talpa, her mind churning with disturbing questions. Did Neil know Lenore had come back? Probably not, since he'd been away in Dallas. But what if he had known? Who would have been dining with him tonight at the Taos Inn—Lenore or Terry? Lenore might claim the relationship was ended, but did she really believe it? Would she really be hanging around here if she didn't think there might be a chance to revive it?

Terry drew a deep breath, trying to clear her mind of its emotional turmoil. What good did it do to plague herself with unanswerable questions? Lenore's disturbing hints had taught her one thing: how very much she wanted to see Neil. In two hours from now, that wish would be granted. And this time she wouldn't allow her fears and suspicions to spoil what was going to be a marvelous evening.

CHAPTER TWELVE

TERRY STEPPED out of the shower, her skin still tingling with delicious refreshment. Hugging the thick, plushy bath towel around her body, she peered at her steam-clouded image in the full-length mirror on the back of the bathroom door. Gradually she relaxed her grip on the towel and let it drop away until she stood completely naked.

She felt a surge of unfamiliar satisfaction at the sight of her own body: her wide elegant shoulders tapering down to a narrow waist, her tip-tilted breasts with their small brown buttons ringed with rosy halos, the gentle swell of her hips, the long sleek line from thigh to ankle. Was this enticing stranger really Terry Morrison? She realized with a shock that it had been literally years since she'd looked at herself like this. She'd done her best to completely ignore her body, but tonight she felt invigorated. But no, it wasn't through her eyes that she'd just been assessing her body. She'd been seeing herself through the eyes of Neil Brewster.

She caught her breath, overcome by the powerful image—Neil's eyes on her, alive with love and wonder, in the trembling moment before both their bodies dissolved into one. . . .

She snapped into sudden alertness, appalled by the languorous daydream toward which she was drifting. Was this what she really wanted? To stop fighting against his overwhelming attraction, yield to the yearning hunger she felt within her, merge herself with that powerful magnetic body?

She felt herself grow icy with sudden panic but threw back her head in a reckless gesture. Yes, this *was* what she wanted. She'd wanted it from the very moment she met him. She had tried for too long to suppress this urgent wanting—even to the point of trying to drive him away. But that brush with Lenore today had released something primitive in her. The very thought of Neil with another woman made her react like a lioness with all her claws out. All her caution dissolved in a fierce determination: whatever Lenore was up to, she wasn't going to take Neil from Terry!

She flung herself into the bedroom and scrambled into a bra and panties. Her newest western shirt and best-fitting pair of jeans were laid out on the bed, the usual dinnertime outfit here in Taos. Ignoring them, she flung open the doors of her built-in closet, riffled through the tailored blouses and slacks and snatched out a flame-colored dress of Mexican cotton, pulled it down over her head and shoulders, then went back to the bathroom to look again in the mirror.

She appraised the dress with critical eyes, noting the low-scooped neckline ringed with intricate white embroidery, the ballooning sleeves caught in with tight cuffs that reached almost to her elbows, the softly gathered skirt flaring out from a tightly cinched waist in three tiers of flounces. She'd bought it on impulse the last time she'd gone to Juárez but had never had the nerve to wear it in Taos. It had seemed too garish, too blatantly flirtatious. It still seemed a little vulgar, overstated. If only she'd kept a few of those old dinner gowns—the sleek, uncluttered green velvet, the clinging black crepe with the mandarin collar, the plain turquoise sheath that Paul had brought back from Monaco....

There you go again, Terry, trying to resurrect that old dead life. Tonight you're going to take the first step toward a new one. And this dress will do very well to take that first step in.

She stared at herself once again, trying to see herself through Neil's eyes. The silver blond coil piled on top of her head struck a jarring note—too neat, too austere, too prim and proper. Swiftly she pulled out the pins, snatched up a brush and groomed her hair into a shining mass that flowed down over her shoulders and halfway down her waist, all the while remembering Neil's stroking fingers.

"Alice in Wonderland...who's just taken a bite of the mushroom." A breathless giggle emerged from her smiling lips. The mushroom had turned little Alice into a giant. Well, this night's Alice was going to grow up a little, too.

"Alice in Wonderland...." That's how he'd seen her last Monday night, a figure out of a children's story, rejecting the role of an adult woman. She smiled at herself in pleased anticipation. This night's Alice was going to grow up a little.

She rummaged through the bathroom cupboard

and came up with a pile of makeup she'd almost discarded. She smoothed on the creamy foundation, used blusher to highlight her cheekbones, outlined her lips with a brighter than usual coral. Then she paused for a moment, remembering the careful gradations of shadow and accent that made Lenore's eyes seem so luminously inviting.

She could do that, too, if she wanted. She had all the materials, bought years ago to appease Paul who had always taunted her about her lack of sophistication. But why should she copy Lenore? She didn't need to. It wasn't Lenore he had held in his arms last Monday, had murmured those marvelous words to.... "As though I was coming home...." "An empty spot in my life, and I want you to fill it...."

With a rising sense of elation, she turned to her mirror again. A flick of pencil, a trace of liner, the lightest film of mascara—there, that should do it. Or maybe a little touch of this gray blue shadow to accent the cerulean glow of her eyes.

Before she could make her decision, she heard the buzz of the door bell. She glanced down at her legs in panic. There wasn't time to hunt for pantyhose—and besides, she wasn't sure she had any without runs in them. Bare legs would have to do. Thank goodness she'd bought those high-heeled beige sandals last summer.

She threw a last look at herself in the mirror, then dashed through the bedroom, stopping en route to shove her feet into the sandals. She slowed down to a walk as she reached the front door. She didn't want

Neil to see her this breathless, or realize how quickly her heart was beating.

She saw his eyes widen in pleased surprise. "Hello, Terry," he murmured softly. "You look terrific. I can see this is going to be a special occasion."

If you only knew how special! Terry smiled casually to hide her growing elation. "I do get out of my work clothes once in a while. Would you like to come in for a drink? I'm dying to hear your important news from Dallas."

"Dallas can wait. Right now, just being with you is more important." He started to reach for her hand, then checked himself and nodded his head toward the waiting Blazer. "Let's have our drinks down at the inn, before we tuck into some of their famous *gallina rellena*."

Moving as though in a dream, Terry walked toward the car, conscious in every pore of how closely he was following behind her. Halfway into town, she realized she'd forgotten to bring a coat or jacket. But tonight the air was so balmy, she didn't need it.

She felt a new upsurge of pleasure, realizing that this was one of those magic June nights when the usual spring-evening chill was replaced by a premature foretaste of languorous summer weather. When they reached the rambling adobe inn, just a block from the plaza, they found the outdoor patio full of people. Clustered under the vivid umbrellas, they seemed to glow with the same subdued excitement Terry was feeling. Even the waitress's eyes had an extra sparkle as she told them that, for the first

time this season, dinner was being served at the outdoor tables.

The whole scene seemed especially arranged to fit
in with Terry's exhilarated mood—the bright-colored
Japanese lanterns strung around the three sides of the
courtyard, the scent from the lilac bushes, the cluster
of pale yellow roses surrounding the fat green candle
that lighted their table, the sounds of flamenco guitar
drifting out from the indoor dining room, the soft
night sky above them, fading slowly from blue to
gray to deep charcoal.

The *gallina rellena* was perfect. As they ate their
way through the traditional holiday dish—tender
roast chicken stuffed with chopped beef and piñon
nuts and flavored with unsweetened chocolate, wine
and spices—Terry kept up a running account of campaign happenings. When she came to David's success
at wheedling information out of Reuben Abeyta,
Neil beamed his approval. "Good man, that David
Quayle. He hasn't lost his skill at interrogation."

Terry knew she should tell him it was really Lenore
who deserved the credit, but she couldn't bring
herself to mention the other woman's name. She was
sure her very inflection would betray how much
Lenore's return had disturbed her. And she didn't
want to shadow this lovely night with those awkward
questions: Did he know she was back in town? Was
he telling the truth when he said she was leaving?

Over coffee and brandy, Neil finally got down to
his business in Dallas. "Just what I was afraid of.
Southwestern Towers is part of a much bigger outfit,
a huge conglomerate called Stanton Odessa. It owns

a whole network of companies, scattered all over the map—a tractor factory in Kansas, a couple of TV stations in Arizona, a baby-food plant in Black River Falls, Wisconsin. That means they can risk a tremendous amount of money, so long as there's any chance of a future profit.''

In the flickering light of the candle, his face looked somber and brooding. Terry shivered a little with apprehension. ''You're really worried about them, aren't you, Neil? But wasn't that what you expected when you went down there? You'd already guessed about the conglomerate.''

Neil nodded glumly, his eyes staring past her shoulder out into the gathering darkness. ''I haven't told you the most disturbing detail, something I *didn't* expect when I went down there. Guess who's the latest addition to Stanton Odessa's stable—my old bête noire from New York, Olympia Tires.''

A jolt of alarm shot through her. No wonder Neil looked discouraged. She knew how much that defeat in New York had cost him. Now he found himself back in the same arena. Would he think the risk was worth it? Or would he decide to drop out of the battle and leave the field to the victorious giant?

As though he had read her mind, he raised his head and looked straight into her eyes. ''Don't worry, Terry. I'm not going to throw in the towel. This thing about Olympia only makes me more determined.'' A shadow of pain flickered in his eyes. Then they hardened into a look of steely resolve. ''They dealt me a low blow last time. I ran away when I should have stayed and fought them. Now fate has dealt *me* another chance. It's not just the future of Taos I'm fighting for now. I've got some personal scores I want to settle."

"I'm so glad you're not giving up, Neil," Terry said with relief. A rueful smile touched her lips. "It's kind of ironic, isn't it? You came out here to forget them—and now you're back in the thick of the same old battle."

Neil's stern frown softened into an answering smile. "There's no such thing as escape, Terry. Running away only increased their power over my life. They forced me into a sterile empty existence—turned in on myself, barring my door against the rest of the world."

"And now you've decided it's time to unbar the door?" Terry tried to keep her voice light, but she couldn't prevent it from trembling a little.

"That's right, Terry." Keeping his eyes fixed on hers, he reached across the table and grasped her hand. "You belong in my life. How could I ever bar any doors against you?"

Rays of warmth seemed to radiate from his hand to hers, spreading all over her body. The air seemed to vibrate with high-pitched ethereal music. The people around them faded into the background, leaving only herself and Neil, alone in the hush of the oncoming night.

His hand tightened on hers. "Where do we go from here, Terry?" His voice had an edge of hoarseness. "You're the one who's calling the shots."

Terry took a deep gulp of air, trying to ease the sudden tightness in her chest. "It's such a beautiful

night. Why don't we go up to your house and look at
that marvelous view from the edge of the mesa?''

His eyes, trained on hers, were brighter than she'd
ever seen them. "Is that what you really want?
You're sure of that, Terry?''

She was filled with joy. She couldn't bear all the
empty space stretching between them. "Yes, Neil.''
There was no tremor now. The words spoke themselves with no effort. "I'm very sure that's what I
want.''

THEY STOOD ON THE EDGE of the mesa, looking across
the shadowy farmland below them to the sparkling
explosion of lights that was Taos, its bright assertion
of human presence overshadowed by the dark impersonal bulk of the northern mountains. Off to their
left, hanging over the vast flat stretch of sagebrush,
the honey-gold ball of the moon looked improbably
near, almost as though they could reach out and
touch it. Behind them, the long low line of the house
blended into the darkness, its foot-thick walls as
sturdy and protective as they had been a hundred
years before.

She felt Neil stirring beside her, turning back
toward the driveway. Terry reached out and laid a
hand on his arm. "It's so lovely here, Neil. Let's stay
outside for just a few minutes.''

Neil nodded silently, looking gravely down into
her upturned face. The moonlight threw the strong
line of his nose and jaw into sharp relief, and she saw
he was frowning a little. "I don't want to push you,
darling. I meant what I said about being willing to

wait. That's why I suggested the inn rather than your place or my place.''

His eyes kept probing hers with an unspoken question. Terry's heart fluttered. She could feel her palms perspiring. She hated herself for being so nervous. What on earth was the matter with her? With every inch of her body still clamoring to fling itself over the precipice, some deep-buried part of her kept sending out warning signals.

''That's why you didn't come in for a drink when I asked you?''

Neil nodded ruefully. ''The way you looked in that doorway, I knew I wouldn't be able to keep my hands off you.''

''That was very nice of you, Neil.'' The words sounded stupid, banal. *Terry, you fool,* she thought, *what on earth are you doing? You know you came here to have him make love to you.*

He was staring at her intently, as though trying to etch each of her features onto his memory. ''Nice? I don't think so. More like self-protection. If you'd pushed me away again, I couldn't have stood it.''

The wistful look in his eyes touched some hidden spring deep inside her. All her long-denied need rose up in a fiery torrent. She reached out both arms to him, pulling herself close against his taut warm body. ''I'm not going to push you away, Neil. I must have been crazy. I'll never push you away again...never, never, never.''

His lips came down to claim hers. His arms closed around her so tightly she found it hard to breathe. Then he loosened his hold and cupped her chin in his hand, tilting her face up to look at the sky above them. "Look at the stars tonight, Terry. They're putting on a show especially for us." He led her out of the shadowy piñons to an open spot, from which they could see the whole vast black bowl of the sky, glittering with its intricate pattern of stars.

They stood side by side, staring silently up at the heavens. The stars seemed to pulse with life, like sentinels welcoming them into the tension-charged silence. Her hand clasped in his, Terry delighted in the current of strength that flowed between them, savoring the warm breath of night on her skin, the spicy scent of the sagebrush and piñons rising around them.

She felt a tremendous sense of awe. How many lovers had stood there as they were standing, watching the same constellations, touched by the same perfumed breath of the southwestern night? Those hardy generations who'd lived in the old house behind them, and long before they had come, there had been the Indians, and before them, an earlier people, lost now in the depths of prehistory, only alive in a few cloudy legends.

The very earth around them seemed to be full of magic, enfolding them, inviting them into some deep elemental embrace. To Terry's reeling senses, it seemed to be holding its breath, waiting for some tremendous event to happen. She turned to Neil with a little gasp, her eyes meeting his in an unspoken question. He instantly grasped her meaning. Without a word, he turned away toward the Blazer in the driveway. A second later, he reappeared at her side, a

folded blanket under his arm. Wordlessly he spread it
out on the ground, then rose and stood looking down
at her somberly, as close to her as he could get without their bodies actually touching.

"Terry," she heard him murmur. He reached out
both hands and grasped her waist. She swayed a little, feeling her bones almost literally turn to water.
He pulled her roughly against his eager body, his
hands stroking her back, caressing her shoulders, the
nape of her neck, weaving a golden web of sensation
around her.

Then she felt his hand drop from her neck to her
long back zipper, and her muscles went suddenly
tense. She found herself in the grip of unexpected
panic. Neil instantly sensed her growing unease. His
hands dropped back to her waist. He gazed down at
her, concerned. "You've got to trust me," he whispered. "I'll never hurt you. I'm going to see that
you'll never be hurt again."

Confidence and a sense of well-being took over
then. It was going to be all right. This time it
was going to turn out all right. She drew a deep
breath and felt all her muscles relax. Then she
reached her own hand up to the zipper and slowly
pulled it down the length of her back. Buoyed by
warm elation, she shrugged the dress off her shoulders, let it fall in a billowing circle around her
ankles, then stepped carefully out of the circle,
conscious all the while of Neil's spellbound eyes
on her, tender, adoring. A moment later she was
flinging her bra to the ground to join her dress. The
moonlight bathed her naked breasts and torso, its

silver touch highlighting each curve and hollow.

Neil stood for a moment as though transfixed. Terry felt her heart begin to beat even more wildly. She could feel his eyes drinking in the sight of her body, and gloried in the adoration she saw there.

Then slowly, deliberately, he reached out one hand and touched the hollow above her collarbone. From there his fingers moved lightly to one of her breasts, tracing the pear-shaped globe in narrowing circles, moving toward the tautly expectant nipple, then retreating to whisper across every inch of her neck and shoulder, raising prickles of sensation wherever they touched, until Terry felt her skin come newly alive, glow with the warmth generated from within.

She felt her desire call out to his, reach out across the few inches of space between them—inches that seemed to be widening into an aching abyss. Then his mouth came down on her nipple, bringing with it a marvelous feeling of warmth and closeness. With a little groan, she pressed herself against him, intent on joining every inch of their bodies as they sank together down onto the waiting blanket.

After long moments of throbbing closeness, Neil moved away, wrestling with the buttons of his shirt. A cool current of air rushed over her for a moment, a welcome relief from the surging heat within her. Then he was back again, his naked chest pressing down on her breasts. Her body arched to meet his as she yearningly claimed his lips. She moved her hands softly over his back, pressing him even closer, learning by heart each new inch of flesh and muscle.

She rolled over on top of him, their legs intertwining in sinuous motion. She felt his hand in the hollow above her hips, pulling down on her panties' elastic waistband. She helped him pull the flimsy material from her, toss it away into the darkness. She felt the harsh scrape of his denim jeans against her naked legs, the sharp edge of a buckle pressing into her skin. Her hands were moving without any conscious volition, urging him out of his clothes, desperate to remove that last barrier between them.

He pulled her to him with a groan, pressing urgent kisses all the way down her throat, her shoulders, her tingling breasts. Then his hand began to travel along her hips, down the inside of her thigh, aiming inexorably.... With each maddening touch her exultation mounted. She felt as though she were soaring through the perfumed air, cradled in liquid moonlight, lost in the vast embrace of primordial night.

Then, after what seemed like hours of breathless longing, she felt his welcome touch at her deepest core. Her body flared up like a rocket. The world exploded in a dazzling haze. There was no more night, no more sky, no more watching stars—only this pulsing hunger driving them on, fusing their separate selves into one being....

The change in the light came like a blow in her face. What had been golden was suddenly garish. Her mind quickly grasped the reality: a car on the driveway, its headlights slashing harshly into the black velvet night.... A small green MG roadster parked just behind the bulky shape of the Blazer....

Terry reached for her dress, not quite comprehending what was happening. Neil was awkwardly scrambling into his jeans, swearing softly under his breath. Then he was on his feet, walking away from her toward the blazing headlights.

The intrusive circle of light seemed to stop just short of the edge of the blanket. Terry was mortified. Had the MG's driver seen them there under the stars, secure in their mad conviction that no one else existed? Who was he anyway, this sudden intruder? Someone who would spread the story all over Taos?

She felt around on the ground for her sandals, snatched them up and made a dash for the Blazer. Safely hidden inside, she strained her ears to pick up the sound of voices.

At first all she heard was a low indistinguishable murmur. Then Lenore's voice lashed stridently into the darkness. "I just couldn't stand to leave you. Oh, Neil, why must you be such a bastard? Don't you see how it tears me apart?"

"Keep your voice down, damn you!" Was that really Neil shouting? He sounded incredibly vicious. Evidently Lenore found him as frightening as she did. Her voice dropped back to a quiet whisper. Neil's voice became quieter, too. Terry could tell from his tone that he was angry but couldn't get a hint of what he was saying.

Then he was shouting again, his voice harsh and distorted. "You bitch! You no-good piece of trash!"

Terry stiffened in shock. She was suddenly back in her Los Angeles apartment, crouched miserably on the expensive Danish sofa, hearing Paul shout at her, his face red and blotchy with anger. "You're just no good for me, Terry. You stupid bitch, you're nothing. You're less than nothing...." She'd tried to shout back at him, remind him that he was the one who had wanted the marriage. But the tears were coming too fast, her crumpled body leached of all its strength. She heard herself whining abjectly, "I'm sorry, I'm sorry. I need a little more time, Paul."

Devastated by the searing pain of that memory, she no longer heard even the murmur of voices. She was back in the pit of darkness, sick with disgust at that whining clinging creature who pleaded for love from a man who obviously loathed her.

Lenore's piercing wail jerked her sharply back to the present. "Darling, darling, after all we've been to each other...."

Terry winced, ashamed of being a witness to Lenore's private anguish. "He tends to go through his women pretty quickly." Lenore had warned her of that. But she hadn't warned her how cruelly he turned on them, how "I want you" gave way to "You no-good piece of trash." *Better keep listening, Terry. Listen and learn. How long will it take till he starts lashing out at you?*

She focused her attention once more, trying to pluck more fragments out of the darkness. Lenore's voice was subdued again. Terry's straining ears caught only an occasional phrase. "What a fool...." "I need you...." "Your life...." Then the murmurs swelled into a wailing crescendo. "Neil, I want you—I need you. You can't just drop me like this."

The slap of palm against cheek cracked through the silence. Abruptly Lenore stopped wailing. Then came Neil's voice, harsher than ever: "That's enough, Lenore. I wish to God I had never met you."

Terry's mind went blank with desolation. Was this the man she'd been about to make love to? Sickened yet impelled, she strove to hear Lenore's reaction. Would she go on clinging and crying, pleading with him as abjectly as she herself had with Paul?

"All right, Neil, you win." Terry felt a surge of reluctant admiration. Lenore was stronger than she was. At least she wasn't about to dissolve into tears.

"I'll leave you alone, if that's the way you want it. I can't fight physical force. That's a field where men always have the advantage."

Huddling numbly against the door of the Blazer, Terry heard the sound of a car door slamming. The MG's motor coughed into action. The headlights receded, faded into the darkness. She heard Neil's returning steps, saw him peering at her through the open driver's window. His face, hollowed out by the moonlight, looked grim and set. "Sorry you had to hear that. But I had to explain to Miss Hitchcock what goodbye means."

From some source deep inside her, Terry summoned the courage to sit up and face him coolly. When she spoke, her voice was calm and free of emotion. "The world is full of women who don't understand what goodbye means. Fortunately, I don't happen to be one of them. Thank you, Neil, for a lovely evening. Now, if you'll just take me home—"

She saw his eyes widen in shock. Then he was wrenching open the door of the Blazer and grabbing her by the shoulders. "Don't be an idiot, darling. That woman has nothing to do with you and me. If you'd only let me explain...."

His arms were around her, crushing her to him. Terry let herself drift for a moment, bewitched by the magical pull of his body's closeness. She felt his lips on hers, her own mouth probing his in hungry welcome.

"He tends to go through his women pretty quickly...." From out of nowhere, the warning flashed stubbornly across Terry's mind. She forced her melting body into stiffness, twisted her head to escape his demanding lips.

"Let me go, Neil." Her voice was breathless. Using all her strength, she struggled against his grasp and finally got a few inches of space between them.

"I mean it, Neil. Let me go." The words were tinged with a ragged edge of panic. His arms dropped away abruptly. He leaned back against the seat, staring at her with a slightly dazed expression. Then he heaved a deep sigh and turned from her to stare grimly out into the shadows.

"I told you once I wouldn't let you spoil things. It seems I underestimated your talents in that direction."

I'm not the one who spoiled things! Terry bit her lip, suppressing the angry retort. She felt suddenly very lonely, an empty space yawning inside her. As the Blazer jerked into motion, she drew herself up, stonily erect, telling herself to make her mind a blank.

The pain in her heart felt achingly familiar. She knew when she'd felt it before—on that silent awkward ride coming down from Midnight. She'd vowed at the time it would never happen again. Apparently, she hadn't learned her lesson. She'd tumbled headlong back into quicksand. Well, thank God that Lenore's intrusion had opened her eyes. Two of these silent rides were more than enough. She'd make very sure there would never be a third.

CHAPTER THIRTEEN

"SO IF WE CAN GET the court to rule on this injunction, it may raise some serious doubts about the legality of the whole procedure...."

As David's earnest voice rang out through the small auditorium of the Taos Art Association, Terry nervously glanced around to count the attendance again. The last time she'd counted only fifty people, a disappointing turnout. They'd expected a crowd of two hundred.

Cecilia was sitting beside her in the front row of seats below the stage, her face glowing with pride as David concluded the report of the legal committee. She hadn't seemed too upset at the lack of response to her recruiting efforts. "It's really not bad for Taos. People aren't gung ho about going to meetings. But we've got a lot of support behind the scenes."

The burst of applause as David stepped down from the platform helped reassure Terry a little. They may not have drawn many people, but those who had come were clearly enthusiastic. Her gaze flicked back to the center-stage chairman's table. Paco Reyes was on his feet, ready to introduce the evening's next speaker. Lenore Hitchcock, sitting beside him, was scribbling away on a yellow legal-sized pad. Terry looked at her with grudging admiration. She still couldn't bring herself to really like her, but she'd had to revise her assessment of Lenore's motives. She was obviously not so phony as she had seemed. After that bitter scene the previous Thursday, Terry had half expected she'd give up on Taos. But she seemed more involved in the protest campaign than ever. She'd worked long, hard hours this past week with Paco and Skeeter, falling naturally into the role of the campaign's office manager and record keeper.

I suppose that's the job she used to do for Neil. The thought summoned up an instant vision: Lenore behind a desk in some New York skyscraper office, Neil leaning over her shoulder, murmuring into her ear as he checked some figures. She felt the familiar tremor of pain go through her, the same sick anguish she'd been feeling all week, each of the hundreds of times she'd recalled Neil's disturbing image.

It doesn't matter, she told herself fiercely. It really doesn't matter anymore. But she still couldn't keep herself from looking toward the back of the auditorium. Yes, he was still in his seat, staring straight ahead at the chairman's table, his eyes apparently fixed on Lenore. There was something unusually grim about his expression. After that scene last Thursday, he'd probably expected Lenore to knuckle under, quietly fade from the scene and leave him in peace. He must be amazed and chagrined that a woman would dare to defy his arrogant orders.

As her eyes lingered on his face, she saw him become aware of her attention. He nodded coolly, raising a questioning eyebrow. She snatched her eyes away, feeling her cheeks grow hot with embarrassment, and tried to bring her whirling thoughts into focus.

Skeeter was up on the stage now—evidently had been there for the past several minutes. She'd been so involved with Neil that she hadn't heard a word of what he was saying. Now she forced herself to concentrate on the appeal he was making.

"So I say it's time to make them come out in the open—flushed out by my big exposé in the *Taos News* next Thursday, leading up to the monster protest rally on Friday." He turned to Paco, his long blond mustache quivering. "With your permission, Mr. Chairman, I'd like to make my plan an official motion."

Paco's thick dark eyebrows came together in obvious disapproval. "I'm not sure that motion's in order. When we announced this meeting tonight, we said it was merely to pool all our information."

"With all due respect, Mr. Chairman, I think you should let our audience decide that." Lenore's voice had an edge of oily sweetness, as though daring Paco to contradict her.

"Yes, Paco, Lenore is right." Skeeter was glaring at him belligerently. "People are getting tired of all this waffling around. That's probably why so few of them showed up tonight. The people of Taos are already ripe for action. I say we should give them the chance to really do something."

Paco looked disconcerted. He obviously wasn't used to opposition from Skeeter. He hesitated a moment as a ripple of murmurs ran through the auditorium, then banged down his fist on the table in lieu of a gavel.

The gesture served its purpose, shocking the audience into startled silence. "I know, as the chairman, I'm supposed to stay neutral—" his resonant voice seemed to fill the small auditorium "—but I can't stand by and see this movement stampeded. I think it's too early for this kind of mass protest. We're doing a lot of good work behind the scenes, using our legal tactics, zeroing in on accurate information, presenting it to the various council members. Most of them seem to be very open-minded. We may already have enough votes to block the proposal."

"Oh, come on, Paco. You heard what David told us. You know the way Southwestern Towers does business. All it would take to close those open minds would be a small wad of money under the table."

Paco's eyes narrowed with anger. "Are you saying the council would trade their votes for money? Where's your evidence for that accusation?"

Skeeter gave a sardonic chuckle. "They're politicians, aren't they? What makes you think they'd be above temptation?"

Paco's expression had turned one or two shades darker. "Is that how you see us, Skeeter? A bunch of small-town tinhorn politicians? That's a typical outsider's viewpoint, condemning us without even trying to know us."

Skeeter glared at him fiercely, apparently forgetting the crowd below them. "You're calling *me* an outsider? When I'm the one who started this whole campaign? What kind of dirty pool are you playing, Paco? Just because I'm an Anglo—''

Terry stiffened in shock, feeling the tide of uneasiness rising around her. *Stop it,* she wanted to shout. *We can't start fighting among ourselves.* But before she could get the words out, Cecilia's clear cool voice cut through the growing tension.

"Come on, you guys, let's not get sidetracked. I understand what's got Paco's back up. We all know some politicians are crooked. But these are folks we've grown up with; we've known them all our lives—them and their families. We can't just assume that they're on the enemy's side. People like Reuben Abeyta, Sam Sanchez, Linda Fernandez—I think they can be persuaded, if we can show them the reasons against the project.''

"Right on, Cecilia.'' The voice came from the other side of the auditorium. Leo Martinez was on his feet, his face concerned and anxious. "You all know my uncle, Ben Montoya. We've been talking about Southwestern Towers. He hasn't come to any final decision, but I'm pretty sure he's leaning our way. He's got a lot of clout in political circles. If he makes a public statement against the project, I'm sure the whole council will vote it down.''

"It must feel good to be so naive and trusting.'' Lenore was on her feet now, moving to the front of the stage, talking directly to Leo. "But we can't afford to depend on friendly persuasion. You've never come up against one of these giant outfits. You don't understand the methods they use. While we keep meandering on with these half-hearted efforts, hard-headed businessmen like Ward McKevitt are already adding up their share of the profits.''

''What's that about Ward McKevitt?'' Neil's voice rang out like a whiplash. ''You mean the head of the First Commercial Bank? How does Ward McKevitt come into the picture?''

Lenore, taken off guard, seemed to waver a moment. Then she quickly rallied her strength to answer his question. ''I only used Ward as one example. He hasn't come out on our side, so we've got to assume he's backing the project.''

''You admit that statement of yours was pure speculation? And yet you want us to follow you into battle? What kind of fools do you think we are?''

His voice fairly dripped with contempt. Lenore glared back at him in grim defiance. Terry could feel the hostility flowing between them. The audience, caught in the middle, was shifting restlessly and starting low-voiced arguments with each other. Couldn't Neil see how much damage he was doing, letting his own private feud feed into the rising tide of anger?

''Mr. Brewster is right.'' Paco had to shout to be heard over the hubbub. ''You big-city folks may think we're pretty dumb, but we don't need any advice from you smart outsiders.''

Skeeter, fists clenched, moved over to face him across the chairman's table. ''So you'll stick your head in the sand, refuse to even listen to an expert—''

''Expert on what? She's not an expert on Taos.'' Paco's bull-like frame moved threateningly toward his looming opponent. The sense of impending violence shook Terry loose from her shocked paralysis. She leaped to her feet, surprising herself with the volume and strength of her protest. "Look, everyone, we can't go on fighting like this! That's just what Southwestern wants—divide and conquer. Can't we agree on a compromise? Lenore, you've proved you're a good negotiator. Why don't you and Paco team up and go try your luck with Ben Montoya?"

"I think that's a lousy idea." Terry's head swung around to stare blankly at Neil. "Miss Hitchcock has shown us how addicted she is to highly dramatic gestures. To send her to talk to Montoya would be a disaster."

A chorus of approbation rose around him. The crowd was clearly turning against Lenore. Terry sank back into her seat, seething with fury. How could he be such a hypocritical bastard? Pretending to speak for the good of the protest campaign, while all the time he was venting his personal anger!

Paco sensed the crowd's change of mood, and seized the opportune moment. "Let's have a vote," he cried. "Should we keep on the way we're going, or switch to Skeeter's confrontation tactics? If you'll quiet down for a minute, a show of hands will tell us where we all stand." He waited for several minutes while the noise from the crowd subsided. "Okay, let's get this settled. All in favor of Skeeter's big confrontation?"

Without taking time to consider, Terry put her hand up. Looking around the auditorium, she saw she had only a sprinkling of fellow voters. But when Paco proposed they continue their low-profile tactics, the crowd's response was a sea of upraised hands. One of the hands belonged to Cecilia. Terry could feel her friend's questioning eyes upon her. She felt a pang of disquiet. Why had she disregarded Cecilia's advice? She realized she had voted on sudden impulse, impelled by the need to defend Lenore against Neil's anger. And here she'd been blaming *him* for injecting his private emotions into the meeting!

Through a fog of confusion, she heard Paco's confident voice adjourning the meeting. The crowd was breaking up, drifting along the aisles to the exit or clumping in little groups to discuss the vote's outcome. Terry stumbled to her feet, heading for the exit. She didn't wait for Cecilia to follow her out. Right now she wasn't quite ready to face her unspoken questions.

She felt a hand on her elbow, and turned to see Lenore smiling warmly at her. "Thanks a lot for your support. I really appreciate it. It's nice to know I still have one friend in Taos."

A sudden rush of emotion blurred Terry's vision. How unfair she had been to Lenore! Caught up in the grip of those primitive jealous feelings, she had seen her only as a powerful rival, ignoring the vulnerable woman who hid her suffering behind that glossy exterior. Impulsively she put her hand out to grasp Lenore's. "I am your friend, Lenore. I'm with you all the way. I'm sure neither of us is a dyed-in-the-wool women's libber, but there are some times when women have to stand together.''

Lenore's eyes gazed into hers with infinite understanding. Terry knew what she was thinking. Though neither of them would say it aloud, a secret bond had drawn them together. They'd both made the fatal mistake of falling in love with Neil Brewster.

Skeeter came down the aisle toward them, his mustache drooping with obvious disappointment. His face lighted up when he saw them standing together. ''Terry! Glad to have you on our side. Thanks for your vote, old girl. What say we all go next door to the Taos Inn and lick our wounds over a drink or two?''

''Not me, thanks. I'm really exhausted.'' Lenore flashed her dazzling smile. ''But I'm sure our friend here will join you, won't you, Terry? Our wounded warrior deserves a little comfort.''

The last thing Terry wanted just then was a drink with Skeeter, but she could hardly back out without seeming ungracious. ''Fine,'' she said. ''I'd love that.'' The smile on her lips felt stiff and phony. She let Skeeter take her arm and guide her through the crowd to the exit. Lenore stayed behind, surrounded by a few of her other supporters.

When they entered the Taos Inn, she went through a few bad moments as Skeeter started to head for the patio. Terry was struck by a sudden disabling vision; herself in that blatantly feminine dress, Neil leaning toward her over the table, both of them wrapped in a cloud of enchantment. She laid her hand on Skeeter's arm, trying to think of some reasonable-sounding objection. Luckily, just at that moment R.C. Gorman called out to him from the inside bar, deflecting the two of them in that direction.

Perched on one of the bar stools, Terry listened absently to the men's conversation, wondering how soon she could decently make her exit. Then Gorman was called away to the phone, and Skeeter turned back to her, his usually genial face looking uncharacteristically solemn. "Have you had some kind of fight with Neil Brewster? I notice you two don't seem to be speaking these days."

Terry went stiff with resentment. Why was Skeeter poking into her private affairs? "Is that how it seems to you?" she parried. "I wasn't aware I was treating him any differently than usual."

"Oh, come on, Terry. I saw the stars in your eyes that night at Paco's. And the whole town's buzzing with gossip about the way you looked when you came here for dinner last Thursday. I wish I'd been here to see that. Apparently you looked pretty sensational."

Terry felt her cheeks reddening. "I get so sick of all this gossip. It really isn't anyone else's business."

Her voice was sharp edged with tension. Skeeter flinched a little. "I didn't mean to make you angry. I'm just glad that you seem to have come to your senses." He peered at her earnestly, his boyish eyes full of concern. "The guy is all wrong for you, Terry—cold and hard, insulated from human feelings."

Cold and hard.... A lot you know about him. You've never seen him as I have, that night on the mesa. . . . Terry drew a deep breath, fighting against the grief that was threatening to overwhelm her. "If you don't mind, Skeeter, let's drop the subject. When it comes to my private life, I'm quite capable of making my own decisions."

Skeeter drew back as if she'd slapped him. "Don't get mad at me, Terry. It's just that I'd hate to see you get hurt."

"Skeeter, please!" A tremendous pressure was welling up inside her. Another few minutes, and something was going to burst. She got to her feet, almost stumbling in her haste to get away from him. "I'm awfully tired. I've got to get home now. My truck is just down the road in front of my office."

"Terry, wait!" she heard him calling to her as she threaded her way through the tables. Once out on the street, she paused and drew a deep draft of the cool night air. Skeeter appeared beside her, looking morose and contrite.

"I didn't mean to upset you—honestly, Terry. Let me walk you down to your truck." He forced a painful smile. "You can stand my annoying presence for that long, can't you?"

A wave of guilt and remorse rushed over Terry. Dear, good, loyal Skeeter. Was she going to let her disastrous feeling for Neil alienate her from all her friends in Taos?

"I'm really sorry, Skeeter. I shouldn't have flared up like that." She reached out for his arm and hugged it to her. They started walking along the deserted street toward her office.

"I know I was out of line." Skeeter was speaking

softly, meditatively. "What happens with you and Neil Brewster is none of my business. But when I saw the big romance had suddenly grounded, I thought it was time to push my own interests a little."

Terry stopped walking abruptly, staring up at Skeeter's moonlit face. His eyes looked pleading and serious, like a spaniel puppy's. "What do you mean, your own interests?"

"Is that so astonishing? That a hick-town cub reporter should dare to fall in love with a high-powered lady architect?" His voice turned hard and bitter. "I realize I'm pretty small pickings. Not all of us are lucky enough to inherit millions of dollars."

"For heaven's sake, Skeeter! You know it's not the money I care about. It's just that I didn't expect this. I've always thought of you as a kind of brother."

Skeeter tried to smile but didn't quite make it. "Yeah, I know—the usual reaction. I seem to come on like everyone's little brother." He stared out into the shadows for a moment, his shoulders drooping in obvious misery. Then he turned back toward her, his voice taking on a new ring of resolution. "Listen, Terry, you've got to think about this. I'm sure we're right for each other. We believe in all the same things—living close to the earth, turning our backs on all those big-city values. We've both been through the mill, too—learned not to expect some big earth-shaking romance." He reached out a hand and gently touched her cheek. "We both know each other so well. We don't have to be afraid of any nasty surprises.'' He lowered his lips to hers. The first kiss was soft and fleeting, as though he were wary of closer involvement. Then his arms went around her. He pulled her close, his lips grinding down on hers hungrily.

She wanted to push him away but hesitated, afraid of hurting his feelings. She stood there unmoved in his encircling arms, trying her best to imagine him as a lover. He was right; they did have the same values. And the prospect of no surprises—that should have been very tempting, considering the kind of disasters she seemed to be prone to. She did feel very safe here, with his arms around her. He was kind, dependable, comforting—as comforting as a nice warm cup of cocoa.

"Terry.... Terry, darling," he was murmuring into her hair now, still holding her close against his lean hard body. Terry felt a sudden surge of revulsion. *This is wrong, all wrong,* she thought wildly. *These aren't the arms that belong around me. If I can't have Neil, I don't want anybody.*

She started to struggle, trying to wrench herself away from his grasp. She had to pound on his chest to make him realize that she really meant it. They stood there in the moonlight, gasping a little, staring at each other in confused exasperation.

"I'm sorry, Skeeter. I guess we moved into that a little too quickly. It takes me a while, getting used to new ideas."

Skeeter stared at her glumly. "Don't apologize, Terry. I know I came on too strong. But I did mean what I said. I think we'd be good for each other.

Will you promise me you'll try and think about it?''

"Yes, I'll think about it. I promise you that." She
turned away from him, walking away down the street
toward her pickup. She felt his eyes on her, knew
they must be full of that puppylike yearning. Her
promise weighed her down like a heavy burden. She
would keep it, of course. She'd try to imagine him as
a part of her life. But where would she find the time
to think about Skeeter while her mind was so wholly
obsessed with Neil?

CHAPTER FOURTEEN

TERRY DROPPED DESPONDENTLY into the swivel chair, flinging the pile of mail she was carrying onto her desk. She stared blankly out at the mountains, just beginning to emerge from the morning mist, while her mind went over and over the last few minutes she'd spent at the post office.

There was no doubt about it; Rick Barton had snubbed her. Turning away like that, pretending not to see her, hear her greeting. He'd heard her, all right, but he'd deliberately ignored her. She'd already been a little concerned about him after he skipped last Friday's committee meeting. She'd tried to get in touch with him over the weekend, but he'd always been "out of the house" when she called.

She was worried. Could Southwestern Towers have approached him, made him an offer that tempted him to switch sides? She brushed the suspicion away impatiently. Rick would never accept that kind of bribe. He was far more fanatic then she was about holding fast to traditional architecture.

No, this coldness of his had a simpler explanation. That vote of hers at the meeting last Thursday night seemed to have alienated a lot of her friends.

She felt a shiver go through her as she let her mind drift back over the long lonely weekend. First, Cecilia's call on Saturday morning, canceling the invitation to dinner. She'd murmured some vague excuse about Gito's illness, but when Terry, alarmed, had asked if the asthma was back, she'd sounded embarrassed and hung up the phone abruptly.

Then, a few hours later, she'd met David coming out of the Plaza Drug Store. He'd given her a curt hurried greeting, hadn't bothered to stop for the usual conversation.

Still puzzling over his reaction, she'd gone into the hardware store to talk to Paco. His smile had been dismayingly stiff and formal. When Terry, fighting a growing sense of disquiet, started to tell him about her committee meeting, he'd brushed her off in a brutally obvious manner, pretending to be too busy to listen.

Yes, it all fitted into a pattern. That vote Thursday night had split the protest campaign. Where there once had been unity, there were now two warring factions—the majority who had sided with Paco, the minority who had followed Lenore. That was the reason her friends were turning against her—just because she'd expressed her honest opinion by casting her vote for Lenore's more aggressive proposal.

Your honest opinion? Oh, Terry, come off it! You voted that way because you were furious with Neil. Terry tried to silence the nagging voice of her conscience, but the memories, once triggered, came thronging inexorably back, vivid in every detail.

Once again she relived that ugly scene on the mesa, heard Lenore's pleading voice: "I want you. I need you;" Neil's harsh reply: "I wish to God I had never met you."

Why had those words disturbed her so deeply? They'd been meant for Lenore, not for her. But they'd touched some sensitive spot in her inmost being, stirred some fierce unnameable emotion. She'd thought all this time it was anger. Now she was forced to acknowledge a far more dismaying emotion. Fear, a sharp sickening fear—that's what it had been. The fear of losing Neil had sent her into a tailspin. The thought that he might someday say those harsh words to her had made her draw into herself in sudden panic. Love was too painful a risk. Better reject him now than wait till the awful day when she'd be rejected.

She fought against the stinging realization, telling herself it hadn't been like that at all, that she'd merely been shocked at seeing Neil's true colors, that she'd had a lucky escape, finding out she'd been right after all in her first impression. Arrogant, self-centered, cruel—that's what Neil Brewster was and always would be. She'd been really stupid, falling in love with him. But she shouldn't have been such a slave to her emotions as to let them come between her and her old friends.

At that moment Terry made a firm resolution. She'd called Cecilia now, apologize for voting against her. Eagerly she started rehearsing her speech: *I was pretty mixed up, I'm afraid—some personal problems I won't go into right now. But you*

*were right, Cecilia, in siding with Paco. Lenore's too
pushy, too strident. She doesn't understand the people in Taos....*

She reached out to pick up the phone, then let her
hand drop abruptly. This wasn't the sort of thing you
could do on the phone. She had to talk to Cecilia face
to face. But not now, not right this moment. Maybe
tonight she'd be able to do it, swallow her pride, coax
back Cecilia's friendship. Right now she was sick of
it all—the petty conflicts, the tension, the pervasive
sense of distrust.

There was only one way to put all these problems
behind her—work, her unfailing refuge. She'd go up
to the mesa, see how Leo's and Sandra's house was
coming along. It was all very well to be a noble
crusader, to spend all one's time preserving the
sacred image of Taos. But not if it meant neglecting
her own profession. Work, hard work—that's what
she needed now, the work she knew she was good at.
It might not dispel her stupid obsession with Neil, but
at least it would give her the sense of accomplishing
something, not floundering around in this futile
swamp of emotion.

SHE DIDN'T SEE NEIL when he first appeared at the
house site. She was too busy checking the vent where
the blower would fit into the solar heating system.
She looked up suddenly to see him standing beside
Gus Pickett, who was proudly pointing out how the
house was progressing.

When he saw her looking at him, he came over and
joined her. "I'm amazed at how fast Gus and his

men have been working. He tells me Leo and Sandra will probably be able to move in this weekend.''

Terry gazed at him warily. Why was he suddenly acting so cordial? He'd ignored her that night at the meeting, had been ignoring her since that fatal night on the mesa. Now he was making a point of seeking her out.

''It's going according to schedule.'' She kept her voice noncommittal. ''There's still a lot of work to be done on the inside, but at least they'll have a roof over their heads.''

She started to walk away, pretending she wanted to check the big front-window openings. Neil laid a hand on her shoulder. ''Terry,'' he said, ''come up to my house for just a few minutes. I need to talk to you about something private.''

His touch, as usual, stirred up a small explosion. Her heart started racing; her veins seemed to pulse with intolerable tension. She reached up and pushed his hand away. ''I don't want any private talks, Neil. We have nothing to say to each other.''

Neil's face clouded with anger. ''Don't get on your high horse, Terry. I wasn't intending to force my attentions on you. What I want to tell you is strictly campaign business. I'm worried about what Lenore is doing.''

''You made that very clear at Thursday night's meeting.'' His biting tone whipped up an answering anger in her. ''Haven't you done enough to hurt Lenore? Did you have to launch that personal attack against her?''

The hazel eyes widened in shocked surprise. ''You

think I attacked Lenore out of personal motives? You're absolutely crazy. Can't you see she's doing her best to wreck the campaign? She's got Paco and Skeeter snarling at each other, even got you to vote against Cecilia.''

In spite of her outrage, Terry felt her conscience prickle. She knew all too well that her own vote had been triggered by personal motives. But she wasn't about to admit that fact to Neil.

''What if I did choose to vote against Cecilia? Is she some kind of infallible oracle? It seems to me we're being much too cautious. Maybe we need some of Lenore's impetuous courage.''

''Impetuous? Is that how you see her?'' Neil glared at her in exasperation. ''Listen, Terry, I know her better than you do. There's nothing impetuous about Lenore. All her moves are based on careful calculation. She wants this campaign of ours to be defeated.''

''What an awful thing to say!'' Terry's voice was louder than she had intended. She saw some of the workmen's heads turn toward them, and lowered her tone to an urgent whisper. ''You think you can get away with anything, don't you? First you brutally reject a woman who loves you, then you do your best to turn her new friends against her.''

Neil's jaw tightened grimly. ''So we're finally going to discuss that night, are we? You really think Lenore loves me? That act she put on really fooled you?''

He was staring at her as if his worst fears had been confirmed. Terry's outrage swelled up into fury.

What was he doing, trying to make her think Lenore didn't love him? After she'd heard that voice pleading in bitter anguish, did he really think she was stupid enough to trust him?

"You self-centered, arrogant bastard! You don't deserve a woman like Lenore. After all those years she spent working for you, all her self-sacrifice and dedication."

A sad little smile spread over Neil's face. He stared at her for a moment as though he wasn't sure she deserved an answer. Then he said in a quiet voice, "You know something, Terry? You look very beautiful when you're angry."

She stopped her attack in mid-sentence, shocked by her own irrational feeling of pleasure. Then she realized what he was doing—trying to cut her off by changing the subject.

"Don't try to butter me up," she said in a low fierce whisper. "I'm wise to those tactics. That's the sort of thing Paul always used to do."

The smile disappeared. He gazed at her for a long silent moment. He didn't look sad now, just unutterably weary. "I'm getting a little tired of being blamed for all your ex-husband's sins. Okay, so I once made the same mistake myself. Because I found out Lenore was cruel and dishonest, I read those qualities into every new woman. I even did it with you, that day at Midnight. But now I'm over that, Terry. I trust you to be yourself, not some other woman's reflection. Can't you do that with me? Can't we both put the pain behind us and go forward together?"

Terry drew a deep breath and looked around her. The workmen had obviously been listening. They all made a hasty show of pretending to concentrate on what they'd been doing. Neil's pleading words seemed to hang in the silence between the two of them. Tempting, very tempting. "Go forward together." Wasn't that what she wanted, deep down inside? But now that she knew the price Lenore had paid, how could she take the risk of trusting Neil?

"I'm sorry, Neil. I'll have to ask you to leave now. The men and I have to get on with our work."

His chin thrust out at a stubborn angle. "Terry," his voice rang out over the mesa, "I'm not going to let you do this! You've got to listen. You've got to let me explain about Lenore."

He reached out to take her arm. Just in time, she flung herself out of range. She realized it was no use trying to argue. He was clearly determined to make a public scene. She ran to her waiting pickup, jumped in and started the motor. As she drove away, she could feel the men's eyes upon her.

Damn Neil Brewster! What must those men be thinking, seeing him drive their boss away in hysterics? It wasn't enough he had ruined her private life. Now he was messing around with her profession!

TERRY UNLOCKED THE DOOR to her office and paused on the threshold, caught in the grip of an overpowering memory. She could almost see Neil's tall plaid-shirted figure, the way he'd looked that first day, glowering at her while he leveled his threats of legal action. She'd seen him then for what he was—arrogant, selfish, contemptuous of anyone else's feelings. How had she let his charm blind her so quickly, let herself be carried away on this dizzying roller coaster of emotion?

She brushed the image away and walked resolutely into her inner office. The pile of unopened mail was on the desk where she'd thrown it this morning. She picked up the first envelope and saw the return address: First Commercial Bank. A tremor of apprehension ran along her spine. Why were they writing her now? She'd already paid them this month's interest. She'd felt bad about not being able to pay the loan back in full, but Ward McKevitt had been very nice about granting that six months' extension.

She slit open the envelope and unfolded the neatly typed letter. The words seemed to leap out at her from the page.

Dear Miss Morrison:
I regret to inform you that, due to unforeseen circumstances, this bank must reconsider the extension of your loan we recently granted you.

Before we reach any final decision, I would like to have a personal discussion with you about this matter. Please call me at your earliest convenience to set up an appointment.

Sincerely yours,
Ward McKevitt

She needed that six months' extension! By the end of the summer, with eight new houses completed and paid for, she'd have plenty of money to pay back the loan in full. But right now, a demand for repayment would mean disaster.

She reached for the phone, dialed the bank's number and was quickly put through to Ward McKevitt. "Ah, yes, Terry, how are you?" His heavy western twang boomed along the line. "It's good to hear from you. I've been expecting your call."

"Then you know what I'm calling about. What's all this about canceling my extension? You know how my business works. I don't get paid until these houses are finished."

There was silence for a moment. "Well, frankly, Terry, there's some concern around here about whether or not they *will* be finished. It appears to us that you haven't been spending much time at your work these past few weeks. You've been too busy with other interests."

It was only too clear what Ward was implying— that he didn't approve of her part in the protest campaign. "Powerful forces," Neil had warned her. But she hadn't expected an attack from this particular quarter.

She wanted to answer him defiantly, tell him he couldn't scare her, that she didn't need his money. But the truth was, she did need it. So she decided to play things cool, at least for the moment.

"I'm not sure I understand, Mr. McKevitt. Are you talking about the time I spent on the protest campaign? I didn't know you were one of Southwestern's supporters."

"I have no opinion on that project, one way or the

other." He sounded a little nervous, as if he hadn't anticipated so direct a challenge. "I just hate to see you make a fool of yourself. Getting involved with all these wild-eyed protesters is bad for your business. Believe me, Terry, you don't know what you're getting into. Now why don't you be a good girl, stick to your architecture, and forget about all this political nonsense."

Terry hesitated. She wasn't quite ready for open defiance. She heard his voice turn soft and wheedling. "Believe me, Terry, I feel very bad about this. I'm as fond of you as if you were my own daughter—"

"That's enough, Mr. McKevitt. I've already got the message."

She could hear what sounded like a sigh of relief. "You're a smart girl, Terry. I'm glad you're going to be reasonable about this."

"Don't go so fast. I haven't decided yet. I need a little time to think things over."

"I'll give you till Wednesday morning at ten o'clock." The wheedling tone was gone. The hard-headed businessman was back in the saddle. "Think very carefully, Terry. I hope, for your sake, that you make the right decision."

The phone clicked before Terry could answer. She sat there holding the receiver as her mind searched feverishly for a possible solution. How much of the principal was still unpaid? Only about twenty thousand. A mere bagatelle to someone like Neil Brewster....

No, not that. She wouldn't go crawling back to

that arrogant bully. There were other banks, after all—banks in Santa Fe, Albuquerque. Her business was well established. It wasn't as though she was just getting started, like the Janus Gallery, for instance—

The gallery! Terry went cold with apprehension, remembering Cecilia's worried remarks about the mortgage. Was Ward McKevitt trying to pressure her, too? For herself, it would mean just a temporary setback. For Cecilia and David, it might mean disaster.

She started to dial the gallery's number, then put down the phone and headed out of the office. This wasn't the kind of thing to discuss over a phone line. If what she suspected was true, they needed to meet in a council of war.

CECILIA'S DOLEFUL FACE as she opened the door told Terry the ax had fallen. "Ward McKevitt?" she asked.

"Ward McKevitt." Cecilia waved her into the living room. David looked up as she entered, then turned away and stared silently out the window.

Terry looked around at the big low-ceilinged room. For her, it had been the scene of many happy occasions—dinners, parties, long afternoons of conversation. But how much more it meant to Cecilia. Her father's hands had helped shape the adobe bricks for the walls, had chiseled the Hopi designs into the roof beams. Her mother had laid the Mexican tiles that framed the corner fireplace. She and her brothers had spent almost all of their lives there.

Was it going to be snatched away now, just because she opposed the schemes of this faceless financial giant?

Cecilia dropped onto the sofa, her lips compressed in a wry painful smile. "He got to you, too, did he, sweetie?"

Terry nodded. "He's threatening to cancel my loan extension—said I hadn't been attending to business. What did he say to you?"

"Pretty much the same thing, I guess. 'Stay home and take care of business. Artists shouldn't be dabbling in politics.' But with us, it's not just the loan. He's already started foreclosure proceedings."

Terry looked at her in horror. "But how can he do that? So long as you're making your regular payments—"

"That's just the trouble. We haven't been." Cecilia looked a little embarrassed. "Last month we paid only half of what we should have. He said then it was okay, that he'd even waive the next month's payment. Now he's suddenly done a flip-flop and sent us this threatening letter."

"Cecilia, that's awful! Couldn't you borrow the money to make up the rest of the payment? Maybe your brother in Denver—"

"I thought of that right away. Things are pretty tight with Roger, but he said he was sure he could scrape up the money—especially since it was needed to save the old homestead. But then, when I talked to McKevitt, he wouldn't accept that—said the only terms he'd accept to stop the foreclosure would be a repayment of the total amount of the mortgage."

"Or quit the protest campaign."

"He didn't come right out and say that, just waffled around the subject, told me I didn't understand how things worked in Taos. Me, a Rampion! My family has been here for three generations. And now this rank outsider, who came here ten years ago, dares to tell me I don't know my way around Taos."

David turned around to face them, his usually genial face set in lines of bitter defiance. "I've only been here three years. That makes me more of a rank outsider than he is."

Cecilia looked up at him, startled into compunction. "Oh, sweetie, you know I don't mean it that way. You could never be an outsider. You're an artist. You've always belonged here from the very beginning."

"Have I? I'm beginning to wonder. Maybe you have too much faith in me, Cecilia. All my so-called artistic talent hasn't helped us to make a decent living. I'm as much of a flop as a husband as I am as a father. My wife is about to lose her family's home, and my son wants to go and live with crazy old Pedro." He turned away abruptly and stared moodily poking the glowing coals in the fireplace.

Terry looked blankly at Cecilia. "What's all this about Gito?"

"It's nothing, really." She gave an impatient shrug. "He's just going through one of those phases. He sulks in his room, won't talk to David, just keeps playing that stupid game with those battered old clothespins."

"Cecilia, that sounds serious. Don't you think it might help to let him go visit Pedro?"

Cecilia's jaw set glumly. "No, I don't. I agree with David. Pedro's obviously done some bad things to Gito's psyche. But kids are resilient. I know he'll outgrow it." She waved her hand in an impatient gesture. "All that is unimportant. The big problem now is this bastard McKevitt."

"He's got you over a barrel," Terry said slowly. "Maybe you ought to just forget the campaign. You've done a lot more than your share already."

Cecilia looked up, her eyes flashing. "How can you say that, Terry? Don't you think the campaign is important?"

"Of course it's important. But not important enough to risk your whole heritage for it."

Cecilia threw out her arms in an expansive gesture. "My heritage? My heritage is Taos. If that goes down the drain, one crumbling old house doesn't matter. David and I don't intend to surrender. We'll fight like those settlers back in the times of DeVargas. Where would we be today if they'd given up and left the place to the Indians?"

Her face was suddenly alight with exhilaration. Then an impish gleam crept into her eyes. "Listen to me, casting Ward McKevitt as one of the Indians. Any self-respecting Indian would consider that a deadly insult."

Terry felt herself being won over by her friend's enthusiasm but fought against it. All this brave talk about settlers and Indians wouldn't help avert imminent disaster. "Look," she insisted, "we've got to do something about this foreclosure business. If you won't give up the campaign, then you'll have to find enough money to pay the whole mortgage. Have you thought about asking Neil—''

"No!" David was on his feet, shouting. "I won't go begging another man for favors."

"But David, you wouldn't be begging. It would only be a loan. You'd pay back the money, sooner or later. You said you might be getting that big commission—''

"That's right," Cecilia broke in. "And we are going to get it. Mr. Enderby loved David's sketches and slides. He's coming to see him sometime this week. Once he signs on the dotted line, all our troubles will be over. With that kind of contract behind us, we could even get a loan from Chase Manhattan. Just you wait and see, sweetie. We can tell Mr. Ward McKevitt to go to Hades."

Terry thought there were too many "ifs" in that whole situation, but she didn't want to dampen Cecilia's high spirits. "That really sounds great, Cecilia. But all that is going to take time. We don't know how fast McKevitt will move. Maybe you ought to ask Neil, just to tide you over."

"Keep your advice to yourself, Terry. I don't want any help from phonies like you and Neil." David banged the poker down onto the hearthstone and stalked angrily out into the kitchen.

Cecilia shot a quick glance at Terry. "Don't pay any attention to David, sweetie. He's just in one of his moods. It really bugs him to have to ask people for favors."

"But can't he see this isn't a personal favor? It's all part of our campaign. Neil warned us this kind of thing might happen. You know how determined he is to beat Southwestern. Helping take the pressure off you would simply be a part of our campaign tactics."

"The same goes for you, Terry. Are you going to ask Neil to help you stymie McKevitt?"

"No! Never!" The words were out before Terry could stop them. Chagrined at revealing so much naked emotion, she groped for an explanation. "It's different with me, Cecilia. I have other ways of getting the money I need."

Cecilia was smiling that all-knowing earth-mother smile. "I understand, Terry. You have your personal reasons, just like David." Her eyes turned opaque and thoughtful. "Speaking of personal reasons, what about McKevitt's? What does he stand to gain if Southwestern Towers goes through with the project?"

Terry had a flash of illumination. "Lenore must know something about it. Remember what she said Thursday night at the meeting?"

Cecilia looked puzzled at first. Then she remembered. "Something about counting up his share of the profits. Does that mean she thinks he's made a deal with Southwestern?" She beamed at Terry. "But this is fantastic. It gives us a perfect handle on McKevitt. You know half the town is in debt to First Commercial. If we can prove he's getting paid by Southwestern for starting foreclosure proceedings on poor starving artists, we can turn the whole population against the project."

She paused for a moment. A new thought had obviously struck her, and her beaming smile gave way to a worried frown. "The trouble is, how are we going to prove it? We can't just go around making accusations. Ward is likely to slap a whopping big libel suit on us."

Terry *was* getting caught up in her friend's enthusiasm now. "I'm sure Lenore knows something. If Neil hadn't hit her so hard, she might have explained it."

"She admitted she didn't have any evidence."

"It wouldn't have to be something put down on paper." Terry's mind was racing, considering all the possible lines of attack. "And we don't need to shout it from the rooftops. All we need to do is convince a few key people—Ben Montoya, for instance. If he thought our local banker was acting under instructions from people in Dallas—"

"Oh, yes, Terry, you've got it! The old man wouldn't stand for that kind of threat to his power. Now all we've got to do is find out what Lenore knows."

"You know where she lives, down in one of those San Geronimo apartments. Let's go down right now and get the ball rolling."

A guarded look came over Cecilia's face. "I'm afraid where Lenore is concerned, David and I are kind of personae non gratae. She didn't take kindly to seeing us vote against her." She cast an apologetic glance at Terry. "You might be in a better position, seeing as how you came out on her side and all."

Despite Cecilia's friendly manner, she sensed that her own vote for Lenore still rankled, and she couldn't help feeling guilty. But this wasn't the moment for complex explanations. "All right," she said. "I'll go see Lenore right now. If she knows what I think she knows, Ward McKevitt may turn into our biggest campaign asset."

CHAPTER FIFTEEN

TERRY DROVE SLOWLY along the private road behind the San Geronimo Lodge, wondering which of the four small adobe houses Lenore had rented. Then she saw something that answered her question: Skeeter's red VW van, parked in front of the furthermost apartment.

She hesitated a moment, obscurely disturbed by Skeeter's presence. She knew she should have been glad to see him there. As one of the campaign leaders, he should be informed about the threats from McKevitt. But his declaration last Thursday night had made things awkward between them. Still, he'd hardly return to that subject in front of Lenore. With the news she was bringing, there should be no trouble in confining the conversation to campaign business.

She hopped down from the pickup and rang the doorbell. Lenore came to the door and ushered her in, looking pleased and excited. "Terry, darling! We were just going to call you. A terrific thing has just happened. Reuben Abeyta is calling a special council meeting this Thursday. He's agreed to lay the whole project before the public."

"This Thursday!" Terry stared at her blankly.

"Isn't that pretty short notice? I thought he told you and David that he was going to bring it up at the council's regular meeting, two weeks from now."

"That's what he said at the time—" Lenore was smiling smugly "—but Skeeter's article made him change his mind."

"Your article? You mean the one accusing the council of taking bribes? But I thought we agreed at the meeting that you weren't going to print that."

"You're right, we agreed not to print it. But we didn't promise not to show it to Abeyta." Skeeter was glowing with self-satisfaction. "Lenore and I just did a little genteel arm-twisting. Reuben decided to beat us to the punch by bringing the whole thing out in the open."

Terry was dismayed. Why had Lenore and Skeeter gone ahead on their own after that very clear decision at the meeting? "Does Paco know about this? Or Neil? They both thought we needed more time for organization."

"Paco Reyes has far too much faith in his fellow townsmen." Lenore sounded contemptuous. "As for Neil Brewster—he has his own private reasons for wanting to slow our momentum."

"What do you mean?" Terry demanded sharply.

Lenore looked quickly at Skeeter, then shrugged her shoulders. "Skeeter knows what I mean. But we've both agreed this is no time to open that particular can of worms. It would only get us sidetracked from the central issue. But what about your news, Terry? You look like you have something momentous to tell us."

What can of worms? What was all this about

Neil's private reasons? Terry forced herself to bite back the questions. Lenore was right. They should keep their eyes on the central issue. And right now Ward McKevitt's position was certainly central.

She quickly filled them both in on the banker's attempt to pressure her and the Quayles. "So you see," she concluded, "it seems pretty clear that he's made some kind of deal with Southwestern Towers. What do you know about it? You started to say something last Thursday—"

"And Neil Brewster took very good care to make sure she didn't get a real chance to say it," Skeeter announced self-righteously. Once more, he and Lenore exchanged meaningful glances.

"Lenore, you do know something, don't you? Won't you and Skeeter please tell me? Maybe we can make McKevitt's threats backfire against him."

"I didn't intend to use this unless I had to." Lenore spoke slowly, her gaze averted from Terry's. "Yes, McKevitt does have a deal with Southwestern. He and a silent partner are handling the financing for the whole project. Southwestern has promised them a generous slice of the profits."

Terry nodded glumly. "That's just what we thought must have happened. But how do you know all this, Lenore? You said Thursday night that you had no documentation."

"That's right. I have no real evidence—nothing on paper, that is. But I do have the word of McKevitt's silent partner."

She raised her eyes to Terry's. Terry was startled to see they were full of pity.

"Oh, come on, Lenore, tell me. There's no point

in keeping this a deep dark secret.'' Skeeter glared at
Lenore demandingly, but she made a weak little gesture of protest. He sighed in exasperation. ''If
Lenore won't tell you, I will. She heard about the
deal from your friend, Neil Brewster. He was trying
to get her in on the partnership with him. He offered
her ten thousand dollars to forget the campaign and
get out of Taos.''

Terry felt weak and dizzy. The walls of the room
seemed to close in around her. ''Neil is in on the project? I don't believe you. Why, he's the one who discovered the link with Olympia.''

''Discovered? That's hardly the word. Neil knew
about Olympia from the beginning. Why do you
think he came down here in the first place? So he'd
be on the spot to help his friends at Stanton Odessa.''

''But he hates Olympia! You know that! He's
always regretted backing out from that fight.''

Lenore's dark eyes were soft with compassion.
''I'm sure this comes as a shock, Terry. I know how
you feel about Neil.''

Terry drew herself up stiffly. ''My personal feelings have nothing to do with the matter. I just don't
believe he could be this two-faced.''

''You don't have to pretend with me, darling. I
saw you with Neil that night up on the mesa.''

Terry felt her cheeks go scarlet. She looked at
Skeeter. He was ostentatiously staring into the fireplace. How much had Lenore told him? The blanket
under the stars, the eager bodies entwining? No
wonder he'd been so sure that she was in love with
Neil.

"It's nothing to be ashamed of, Terry. The Brewster charm is pretty overpowering. You heard *me* that night, I'm sure. Even with all I knew about his deal with Olympia, I still came crawling back like a poor whipped puppy."

"What deal with Olympia?" Terry braced herself, determined to hear the truth, no matter how painful.

"The deal they made to get him to call off his suit—a big block of stock in Stanton Odessa."

"That's crazy. I don't believe it. Why would Neil do a thing like that? He has more money now than he knows what to do with."

"Neil doesn't care about money. It's power he's after. He thought he had found it in championing the consumer. One brave man, standing up to all those giant corporations. It worked for a while, I guess. But then he came up against Olympia Tires. When he saw that he couldn't beat them, he decided to join them. That's how he got in on the ground floor with Stanton Odessa. It's a much more powerful outfit than anything in the so-called Brewster empire."

"He knew about Stanton Odessa all along? Then why did he bother going down to Dallas?"

"Ah, yes, that famous trip. That was pure window dressing, pretending to be a big help in our campaign. And all the while he's been secretly working against it. You saw how he dragged his feet at the meeting on Thursday. And I know he's been talking to Paco, making trouble between him and Skeeter. Now he's turned Ward McKevitt loose on you, just because you dared to vote against him." Lenore's face was suffused with sadness. "I really didn't think he would stoop that low. But he's always been pretty ruthless with his women.''

"The guy's a real bastard, Terry." Skeeter's voice was heavy with condemnation. "You remember, I tried to warn you.''

Terry felt a new sense of grief, ready to overwhelm her. She wanted desperately to get away from both of these people—Skeeter with his self-righteous air, Lenore with her all-knowing compassion. At home, by herself, perhaps she could think more clearly, come to terms with this startling new view of Neil. *He never loved me. He only pretended to love me. All the time he was secretly working against me....*

She jumped up from her chair, ready to head for the exit. Then she remembered why she'd come. The campaign, that was what mattered. If she let her personal feelings sweep her away, that would really be a victory for Neil Brewster.

"Okay, you guys, you've convinced me. Now let's go convince Ben Montoya. Once he sees the kinds of tactics Southwestern will stoop to, I'm sure we can get him to come out against the project.''

Lenore's eyes widened in sudden alarm. "Wait just a minute, darling. Do we really need to do that? Why don't we wait till after the council meeting? We've got the people behind us. The council will probably vote our way without our exposing all this underhand business.''

"But it's not just the project now. It's the threat to Cecilia and David. We've got to get McKevitt out in the open. It would only take a few words from Ben

Montoya to lose him half of his most profitable business.''

Lenore's mouth was compressed to a thin firm line. "I'm sorry for Cecilia and David, but they do have an option. So do you, Terry. None of you really needs to appear at that council meeting. If you tell McKevitt you're quitting the protest, I'm sure he'll drop the whole matter."

"Not appear at the meeting? But that's crazy, Lenore. I've got to appear at that meeting. Everyone knows I'm the head of the architects' committee."

"Terry, dear, you're not indispensable. Someone else can give your report to the council. The same with Cecilia and David. Somebody else can make their presentations."

"But how would that look to the public? The campaign's three staunchest supporters not even showing up at the council meeting?"

Lenore raised a quizzical eyebrow. "It wouldn't be the end of the world. Skeeter, you know, is a very good speaker. I'd do my best, too. And after all, the facts do speak for themselves. Things might turn out better without so many local undercurrents."

Something wasn't quite right here. Lenore was taking this all too calmly. And what was all that about local undercurrents? Was she saying Cecilia's network of friendships wouldn't be useful? And Paco? What about Paco? Wasn't it strange that he wasn't here to discuss their plans for the council meeting?

"I have a suggestion," she said, trying to keep the growing doubt out of her voice. "Let's go talk things over with Paco. We'll tell him about Neil's deal with

McKevitt and see how he feels about going to Ben Montoya.''

"I'm not sure that would be wise." Lenore's face had assumed a stubborn guarded look. "There may be new factors here that you haven't considered."

Terry waited for her to describe these mysterious new factors, but Lenore seemed reluctant to do any further explaining. Skeeter leaped into the breach, his voice growing sharp and defensive. "Lenore and I don't trust Paco. He and Neil have become close buddies. He's likely to go tell Neil we know what he's up to."

"What if he does?" Terry's suspicions were growing stronger by the minute. "If he's really working against us, we should make the whole deal public. At least Neil would have a chance to defend himself."

The corners of Lenore's mouth turned down contemptuously. "There you go again, Terry—putting your feelings for Neil above the campaign."

Terry's first instinct was to lash out angrily at the other woman. What right did anyone have to make that accusation? Then she suddenly realized what Lenore was doing. By turning the heat on her, she was shifting the argument away from the real subject. A clever ploy. It had almost worked.

She could hear Neil's words now, beating a small refrain in her ear: "All her moves are based on careful calculation.... She's doing her best to wreck the campaign...." She'd brushed off the words as the product of personal spite, but now she began to wonder. This rift between Skeeter and Paco—Lenore had said it was Neil who had caused the trouble. But had it really been Neil? Hadn't it been Lenore who'd egged Skeeter on to rasher and rasher action, ignoring Paco's advice, pushing him into a premature confrontation?

"I'm sorry, Lenore," she said, "but I don't think I'm qualified to make these decisions. I'm going to have to talk to a lot more people before I decide what I'm going to do."

"You're going to see Paco, are you? After what we've just told you?" Anger flared in Lenore's dark eyes. Anger, and something else.... Fear? Calculation? It looked like a mixture of both.

"Yes, I'm going to Paco. He started this campaign. He knows the people of Taos better than we do. But before I do that, I'm going to do something else. You've told me what Neil Brewster did in that fight with Olympia. I think it's time I let him tell me what you did."

CHAPTER SIXTEEN

"WHAT A PLEASANT SURPRISE." Neil rose from the
carved wooden bench on his *portal*, gravely watching
Terry come toward him along the driveway. The
words sounded cordial enough, but his face looked
stiff and wary.

"Don't worry, Neil," she said lightly. "I'm not
going to throw another tantrum. I just came here to
ask you a couple of questions."

The last few words had a definite ring of challenge.
She saw his face tighten up even further. *He knows,*
she thought with a pang of dread. *He's guessed that
Lenore has exposed him. He's trying to think of
some way to convince me she's lying.*

Firmly she brushed aside that damning explanation. Why was she always so ready to think the worst
of Neil? That wary look didn't have to mean he was
guilty. There was a likelier, more innocent explanation. Three hours before she'd been shouting at him
in anger. Now she was back, talking grimly about
asking questions. Surely that was enough to make
any man look defensive?

Remembering that earlier flare-up, she found herself wondering why she had been so furious. Lenore
was no friend of hers. Why should she mind Neil's

diatribe against her? Merely because she thought he was being unjust to a vulnerable woman? But how did she know he was being unjust? She'd brushed him off whenever he'd tried to tell his side of that story—that first night, here at his house, then over drinks at Que Sera, and once again this afternoon down at the house site.

Sudden panic seized her. Did she really want to hear that explanation? One of them had to be lying— Neil or Lenore. Suppose the story he told didn't convince her? Suppose she was forced to believe what Lenore had said—that she'd been tricked into loving a two-faced schemer?

The questions were there, clamoring for an answer. *Did you really make a deal with Olympia? Were you working for Southwestern Towers from the very beginning?* But she found herself backing away, making small talk, praising the carved wooden bench, a new acquisition, telling Neil he'd been really lucky, finding it down at that Chimayo auction.... And look at those morning glories, how nicely they were starting to climb up the wooden pillars.... And yes, it looked like rain over there in the mountains. But out in the west, look at that lovely sunset....

Neil dutifully offered her a glass of white wine. She accepted it gratefully, settling herself on the bench, sipping nervously from her glass as they both gazed out over the valley. Finally they seemed to run out of subjects. The silence thickened between them. The closeness of Neil's too-familiar body began to make Terry feel as though she were smothering. But she still couldn't move to the point of the crucial show-down.

It was Neil who finally broke the awkward stale-mate. "What about it, Terry? Don't you think it's time you started asking those questions?"

She could feel her heart beginning to pound er-ratically. "We'll get to them in a minute. Right now I'd just like to sit and watch that sunset. You have such a fantastic view here—on one side that explo-sion of purple and gold and scarlet; on the other that jet-black mass devouring the mountains. . . ."

"Absolutely terrific." He cast a quizzical glance in her direction. She knew he could tell she was stalling. "I've been thinking of glassing in this whole *portal*— something along the lines of that room you built onto Mrs. Romo's house. When you get the time, you might draw me up a few sketches."

A sliver of ice seemed to slip between Terry's ribs. Was this what she was to Neil now, merely a source of professional services? Three weeks before, she would have leaped at his suggestion. Now it seemed insulting. After all those golden moments she'd spent in his arms, she couldn't stand to be pushed back into a merely professional role.

She drew a deep breath, feeling that her whole future depended on the next few minutes. If Lenore's accusations were true, she would have to cut him out of her life forever. If Lenore had been lying, that still didn't make that night on the mesa any easier to understand. But at least it meant he might have been halfway sincere, that those intimate moments weren't part of a callous scheme to use her for his advantage.

"I didn't come here to talk about architecture." Despite her hammering heart, the words emerged without any telltale tremor. "I came to ask some questions about Lenore Hitchcock. She's just been telling me a fantastic story. She says you and Ward McKevitt have made a financial deal with Southwestern Towers."

"Lenore told you that?" He looked genuinely astonished. "Good Lord, what a really tremendous imagination." A wry smile twisted his lips. "Now why would I do a thing like that? Surely she didn't suggest I needed the money?"

"She said you wanted power—that you thought you could get it through Stanton Odessa—that you'd dropped the Olympia suit because they offered you a tempting stock deal."

Neil let out a whoop of incredulous laughter. "Fantastic! Simply fantastic!" Then his face hardened. His steely eyes drilled relentlessly into Terry's. "You're not going to tell me you really believe that, are you?"

"I don't know what to believe." Terry kept her eyes on his, her gaze unflinching. "I can't make up my mind till I hear your side of the story."

Neil winced as though she'd slapped him. "Well, thanks a lot, Terry. You really have a lot of faith in me, don't you."

The pain was like a knife twisting inside her. "Please don't be angry, Neil. I'm only trying to get at the truth." She hated the pleading note that had crept into her voice. Was she looking as crushed and miserable as she was feeling? She hoped not. He'd think she'd come begging to him, the way Lenore had.

"You want the truth, do you?" A new note rang out in his voice, a note of grim decision. "All right, Terry, here goes. Has Lenore ever told you how we happened to meet? She came to work as a volunteer in my office. I was just beginning the fight against Olympia. We were still in the research stage, collecting complaints, lining up the experts, probing for information within the company. Lenore was a tireless worker. She kept everyone else ablaze with enthusiasm. So I offered her a job as my assistant. We wound up spending most of our time together— working all day, relaxing and talking at night. I thought I had never met such a wonderful woman— so warm, so sympathetic, someone who shared all my dreams and ambitions."

His mouth quirked up a bitter grimace. "Naturally, I fell in love with her. I suppose that was what she intended." His eyes clouded over. He paused for a moment, intent on some inner vision. Then his voice turned crisp and matter-of-fact.

"We had a lot of good luck in building our case against Olympia. We found some reliable sources within the company. They provided us with all sorts of evidence—interoffice memos, test results, reports of special consultants. They made a damning indictment against Olympia, showed the company knew all the time their tires were faulty. One look at that stuff, and any judge would have to rule against the corporation."

The wry mirthless smile was back on his lips. He

stared out across the valley, his eyes fixed on the bright orange half circle precariously poised above the deep purple horizon. Terry could feel all his muscles tensing, as though to ward off some approaching danger. "Then a funny thing happened. I usually kept all that evidence in the safe in the office. But the night before the first hearing, Lenore volunteered to keep it in her apartment. That way she wouldn't have to stop off on her way to the courtroom next morning, she said."

He turned to her, his eyes somber and brooding. "Unfortunately, someone broke into her apartment while she was asleep. When the alarm clock woke her up the next morning, she found someone had stolen all our documentation."

"What terrible luck," Terry groaned. "Lenore didn't mention that part of the story."

"I'm not surprised. It turned out that the so-called break-in never happened. Lenore staged the whole thing herself, even jimmied the lock to her own apartment."

"Wait just a minute, Neil." Terry's mind was reeling. "Are you trying to say Lenore sabotaged your whole case? That was the reason you had to drop it?"

"That shocks you, does it? Then you can imagine how I felt when the truth finally hit me. I wouldn't believe it at first. I kept thinking Olympia must have hired someone to do the break-in. I spent a lot of money on private detectives, hoping to prove that. They did a good job, those men. They brought me back copies of two canceled checks from Olympia's personnel department. Each of them was for ten thousand dollars. Both of them were made out to Lenore Hitchcock.''

Terry tried desperately to weigh the two wildly contrasting stories. On the one hand, Lenore claimed Neil was a double agent, pretending to fight the forces he was secretly backing. On the other, Neil claimed Lenore was the traitor.

She looked at the man beside her, trying to see him as part of Lenore's scenario. A hundred moments flashed through her mind, forming a kaleidoscopic image. Neil at El Patio: ''Out here I hoped to find something truer, more honest;'' Neil accepting the campaign challenge: ''I'm in this all the way;'' Neil's grim face denouncing Olympia: ''I've got some personal scores I want to settle.'' Could that really have been all playacting? Had the trip to Dallas been part of an elaborate cover-up, the money and time he'd poured into the campaign merely a lure to earn him a leadership niche in the protest movement and put him in a good position to sabotage it?

She backed away from that question and considered Lenore in the light of Neil's revelations. From the very first, there had been something phony about her—that too-bright smile, that gushing enthusiasm. Now *there* was a cover-up for you. It was easy to picture her as a two-faced schemer, with that glossy facade hiding her real intentions.

Terry felt excitement building inside her. She remembered the way Lenore had brushed off any questions about her background, had tried to play down her relationship with Neil. And with all her enthusiasm, what had she really done to help the campaign? They'd started out as a unified popular movement, their careful planning geared to the special conditions of Taos. Now they were fighting each other, rushing toward a premature confrontation. And Lenore stood right at the center of all that trouble.

A tremendous wave of relief swept over Terry. Neil was telling the truth! She should never have doubted him for even a minute. She should have trusted her basic intuition. Arrogant he might be, relying too much on the power of his money. But the side of him that had first drawn her to him—the man searching for a cause that he could believe in—that side was real. That side of Neil Brewster a woman could really depend on....

She caught herself up with a start. *Terry, you fool! You're going too fast again. This puzzle still has a lot of missing pieces.*

"Do you mean what I think you mean, Neil—that Lenore is still being paid by Olympia Tires?"

"Olympia, Southwestern Towers—they're both owned by Stanton Odessa. Of course she's still working for them. Why else do you think she came here to Taos?"

"I always assumed she followed you here. It was obvious there had been something between you."

Neil smiled bitterly. "Now you understand what that something was—treachery, lies and deception. No, Lenore didn't follow me here. When I left the city behind me, I went to a lot of trouble to keep my whereabouts hidden. Looking back now, I can see that Lenore's betrayal had sent me into a deep depression. My whole life seemed useless to me. My old crusader role seemed empty and stupid. The simplest everyday actions—getting out of bed in the morning, shaving, brushing my teeth—all seemed to require an enormous amount of effort. I knew I should use my evidence to see Lenore brought to justice, but the mere thought of setting foot into a courtroom made me feel nauseous.''

He smiled wryly at Terry. ''Now you understand why I behaved like a hermit those first few months in Taos. Then, just as I started emerging from hibernation, I ran into Lenore one day in the Taos plaza. I'm sure she was as startled as I was. The last person on earth she wanted to see was someone who knew about her job with Olympia.''

''You guessed, then, that she was working for Southwestern Towers?''

''Knowing Lenore, I thought she was up to something. But I had no idea at that time of the tie-up with Stanton Odessa. We did a little reprise of the scene we'd played in New York after I found the checks she'd received from Olympia. I told her to get out of town or I'd have her hauled back to the city to face legal charges. I thought I'd convinced her. She looked pretty shaken the day I saw her drive off to Albuquerque. I'm still not sure why she came back. My guess is that her corporate bosses upped the ante, and she thought she could bluff her way through the whole situation.''

''When did you realize what she was really up to?''

''After that trip to Dallas, everything came into

focus—especially when I got back and found she'd become the campaign secretary.''

"Why didn't you speak out then—warn us all she was working for Southwestern?"

"That's what I should have done. But I somehow convinced myself it was better to wait till she actually pulled some dirty tricks before I went as far as blowing her cover. My stupid pride must have warped my judgment. To expose Lenore, I'd have had to expose myself, let the whole world know what a fool I'd been.''

"But that wasn't your fault! You couldn't have known Olympia would try to bribe her."

Neil shook his head in exasperation. "Don't you understand yet? She was working for them even before I met her. That's why she wormed her way into my office, and into my life. That's the part I can't stand anyone knowing—that I let her twist me around her little finger, fell in love with her right on schedule, still loved her for a time even after I knew she'd betrayed me."

He turned away and stood up, staring gloomily out over the valley. The bright orange disk had dropped below the horizon. Shifting layers of rose and cobalt were mimicking the shapes of a distant fairy-tale city. Terry saw the lines of suffering etched in Neil's rugged face and understood what he'd meant by all those warnings about how Southwestern might hurt them. She'd been thinking in terms of material harm—loss of customers, legal harassment, the sort of tricks Ward McKevitt was playing. But Neil had been hurt at a much more basic level. He'd cast

Lenore in a loved and cherished image—and that image had been shattered. She knew all too well how devastating the blow must have been. She'd got a taste of it when Lenore had tried to make her see Neil as a double-crossing schemer.

Love and compassion swelled within her, and those feelings were almost ready to burst out. She wanted to reach out and touch him, smooth away those troubled lines from his forehead. But she knew she mustn't do that until he answered the question that had been nagging at her from the moment he'd started talking.

"That night she came and found us here in the moonlight, I heard a lot of what she was saying to you. She sounded then as though she really loved you."

He swung around to face her, his eyes blazing with anger. "That damned melodramatic scene! That's what Lenore intended. Those theatrical shrieks and groans must have been pretty impressive. You couldn't see what I saw, the mocking smile that went with those pleas of devotion. I was half-mad with anger already; that smile pushed me over the brink. I'd never hit her before, much as I'd longed to. But that night she kept goading me on till I lost all control." His eyes turned cloudy with bitter reflection. "I suppose she intended that, too. It was all part of her plan to turn you against me."

"But she must be in love with you, Neil. Why else would she go to such lengths to split us apart?"

Neil stared at her incredulously. "You think she did all that because she was jealous? Absolutely not,

Terry. That woman, believe me, is as cold as ice. Her only goal is to wreck the protest campaign. She wanted to drive a wedge between us—the way she did between Paco and Skeeter. It worked pretty well, didn't it? She made you furious with me. Wasn't that the real reason you voted with her Thursday night?''

Incredible, the way Neil could sense all her thoughts and feelings. "I've been such a fool," she murmured. "I let myself turn against you without even giving you the chance to explain. If you'd told me all this that night, everyone could have pitched in and stopped her before she drove the campaign to the edge of disaster."

Neil became alert then. "But I thought we had stopped her, Terry. That vote Thursday night—"

"What does she care about votes? She knew that Paco was right. The worst tactic we could use is open confrontation. So she egged Skeeter on to do just that. Now the council has moved up its meeting to this Thursday night. That doesn't give us much time to get ready."

Neil gave a long low whistle. "Things do sound pretty bad. But now that we know what Lenore is up to, we still have time to organize our forces and get the campaign going our way again."

"That may not be too easy. With Ward McKevitt pulling his dirty tricks, we may find a lot of our people don't dare to support us."

"What's all this about Ward McKevitt? He really does have a deal with Southwestern Towers? That wasn't just part of Lenore's fancy embroidery?"

"He's in with them up to the hilt. He's threatened

to cancel my loan extension and has started foreclosure proceedings against the Quayles—which means a lot of our other supporters may have been getting similar warnings.''

Neil's jaw tensed in defiance. ''So they're starting to use their usual tactics, are they? That must mean we've got them worried. But we'll show them that they can't scare us. This is one time I'm glad to have all that money. We'll have to fight fire with fire. Tell all the people they've threatened that I'll make good their losses if they'll stand firm—''

He broke off abruptly as a new thought struck him. The look he turned on Terry was a complex mixture of hurt and disbelief. ''Lenore made you think I was in on a deal with McKevitt. That meant I must have suggested that threat against you. Did you really believe that, Terry—that I could do something like that to the Quayles and you?''

Terry nodded, feeling guilty and miserable. Now that she was here with Neil, that lapse in trust seemed like criminal folly. ''She sounded so convincing. I guess I did believe her, there, for a while.''

He shook his head bewilderedly. ''But you hardly knew Lenore. And yet you trusted her instead of me. How could you do that, Terry? Do I really seem like that kind of callous bastard?''

Terry felt the sting of tears beneath her eyelids. ''Oh, no, Neil, no! No matter what other faults I thought you had, I always believed that you were completely honest.''

''And yet when Lenore said I wasn't—''

"Oh, damn it, Neil, don't you understand? It was all because of that scene out here that night. When I heard her pleading and begging for you to love her, it reminded me of how I did that with Paul. I identified with Lenore. I felt as though I was suffering along with her."

The hurt angry look faded out of Neil's eyes, leaving them warm and thoughtful. "The woman scorned—is that how you saw yourself?"

Terry nodded mutely, still reproaching herself. "It's the way I've been seeing myself for the past five years."

"But that's all over, darling." Suddenly his arms were around her. He pulled her gently to her feet, his tender gaze probing her face. "Damn it, Terry, how many times do I have to say it? I love you, I want you, I need you. I want you to live with me for the rest of my life."

Deliriously happy, she turned her lips up to his in a hungry gesture, and he drew her close for a long, long kiss. It seemed to bring with it a tremendous sense of comfort, dissolving all the pain and hurt she'd been carrying inside her.

Finally he released her, looking down at her with a quizzical smile. "You do love me, Terry. I can feel it. Your head may be full of a lot of crazy ideas, but your body isn't fooled by all that nonsense. Why don't you just trust me, darling? These emotional flip-flops get pretty confusing."

Terry pressed herself close against him, rejoicing in the healing warmth of his body. "Oh, Neil, I've been such a fool. I've wasted so much time learning to trust you. But I really do trust you now. I promise you I'll never doubt you again.''

He was kissing her neck, the hollow of her throat, nuzzling his face into her hair. ''You're letting me off too easy.'' His whispered words were soft in her ear. ''I did a few flip-flops, too. Do you understand now what happened up there at Midnight?''

She raised her hand to dreamily trace the line of his cheekbone. ''Of course I do. You got me confused with Lenore, just as I keep getting you mixed up with Paul.'' She pulled away a little, gazing solemnly up into his hazel eyes. ''This afternoon—down at the house site—you said we ought to put all that pain behind us.''

''You wouldn't listen to me.'' He reached out and pulled her into his lap as he sat back down on the bench, settling her head against his shoulder, his hands moving softly over her back and hips. ''Are you ready to listen now? Are you, Terry?''

''I'm listening,'' Terry murmured, nestling against his chest. She could hear his heart thudding against her ear. The pulsing sound seemed to invade her bloodstream, making her body throb to the same pounding rhythm. She took his hand and held it to her breast, willing him to feel how finely in tune their bodies were, then opened the top button of her shirt and slipped his hand inside it.

He groaned softly, his arms closing around her so tightly she gasped for breath. Then his hand left her breast and slipped under her legs. A second later, she found herself airborne as he swung her up from the bench and carried her along the *portal*.

Kicking the front door open, he strode along the hallway into the low-ceilinged *sala*. She felt dizzy, disoriented, but at the same time, full of tremendous joy. The moment of sudden panic when the solid earth dropped from beneath her gave way to a sense of soaring confidence. How marvelous to feel the strength in those cradling arms, to feel his love for her.

He carried her through another doorway, stooping a little under the low-placed lintel. After the vast expanse of the *sala*, the bedroom seemed tiny. She caught a glimpse of the carved and gilded headboard, and then she was sinking into the mattress's softness, reaching out to draw him down to her hungering body.

They lay there entwined for a moment, delighting in the closeness of their embrace. Then with one lithe movement, Neil flung himself off the bed and across the room. She heard the sound of a key being turned in the lock. A moment later, he was back beside her, pulling her close, running his hands down her back and sides. "Just making sure," he whispered. "This time you're not going to leave me. You'll never leave me again. I'm not going to let you."

She was finally at peace. The treacherous world outside faded away. All that was left were the four thick walls of the shadowy bedroom, dimly lighted by one small square window, the sheltering thatch of the ceiling's *latillas* curving above them. She was safe here, protected and guarded, safe in the arms of the man she would love for the rest of her life.

A pervasive languour enveloped her body, and she

felt herself drifting.... Through a soft warm mist of pleasure, she was vibrantly aware of his hands moving gently around her shoulders, easing her shirt away from her tingling breasts. They began to undress each other slowly until they were both breathless with anticipation, until at last there were no more barriers between them and her eager skin could feel every inch of his taut body.

The certainty, the marvelous sureness that came with the joining of their bodies made her feel that she had reached a long-lost home after years of a bleak exhausting journey. This was what she had sought all those long lonely years. This was what she'd come seeking in Taos. And Neil had come seeking, too, escaping a world where love crumbled to ashes, searching as she had been searching for this same certainty, this same sureness.

Neil's tender words reflected her thoughts. His cheek pressing against hers, his warm breath soft on her listening ear, he murmured, "Oh, Terry, my darling, why did it take us so long to find each other?"

She struggled for words to express her newfound sense of trust, her belief in the glowing future that seemed to be opening before them. But all that came out was a whispered, "I love you, darling."

For Neil, that was more than enough. She could feel the rising passion inflaming his body. Joyously she opened herself to him, drew him into her urgent center. Nothing existed for her except Neil's hard body. They had once been strangers. Now they shared one skin, one bloodstream, one heartbeat....

The ringing of the phone dissolved the rosy haze of

pleasure, bringing her harshly back to earth. "Ignore it," Neil growled in her ear. But she couldn't ignore it. The insistent ringing kept nagging at her, warning her that they couldn't escape intruders. That feeling of safe homecoming had been an illusion. The world of conflict and pain was still waiting out there.

"Answer it, Neil," she whispered. "It must be something serious. Otherwise they wouldn't keep ringing this long."

He muttered an oath, then rolled away from her and reached out a groping hand for the receiver. She saw his unfocused eyes turn sharply alert, his forehead crease in a puzzled frown. "Yes, she's here," he said curtly. He held the receiver toward Terry. "Leo Martinez. He says it's very important."

Terry suddenly felt absurdly self-conscious. As she reached up to take the phone, she grabbed awkwardly for the bedspread and pulled it over her naked body. "Yes, Leo?" she said in a breathless voice.

"I hate to disturb you, Terry, but something strange has just come up. Uncle Ben is very upset, keeps muttering about 'those treacherous Anglos.' He insists he's going to make a public statement, but I've persuaded him to wait till he hears your explanation."

"*My* explanation? My explanation of what?"

"We can't discuss it over the phone." Leo's voice sounded stiff, almost hostile. "You've got to come to his house right now and see him in person. It's easy to find—just past the church in Ranchos." Brusquely he rapped out the directions, then clicked down the phone without waiting for Terry's answer.

She turned and looked blankly at Neil. "I've got to go talk to Ben Montoya. Leo wouldn't say what it's about, but it must be something about the Southwestern proposal."

Neil lay back on the bed, one arm flung despondently over his face. "One more black mark against Stanton Odessa. Can't they leave us in peace for even one night?"

"Oh, darling, you know how I hate to leave you. But Leo sounded so strange. I'm afraid something terrible's happening."

Neil looked up at her, suddenly concerned, then rolled to the side of the bed and started reaching for his abandoned clothing. "Of course you have to go, Terry. But you're not going to leave me. I'm going with you."

Terry was comforted by his gesture. How good it felt not to be alone anymore, to have someone who wanted to help her fight her battles. Then she remembered Leo's mysterious words about "treacherous Anglos." "That might not be such a good idea," she said reluctantly. "Leo knows the old man better than we do. He asked specifically for *my* explanation. If he'd wanted you there, too, surely he would have said so."

Neil was just in the process of buckling his belt. He looked up at her in hurt surprise before his face slowly relaxed in a grin. "Isn't that just my luck? Falling in love with an independent woman. Okay, Terry, you're on your own. But I'll keep you company as far as Ranchos. Then I'll drive on into town. I've got a few of my own little problems I ought to attend to."

Terry gave him an answering grin. They finished getting dressed in companionable silence. A few minutes later they walked out to Terry's pickup, their arms around each other.

"*Hasta la vista*, Terry." Neil pulled her close to give her a warm drugging kiss. "I should be back here in an hour. Finish your talk with Ben, and come back here quickly. We've got some unfinished business to attend to."

She laughed softly in agreement and moved out of his arms into the chilly truck cab. The last sight she had were the lights of Neil's Blazer, following her along the dirt road to the highway.

CHAPTER SEVENTEEN

TERRY PASSED THE GARISH NEON LIGHTS of the road-side bar, turned right after the massive eighteenth-century church of San Francisco d'Assisi and continued along the narrow tree-shaded lane, trying to remember Leo's instructions. Then she saw the ten-foot wall loom up to her left, the colorful Mexican tiles embedded in the adobe gateposts. Pulling the truck as far as she could onto the lane's sandy shoulder, she parked it.

She pushed the bell set into one of the gateposts. Here in the darkness, away from the lights of the highway, she felt as though she'd stepped back a few centuries into that valiant era when walls like the one surrounding Montoya's house had been built as a bulwark against marauding Indians.

The heavy gate creaked open. Leo's face looked grim and pale in the moonlight. "Hi, Leo," she said. "I'm here. Now what's this mysterious problem I'm supposed to explain to your uncle?"

"Come on in, Terry." He turned away abruptly and started to lead her in between the neatly trimmed shrubs that lined both sides of the flagstone path.

"Wait just a minute, Leo. You said your uncle is

very upset. I can't just go in there cold. I've got to
know what we're talking about.''

Ahead of her on the path, she could see the silhou-
ette of Leo's lean body, his shoulders squared in obvious tension. He peered away from her toward the
low adobe house, where light was streaming out of
the open doorway. ''Sorry, Terry—'' he flung the
words over his shoulder ''—Uncle Ben's orders. He
wants to show you this thing himself.''

Show me this thing? What thing? Terry's mind was
buzzing in circles, searching for a possible explanation. What could have happened to turn the old man
against them? Some kind of financial threat from
Ward McKevitt? No, Montoya was too powerful a
man for that kind of pressure. Skeeter's brash challenge to Reuben Abeyta? But he wouldn't call her to
answer for that; he'd call Skeeter. Whatever it was, it
must be really serious. It wasn't just Ben Montoya
who'd turned hostile. Leo obviously shared the old
man's anger.

She followed Leo into the house, down a long hallway and into a small square room. Its walls were
lined with bookshelves. In one corner stood an old-
fashioned rolltop desk. Ben Montoya was bending
over the desk; he was clad in a blue denim work shirt
with bright red suspenders. He swiveled around to
face her. She'd met him before and always found him
impressive, with that silvery shoulder-length hair falling away from a central bald spot, forming a leonine
mane around his craggy face. He stared at her for a
long silent moment as his dark eyes peered intently
back from under heavy jet eyebrows. She heard Leo

nervously clearing his throat behind her. "Uncle Ben, I think you've already met Miss Morrison."

The massive head inclined a bare half inch. "*Buenas noches*, Miss Morrison. *Bienvenida a mi casa.*"

"*Buenas noches, Señor Montoya.*" Terry sent a glance of anxious appeal toward Leo. Were they going to conduct this whole conversation in Spanish?

Ben Montoya intercepted her glance, his eyes lighting up with a gleam of sardonic amusement. "A pleasure to see you again." He held out one large hand in her direction. "Forgive me for not getting up. These old legs have served me so well that I try to keep them from bearing too much of a burden."

Terry grasped the proffered hand, feeling the wiry strength of the old man's muscles. "A pleasure for me too, sir. Leo said you wanted to show me something?"

"All in good time. All in good time." Montoya was not to be hurried. His calm appraising gaze made Terry feel even more nervous. He seemed to be sizing her up, measuring her against some inner vision. "I liked that house you built for Elvira Sanchez. Very nice, your treatment of that *portal*. You have a genuine feeling for our traditions."

"Thank you, Mr. Montoya. Coming from you, that's really a compliment."

"I wish I could say the same about all your other new houses. That one of Steve Galliard's, for instance—the one that looks like a launching pad for a missile. But at least you had the good sense to build it way out on the mesa." The deep-set eyes were glow-

ering at her now, filled with sudden inexplicable
anger.

Terry's brief moment of pleasure gave way to
another upsurge of apprehension. "That's the whole
point, Mr. Montoya. I always try to fit my design to
its setting. I'd never have built Steve's house in
downtown Taos."

She thought she saw his eyes soften a little and
plunged ahead, eager to seize the opening. "That's
why I'm fighting this Southwestern Towers proposal.
Surely you share my feelings, Mr. Montoya? A
modern apartment building, so completely out of
scale with the rest of Taos—don't you agree that
would be a total disaster?"

The dark eyes stared fixedly into hers as though he
were trying to read her mind. "Is that what you
think, Miss Morrison? So did I, when I first saw the
plans. Since then, however, I've had to revise my
opinion. Much as I'd hate to see them take over Kit
Carson Park, it might be the lesser evil."

"The lesser evil?" Terry was flabbergasted. "A
fifteen-story building right in the heart of Taos? For
heaven's sake, Mr. Montoya, I can't imagine anything worse than that."

"Can't you, Miss Morrison?" The words came out
as a growl of contempt. "Then let me show you
something." He swung around to his desk and pulled
a roll of paper out of one of the pigeonholes. He gestured to Leo, who took it and gave it to Terry. Turning back, Montoya stared accusingly at her, his head
drawn down into his shoulders like a bull preparing
to charge. "Perhaps you might like to have a look at

that? If I'm not mistaken, you'll find it quite familiar.''

Terry took the paper and slowly unrolled it. It turned out to be what she had expected, a print of an architect's drawing. But she hadn't expected this particular drawing.

She stared at it, openmouthed, as shock burst through her. Her apartment design, the one that had earned first place in that student contest! What was it doing here in Montoya's study? And what were these other buildings drawn in around it?

She assessed the drawing more closely, and suddenly recognized the encircling buildings. The nape of her neck began to prickle. La Fonda Hotel, La Cocina, the old county courthouse, the colonnaded *portal* arching over the sidewalk. A meticulously detailed sketch of all the buildings that ringed the Taos Plaza.

But where was the brick-cobbled expanse of the central plaza? Where were the giant cottonwoods and pin oaks? Where was the octagonal bandstand, where mariachi groups played during fiesta? Where was the flag that had flown day and night since that Civil War skirmish back in the 1840s? Where were the cast-iron benches where Taoseños and tourists alike sat in the shade of the trees to watch the life of the town unfolding around them?

Gone, all gone—their space usurped by the bulk of that monstrous building, its fourteen stories rearing up in sharp-angled contrast to the smooth flowing lines of the flat-roofed earth-hugging adobes.

Her fingers trembled uncontrollably. She lifted her

head and met the eyes of Ben Montoya. "But this...
this is crazy." Her mouth felt as dry as a desert
hiker's. "Someone must be playing a practical
joke—"

"Look down in the right-hand corner." Leo's
voice came to her as though from a very great
distance. Her eyes flicked down to the corner, knowing with nightmarish certainty what she would find
there. The damning signature swam before her eyes.

"But I tell you, I didn't draw this," she whispered
hoarsely. "Someone has obviously been forging my
name."

The old man's eyes were hard and unyielding.
"That center building isn't your design?"

The small square room seemed to close in around
her. Terry felt as though she were drowning, sub-
merged in a sea of misunderstanding. "I *did* design
that building," she admitted. "But that was years
ago, back in California. It had nothing to do with
Taos. Somebody else drew those plaza buildings
around it."

She stared earnestly into the old man's eyes, and
met a solid wall of disbelief. "Really, I didn't do
this." Her voice rose shrilly. She looked desperately
over at Leo. "You know that, Leo. You know it's all
some kind of grotesque joke."

The eyes that stared back at her were the eyes of a
stranger. "It's no use, Terry. You've just admitted
it's your design."

She swung her gaze back to the man in the swivel
chair. "But I didn't draw these plaza buildings
around it. Someone else must have drawn those and

superimposed my apartment design in the middle. It would have been easy to do. All you'd need is the right photographic equipment.''

Ben Montoya's only answer was a tiny quirk of one bushy black eyebrow. ''Look,'' she said, desperate to convince him, ''where did you get this drawing? It must have come from someone at Southwestern Towers.''

''That's a very good guess, Miss Morrison.'' The anger was gone from the deep-set eyes. The craggy old face looked drawn and tired. ''One of their emissaries came to see me this afternoon. He said he wanted to tell me something about the motives of their opponents. Then he showed me this drawing and told me you'd brought it to them several months ago, suggesting that they adopt it as one of their projects. The company, he told me, wouldn't dream of invading such a hallowed historical site. It was shortly after they rejected your plan that you started campaigning against the Kit Carson proposal, which I assume they consider not nearly as sacrosanct.''

''Don't tell me you believed him! Can't you see he had his own ax to grind?''

The old man shook his head scornfully. ''I learned long ago not to trust any Anglo. That's what disturbed me about this protest movement. Could so many Anglos really care about our old traditions? Or was there some hidden agenda, some other reason for them to be fighting Southwestern? This drawing shows I was right in my suspicions.''

Terry felt weak and dizzy. ''But this is completely fantastic. I could never dream of committing a crime like this.''

"Oh, come off it, Terry." Leo's voice was cold and hostile. "It's your design, after all. You must have submitted it to them. How else would they have got their hands on that drawing?"

A ribbon of memories unreeled in Terry's mind. That night in the candle-lighted study.... Neil's hand lifting the rolled-up sketch from the nail keg.... The excitement in his eyes as he looked at the drawing.... And that earlier moment, back in the greenhouse, when she'd told him she never bothered to lock her doors....

"Someone must have stolen it out of my study." Could she have spoken those words? They sounded so faint and breathless, as if they'd been shouted across an enormous distance.

"Any particular someone?" the old man snapped. "Maybe you can suggest a convenient suspect— someone who'd seen your drawing? Someone who knew where you kept it in your study?"

The answer was etched on her brain in burning letters. There was only one person in Taos who fitted Ben Montoya's description. *Oh, no, Neil, not you! I can't stand it. I won't believe it—I won't. Just when I got through saying I'd never doubt you....*

A sudden thought pierced through her anguish. Lenore! This must be her doing! But how had she known about that contest design? No matter—she'd found out somehow. She'd already proved she would stop at nothing. Stealing the sketch from her study would have been child's play. Lenore... yes, that was the answer. It must be. It must.

Terry drew a deep breath, trying to pull herself together. Then she looked directly at Montoya, forc-

ing herself not to flinch under his challenging gaze.
"I think I know who did this. It's someone who's
played a big part in our campaign. Southwestern
Towers has paid that person to sabotage it."

"There, Uncle Ben. I told you she'd have an answer." Leo's voice was jubilant with relief, and Terry
realized how much her apparent guilt must have dismayed him.

"You call that an answer? I don't." The old man
glowered fiercely at his nephew. "I need some solid
proof of that accusation. What's his name, this so-
called saboteur?"

"I can't tell you that right now. I've got to be really sure that's the person who did this. As for solid
proof, that's going to be difficult. But I'll find some
way to get a confession."

The shrewd old eyes scanned her face for a long
silent moment, assessing the truth of what she was
saying. Then the leonine head slowly nodded. "I'll
give you till ten o'clock tomorrow morning. After
that, if I'm not convinced, I'm going to announce my
support of Southwestern's proposal."

"Oh, no, you can't do that! Just because you distrust my motives, that doesn't mean you should back
Southwestern."

Sadness clouded Montoya's eyes. "I'm an old
man, Miss Morrison. I've seen many changes in
Taos. Most of them have not been for the better. The
way of life I grew up with is gone forever. I've seen
the town I love invaded by strangers—restless
pushing strangers who despise all the values my
ancestors cherished. I've fought these changes as

much as I could, but I've learned that I can't really
stop what you outsiders call 'progress.' The best I
can do is keep it within certain limits. You people will
build your condominium somewhere. I'd rather give
Southwestern Kit Carson Park than have you or anyone else come back next year and destroy our plaza.''

Terry felt an icy chill ripple through her. She felt
forlorn and abandoned, as though the door of a
brightly lighted house had been slammed against her,
leaving her alone outside in the darkness. She wanted
to cry out in protest, tell the old man she wasn't really a stranger, that she did belong here in Taos. But
she knew suspicion had closed his ears against her.
Her only chance of getting behind that slammed door
was to prove she hadn't conceived that abominable
drawing.

''I think you're wrong, Mr. Montoya. But right
now, I'm in no position to argue. I'll get back to you
as soon as I can—and bring you proof that Southwestern is trying to frame me.''

The old man waved his hand in dismissal. Leo
opened the door to the hallway and walked silently
by her side until they came to the big front door.
''It's up to you now, Terry. I sure hope you can
prove what you said in there.''

''I can prove it. I know I can prove it.'' She looked
anxiously up at Leo. He still looked withdrawn and
wary, but she sensed he really wanted to believe her.
He shrugged slightly and pushed the door open. The
cool night air rushed in and surrounded them. Then
Terry was standing alone on the *portal* and Leo was
back inside, safe within his ancestral shelter.

Terry paused for a moment, looking up at the stars, a handful of silver confetti flung against the charcoal sky. Beneath its vastness, she felt like a tiny insignificant creature. "I can prove it. I know I can prove it." The brave words she'd flung at Leo returned to taunt her. Exactly how was she going to prove it? She'd have to force Lenore into confessing. And how was she going to accomplish that? Merely accusing her wasn't the answer. She'd have to apply some kind of enormous pressure. But what kind of pressure could crack that glossy facade and expose the duplicitous schemer behind it?

It came in a sudden flash: those checks from Olympia. Neil had implied that they'd provide enough basis for legal action. Given a choice between the courts and Ben Montoya, Lenore would surely reveal her part in faking that drawing.

Quickly Terry made her plans. She'd go back to the house on the mesa and wait for Neil. Then the two of them would confront Lenore together. The thought of his warm vibrant presence brought sudden strength to Terry's body. She wasn't really alone, a rejected stranger. Now that she had Neil, she would never again be alone.

She groped her way down the path to the gate in the outer wall. As she stepped out into the road she found herself caught in the glare of approaching headlights. She stayed close to the wall, expecting the car to drive on past her. Instead it swung over and stopped just behind her pickup. Then she saw its boxy shape, and knew who the driver was.

"Skeeter!" She went back to the van and peered

into the driver's window. "What on earth are you doing here?"

"Leo phoned Lenore's house when he was trying to find you." Skeeter's mustached face in the shadowy moonlight reminded her, once again, of a frontier desperado. "He sounded pretty shook up, so I thought I'd come over and find out what was happening. You just saw old man Montoya? What's bugging him, Terry? Anything serious?"

"Worse than serious, Skeeter. It could be disastrous." Quickly she sketched in the high points of her confrontation with Ben Montoya—the phony drawing, Montoya's suspicions, his threat to announce his support for Southwestern's project.

Skeeter listened in growing consternation. "This is really the pits," he burst out as she paused for breath. "What can we do to convince him you're on the level?"

"We've got to confront Lenore, get her to make some kind of confession."

"What do you mean, some kind of confession? What's Lenore got to do with this mess?"

"Lenore is a phony, Skeeter. She's working against us. She's getting paid by Southwestern Towers."

"The hell she is! Are you going crazy?" Skeeter's face was contorted with anger. "Lenore is the driving force behind this campaign. If it weren't for her, we'd be getting no place."

Terry's shoulders sagged with sudden fatigue. Did she have to waste time explaining it all to Skeeter? She should be with Neil, making plans about how to force Lenore into confessing.

"Look, Skeeter, I know this is hard to believe. But Neil has proof that Lenore is working against us. She was helping him on the case against Olympia. Just at the crucial moment, she did away with the evidence they needed. Through a couple of private detectives, he got positive proof that Olympia had paid her for it. You know about Stanton Odessa—it owns both Olympia Tires and Southwestern Towers. Isn't it obvious she's still on its payroll?"

Skeeter's expression had been growing more and more sullen. "You're softheaded!" he finally exploded. "Don't tell me you really swallowed all that garbage. You heard what Lenore said about Neil. *He's* the one who's tied up with Stanton Odessa. When you split from Lenore's place, you were all fired up to confront him. Now all of a sudden, Lenore's turned into the bad guy and your rich playboy friend is the knight in shining armor."

Terry heaved a sigh of exasperation. "This is no time to stand here and argue. I know Lenore is lying. She's working for Southwestern Towers. She must have had something to do with faking that drawing. What we've got to do now is find some way to prove that. I'm going to pick up Neil, get him to tell her he'll take her to court—"

"Wait just a minute, Terry. Aren't you jumping the gun? Shouldn't you hear Lenore's side of the story? She may have a perfectly innocent explanation."

"Innocent? For stealing my design? For making it look like I planned it for the plaza?"

"When did she steal your drawing? She's never

been out to your house. I doubt if she even knows how to find it. And high-rise buildings aren't really your style. How could she know you'd ever designed one?"

Terry's mouth was set in a stubborn line. "Oh, shut up, Skeeter. I know I can't answer those questions. But I feel in my heart that Lenore comes into this somewhere."

"You feel in your heart," Skeeter mimicked her words in a mocking falsetto. "You mean you're so hot for Neil Brewster that you'll instantly swallow any old lie he tells you."

"He's not lying, Skeeter. He's heart and soul behind the campaign."

Skeeter smiled at her in condescending pity. "You poor sweet gullible fool. Then how come I just saw your hero's car parked in front of Ward McKevitt's house out near the Dram Shop?"

The unexpected question threw Terry off balance. "Ward McKevitt's house? He didn't say he was going there—"

"You bet your life he didn't. If he'd told you he was rushing off to see his good buddy, you might have suspected Lenore was telling the truth."

Encouraged by Terry's shocked silence, Skeeter plunged ahead with his accusation. "I thought that would shake you. Maybe he's not such a hero after all?" His eyes lighted up as a new idea struck him. "And how about that mysterious drawing? Lenore's never been to your house. But I bet Neil's been there, hasn't he?

"Yes, I thought so," he said smugly when it was

obvious that Terry couldn't answer. "And while he
was there, I bet you showed him that drawing?"

Terry tried to free her face of all expression, but
the very effort gave her away. "There, you see!" he
crowed triumphantly. "You've got no evidence
against Lenore—but plenty against Neil Brewster.
Don't you think, before you fall back under his spell,
that you should hear what Lenore has to say about
this?"

All the doubts she'd brushed aside in Montoya's
study came flooding back to mock her. Had her first
instinctive guess actually been the right one? Was she
clutching at straws in trying to blame Lenore?

No, she couldn't believe that. Neil couldn't be that
dishonest. The love she'd felt when he'd held her in
his arms—that had to be real. There was no way on
earth he could have been faking.

Renewed confidence welled up from deep inside
her. Lenore *must* be lying. She didn't need Neil to
confront her. She'd go face her now, fling out her accusation, read the inescapable truth in those luminous eyes.

She turned away from the van, afire with sudden
impatience. "Come on, Skeeter," she shouted over
her shoulder. "Follow me to Lenore's house. I want
you to watch her face when I ask her how she faked
that drawing."

TERRY SLOWED HER TRUCK as she turned off the
highway onto the private road. She peered ahead into
the darkness, trying to see if there were lights in
Lenore's windows. When she first caught sight of

Neil's Blazer standing in front of the little house, relief flooded through her. With Neil beside her, ready to back her up with his evidence, she could surely make Lenore confess.

Parking the truck, she hurried toward the little porch of Lenore's adobe. To her surprise, she found the door standing open. She heard the low murmur of voices, from somewhere inside the house.

Drawing a deep breath, she started up the steps. How good it would be to finally get this whole affair settled, force Lenore out into the open, stop her insidious sabotage of the campaign.

Peering in through the doorway, she caught a glimpse of Neil. He was standing with his back to the door, talking to Lenore in a hushed confidential tone. Something about the scene alarmed Terry inexplicably. Lenore was listening to him so intently, almost as if she were mesmerized. What on earth could Neil be saying?

A few of his words drifted out to her straining ears. "Here's what you're going to do," she heard him say, and then, "the Thursday-night meeting," and then, raising his voice so that Terry heard him very clearly, "copies to all the council members."

Copies of what? The question flashed through her mind, followed almost at once by the stunning answer, as she caught a glimpse of the familiar roll of paper clutched in Neil's hand.

She felt the blood pounding in her ears as she stepped through the doorway. Lenore's eyes suddenly shifted, leaving Neil's face to focus on Terry. "Well, look who's here." Her voice held an edge of sarcastic amazement. "Come right in, Terry, darling. Neil and I were just talking about you."

"Terry!" Neil swung around to face her. "What are you doing here, darling? I didn't expect you—"

"No, I'm sure you didn't." Terry forced her voice to stay steady. How could he manage to look so innocent? "Would you give me my drawing, please? I gather you've already made sufficient copies."

A puzzled frown wrinkled Neil's forehead. "Terry, what's going on here? Where did Lenore get your drawing? What's she using it for?"

"Oh, Neil, there's no use pretending." Lenore's cool drawl cut through Neil's string of questions. "Terry's caught us red-handed. Luckily, there's no way on earth she can prove it."

Terry stood there dazed for a moment, dazed and enraged. *Oh, Terry, you fool, you fool! Now you know the answer to all your questions. Both of them are working for Southwestern. Both of them are two-faced liars!*

And that scene in the little bedroom, those kisses, those loving touches, that firm assertion that he'd never let her leave him—had that all been an act, too, a red herring to distract her from her suspicions?

"Terry, don't listen to her. She's lying." She saw Neil start to move toward her, the drawing still clutched in his hand. The sight of it rekindled her anger. It seemed like a part of her life he was holding, ready to use in his cynical manipulations.

She reached out and snatched it from him, then whirled and ran out the door, clutching the roll of paper close to her chest. As she came down the steps of the little porch, she collided with Skeeter.

"Terry! What happened? You're crying." His arms closed around her.

"Let me go!" she shouted, lashing out at him blindly with her fists, feeling the tears rolling down her cheeks, the intolerable pain exploding inside her. With a final tremendous effort, she twisted out of his grasp, jumped into her truck and gunned the engine.

"Terry, come back!" The shout followed her into the darkness. Was that Neil's voice or Skeeter's? She didn't know and she didn't care. All she wanted right now was to be alone in the darkness, alone with the grief and pain of finally learning the truth about Neil Brewster.

CHAPTER EIGHTEEN

IT WASN'T UNTIL SHE CAME down the hill into Questa that she realized where she was going. She'd driven around in a daze for almost an hour, trying to think of a place where she could be free of intruders. She longed to drive down to her house in Talpa, lock all the doors, dive under the bedclothes. But Skeeter was probably there already, waiting for her on her doorstep, a living reminder of how wrong she'd been about Neil.

Now she was heading north, the lights of Taos already far behind her—ahead of her the brooding lonely mountains. And up on one of those mountains, a ghostly circle of ruined cabins beckoned, drawing her inexorably toward them.

She slowed down the truck for a moment, trying to shake herself free of this strange compulsion. What on earth was she doing, speeding like this through the night on her way to Midnight? Wasn't the pain bad enough? Why rub more salt in her wounds by going back there?

But perhaps more pain was exactly what she needed. To feel her loss to the full—come face to face with it. That was the way to exorcise her demons. By reviving that ardent memory in all its power, she might finally break loose from its spell and put Neil Brewster out of her life forever.

She pressed her foot down on the pedal. The truck rushed past the scattered lights of the sleeping village. As she turned off onto the bumpy dirt road, the night closed in like a dark cocoon, shutting her off from all other living creatures. Feeling a sudden need for human contact, she reached for the radio knob and clicked it on. The lyrics stabbed into the darkness:

> The love that I've found,
> Ever since you've been around,
> Your love's put me at the top of the world....

Her mind came alive with incredulous protest. Oh, no, it couldn't be—not now, not here, not after what had just happened.... She reached out to switch off the radio, but some inner force seemed to stop her hand in midair. The Carpenters' voices rode on with her through the night:

> There is only one wish on my mind,
> When this day is through I hope that I will find,
> That tomorrow will be
> Just the same for you and me....

Terry gripped the wheel, gritting her teeth against the lancing pain. Tomorrow. For her and Neil there would be no tomorrow. Perhaps up there at the top of the world, she'd find the strength to face that lonely dawn.

TERRY WOKE UP cramped and shivering and blinked
blearily out at the cold gray morning. Hugging her
nylon Windbreaker more closely around her, she
turned on the pickup's heater and let the rising
warmth gradually thaw out her stiffness.

She realized she'd been sleeping for three or four
hours. That was surprising. She had been sure her
anguished thoughts would keep her awake all night.
She must have been really exhausted from all of
yesterday's catastrophes.

Gingerly slipping down out of the truck cab, she
stretched her limbs to relieve the cramping in her
muscles. She looked at the scene around her, bracing
herself against the memories. How different everything looked on this misty morning. She knew the
waves of blue mountains must still be out there,
stretching away to the southern horizon. But all she
could see was a vast expanse of billowy gray, blotting
out the world she'd left below her. The green knoll
she stood on seemed like a tiny island. She felt like a
shipwreck survivor, marooned in a silent ghostly sea.

Far off in the distance, she heard the soft rumble
of thunder, and a tremor of apprehension shot
through her. What was happening down there in the
hidden world below her under that lumpy layer of
gray cotton batting? Perhaps it was already raining,
the impetuous deluge streaming down the steep
wooded hillsides. The thought of the rutted dirt road
melting into slippery treacherous mud made her
shiver again.

Terry took a deep breath of the cold thin mountain
air, telling herself not to worry. The thunder was so

far away she could scarcely hear it. The storm wouldn't hit for another few hours. She still had time to finish the task that had brought her up here, perform the burial rites for that short-lived illusion that had sprung into hectic bloom in the midst of these ruined cabins.

She had parked her truck on the patch of hard level ground beside the skeleton of the old hotel. Now she started retracing the steps of that fateful encounter, picking her way through the naked floor joists till she reached the doorpost and leaned her cheek against its smooth weathered surface, now cold and clammy with condensation.

Once again, reliving that first tumultuous embrace, she felt the liquid fire spreading through her veins, the searching hands caressing her melting body, the compelling lips arousing that urgent hunger. This time she made no attempt to suppress the onslaught of sensual feeling. Deliberately she let it take over, let herself float away on a cloud of remembered sunlight igniting into a hot blinding feeling of oneness.

Oh, Neil.... An icy spurt of pain zigzagged through her heart, shocking her back to the dark chilly present. That kiss had seemed so spontaneous, as natural as an earthquake or a cloudburst. Now she understood that it must have been carefully planned, the first devious move in Neil's secret chess game. Once he'd felt her response—so pathetically eager—he'd gone on to the next move, that brutal rejection. It had all been part of the winning gambit, designed to leave her dissatisfied, wanting more, and therefore, under his control.

She pressed her forehead against the doorpost, racked by hopeless longing in spite of herself. Her arms went out to wrap around the unyielding wood as the hurt took over, releasing a flood of healing tears. She let them roll out unchecked, feeling them wash away the intolerable tension. And gradually Terry attained a strange sort of solace. Here on her lonely island, hidden from all human eyes, she could finally let herself admit her innermost feelings, swallow the bitter dregs of humiliation.

The sound of a motor shocked her into alertness. Her hands flew up to her face, scrubbing away at the telltale tear marks. She pressed close to the doorpost, trying to hide behind it, holding her breath for fear of betraying her presence. A minute more, and the car would be past her, would disappear on up the wild mountain road, and she'd be safe again on her little island.

Just as she thought it had passed her, the motor coughed for an instant and died away. She glanced out quickly from behind the sheltering doorpost. For a moment, her mind refused to believe what she saw. Had she reached the stage of hallucinations?

But no, the red Blazer was real. And so was the man who'd just jumped down from behind the wheel, now walking toward the ruined cabins. Her hiding place was no longer safe. He must have already seen her. She flushed with shame, realizing how easily he'd read her mind. Now he was probably relying on this spot's remembered enchantment to make her swallow more of his clever lies.

Releasing her grip on the doorpost, she started

picking her tortuous way back through the floor
joists, till she finally stepped over the old front-door
threshold and reached the grassy spot where Neil was
standing. "It's no use, Neil," she said coldly. "I've
had enough of your so-called explanations."

He stared back at her just as coldly. The hazel eyes
were hard and opaque. "You think I came up here to
defend myself? Forget it, Terry; I don't need to. This
time you're the one who's going to do the explaining."

"Me? Well, isn't that just like the high and mighty
Neil Brewster! You think you can get away with
anything, don't you? Just because you have all that
money, you think the whole world will come groveling at your feet."

A flash of pain flickered in his eyes. "The whole
world? I'm not that ambitious. All I'm interested
in is this one small corner, a corner that seems to be
doing a very good job of shutting me out completely."

"Don't pull that wistful act," Terry said bitterly.
"You've got this whole town in the palm of your
hand."

"You think so, do you? When all the people I
thought were my friends have turned against me?
Skeeter Phillips, David Quayle, Paco Reyes—not to
mention your own inimitable self—"

"What else do you expect? You were plotting
against us all the time!"

"You're so very sure of that, aren't you, Terry?
Yet just a few hours ago you were making a solemn
promise that you'd never doubt me."

Terry steeled herself against her own guilt feelings, remembering how sincerely she'd meant that promise, and how quickly her former distrust had taken over. Too quickly, perhaps? Maybe he really did have some explanation. There was a hollow feeling in the pit of her stomach. Could she possibly have misjudged him? Had all those loving words really been sincere?

Watch out, Terry. The Brewster charm is getting to you again. Doggedly she clutched at her fading anger, conjured up a scene guaranteed to revive it: Neil standing there at Lenore's, Terry's sketch in his hand, talking about the copies he'd make for the council. . . .

"Are you trying to say you didn't steal my drawing? You're the only person in Taos who knew it existed. And what about Ward McKevitt? Skeeter saw your car in front of his house."

Neil's face hardened into a stony mask. "I've already told you—I didn't come here to explain my actions. If you don't have faith in me, I don't give a damn what anyone else thinks."

Terry stared at him contemptuously. "You refuse to explain, yet you expect me to trust you? What do you think I am—one of those spineless women who thinks the sun rises and sets in her lord and master's eyes? 'My man, right or wrong'—is that what you want me to say? Forget it, Neil. That kind of thinking went out with hoopskirts."

A quizzical look softened the hazel eyes. Neil shifted his gaze from her face and let it roam over the circle of ruined cabins. "Remember the day we came up here?'' His voice held no anger now. It was soft and insinuating, pleading with her to retrieve that shared memory. "You talked about the women who lived in these cabins, how they left everything behind them to share a new life with their husbands. You said it must have taken tremendous courage. But it took something else as well—tremendous faith. Those women must have really believed in their men, to stick with them in the face of disaster.''

Terry couldn't deny the pain she felt at his words. How dare he do this, use her own words against her? He knew how she'd been feeling when she said them—still weak and shaken by that kiss's fierce enchantment. And now he was callously trying to conjure up that memory, use that weakness against her.

"All that impressed you, did it?" She was lashing back at him now, intending to hurt him. "I must have been reading you pretty well. That's the sort of woman a man like you would look for. Someone with no mind of her own. Someone who would bury her talents, throw away all her hard-earned skills, be content to spend all her time gazing adoringly at the great Neil Brewster.''

"There you go again. You're not talking to me; you're talking to your ex-husband—just as you've done since the day I met you.''

The words hit home with the sting of truth. Neil was right. It really was Paul those words had been aimed at, but her stubborn anger wouldn't let her admit it.

"If I get you confused with Paul, it's because

you're exactly alike—arrogant, selfish and domineering. I used to have a weakness for that sort of man. But now, thank God, I've finally learned my lesson.''

"You haven't learned anything, Terry," Neil stated harshly. "You keep clinging to that old marriage like some kind of security blanket. The moment anyone threatens to get too close, you shut them out by turning them into Paul."

"You're a fine one to talk," Terry shot back, goaded beyond endurance. "Remember that first afternoon you brought me up here? Who did the shutting out that day?"

"You won't let me forget that, will you? All right, I admit it; I let Lenore come between us. But only that one time. After that I got rid of my ghosts. You didn't get rid of yours, though. You kept on using Paul as a shield between us."

"Using Paul as a shield! What a crazy thing to say. When I think of how hard I've tried to forget that miserable marriage—"

"Have you, Terry? I don't really think so. Misery can represent a kind of safety. If you only expect the worst, you'll never have the chance to be disappointed." He stared intently at her, his eyes dark and brooding. "I guess that's where I made my mistake with you. I thought you were ready to risk being happy."

She looked up at him, stupefied. Could he really be this brazen—glossing over all his deceptions by pretending she was the one who had failed him?

He jerked his head away impatiently to gaze out over the mountains. "What the hell am I wasting my time for? I didn't come up here to talk about you and me. All I care about now is winning this blasted campaign.''

"You dare to say that? You?" Terry's eyes were blazing with indignation.

"Look, Terry—" he heaved a sigh of exasperation "—I'm just too tired to keep playing your games. I've spent half the night talking to people, trying to straighten this out—Skeeter, Paco, Leo, Ben Montoya. All of you seem to distrust me for different reasons. So just cut the dramatics, please, and give me a chance to ask *you* a few questions.''

She noticed then what she should have noticed before—how pale and drawn his face looked, his drooping posture. This tiredness of his was obviously no pretense. And talking to all those people—especially Ben Montoya. Why would he have approached the old man if he was really the one who had stolen the drawing? Surely he would have let matters ride, knowing that Ben was about to come out for Southwestern?

Staring up into his haggard face, Terry felt her anger dissolve into compassion. She reached out toward him in a vague gesture, then drew her hand back in confusion. That wistful charm! Was it getting to her again?

"Go ahead, Neil." She kept her voice cold and level. "Fire away with your questions. You know very well *I* have nothing to hide."

His weary eyes were devoid of anger now. "I don't know anything, Terry, unless you tell me. I was astonished tonight when I saw that drawing. Lenore didn't expect me, I guess. It was lying out on the table when I arrived there. She tried to say you'd given it to her. I couldn't figure out why you'd do that. Then you came in and flew into your tantrum, then rushed off into the night before I could stop you. Just after that, Skeeter burst in like a madman, demanding to know what I'd done to his darling Terry. I managed to calm him down till he told me about the business with Montoya. Then I knew this was just one more of Lenore's dirty tricks."

A tiny glow of hope was growing within her. Could it really be true? Could Neil really be blameless? He made it sound so very plausible.... Then the damning words came back to her: "copies to all the council...."

"But I heard you, Neil. You said you were going to send copies to all the council members."

"Copies?" A little frown furrowed his brow, then disappeared. "I was talking about the checks, the ones Lenore got from Olympia. I told her if she didn't leave town immediately, I'd expose her for what she is, a two-faced liar."

She stared at him doubtfully, clinging to her skepticism. Didn't that sound like much too pat an answer? Then she remembered the other crucial question. "Just a minute," she said. "How did Lenore even know that drawing existed? You're the only person who's ever seen it."

"The only person in Taos. But what about California? That drawing must have been seen by hundreds of people—your fellow students, your college instructors, the contest judges, the people who gave you a job with that fancy outfit.''

"Oh, yes, Neil, you're right! And the library, too—the college library. They keep copies on file of each year's winners!''

Neil's eyes lighted up with excitement. "We've got it, Terry. That's where she must have found it. Where is that copy now? You looked as if you were going to tear it to pieces.''

Terry was already racing toward her pickup. She snatched up the sketch and unrolled it. Neil followed closely behind her and stood peering over her shoulder. The closeness and warmth of his body seemed to envelop her. She shoved the sketch into his hands and took a few steps away, leaning against one of the weathered timbers, hoping he hadn't noticed how much his nearness disturbed her.

He was staring down at the sketch, oblivious to his surroundings. "What's this?'' he said sharply. "You see that number? Was that part of your original drawing?''

He held out the sketch so that Terry could see it, pointing to the string of black figures across the upper right-hand margin. "No, I didn't put that there,'' she murmured. "It looks like some kind of rubber stamp.''

"That's it!'' Neil snatched back the drawing, gazing at it triumphantly. "I bet that's the library's acquisition number.''

"Of course,'' Terry breathed. "That's how she must have done it. She got it out of the files and made her own copy.''

Neil looked doubtful. "Wait just a minute, now. You mean they'd let her take this out of the library? How could she manage that? She wasn't even a student."

Terry was suddenly euphoric, amazed at the simplicity of the solution. "She didn't have to take it out. They've got a huge copy machine up in the art department. For fifty cents she could make a perfect copy. Once she had that in her hands, she could easily find someone to draw in the plaza buildings around it."

"Okay, so we know how she did it. The question is, how do we prove it?" Neil's eyes narrowed in concentration. "You know how that library works. What's the procedure for getting things out of the files?"

Terry struggled to recall her student days, fighting an overwhelming surge of remorse. She was sure now that Neil wasn't guilty. How could she have been so quick to distrust him? "Oh, Neil," she burst out, "I'm so sorry. I should have known you couldn't have stolen that drawing. But you did seem the likeliest person. And then, when Skeeter mentioned your visit to Ward—"

"I'm not interested in your excuses." Neil's voice was sharp with distaste. "I just want to win this campaign and then pack my bags and get the hell out of Taos."

Terry stared at him blankly. "Get out of Taos? What on earth do you mean? You belong here now. You've put so much of yourself into saving this town."

Neil's face twisted into a wry grimace. "God knows, that's what I've been trying to do. I thought I had finally found a home here. But now I know this place will never accept me. You said it yourself, that first day. I'll never fit in here, not in a hundred years."

Terry winced with pain, remembering the outraged woman who'd flung that taunt at him. How long ago it seemed, that ecstatic encounter. Who could ever have dreamed that three short weeks later she'd be standing here, longing for him, knowing that this was the only man in the world she could ever love—and knowing, too, that if she lost him it would be because she deserved to lose him.

She stared at Neil, groping desperately for some way to keep him near her. "Give me a little more time," she wanted to say. "You don't have to love me—just don't go out of my life forever."

He had turned away and was gazing out over the mountains, now just emerging from under their blanket of fog. The dark clouds to the south seemed to be moving toward them. The sky was a darker gray; the air felt heavy with moisture.

"I don't like the looks of that storm," he said tersely. "Let's get out of here before it hits us." He reached out and grasped her wrist. "Don't just stand there, staring at me like some kind of idiot child. Get into the Blazer, quick. When that road starts turning to mud, the four-wheel drive will get us through it."

Terry closed her eyes for a moment, brought alive again by his touch. And now he was taking it from her, that powerful magic. She'd never feel it again, the waves of sensation, the rising sensual excitement.

All that was left to her now was the awkward silent ride down out of the mountains, sitting stiffly beside him, her body avoiding his as if his touch were poison.

Compressing her lips to hold in a scream of denial, Terry wrenched herself from his grasp and stumbled toward the door of her pickup. Ignoring his shout of protest, she gunned the truck into action, swinging it blindly down toward the rutted dirt road that led back to Taos.

CHAPTER NINETEEN

SHE HAD DRIVEN ONLY THREE MILES when she heard the first clap of thunder. Five minutes later the cloudburst hit, pelting down on the roof of the truck like machine-gun bullets, cutting the visibility down to almost zero. Terry knew what she ought to do—pull to the side of the road and wait for the rain to let up a little. But if she stopped to do that, Neil would surely insist that she switch to the Blazer.

She slowed the truck down to a bare ten miles an hour and crept slowly forward, peering out at the six feet of muddy road just in front of her windshield. Snatching a glimpse in the rearview mirror, she saw a pale blur far back in the distance, which she guessed must be the headlights of the Blazer. She rounded a curve, and the blur disappeared behind the side of the mountain. She carefully kept herself from glancing out her side window, knowing only too well what was out there, veiled by the gray wall of rain: a sheer drop down the rocky hillside to the bed of Cabresto Canyon, almost a thousand feet below her.

Feeling the wheels start to slither across the road, she fought the impulse to slam her foot down on the brakes. In this slick adobe mud, a sudden stop could send the truck into a skid. Struggling to keep the wheel steady, she geared the truck down into first and drove even more slowly.

She was startled by a sudden rushing sound in her ears, as if a huge gust of wind were sweeping through the pine forest. She saw, too late, that it hadn't been wind. Her shocked gaze encountered, two feet ahead of the truck's front wheels, a torrent of rushing water.

She slammed her foot down on the brakes, acting on ingrained reflex. The truck spun around like a lightweight toy, its nose pointing out toward empty space. Desperately she shifted into reverse, but the slippery mud gave the tires nothing to grip.

Horrified, she felt the truck begin to slide forward, the force of gravity pulling it downward. The front wheels bumped slowly across the rocks on the narrow shoulder; then suddenly there was no more ground beneath them.

Terry's paralyzed brain suddenly started to function. She grabbed the door handle beside her, jammed it down, felt the door give way, flung herself through it. The next thing she felt was the scrape of rocks and gravel against her stomach. She was splayed out against the scree-covered side of the mountain, grasping desperately at the treacherous gravel beneath her, feeling it shift and give way beneath the weight of her body. Her boots felt as though they were full of cement, dragging her down toward the void below her. Her hands closed around a protruding spur of what seemed like solid rock. She clung to it, oblivious to the pelting rain, ignoring the way the sharp edges of rock cut into her hands. But a creeping numbness finally loosened her grip, and she went tumbling helplessly down toward the bed of the canyon.

Her mind went blank with panic. She was falling rapidly now, rolling over and over, her speed increasing with every second. Then something came up and hit the left side of her body. The impact left her gasping for breath. When her mind cleared, she realized what had happened. She'd been caught by a rocky ledge jutting out of the side of the mountain.

Hearing a crashing noise far below her, Terry cautiously opened her eyes to peer down toward it. She shut them again, appalled by the sight of her battered pickup, tumbling over and over, hundreds of feet below her.

Then she looked up toward the road. All she could see was the gray expanse of treacherous scree. Her eyes closed again. She felt with her hands around the rocky ledge. It seemed to grow wider in front of her. Inch by inch, she pulled her body forward, expecting every second that the rock beneath her would crumble away and pitch her into the emptiness of the canyon.

"Terry! Don't move! Stay right where you are!" Neil's voice drifted down from someplace high above her. Just the sound alone was enough to blunt the edge of her panic. She raised her head and peered up toward the road, feeling the knife blades of rain slash down on her upturned face.

She saw him leaning over the side of the roadway, and her stomach tightened in horror. Too close! Too close! Any moment now, she'd see him hurtling down the mountainside toward her.

He disappeared for a moment, then reappeared almost immediately. Terry gazed up at him longingly. How could he be so agonizingly near and yet so far out of her reach? Then her attention veered to the brown snakelike object moving down the hillside directly below him. She followed its progress in fascination for what seemed like hours. Finally the big loop of heavy rope touched the ledge in front of her face and dropped flat.

"Terry, take hold of the loop! Try to get your arms through it." The sound of his voice quieted her racing heart, gave strength to her flaccid limbs. Obediently she reached out and clutched the scratchy rope just above the knot that formed a loop. Pulling the coil toward her, she started wriggling her upper body through it.

When she felt its roughness securely under her armpits, she raised her face again. The rain appeared to be slacking off a little. She could see him clearly now, the lean rugged face tense with concern. "Okay, I'm ready!" she shouted.

"Good girl!" she heard him shout back. "Hang on as tightly as you can. I'm going to start pulling." His head disappeared again. A moment later she felt the rope start to tighten under her armpits. She clasped both hands securely around its shaft, feeling the top of the knot press up below them.

Her body straightened into a vertical position as Neil began hauling her up. Despair gave way to elation, as inch by inch she moved up through the muddy gravel. Up, up, up. The rope was searing the flesh off the palms of her hands. She fought against a wave of nauseous blackness that threatened to overwhelm her.

"Hold on! For God's sake, hold on!" Neil's voice stabbed through the blackness, giving her renewed courage, until at long last the rough rope under her armpits gave way to strong hands that grasped her and pulled her upward. She dug her toes into the hillside and found a spot that gave her a little support. With a last burst of strength, she pushed herself over the edge of the roadbed and felt the blessed ground leveling out beneath her, felt Neil's arms pulling her close to his lean hard body.

"Oh, Terry... my darling Terry." His lips were crushing hers, his arms taut and demanding. They clung to each other, gasping, oblivious to the thick clay mud that sucked at their outstretched bodies. Terry drifted mindlessly, knowing only that she was back in the place where she needed to be, luxuriating in the comforting warmth of Neil's embrace.

Then, without warning, the warmth wasn't there anymore. Neil had pulled away abruptly, letting in the cold sting of rain. He was standing above her, his face an impassive mask. Silently he reached down to help her to her feet. She clutched his hand and struggled to a kneeling position, then finally managed to pull herself onto her feet. Dazedly she turned and looked down the side of the mountain with some vague idea of looking for her pickup.

"It's gone, Terry—totaled." Neil's voice rasped in her ears. Terry swung her eyes around to the road

ahead. But there was no road there—only that torrent of pounding, surging brown water.

"What happened?" she asked in a shaky voice.
"Where did it come from, all that water?"

"A flash flood." Neil stood beside her, gazing
across the ten feet of roaring water. The rain was
much lighter now. She could clearly see the road on
the other side, curving around the mountain toward
Taos and safety. Neil gestured toward the hillside
above them. "This must have been a dry stream bed.
When the sky opened up, it turned back into a river.
The big clay culvert that was supposed to carry the
water under the roadbed was torn loose by the flood
and tossed down into the canyon."

Terry's head was starting to whirl, and she felt her
knees giving way beneath her. The enveloping blackness was closing in again. Neil must have seen her
ominous change of color. He reached out and
grabbed her around her waist, then slung her quickly
over his shoulder.

"No!" she gasped. "You don't need to do that. I
can make it—"

"You've caused enough trouble already. From
now on, you're going to shut up and do what I tell
you." She felt herself being dumped on a hard
leather seat. A moment later, Neil climbed in beside
her, and she heard the cough of the Blazer's engine.

"Wait, Neil," she cried in sudden panic. "Where
are we going? Can't we stay here till the storm is
over?"

"Sure we can, if you want to get caught in a rockslide." Neil was staring grimly ahead, all his atten-

tion focused on his driving. "We've got to get out from under this mountain. We'll wait it out on that big plateau at Midnight."

He was hunching over the wheel, his shoulders sagging with obvious exhaustion. Terry felt a pang of remorse. Why had she been so stupid, dashing off like that in her pickup? She might have got them both killed.

The rain had almost stopped, but a fierce gusty wind had sprung up, pushing angrily at the sides of the Blazer. Every few seconds Terry could feel the car rocking. She gripped the edge of her seat with nerveless hands, breathing a silent prayer as she watched Neil battle to keep control of the steering. They were inching along with agonizing slowness, but the four-wheel drive was providing just that extra bit of traction they needed.

Then, after what seemed like hours, the wind dropped away abruptly just as they came in view of the ruined cabins. Neil whistled between his teeth in appreciation. "Pretty smart guys, those old miners. They built their town in a natural windbreak." He angled the car off the road, bumped over the grassy plateau and came to a stop beside the old hotel. "Good drainage, too." Relief had smoothed the furrows out of his forehead. "This ground feels pretty firm underneath us. We won't have to waste our time digging the Blazer's hubcaps out of the mud."

Terry started to ask how long they were going to stay there, but halfway into her question her body was racked by a series of sneezes. Neil looked up at her sharply, discarding the road map he'd been perusing. "Good Lord, woman, you're freezing," he growled. "Get out of those wet clothes this minute. There's a sleeping bag in that pile of gear just behind you."

The thought of taking her clothes off triggered an instant image: the shadowy bedroom up on the mesa, Neil's eyes and hands caressing her naked body. She flinched away in protest. "Oh, Neil, that's not necessary. I'll be all right in a minute."

Neil glared at her in undisguised irritation. "Shut up and take off those clothes, Terry. The next few days are going to be full of problems. We can't afford to have you come down with pneumonia."

Terry realized that she was gritting her teeth, trying to keep herself from shivering. She looked down at her clothes and saw with a shock how filthy they were, caked with sticky red mud, even torn in some places. She nodded meekly and started to open the door beside her.

"Not that way," Neil muttered brusquely, reaching across to stop her. "No sense in getting another chill. Climb over the back of the seat. The sleeping bag is in a dark blue stuff sack."

Terry followed his instructions, scrambling into the back and pulling the fluffy down bag out of its covering. She slipped off her jacket and shirt, then paused for a moment, feeling exposed and self-conscious. She flicked a glance toward Neil and saw he was poking around in the glove compartment, apparently oblivious to her presence.

Again the searing memory rose to taunt her: the bedroom, his hands on her breasts, their naked bodies clinging together.... She brushed the image away and quickly unhooked her bra, then pulled off her boots, along with her jeans and panties. The sleeping bag's nylon lining made her feel icy cold for a couple of seconds before the blessed heat began seeping through her body, soothing her aches and bruises, giving her a cozy sense of well-being.

Neil's face appeared over the seat. "That's better," he said. "Now throw me those dirty clothes. I'll go wash some of the mud off. They'll dry soon enough if I put them under the heater."

She started to tell him she'd rather do her own washing, then saw how silly that was and wordlessly bundled up the pile of damp clothes. His head disappeared briefly below the front seat. Then he emerged again and handed her a blue-enameled tin mug. "Careful," he said. "It's hot."

Terry sniffed incredulously at the steaming liquid. "Coffee!" she said. "Where on earth did that come from?"

Neil's weary face relaxed in a crooked smile. "I believe in being prepared. That's why I always carry this useful gadget."

Terry leaned across the back of the seat and saw the glowing red ring of the little hot plate that he'd plugged into the cigarette lighter. A jar of instant coffee stood on the seat beside it, along with some packets of sugar and powdered creamer. "Fantastic!" Terry breathed. She took a cautious sip, followed by several swallows, feeling the heat radiate through her.

Watching her approvingly for a couple of seconds,

he then reached into the glove compartment and handed her a foil-wrapped package. "You'd better have some breakfast. These Cadbury bars have a lot of quick energy." He picked up the bundle of clothes, slid down from the driver's seat and walked away toward a nearby stream.

Terry unwrapped the bar of chocolate, suddenly aware that she was ravenously hungry. How long had it been since she'd eaten? She'd shared Gus's tuna-fish sandwich out at the house site. After that, things had started happening too fast for her to think about eating. More memories surged up relentlessly: the quarrel with Neil and her flight from the house site, the letter from Ward McKevitt, Lenore's shocking accusations, her relief at Neil's explanation, and then, those glorious moments in the little bedroom, Neil's urgent whisper, "You'll never leave me again...."

But now Neil was the one who was leaving. She felt the tears prickle behind her eyelids. If only she'd had more faith, hadn't let all those stupid suspicions overwhelm her....

The chocolate bar had the taste of ashes, but she forced herself to swallow the last few bites. By the time Neil came back to the car, she was in control of her emotions.

"That was marvelous," she said brightly. "Your traveling kitchen gets three big stars in my guide-book."

He nodded acknowledgment as he moved the hot plate down to the floor of the car, making room for her clothes on the seat in front of the heater. Once they were laid out to dry, he busied himself with making his own cup of coffee, pouring the water out of the gleaming aluminum flask that he'd just refilled from the mountain stream.

She watched him silently, admiring the deftness of his strong, sun-tanned hands. How could anyone accuse this man of being merely a playboy? "You're really full of surprises. Next thing I know, you'll be dishing us up a meal of milkweed roots and wild mushrooms."

Neil's mouth crinkled into a grin, and for a moment the cold distant look turned almost friendly. "I can do better than that. How about this?" Reaching into the glove compartment, he tossed her another packet that looked like a small-size bag of potato chips. Turning it over, she saw the taste-tempting picture—a steaming dish of spaghetti and meatballs.

"It's freeze-dried food. You don't have to cook it—just pour on some boiling water. I've got enough of this stuff to last us a week."

Terry looked up at him in surprise. "You don't think we'll have to stay here that long, do you?"

"I certainly hope not." The grim tired expression returned to his face. "It all depends on the weather. If the rain holds off, this wind should dry out the road pretty quickly. We might be on our way in another three hours."

"But that place where the flash flood came through—even if the stream dries up, there's still that break in the roadbed. You aren't going to try to drive the Blazer across that?"

"We're not going in that direction," he explained

in long-suffering patience. "The other end of this road leads down to Red River. From there, the highway is paved all the way back to Taos."

Terry knew she ought to feel pleased at the thought of getting back to a nice hot shower and having a chance to solve all those campaign problems. But she actually felt miserable at the prospect. Despite Neil's studied coldness, it felt very good to be here with him, as if they were two shipwreck survivors, marooned in this lonely spot, cut off in their world on top of the mountain.

She scanned the sky, secretly hoping to see more thunderheads. The sky above was still gray, but out on the southern horizon it was rapidly changing to brilliant blue. She saw range after range of mountains emerge from their veils of moisture. The real world was back around them, pulling them inexorably toward it. They'd leave in a few more hours, try to undo the harm Lenore's deception had caused. Thursday night would bring the final decision. The bitter defeat or the longed-for victory—which would it be? To the weary aching woman stretched out in the sleeping bag in the back of the Blazer, that once urgent question no longer seemed important. Even the fact that Neil had saved her life now appeared to be supremely ironic. What good was her life if Neil wasn't there to share it?

Was he really going to leave Taos? Surely there must be some way to stop him! She struggled up to a sitting position, ready to launch a last impassioned plea. "Neil," she murmured softly.

But Neil didn't hear her. He was sound asleep,

curled up on the car's front seat. Down on the floor, the ring of the little hot plate still glowed a fiery red. Terry reached over the seat back and pulled the cord out of the dashboard, the effort sending arrows of pain shooting through her aching muscles. Wriggling back into her down-filled nest, she surrendered herself to exhaustion, letting it sweep her away into oblivion.

CHAPTER TWENTY

TERRY AWAKENED BEFORE HE DID, disturbed by a dream in which she'd been careering on a bicycle down a steep muddy road, surrounded on every side by lightning and thunder. She peered at Neil over the seat. He was curled up on his left side, head pillowed on one hand, looking strangely young and defenseless. Still half asleep herself, she watched him for several minutes, imagining how it would be to wake up beside him every morning. As though she'd sent him a telepathic signal, he stirred and opened his eyes, gazing directly up into her watching face.

She detected a look of surprise, then of pleased wonder. He reached up a hand, and she waited breathlessly for his touch on her cheek. Then the hazel eyes went dark with sudden awareness. He swung himself up abruptly into a sitting position and peered out the window.

"Good Lord, what time is it, anyway? Why did you let me sleep so long?"

Terry glanced at her watch, fighting back her disappointment. "It's eleven o'clock. We've only slept for about two hours." Then she realized what had alarmed him. The clouds had come back again, darkening the sky ominously. Far to the south, she heard a soft roll of thunder.

"The storm's blowing up again. We'd better get out of here now, or we'll never make it."

Before Terry could say a word, she felt the Blazer bumping across the grass, then lurching onto the rocky road. Sighing ruefully, she thought of how good it would have felt to bathe her scratched muddy face in that little stream, then come back to the car for a steaming cup of coffee. No time for such luxuries now—only time for watching and praying—watching the road ahead, praying no unforeseen danger would hinder their escape down the rocky mountainside.

Reaching over the seat, she picked up her clothes. They were almost dry, just as Neil had predicted. She dressed herself quickly, this time with no concern that Neil might be watching. He was far too busy scanning the road ahead, his senses alert for impending danger.

They inched down the road for what seemed like hours, though it turned out to be only about forty-five minutes. Finally they reached the town of Red River, its one main street almost deserted, its usual crowd of tourists kept inside by the threatening storm clouds. Terry suggested they stop in a little café for a sandwich and coffee, but Neil merely shrugged and kept on driving.

Terry considered climbing over the seat back, but decided to stay where she was. Better to bear her grief back here alone and unseen than to sit beside him in that terrible stilted silence she remembered so well from their first ride out of the mountains.

By the time they reached the outskirts of Taos, Terry's spirits had sunk to their lowest level. Only a few minutes more and he'd drop her off at her house—and after that, would she ever see him again? Desperately she groped for some way of delaying that parting. "You must be famished," she murmured. "When we get down to Talpa, it's my turn to do the cooking."

"We're not going to Talpa. I haven't got that much time. I'm going to drop you off at the Janus Gallery."

"But, Neil, I look such a fright." Terry's hand went up to her matted hair, vainly trying to smooth out some of the tangles. "Besides, I'm not even sure they'll let me in. David seemed very standoffish the last time I was there."

He glanced at her in the rearview mirror, and the barest hint of a grin lifted his mouth at the corners. "You look remarkably waiflike. They wouldn't have the heart to turn you away. Besides, there's a little job I need you to do there."

Terry felt a spurt of pleasure. In spite of her lack of faith, Neil still needed her for something. "A job?" she asked. "What sort of job?" Then she scolded herself for sounding so eager.

"I want you to give the Quayles this check." He reached into his jacket and pulled an envelope out of his inside pocket. "But first you've got to get Cecilia to promise she's not going to tear it up."

Terry remembered the day before on the old *portal* when she'd told him about Ward McKevitt—how his anger had flared, as he'd said, "We'll have to fight fire with fire."

"Oh, Neil, that's wonderful. We can't let that monster foreclose on the gallery. But what do you mean, tear up the check? I'm sure Cecilia will be absolutely delighted."

"I thought so, too, before last night's little drama. I drove over there while you went to see Montoya—thought I'd do my boy scout deed and reassure them. Cecilia looked pretty happy, but David wouldn't accept it. He said he could stand on his own two feet, that he didn't want anyone else taking care of his family."

"Oh, dear," Terry groaned. "Doesn't that sound just like David! But surely Cecilia managed to calm him down? After all, it's her family home they'd be losing."

"She did her best, the poor woman. She tried to turn it into some kind of joke—you know the old melodrama, with the heroine sighing 'My hero!' and the villain shouting 'Curses! Foiled again!' But David just got more and more obstinate. He asked me how I'd found out about the foreclosure. When I told him I heard it from you, he hit the ceiling—said he was tired of two-faced schemers and told Cecilia to give me back my check. She'd already stashed it away in her apron pocket. She took it out and tore it in little pieces, and before I could stop her, she'd thrown it into the fire."

Terry had stiffened in shock. "David said that about *me*? Just because I voted against Cecilia?"

"It had to be more than that." Neil's jaw jutted

out grimly. "I think our lovely Lenore has been showing that so-called sketch of yours all over town. It would suit her plans very well to have our campaign supporters doubting your motives."

Terry's eyes lighted up in sudden apprehension. "Do you think she showed it to Paco? That might be why he's seemed so cool these past few days."

"He's been pretty cool toward me, as well—kept dropping little hints about Ward McKevitt. I didn't know what he meant until you filled me in on Lenore's cockeyed story."

"You think she's got him convinced that you're really Ward's partner?"

Neil lifted a quizzical eyebrow. "She's raised some suspicions, maybe. But Paco isn't that easy to convince. He's already sensed she's playing a devious game."

Terry's remorse flared up again. If only she had been half as loyal as Paco! "We've got our work cut out for us, then. Only two more days to straighten out all these people."

Neil shot her another quick look in the rearview mirror. "I'm leaving all that up to you. After I drop you off, I'm driving straight down to Albuquerque."

His words were a blow. "Oh, Neil, you're not leaving already! You said you were going to stay till the end of the campaign."

"I don't have to account to you for my movements," he snapped. "What I'm going to do next is none of your business. Your job is here in Taos—and you're going to start it right now, by setting the record straight with Cecilia and David."

I don't care about Cecilia and David. All I care about is being with you. The words were forcing themselves into Terry's throat, but she gritted her teeth, suppressing the anguished cry. It was no use complaining. She'd brought this on herself. At least she'd do better this time than she had with Paul. This time there would be no shameful whining or begging, trying to snatch back a love that had already fled.

"But what if they refuse to listen to me?"

"You'll find some way to convince them. I have great faith in the famous Morrison ingenuity." Before she knew what was happening, his arms went around her, drawing her close in a long passionate kiss. Then, just as abruptly, he was opening the car door and pushing her out. "Off you go, Terry. Give my regards to Cecilia and David."

Still not quite sure what was happening, she found herself in the gallery's driveway, watching the Blazer roar off toward the Santa Fe highway. A tiny flicker of hope stirred inside her. That hadn't felt like a farewell kiss. Then she told herself sternly not to waste time on impossible dreams. Determinedly squaring her shoulders, she pushed open the little gate and started up the path to the Janus Gallery.

She paused in front of the big paneled door, wondering what sort of reception she'd get from the Quayles. Now she understood why Cecilia had looked so embarrassed when David had left the room the day before. Cecilia herself had seemed as friendly as ever, but maybe she'd changed her attitude in the meantime. With all these horrible rumors floating around—

Just as she reached out her hand to lift the knocker, the door was flung open before her, and Cecilia was staring at her in shocked surprise. "Come in, sweetie, come in. What on earth has happened to you? You look like a refugee from a Kansas cyclone."

"It's not quite as bad as that. Just a little brush with the side of a mountain." Gratefully Terry let herself be pulled inside the warm dry gallery, while she poured out her story in brief disjointed phrases— the truck tumbling down the hillside, her desperate perch on the crumbling ledge, the miracle of the life-giving rope, Neil's powerful arms dragging her up to safety, the treacherous trek down from Midnight.

As she went through the hurried recital, she had the sense of living it all again. Now that her senses were no longer numbed by shock, she was hit by the full realization of what had just happened. She felt her eyes filling with tears, her shoulders shaking. "I almost died," she heard herself sobbing. "I almost died, but Neil saved me."

Cecilia held her close in wholehearted sympathy. "It's all right, Terry. You're safe now. But what on earth were you doing up there in the mountains? We were wondering where you'd gone. When Neil came back here last night, he was almost frantic, asking us if we'd seen you. We figured you must have had some kind of quarrel."

A new flood of tears welled up under Terry's swollen eyelids. "Oh, Cecilia," she wailed, "I've made such a mess of things. How could anyone make so many mistakes?"

Cecilia patted her shoulder gently. "Sweetie, you're really exhausted. Come and flop down on the sofa and let me get you a nice hot cup of tea." She put her arm around Terry's waist and guided her into the living room. David was there, sitting in front of the fireplace, staring into the glowing embers. He didn't turn when they came into the room.

"Look who's here, David, sweetie." Cecilia's voice had a challenging ring. "Guess what's just happened to Terry. Her pickup fell off the side of a mountain."

David shot a quick glance at Terry, then turned back to the fire again as though unwilling to meet her eyes. "Hello, Terry," he mumbled.

"You'll have to excuse David," Cecilia said briskly as she settled Terry down on the sofa, tucking some bright-colored cushions under her head. "He's got the jitters, waiting to meet his new patron. Mr. Enderby is due to arrive from Phoenix any minute."

"Don't make excuses for me!" David's angry eyes glared directly at Terry. "The truth is, I'd rather not have you under my roof."

Cecilia's face went pink with embarrassment. "You're really awful, David, the way you jump to conclusions. The least you could do is talk to Terry directly, tell her all your horrible suspicions." She stared down at the floor, biting her lip. Now she was the one reluctant to meet Terry's eyes.

"Look, you two, let's get this out in the open." Terry's voice was firm and determined. "I think I can guess what's thrown you both into a tizzy. Did Lenore show you that design I'm supposed to have drawn, that fourteen-story atrocity in the plaza?''

Cecilia was visibly startled. ''Lenore? You mean Lenore Hitchcock? What's she got to do with all this? The drawing just appeared in our mailbox last Friday—no return address, no note of explanation. I told David there must be something fishy about it, if whoever sent it wouldn't appear in person. Besides, you've never gone in for apartment buildings. I bet you've never drawn such a thing in your life.''

''Oh, yes, I have—back in Los Angeles.'' Quickly Terry told them about the student contest, the library copy's telltale acquisition number, the way Lenore's scheme had taken in Ben Montoya.

David's anger was replaced by cautious interest. ''But why would Lenore pull a stunt like that? She's supposed to be fighting *against* Southwestern.''

''It's just like I told you, David,'' Cecilia explained excitedly. ''She doesn't really want our campaign to succeed. That's why she's forcing the pace, encouraging Skeeter to make all those wild accusations. She's doing her best to turn the town against us.''

David gazed doubtfully at his wife. ''Oh, come on, Cecilia. I'll admit she's a little overenthusiastic. Her aggressiveness has raised some people's hackles. But I don't think she really intended to do that.''

''Oh, yes, she did.'' Terry's voice was sharp with challenge. ''She's trying her best to ruin our whole campaign. Lenore is being paid by Stanton Odessa. They know she's good at this kind of sabotage. She's done it before, when Neil was fighting Olympia Tires.''

David frowned incredulously. ''That sounds pretty

crazy, Terry. Lenore didn't even know Neil before she came here to Taos.''

''That's what she wanted people to think. But she told me herself that she'd been Neil's New York assistant. She pretended she was devotedly trying to help him, when what she was really doing was stabbing him in the back.'' Terry sketched in further details of Lenore's double cross, leading to the loss of Neil's case against Olympia Tires. ''She was being paid by Olympia all the time,'' she concluded. ''If you want more proof, just ask Neil. He'll show you the checks he got from Olympia.''

David shook his head, clearly bewildered. ''That's quite a story, Terry. The whole thing sounds pretty weird to me.''

''It doesn't sound weird to me.'' Cecilia stuck out her chin defiantly. ''It all comes down to one question—who are you going to trust? Terry, who's been our friend for years and years, or this woman we only met a few weeks ago.''

David's face softened, and he smiled apologetically at Terry. ''I'm sorry, Terry. I should have known better. Lenore's little scheme kind of caught me off balance.''

''Okay,'' Cecilia beamed, ''I'm glad we've got all that settled. Now let me get you that cup of tea—and how about a grilled-cheese sandwich, sprinkled with *jalapeños*, the way you like it?''

Without waiting for Terry's response, she bustled off into the kitchen. David and Terry stared silently at each other, both of them still feeling a little embarrassed. Finally David thought of a question to break the impasse. "What's all this about your pickup? It didn't really fall off a mountain, did it?"

"Yes, I'm afraid it did." Terry backed away from repeating the whole painful story, afraid the tears might start flowing again. "It was all my fault, really—just one of those stupid accidents. I got myself into a pickle; Neil got me out of it and dropped me here on your doorstep. He would have come in himself, but he had to get on to some urgent business."

David's face clouded over. "I haven't been very cordial to poor old Neil. I guess he deserves an apology, too."

Terry's spirits perked up. Here was her chance to accomplish Neil's mission. "Does that mean you've changed your mind about accepting his check?" Her hand was in her jeans pocket, fingering the torn-up check's replacement. But David's frown kept her from pulling it out.

"I still feel the same about that. Cecilia and I don't need any help taking care of the gallery. We're doing quite well on our own, aren't we, Cecilia?"

His wife, who had just come back in with the tea tray, blinked a couple of times before she answered. "Of course we are, sweetie. We're doing just super." She set down the tray and smiled brightly at Terry, but Terry thought her enthusiasm sounded a little forced. "Has David told you the wonderful news about Mr. Enderby? You know, his rich admirer who's on his way here from Phoenix? The deal for the mural is practically in the bag. He's already approved the design David sent him. We've even got to the point of discussing money. He's mentioned a princely sum—more than enough to pay off the mortgage. But before he makes things final, he wants to come here and meet David in person. He says that's the way he always does business, that the human factor is far more important than money."

"Imagine a millionaire saying a thing like that," Terry said with satisfaction. "He sounds like our kind of people."

"Doesn't he just!" Cecilia's smile seemed more sincerely triumphant now. "So you see, there's no need for Neil's check. Like David says, we're doing fine on our own."

Terry's hand was still in her pocket, fingering the slip of paper. Despite Cecilia's confident words, she still wasn't sure the gallery was out of danger. Suppose something happened to change Mr. Enderby's mind? But this wasn't the moment to voice that lingering doubt. It might imply that she didn't have faith in David.

"That's really terrific." She smiled at both of them brightly. "When is this paragon supposed to arrive?"

Cecilia glanced at the clock on the mantel. "He said about two-thirty. That would mean in another half hour. But he's driving from Albuquerque, which means that this weather might slow him down a little. Anyway, it won't be very much longer. Isn't it lucky you'll have a chance to meet him?"

"Oh, no!" Terry cried in horror. Her hand raked distractedly through her matted hair, and she looked down at her wrinkled clothes in consternation. "I really have to get home and into the shower. Anyway, I'm dead on my feet. I know I'd make an awful impression.'' She turned apologetically toward David. ''I know it's an imposition, especially right at this moment. But maybe you'd have enough time to drive me home?''

Cecilia jumped quickly to her feet. ''Nothing easier, Terry. We were just about to take Gito down to his baby-sitter. We can operate better without him underfoot—you know, some millionaires aren't very keen on children. David can drop him off at Mrs. Romero's and then run you down to your little nest at Talpa. Why don't I go get him into his coat right now, so you can go home and collapse in comfort?''

David smiled at Terry as Cecilia went out toward the bedrooms. ''You look as though you could use a little sleep. Otherwise, I'd insist on your staying. We could introduce you as one of my models. With that layer of good New Mexican earth you're wearing, you could pose as the spirit of La Tierra Encantada.''

Terry gave him a rueful smile. ''With the shape my hair is in, I look more like a Medusa.''

David chortled with glee. ''Hey, that's an idea. I could paint you as part of a Hopi snake dance.''

Terry nodded laughingly, grateful that they were back on friendly terms. Just at that moment, Cecilia burst into the room. ''David,'' she cried, her voice tinged with panic, ''I can't find Gito!''

David looked up with a puzzled frown. ''I thought he was in his room, playing some more of those crazy games with the clothespins.''

"He was, half an hour ago. But now he's disappeared."

David sprang to his feet, his face tight with tension. "Have you looked outside in the garden? Sometimes he likes to play Indian under the bushes."

"I've looked everywhere, David," she said, heaving a sigh of exasperation. "Gito is gone, I tell you. And he's taken a lot of things with him—that toy backhoe of his and his red anorak, the one with the white-and-blue arrows."

"So he finally went and did it! He ran away to El Loco—or maybe that crazy old man came here and got him."

"Pedro wouldn't do that, take a child away from his parents." Cecilia glared defensively at David. "If that's where Gito has gone, he must have gone of his own free choice."

David started to make an angry retort, but his voice was drowned out by a startling clap of thunder, followed almost at once by a flash of lightning. The three of them stood transfixed, staring out the big living-room window.

"Good Lord, that was close," David muttered. "It must have hit down by the old Taos bridge."

"Oh, David," Cecilia cried shrilly, "that's where Pedro's shack is! If Gito's down there, we've got to go there and get him."

"Don't worry, baby. He's nowhere near that lightning." David laid a soothing hand on Cecilia's shoulder. "That bridge is more than a mile away. Gito hasn't had time to get that far."

"But that's even worse, don't you see?" Cecilia

jerked away impatiently. "Look at those storm clouds, there over the mountains. It's going to start pouring again any minute. If he gets caught in that downpour and has an asthma attack— Well, don't just stand there, David! We've got to go find him."

They stared at each other, horror-struck. The sudden patter of raindrops galvanized David into action. He dashed out of the room and returned with two heavy raincoats. "Come on, woman," he cried, "put this on. The river's at flood height already. God knows what's happening to Pedro's flimsy old shack."

"Wait," Terry exclaimed, following them out of the living room. "What about your man from Phoenix?"

Cecilia was already at the front door of the gallery. "You do it, Terry," she called back over her shoulder. "Use your charm on the old sweetie pie. Prepare the lamb for the slaughter. I don't know when we'll be able to get back," she added in a worried tone.

"Don't worry about anything here," Terry said firmly. "I'll take care of your client." The Quayles were already climbing into their truck as she spoke, and Terry was left alone in the empty house.

Her hand went to her matted hair. She hurried into the bathroom and peered into the mirror, assessing the damage. Her face was streaked with dried adobe mud. Realizing she didn't have time for a shower, she picked up a washcloth and scrubbed until her complexion shone, then used a nailbrush to get the dirt out from under her jagged nails. She stared with dismay at her rumpled clothes. Most of the mud had come out in the mountain stream, but a number of ugly red brown streaks remained.

Hurrying into the bedroom, she opened Cecilia's closet, stripped off her wrinkled jeans and pulled a long flowered skirt down over her head. Checking herself in the full-length mirror, she saw that it was trailing the ground by a good two inches. She rolled it up around the elastic waistband, creating a clumsy bulge around her middle. *Never mind,* she thought. *The tunic will hide that. But my hair? What about my hair?*

She looked around despairingly, saw a bright red scarf on top of the Spanish dresser. Piling her muddy hair up and twisting it into a topknot, she secured it with Cecilia's tortoiseshell comb. Then she wrapped the red scarf around it, turban fashion, and looked at herself again in Cecilia's mirror.

A flamboyant Gypsy gazed back at her. The image made her feel like a usurper. On Cecilia, with her dark hair and tall figure, this style of dress looked striking and romantic. On Terry, it looked pretentious and bizarre. *Oh, well,* she told herself, *Mr. Enderby doesn't know what I usually look like. He's probably one of these dilettantes who gets a kick out of meeting bohemian artists.* Well, she'd do her best to put on a good show for him. It was the least she could do to help her friends save the gallery.

But perhaps there would be no need for her masquerade. Cecilia and David might be back any minute. If Gito had kept to the road, not become frightened and wandered off into the bushes.... An unpleasant image rippled through her mind: a little boy crying, crouched under a rain-swept piñon, or huddled in a leaky hut ringed with shadowy human figures. Sam Geromino, that's what he'd called him. Terry pictured a gnarled aged farmer in faded jeans and a tattered straw hat, hands twisted and callused from wresting small crops of beans out of the rocky hillside. And Mrs. Geromino? She would look like the *curandera* in *Bless Me, Ultima*, wise old eyes in a wrinkled face, mouth crinkling into a toothless smile.

What else had Gito told her—something about the boys that got the spankings? Terry's vision abruptly turned into a nightmare: a willow switch clutched in old Pedro's hand, rising and falling in a steady sinister rhythm, writhing figures on the packed-earth floor of the shack, the river outside inexorably rising, swirling around the cabin, smashing in the flimsy door....

Stop it, Terry! Why was she thinking such crazy thoughts? Her nerves must really be on edge. No wonder, with all she'd been through in the past twenty-four hours. Another image flashed before her—Neil's face in all its familiar detail. Terry's heart lurched.

Desperate to escape from her inner turmoil, she ran to the window to see what the weather was doing. Perhaps the storm had let up? No, the rain was pelting down as hard as ever. Still, that might be a good thing. It would keep Mr. Enderby away a little while longer. No sane man would try to drive through this deluge.

Just as she was about to turn away, she saw a car veer off the distant main highway into the gallery's access road. She stood watching it as it came closer and closer, a gray Mercedes, its original glossy sheen sadly marred by streaks of clinging mud.

Her heart began to beat quickly. This must be the important patron from Phoenix. Why had she wasted all this time daydreaming when she should have been getting things ready for his arrival?

She rushed out to the kitchen, pulled out a tray of ice cubes, dumped them into the sink, then piled them into a hand-thrown bowl made by a local potter. Now, where did Cecilia and David keep their liquor? She rummaged under the sink and found an unopened bottle of Chivas Regal. Quickly she wrestled the top off, licking the cut the sharp foil made in her finger.

She muttered a few choice swear words when she heard the knocker bang on the gallery door, then wrapped a paper towel around her cut finger and hurried out to answer it. Halfway to the big paneled door, she stopped herself short. *Careful, Terry. We don't want our future patron to think we're too eager.* Drawing a deep breath to calm herself, she walked the rest of the way at a measured pace, lifted the heavy iron latch and opened the door.

"Mr. Enderby—" Astonishment cut short the greeting she'd been rehearsing. The man was so very different from what she'd expected. She had pictured him with a sleek tan, a well-tailored suit concealing an incipient paunch, an overall aura of elegant living. What she saw was a small gnomelike creature whose head came only as high as her shoulder, wearing brown suede jeans and a bright purple cowboy shirt with a bolo tie, his wizened face almost lost beneath the brim of what had once been a pure white Stetson, but was now speckled with rain spots.

"Mrs. Quayle, I presume?" The prunelike mouth pinched up in a death's-head grin. He took off his hat and slapped it against his thigh, scattering drops of water all over the doorstep.

"Oh, no, I'm not Mrs. Quayle," Terry said, flustered. Then she pulled herself together and managed a smile that she hoped was suitably charming. "Come in, for heaven's sake. What a shame you had to come on such an awful day. I hope you didn't run into any trouble? No flash floods, no roads under water?"

The little man stepped over the threshold and looked deliberately around the gallery, fixing each painting and piece of sculpture with an eagle-eyed glance that seemed to be assessing their market value. Finally he turned back to Terry. "Young lady, whoever you are, why are you standing there staring? Kindly go tell Mr. Quayle I am here to keep our appointment."

Despite his small frame, his voice was strong and commanding. Terry turned automatically toward the living room. Then she caught herself up with an apologetic gesture. "I'm sorry, the Quayles aren't at home. They had to go out on...some urgent business. Come into the living room, won't you? They should be back any minute. What would you like to drink while we're waiting? We have Scotch and gin and tequila—"

"I never touch alcohol." Mr. Enderby's pale blue

eyes scanned her up and down, making her uncomfortably aware of her unorthodox costume. "If you are not Mrs. Quayle, then who are you? We have not yet had the pleasure of an introduction."

The scorn in the pale blue eyes canceled out any notion that knowing her might be a pleasure. "I—I'm sorry," she stammered. "I'm Terry Morrison, a-a kind of a neighbor."

"You're an artist yourself?"

"No, I'm an architect. As a matter of fact, you're looking at some of my work. I designed this addition when the Quayles expanded their gallery."

Mr. Enderby cast another brief glance around the gallery. "Serviceable, quite serviceable." She could see she'd gone up a notch in his estimation. "I suppose you know Lester Riordan? He's supposed to be the best architect in Dallas. He did the design for the Enderby Library. Now he's working on some kind of project here in Taos."

Terry froze for a moment, struck by a premonition. "Would that happen to be a high-rise condominium—the one that's being planned by Southwestern Towers?"

The sour old face brightened with interest. "Yes, that's the one. You know about it? Maybe you're doing some work on the project, too?"

"No, I'm not." Terry's voice was small and subdued. "As a matter of fact, I'm working against it."

Mr. Enderby looked puzzled for a moment. The frosty look was back in the pale blue eyes. "Lester said there was some local feeling against the project. He didn't seem to be too worried about it."

Terry stifled her impulse to contradict him. She reminded herself that she ought to be charming this man, not arguing with him. "Why am I bothering you with our local squabbles?" She gave him what she hoped was a winning smile. "It's David's painting you're interested in. Please come into the living room. I can make you some tea or coffee—"

"I didn't come here for a social visit. There are many demands on my time, young lady. My schedule provides thirty minutes for Mr. Quayle. Then I'm driving on up to another appointment in Denver."

"But you can't drive up there through all this rain! The roads will be very dangerous up in the Rockies."

His eyes shot out sparks of annoyance. "Your concern for my welfare is very touching. You sound just like that old-maid doctor of mine. He's made me give in and stop flying my Cessna, but despite my great age, I'm not yet reduced to the point where I need a hired chauffeur."

"I didn't mean it that way," Terry assured him, dismayed. "Those roads would be dangerous for any driver—"

He brushed her protest away impatiently. "Don't worry about me, young lady. I'm not going to let a mere rainstorm throw my schedule out of kilter. I thought I had made it clear to Mr. Quayle that a limited time had been set aside for our meeting. But I suppose he's one of these flighty artistic types. No sense of responsibility, no regard for the needs of others—"

"Really, David's not like that," Terry broke in sharply. "He was here, waiting to meet you—practically counting the minutes till your arrival. Then he found out his five-year-old son had wandered out into that storm. Surely you understand that he had to go try and find him?''

''That does sound most distressing.'' Mr. Enderby frowned in shocked disapproval. ''I'm surprised Mrs. Quayle allowed such a thing to happen. When I spoke to her on the phone, she seemed like a refreshingly practical woman, not at all like the usual artist's wife.''

Terry suppressed the urge to spring to Cecilia's defense. Mr. Enderby's feathers were already sufficiently ruffled. She ought to be calming him down, putting him in the mood to sign the contract with David. ''I'm sure they'll be back in just a few minutes.'' She ventured a placating smile. ''Meanwhile, I can show you some of David's paintings. That one over there, for instance.'' She gestured toward the far end of the gallery. ''The coyote dressed in Harlequin costume. Coyote, you know, is the Navaho spirit of mischief—''

''I don't need to see Mr. Quayle's paintings. The slides he sent me were quite sufficient.''

Terry stared at him in amazement. ''You drove all the way here through that awful rainstorm, and now you don't want to see David's paintings?''

''I don't see why that should surprise you. I explained to Mrs. Quayle why I was coming.''

''She said something about the human factor—getting to know the artist as a person.''

''That's it exactly, young lady. After a great deal of sad experience with various artists, I've learned to take certain precautions. I came here to size the man up, see if he operates on a businesslike basis.''

"But Cecilia said—'' Terry gulped in dismay. "I mean, I understood you'd already come to some agreement.''

"I've agreed about how much I'll pay him.'' The little man sniffed with distaste. "But money's the least of my worries. I'm more concerned about his personal habits. Is Mr. Quayle the type who can work against a definite deadline, or will he sit around complaining about lack of inspiration?''

"Surely it isn't a question of inspiration. Hasn't David already sent you a sketch of his mural? From now on, it would be just a technical matter, preparing the wall and painting the fresco on it—''

"I'm afraid it's not quite that simple. After consulting with Mr. Riordan, I find we'll have to make a number of changes.'' He tapped the thin briefcase he carried under his arm. "I want to go over the plans with Mr. Quayle, see how he molds himself to the demands of the situation.''

"The demands of the situation,'' Terry echoed slowly. "Exactly what does that mean in this case?''

Mr. Enderby glanced up at her sharply. "You want me to show you the plans? I'm not sure that's appropriate, unless, that is, you're acting as Mr. Quayle's official agent.'' Again his eyes moved over her gaudy costume, registering distrust and disapproval.

"I'm not exactly his agent, but I am a close friend of David's. I know pretty well how his mind works. It's taken him a long time to develop his current style. He wouldn't want to depart too much from it.''

Mr. Enderby grunted with displeasure. ''One of these stubborn birds, is he? A typical case of inflated ego?''

''Integrity is the word I'd prefer to use,'' Terry said angrily. ''David feels very strongly about not pandering to popular taste. He's stuck to his personal style, even though it meant less business for the gallery.''

Mr. Enderby sniffed contemptuously. ''A small-scale operation like this—I suppose the difference isn't all that important. But when it comes to my library, we're talking about real money. For what I'm offering him, he should be willing to stifle his sensitive ego.''

Terry fought to suppress her sense of outrage. What colossal arrogance, to think that money would buy anything he wanted! And this was the man she'd described as ''our kind of people.''

Cautiously she looked toward the briefcase. ''Of course, if it's a matter of minor changes. . . .''

Mr. Enderby's face was cold and masklike. ''Some minor, some not so minor. First of all, there's the color scheme suggested by Mr. Riordan. Mr. Quayle will have to fit in with that. I believe the artistic jargon is 'change his palette.' Those dull browns and grays he's currently using are simply not adequate for Mr. Riordan's daring conception.''

''But David's palette is an integral part of his style! And it's not all browns and grays. It's raw ocher, burnt umber, cobalt violet—a subtle gradation along the earth-tone spectrum. That's what makes the southwestern landscape so enchanting. David's worked very hard to capture it in his paintings.''

''Is that your opinion, young lady?'' Mr. Enderby arched his skimpy white eyebrows. ''I'm afraid our best designers are veering away from those old clichés. They're beginning to use some much more exciting colors. Not that he'd have to make all that many changes—a bit of magenta, some crimson, some lemon yellow. But I don't make any pretense of being an expert. Mr. Riordan's conveyed his instructions very clearly.''

''Your architect is giving your artist instructions?'' Terry heard her voice growing louder, and lowered it to a more conversational level. ''That's not the usual relationship between the professions. Most architects think in terms of collaboration.''

''That may be so in a small-town practice like yours.'' Again, the contemptuous sniff. ''We're not talking about quaint two-bedroom houses. We're talking about a three-million-dollar building. I'm the one who's putting up all that money. Mr. Riordan is ready to give me what I ask for. If Mr. Quayle isn't willing to go along, I can easily find a more cooperative artist. After all, it's merely a matter of decoration.''

''Merely decoration!'' Terry's outrage could no longer be contained. ''You could say the same thing about the Sistine Chapel. Who was it put up the money for that little project? One of the Renaissance popes, I think. Who even remembers his name now?

People go there because of Michelangelo's paintings.''

Mr. Enderby stiffened, drew himself up to his full five feet two inches and glared belligerently at Terry. "Your attitude, young lady, is very unpleasant. I've been warned about people in Taos. It's said to be full of wild-eyed insubordinate artists. That seems to be true of its architects, too.''

"Insubordinate, Mr. Enderby? That's a very good way to describe us, here in Taos. That's the reason most of us came here. We were tired of kowtowing to people like you, people who think their money can make up for a lack of genuine values—like taste, sensibility, understanding—''

"You've said quite enough, young lady. I didn't come all this way to be insulted.'' Mr. Enderby turned toward the door and started wrestling with the heavy iron latch.

His threat to leave brought Terry back to her senses. "Wait,'' she said desperately. "Please stay here and talk to David. I'm sure you two can work out some arrangement.''

Mr. Enderby was still wrestling with the door latch. Finally he succeeded in pushing it open. Turning on the doorstep, he fixed his cold blue eyes on Terry. "I don't need to meet Mr. Quayle. I've already learned a great deal about him. He doesn't keep his appointments; he allows his son to run loose in dangerous country; he chooses friends who excuse their own shortcomings by the typical ploy of reviling successful people.''

"But that isn't fair!'' Terry cried. "You can't

make a decision based on such irrelevant reasons.''

"Don't tell *me* what I can do. I've managed to build up a billion-dollar business, all based on my skill at making quick decisions. Goodbye, young lady.'' He flicked a glance at his watch. "I seem to be right on schedule. I hope my Denver appointment is more rewarding.''

He swung around and marched down the winding path through the piñons, oblivious to the slashing torrents of rain. A moment later, she heard him start his engine.

Terry stood in the doorway, watching the car jolt down the muddy road and disappear behind a solid gray curtain of water. Then she stepped disconsolately back into the gallery. The empty rooms seemed to be full of mocking voices. David's paintings stared down at her in accusation. *Terry, you idiot,* they seemed to be saying, *why must you be such a bungler? Isn't it bad enough that you've failed the man you love? Now you've just thrown away your best friends' future.*

CHAPTER TWENTY-ONE

THROUGH THE NEXT TENSION-FILLED HOURS, Terry sat
on the living-room sofa, staring out the big window.
She heard the clock strike three, then three-thirty,
then four o'clock. After that, she refused to listen.
She tried to bury herself in a book, but instead of the
printed page she saw visions of swirling water, a
truck helplessly stuck on a muddy road, a tiny shack
overwhelmed by a raging river, David's and Cecilia's
desperate faces, the truck itself snatched away by the
towering flood waves.... Finally, exhaustion took
her. The book fell out of her hands, and her body
collapsed into heavy nightmare-filled sleep.

She awakened with a start from a dream of being
crushed by a tumbling rockslide, and stared incredulously out toward the dark blue mountains, no
longer concealed behind the opaque veil of rain. The
sky was a vivid blue. The garden's piñons cast sharply defined black shadows in the late-afternoon sun.

Thank God, the storm was over at last! But what
was keeping David and Cecilia? If they still hadn't
found Gito, were still desperately searching, even
after the storm was over....

Her mind balked at that point in her speculations.
She sank into a drowsy numbness, watching the sun

as it slipped by imperceptible stages down toward the western horizon.

When she heard the sound of the engine, all her senses came alive. She raced through the kitchen and gallery, through the garden and out onto the muddy road, bracing herself against the possibility of disastrous news. Breathlessly she watched the truck emerge from the distance, saw the pale blobs of faces take shape and resume their familiar features. She let out her breath in a sigh of tremendous relief. They were smiling, all of them—David, Cecilia and little Gito. At least they were safe—even though she'd just shattered David's hopes for his big commission.

She hugged them all as they piled out of the cab. "Thank goodness you're safe, Gito," she murmured to him, then turned to Cecilia. "What took you so long? How far did you have to go to find him?"

"Gito was safe all the time." Cecilia's eyes were dancing. "We found him down in old Pedro's cabin."

"But the river, the flooding water—it didn't rise high enough to do any damage?"

"No flood's going to catch our wise old Pedro Lopez," David responded exuberantly. "His shack is built on an outcrop of solid rock, high above the banks of the river. He's watched floods come and go for the past twenty years."

"Auntie Terry, Auntie Terry!" Gito was jumping up and down with excitement, trying to get her attention. "Sam Geromino is coming to stay at our house!"

"That's right." Cecilia smoothed the little boy's

hair affectionately. "Sam Geronimo and his missus
and all the Geronimo family." A chill evening breeze
ruffled the piñon branches, and Cecilia shivered a little. "I hope you kept the fire going, Terry. Let's go
have some hot whisky punch while we tell you all
about our little adventure."

David was already carrying Gito inside. Terry
started to follow him in, shaking her head in astonishment. Why was Cecilia so delighted by the prospect of sheltering Pedro's mysterious family? And
why was David so fulsomely praising "El Loco's"
wisdom?

The sound of another set of footsteps made her
stop in her tracks and look back toward the pickup.
Pedro Lopez was lifting a heavy bundle out of the
truck bed. Struck dumb, she watched him carry his
burden up the path through the piñons, a cylindrical
object, almost as tall as he was, wrapped in a heavy
tarpaulin.

With Gito safely deposited in the house, David
came out to meet the gnarled old man, evidently
wanting to share the heavy weight. Pedro shrugged
him away, carried the bulky bundle over the threshold, then set it down in the gallery, beaming at it with
a proud possessive smile.

"Terry," David said, "I think you know Mr.
Lopez, don't you? He's just become the Janus Gallery's new client."

"Client?" Terry stared at him blankly. What on
earth was David talking about?

"Show her, Pedro." David's eyes had picked up
the same proud gleam as Pedro's.

The old man nodded shyly at Terry, turned to his bundle and began to unwrap it. As the tarpaulin fell to the floor, Terry gasped in admiration. She gazed at the carved wooden figure of a bearded man, the open book he was carrying, the lion crouching beside him—the traditional pose of the patron saint of Taos.

"San Gerónimo!" she breathed. Pedro nodded emphatically. "What a beautiful piece of work! There's so much life in that face—you feel he's about to launch into a sermon. And the way the folds of his robe follow the grain of the wood...." She looked at Pedro with awestruck eyes. "You carved this, Mr. Lopez?"

He nodded again, a tremulous smile quivering around his sunken mouth. "But where did you learn to do such beautiful work?"

"Pedro's father taught him." David's voice was quietly triumphant. "In his time there were still many *santeros*, artists who carved the images of the saints. But I don't need to tell you that. You know a lot more about the old *santos* than I do."

Terry nodded, her eyes still fixed on the wooden figure. Two years before, when she'd remodeled that old mansion for Bill Hickey to live in, she'd become deeply absorbed in studying this local folk art. She was fully aware of the fabulous prices the old *santos* sold for, which had probably doubled between then and now. But the sculpture that stood before her was far superior to the stiff conventional figures she'd seen in books and studied in museums and churches. This was the work of one of that rare breed of artist whose talent was present from birth, men like Henri Rousseau, who produced masterpieces with no help from any art school. Terry looked respectfully at Pedro, recognizing the fire of genius that blazed within the odd little man.

"Isn't he fabulous, Terry?" David's air of suppressed excitement told her he'd made the same assessment she had. "Pedro's cabin is full of these carvings. He's been working on them for the past thirty years."

"Fabulous isn't the word. Miraculous is more like it." Terry's throat was tight with emotion. "But why isn't he already famous? Do you mean to say we're the only people who've seen this?"

"That's right. Pedro's been keeping his talent a secret," David said with a broad smile, as proud of his newfound client as if he himself had done the carving. "He was too ashamed to show them to anyone else—says his work's not nearly as good as his father's."

"You called him your client. Does that mean he's willing to sell them?"

"Willing and eager. He was delighted to learn that they might be worth money. When Cecilia suggested we handle the marketing for him, he practically kissed her."

"Isn't it marvelous?" Cecilia came in from the kitchen, carrying a tray loaded with five steaming mugs. "We're going to have a wonderful show for Pedro—send announcements out to Los Angeles, Dallas, New York—all the big galleries. It'll be the biggest event of the Taos season."

She said something in Spanish to Pedro, handing him one of the steaming punches. He beamed and nodded, quietly sipping his drink. "I told him he'll be the boss of the whole hacienda. Now, everybody, let's go in by the fire and bake the dampness out of our tired old bones."

Still dazed by the revelation of Pedro's talent, Terry followed Cecilia into the living room and sank down onto the sofa, feeling the heat of the fire seep into her sore muscles. Gito nestled beside her, noisily slurping his cup of hot cocoa. "Do you like Sam Geromino, Auntie Terry?" The child's dark eyes were eagerly searching her face.

"I like Sam Geronimo very much. You have some wonderful friends, Gito. I'm looking forward to meeting the rest of the family." She looked up at Cecilia. "I suppose Mrs. Sam turned out to be Santa Aña, the patron saint of the Taos pueblo?" Cecilia nodded. "And that business about the boys who get the spankings?"

"That's what we think is the most exciting part. Pedro's carved a whole *penitente* procession—you know, that secret cult, up around Mora, where the members parade on Good Friday with one of them playing Christ and carrying a cross, and the rest of them scourging themselves with yucca whips?"

"Wow!" Terry exclaimed. "Won't that cause a sensation! No one has ever photographed those old rituals. The cult members won't allow it. Pedro's sculpture will be absolutely unique. You'll have all the museums in the country bidding against each other."

Cecilia smiled as she sipped from her steaming mug. "It's already given David some great new images for his painting, especially the mural design for the Enderby Library. He's decided to add a new panel—balance the Navaho Blessing Way scene with one showing the *penitentes*, dressed as they were in the time of DeVargas."

"Yeah, I can't wait till he gets here," David murmured. "We'll take him down to the cabin, show him all Pedro's carvings—"

"What's the matter, Terry?" Cecilia interrupted him. "Did that sip of punch go down the wrong way?"

"I'm afraid I have some bad news." Terry swallowed uncomfortably. "Mr. Enderby has already been here and gone. He left about four hours ago."

"But why did he leave so quickly?" Cecilia exclaimed. "Surely you must have explained. Why didn't he stay and talk to David?"

"It's all my fault," Terry groaned. "I started an argument and got his back up." Quickly she sketched in the scene. When she got to the point of repeating her final outburst, David let loose with an Indian war whoop.

"Good for you, Terry," he chortled. "I'd have said the same things myself, if I'd been here with you."

"Right on," Cecilia exclaimed. "Art is made for love, not for money, isn't it, Pedro?"

Pedro nodded happily, said something in Spanish and raised his mug.

"That's an old Spanish toast," Cecilia remarked

in a pleased tone. She, too, raised her mug and clicked the brim against Pedro's. " 'Health, wealth, and love, and time to enjoy them all.' Well, we certainly seem to have plenty of all those good things." Exchanging an affectionate glance with her husband, she then turned briskly maternal. "Come along, Gito, you've had enough excitement. If you're going to stay healthy, you've got to get some rest. You had a long walk to-day, all the way down to Uncle Pedro's."

Gito's lower lip jutted out in sulky protest. "Auntie Terry," he whined. "I want to talk some more to Auntie Terry."

Cecilia sighed fondly, raising her eyebrows at Terry. "Serves you right for pinching my gorgeous outfit. Now Gito thinks you're his other mommie. Looks like you'll have to come and preside at the bathtub. We'll leave these men to their dreams of ar-tistic glory. After Gito's fed and in bed, I'll dish up some supper. All those terrific steaks we laid in for Mr. Enderby—they'll make a fine banquet to enter-tain our new client."

"THAT MEAL WAS WONDERFUL, CECILIA. And wasn't it great how much old Pedro enjoyed it?" Terry said, sipping at her cup of camomile tea. She and Cecilia were sitting in the kitchen, having a bedtime drink after washing and drying the dishes from supper. David was driving Pedro back to his cabin. Terry had gladly accepted Cecilia's suggestion that she spend the night on the living-room sofa. It kept her from having to face the loneliness of her own little house in Talpa.

"Better to please our new client than to waste that good food on snotty old Enderby." Cecilia's face twisted into a comical grimace. "Besides, old Pedro deserves a little high living."

Terry heaved a sigh of pleasure. "It's all working out like some kind of fairy tale. Pedro gets his share of money and recognition; you get enough in commissions to put the Janus Gallery back on its feet."

"It isn't just the commissions. Pedro's work will make the gallery famous. People will come here to see Pedro's carvings. Then they'll stick around to look at David's paintings."

"It's marvelous how things all worked out for the best. But everything happened just in the nick of time. I still think you were taking an awful risk in not accepting that check Neil wanted to give you."

"That was David's decision. I couldn't do anything else but stand by my man," Cecilia replied firmly.

"But it might have meant losing your family home. And all those plans you have for the Janus Gallery—"

"Okay, so what if we lost it?" Cecilia said brusquely. "We'd still be alive. We'd still have each other."

"But to force you to make such a choice. I still think David shouldn't have done that. It was very wrong."

"Look, Terry—" Cecilia set down her cup with a deliberate gesture "—when you love a man the way I love David, right or wrong doesn't matter a hell of a lot. It's like you, falling down that cliff and having

Neil save you. Suppose, instead of Neil, it had been someone you knew was some kind of criminal. You wouldn't pull back your hand just because he was one of the bad guys. You'd have latched onto that rope just the same, knowing it was the only way of saving your life. That's the way things are between me and David. He's like a lifeline to me. I'll put up with any trouble, any disaster, so long as I know I've got him with me.''

Terry was silent a moment. How lucky Cecilia was, bound by this steadfast tie to David, while she was lost and alone—worse than alone, now that she'd known the warmth of Neil's love, and then foolishly lost it.

"Oh, Cecilia,'' she moaned, "I feel so lonely. I wish I had fallen all the way down that mountain.''

"For heaven's sake, Terry, how can you say that? You have a wonderful life, work you love, a rich intelligent boyfriend—''

"But that's the whole point!'' Terry's voice was trembling. "I haven't got Neil. I had him once, but then I got stupid and lost him.'' Grimly she fought back her tears, turning her face away from Cecilia.

Cecilia reached out and gripped her chin, forcing her head around so she could see Terry's tear-filled eyes. "Now listen to me, Terry Morrison. That man is crazy about you. Okay, so you two had some kind of little hassle. I realized that when he came here looking for you. But he wasn't angry, just terribly worried. He wanted to find you, try to straighten things out—''

"He was worried about the campaign, not about

me. That's the only reason he wanted to find me."
Terry's words were flowing out at an uncontrollable
pace, along with the tears flooding down her cheeks.
"Once we beat Southwestern Towers, he's leaving
Taos forever. He says he's fed up with the place, that
everyone here seems to have turned against him—"

"Stop it, Terry. Don't go into hysterics." Cecilia
was holding her, shaking her heaving shoulders.
"Now listen to me a minute. Who is this 'everyone'
you're talking about? You didn't turn against Neil,
did you?"

"Yes, I did, I did." Terry's sobs were growing
louder. "I let him down so terribly. But it's been that
way all along, ever since I met him. I kept distrusting
him—pulling him close, then pushing him away. So
many times he tried to tell me the truth; so many
times I wouldn't even listen."

"So what's new in that? You were following your
usual pattern." Cecilia's brusque words cut through
the fog of emotion, jolting Terry back to a semblance
of calmness. She fixed her tear-swollen eyes on
Cecilia and tried to concentrate on what she was saying.

"Crying's not going to help, Terry. It's up to you
to break out of that dead-end pattern. You've got to
stop burying yourself in that rotten marriage, start
living again, making a life of your own."

"I want to, Cecilia. I want to so desperately. But
Neil is too overwhelming, too much like Paul. I had
one taste of being a cipher, a nothing, living in
the shadow of my husband. I couldn't stand going
through all that again."

Cecilia raised an ironic eyebrow. "So Neil's too strong for you, is he? What kind of man do you want? Would you rather have someone like Skeeter, a really nice guy, so sweet and malleable, who'd let you lead him around by the nose, the way Lenore has been doing? Well, tell me, Terry, is that what you want?"

A pair of images flashed before Terry's eyes— Skeeter's pleading, puppy-dog eyes: "I think we'd be good for each other"; Neil's stern demanding face: "I'm not going to wait forever." With a sinking heart she acknowledged the fact that there was no real choice between them. It had to be Neil for her, Neil Brewster or no one.

"I'd rather have Neil, of course. But why is it always like this? Why do I always fall for men who are too strong for me to handle?"

Cecilia leaned back in her chair with a quizzical smile. "Listen to you, coming on like some shy shrinking violet. You're a pretty tough lady yourself, Miss Morrison. I can't imagine a guy you couldn't handle."

"You don't really know me, Cecilia. You didn't see the way I acted with Paul."

"You're telling the truth there, sweetie." Cecilia leaned forward across the table, looking earnestly into Terry's eyes. "I didn't see you with Paul. For all I know, you could have been just what you claim, a weak driveling idiot, groveling humbly before her indomitable master. But that was a long time ago. I'm seeing you as you are now—strong, self-confident, standing up for what you believe in. Look at the way you confronted that little tyrant from Phoenix. Could some poor spineless female have told him off so superbly?''

Terry grimaced disparagingly. "So superbly I lost the commission. I really messed things up for you and David."

"You didn't mess things up! You were perfectly right to tell him where to get off. I love what you said about insubordinate artists. Why should we leave the big city and come here to Taos if we're going to be pushed around by people with lots of money? Which brings us back to our friends at Southwestern Towers. We've got to start cracking tomorrow if we're going to pull this campaign of ours together."

Terry's forehead furrowed with worry. "You're going ahead with the protest campaign? But Cecilia, what about Ward McKevitt? I know you'll have plenty of money once Pedro's carvings start selling, but what if Ward goes ahead now with the fore-closure?"

A sly smug smile spread over Cecilia's face. "Don't worry. That self-centered boyfriend of yours has already taken care of that little problem." She reached into her apron pocket, took out a piece of paper and laid it on the table in front of Terry.

Terry stared down at it incredulously. "But that can't be Neil's check. He saw you tear it up in front of his eyes."

Cecilia looked a little embarrassed then. "I'm afraid I wasn't quite *that* self-sacrificing. But the atmosphere was so full of melodrama that I just couldn't resist my little theatrical touch."

"So you didn't destroy the check? But Neil said you threw the pieces into the fireplace."

"He saw me throw something." Cecilia's lips quirked into an impish grin. "He didn't know it was only my shopping list. I just happened to have it there in my apron pocket."

Terry gave her a long level look. "So you didn't really have that much faith in David. You were only pretending to let him make the decision."

"I don't see it that way," Cecilia replied defiantly. "It was just because I had so much faith in David that I knew he'd eventually come to the right decision. Once he'd had time to think things over calmly, he'd see there was nothing weak or unmanly in accepting what was only a short-term loan." The impish grin became a full-fledged smile. "Of course, our fantastic new client helped him to see the light a little faster. He's already agreed to accept the replacement check you brought us from Neil."

Terry was flabbergasted. "How did you know I was bringing another check?"

Cecilia chuckled softly. "Honestly, Terry, I sometimes think I know that man a lot better than you do. Once Neil's made a decision, he's not going to stop until he sees it through."

"Once he's made a decision...." Terry was suddenly back in the shadowy bedroom, hearing Neil's whisper close to her ear. "This time you're not going to leave me. You'll never leave me. I'm not going to let you."

Had her lack of faith really canceled out that promise? She remembered the kiss in the car, her sense that it hadn't felt like a real farewell. Besides, Cecilia was right. Neil was the kind of man who would see things through. Whatever his purpose was in Albuquerque, he would surely come back to be in on the campaign's finish. . . .

A tremulous hope began to form. Yes, she was sure of it now. Neil would come back to Taos. Her only problem was how to get him to stay there.

She broke off her meditation, vaguely aware that Cecilia had asked her a question. "Sorry," she said. "I didn't hear what you were saying. All this excitement has got me pretty exhausted."

"That's what I was trying to tell you, Terry, sweetie. It's time you fell into bed. We've got to be up bright and early tomorrow morning. Your boyfriend's ex-girl friend has got our campaign all tied up in knots. We've only got two more days to get it untangled."

CHAPTER TWENTY-TWO

TERRY TURNED HER HEAD to peer nervously toward the back of the meeting room and saw that the last few seats had now been taken. A small group of their supporters had just come in and were forming a standing phalanx against the back wall. She saw some familiar faces and lifted her hand in a comradely gesture.

Cecilia was sitting beside her, wearing one of her colorful skirt-and-tunic outfits. Her eyes were fixed on the long low platform that spanned the front of the room. Six of the nine council members had already taken their places at the conference table, including the chairman, Reuben Abeyta. Some of the men were exchanging joking remarks with each other. The two women sitting together at one end of the table were gravely perusing some official-looking papers.

"What a tremendous turnout," Terry whispered. "Your phone committee must have been very efficient."

She expected an answering smile, but it didn't come. Cecilia looked tense and worried. "That's the easy part—getting them here to the meeting. The question is, will the council listen to them?"

"Surely they'll have to listen," Terry replied apprehensively. "Most of these people are registered voters. They can't ignore the people who put them in office."

"I hope you're right," Cecilia murmured. "But Skeeter's article must have got their backs up. He practically accused them of taking bribes from Southwestern."

"Yes, that was really a shame. And it came out at the worst possible time, the very morning of the council meeting. I'm sure they're not feeling friendly toward the protesters. Let's just hope they can forget their personal feelings and vote on the real issues."

"They may not see the issues the same way we do." Cecilia was looking gloomier by the minute. "I've heard some disturbing feedback from people who've talked to some of the men on the council. They seem to be really impressed by Southwestern's propaganda about all the money and jobs the project would bring into town. You've got to admit that they've done some good PR work—all those expensive brochures, the articles in the Santa Fe paper, those clever TV commercials that look like public-service announcements, and then this business of Ben Montoya. His statement got big play in the Santa Fe media."

"I know we've got problems, Cecilia. But we've also got Paco. I'm sure he'll be able to carry the council with him against Southwestern." She looked ahead toward the first row of seats, where the campaign spokesmen were sitting. Her heartbeat quickened. There was still that empty seat on the right side of Paco. That must mean he was expecting Neil. But who was the gray-haired woman to Paco's left? She started to ask Cecilia, then decided not to disturb her. It was probably Mrs. Cisneros, Lenore's replacement as campaign secretary.

The rest of the row was filled with people she knew: Juan Archuleta, the school superintendent; John Holland, the drugstore owner; Father Haas from the Guadelupe church. Across the aisle sat the Southwestern contingent, a trio of well-groomed young men in citified suits. A slide projector was already in place on a table beside them, aimed at a screen on the platform beside the council table.

Terry looked for Lenore but couldn't find her. She did find Skeeter, though, sitting on his haunches at the end of the row of campaign spokesmen, scribbling away in a notebook, oblivious to the icy looks from the people around him.

Terry turned back to Cecilia. "I still feel we should have approached Montoya again. I wanted to explain about my drawing, but Paco seemed to think that wasn't a good idea."

Her friend didn't answer. She was staring tensely up at the council table. David leaned across in front of her rigid body. "Paco was right. You didn't have any real evidence to take to Montoya. That's why Neil's flown out to L.A., to get more definite proof of Lenore's deception—"

"You're only guessing, David. We don't really know what Neil's up to." Terry shot another glance at the empty seat beside Paco. "It's almost time for the meeting to start, and there isn't a sign of him yet."

David said nothing, only shrugged and leaned back in his chair. His noncommittal attitude annoyed her. Surely he might have said something reassuring. She gazed dully at the people around her, conversing with each other in low intense voices. The feverish enthusiasm that had carried her through the past two days seemed to have faded away, leaving her depressed. She'd been so absurdly pleased with her fence-mending efforts—especially when her explanation of Lenore's ruse had reconciled her with Leo Martinez. She'd done a good job, too, with the architects' committee. Just as she and Neil had guessed, most of them had been sent copies of the phony drawing. And best of all, she'd managed to get through to Paco. It had made her feel really exultant to have him grow friendly again after last Saturday's cool reception, though there was still a strange hint of reserve in his attitude toward her—nothing hostile; she was certain of that—just a glint of quiet amusement, as if he was keeping some secret from her.

She thought it was probably something he'd heard from Neil—at least, she fervently hoped so. That hope had kept her afloat through these two days of hectic campaigning. But now the moment was here, the final foray against Southwestern Towers, the encounter that would decide if they won or lost, and Neil wasn't here to join in the battle. True, that seat was still empty. There was time enough left for him to get here....

Murmurs of curiosity rippled through the crowd. Cecilia's elbow was poking into her ribs. "Look who just came in—Ward McKevitt. Don't tell me that

cagey old schemer's about to come out in the open.''
They watched the pudgy banker walk toward the first
row of seats, expecting him to sit with the Southwestern spokesmen. Instead he turned to his left and
dropped into the empty seat next to Paco.

Terry blinked in bewilderment. David was leaning
forward with a puzzled frown. "Will you look at
that, Cecilia. What is the old buzzard up to now?"

Before Cecilia could answer, the rap of Reuben
Abeyta's gavel called the meeting to order. The
rest of the council members had taken their places.
The whole room was now aglow with electric excitement.

Abeyta paused for a moment, waiting for the
crowd to grow silent. Then his high-pitched nasal
voice sang out from the platform. "I'm glad to see so
many interested citizens here tonight. If no one has
any objections, I suggest we waive the usual order of
business and take up the rezoning proposal recently
submitted to us by Southwestern Towers, a Dallas
development company. As most of you know, our
Santa Fe legislators were so impressed with what this
project would mean to the welfare of Taos that they
arranged for the park commission to sell some of the
state's land in Kit Carson Park.''

"I don't like the way he put that," Cecilia murmured. "Sounds a lot too sympathetic toward Southwestern."

Terry answered with a quick grimace, keeping her
eyes fixed on the council chairman. "However,"
Abeyta was saying, "the final decision was left to
your local council, which, I'm sure you'll agree, is

just how it should be. The future of Taos must remain in the hands of Taoseños."

A chorus of raucous cheers came from a little knot of spectators directly across the aisle from Terry. She turned to survey them with a sinking heart: long hair, ragged beards, an assortment of bizarre decorations—perfect examples of the breed some of the more conservative townspeople referred to disparagingly as "hippies." Some of them were waving placards with anti-Southwestern slogans.

Cecilia frowned grimly. "Where do those idiots think they are? This is no place for sixties-style demonstrations."

Terry caught a sudden glimpse of Skeeter, standing in the midst of the motley group, waving a crudely lettered placard. She decided not to point him out to Cecilia. Her spirits were low enough as it was. She didn't need any more proof of Skeeter's poor judgment.

Abeyta was lecturing the noisy group sternly, telling them they'd be ejected if they interrupted again. One of the bearded men stood up and shouted, "Two-bit politicians!" But before Abeyta could take any action, the protester's companions pulled him back into his seat and urged him to keep his mouth shut.

Terry was uncomfortably aware of disapproving faces all around her, most of them people she knew as campaign supporters. She breathed a sigh of relief as she saw Abeyta turn to the Southwestern spokesmen, inviting them to make their presentation.

They made a very persuasive appeal. The slides of

the building itself were cleverly drawn, avoiding contrast with any nearby structures. The fifteen-story
apartment house seemed to nestle into the landscape,
framed by some vague green blobs designed to make
people think they were cottonwood trees. There were
several slides of construction workers in action,
stressing the many jobs the project would bring to
Taos. The slides of the lavishly furnished apartment
interiors provided a background for describing the
well-heeled tenants who would flow into the town,
enriching its artists and merchants. Several slides
proudly portrayed their landscaping plan—a wading
pool open to Taos toddlers, heavy plantings of lilacs
and rhododendrons, a rosebush hedge surrounding
Kit Carson's grave. As a final touch, they mentioned
the private security force that would make the whole
park safer after nightfall.

As the last spokesman took his seat, Abeyta nodded to him with a friendly smile. "Thanks for that
excellent presentation. You gentlemen seem to understand our local problems."

Terry winced with annoyance. Had Abeyta already
decided to vote for the project? His cordial remarks
pointed in that direction. Ben Montoya's statement
had probably helped to convince him. What a powerful influence that old man wielded!

She forced her straying attention back toward the
front of the room. Paco was on his feet now, beginning his presentation against the proposal. Terry's
hopes began to pick up as she listened. His sincere
low-key manner made a refreshing contrast to the
glib show-biz style of the Southwestern contingent.

"I agree with Chairman Abeyta. Southwestern's proposal is quite impressive. Of course, there are a few drawbacks—like the fact that the jobs they offer aren't the kind Taos needs. The construction jobs are purely temporary, and the permanent jobs, those for maids, custodians, and gardeners, are low-paying jobs without any future.

"But I'm not going to spend my time here tonight stressing the negative side. I'm not going to ride my old hobbyhorse about low water pressure." He paused for the appreciative laughter that followed his remarks. "I'm not going to say nasty things about all those rich strangers who'll come for two weeks and leave, a transient population with no interest at all in solving our local problems. I'm not even going to criticize Southwestern's architecture, with its criminal lack of respect for our old traditions.

"As you young folks say—" he nodded toward the hippie enclave "—I'm not coming here as a put-down artist. I'm going to make a positive counter-proposal—one that will bring us almost the same amount of jobs and money—one based on local needs that won't drain away our water or spoil the looks of our town but will provide for a stable, hardworking population—our own young men and women, people with roots in this community, who need an affordable setting in which to bring up the next generation of Taoseños."

More murmurs swept through the audience. Everyone seemed to be looking at his neighbor, wondering what Paco had up his sleeve. Terry watched him turn to face the Southwestern spokesmen. "Since you gentlemen were so thoughtful as to bring this projector, may I borrow it to show a slide of my own?''

The men, caught by surprise, gave their reluctant agreement. Paco thanked them politely, moved over to the projector and dropped in a slide, then turned on the machine to project the image.

Terry gasped in surprise, staring at that image: her own housing project, the one she'd designed for the land at Llano Quemado, just outside the Taos town boundary! How on earth had it got into Paco's hands? Dazedly she heard him praising its assets— her clever use of difficult terrain, the aesthetic appeal of house sites at varied angles, the solar heat provided by the greenhouses, the water-conserving terraces for the gardens.

A Southwestern spokesman sprang to his feet in protest. ''People of Taos,'' he shouted, ''don't be taken in by this transparent ruse. These agitators have run out of honest objections, so they've dreamed up this amateur notion on the spur of the moment, just to confuse the issue.''

''I beg to correct you, sir.'' Paco's voice was smoothly polite. ''The plan I'm showing you isn't an amateur notion. It was drawn up by a fully qualified architect, someone who's very familiar with local problems. Its author is our brilliant young Taoseña, Miss Teresa Morrison. Stand up, Terry. I want all these people to see you.''

Terry saw hundreds of eyes turning toward her. Reluctantly she rose to her feet, her mind abuzz with speculation. Neil must have stolen that drawing and brought it to Paco. So he was a thief after all, although, admittedly, a thief for a good cause. This must be the reason for Paco's secret amusement she'd found so puzzling.

As she sat back down, Cecilia tugged at her sleeve. "Terry, you sly little fox! Why didn't you tell us?" Her eyes were bright with rekindled hope.

"Don't be absurd, woman." David's voice cut through the surrounding hubbub. "She was right to keep it a secret. If she'd let you know, the news would have been all over town. She had to keep quiet to avoid forewarning Southwestern."

Terry was beset by conflicting emotions. She was pleased to see her pet project being used to challenge Southwestern. But why hadn't Neil and Paco let her in on their plans? Did they share David's wounding assumption that a woman's discretion couldn't be trusted?

The chorus of whispered comments died down a little as another man from Southwestern challenged the crowd. "How do these agitators plan to pay for all this? Their proposal could bankrupt your local treasury."

"I have the answer to that." Ward McKevitt popped up beside Paco, his round red face glowing with partisan zeal. "The money is already pledged. A local citizen is lending it to us. The rents from the houses will eventually pay back his investment—but as a gesture of faith in Taos, he's making the loan without charging any interest."

The Southwestern spokesman smiled incredulously. "Another crackpot notion. These people aren't going to believe that fairy tale. How do we know this benefactor exists? He might be a figment of your imagination.''

"The people here know me a whole lot better than you, sir. They know I've got the bank's assets behind me. If I say we've got the money on those conditions, they know darn well I'm not just whistlin' Dixie.''

Neil must have put up the money. No one else around here could afford that kind of gesture. Terry's mind was racing, adding the facts together. No doubt McKevitt would get a commission for handling the financial arrangements. That would account for his sudden switch of allegiance. Was this what Neil meant by fighting fire with fire?

McKevitt's announcement had triggered a flurry of reactions throughout the room. The council members were conducting hurried conferences with each other. A woman's voice rose imperiously over the hubbub.

"I demand to be recognized, Mr. Chairman.'' Lenore was on her feet, shouting from the back of the hall. "I am the secretary of the protest movement. Ward McKevitt has no authority to speak for us. Our supporters have never been told about this new proposal. Why won't he give us the name of this mysterious benefactor? I ask you, people of Taos, are you going to let some faceless stranger determine your future?''

The glint of battle flared in Paco's eyes. "As you well know, you've been replaced as campaign secretary, Miss Hitchcock. You're a fine one to talk about faceless strangers anyway. You're working for one very important bunch of faceless strangers—the management of Stanton Odessa.''

"Stanton Odessa?" Lenore's assurance faltered a little. Then she squared her shoulders and stared defiantly back at Paco. "Why are you raising all these side issues, Mr. Reyes? I suggest we stick to the Southwestern Towers proposal without dragging in all these distracting red herrings."

"I'm not raising any side issues." Paco's voice, calm and deliberate, cut through the babble of voices, reducing the observers to an uneasy silence. "Stanton Odessa *is* Southwestern Towers. It owns the company, lock, stock and barrel, just like it owns Olympia Tires." He turned away from Lenore to appeal to the council. "Think about it, my fellow townsmen. I'm sure you all remember that big scandal. Olympia was accused of putting out faulty tires, but the company stood its ground and refused to recall them. And six months after all that excitement, our neighbor, Martin Sanchez, died in an accident caused by those faulty tires."

His quiet voice changed to a tone of exhortation. "Who are you going to trust—the strangers whose callous greed killed Martin Sanchez, or the friendly banker we've known for the past ten years?"

"Don't listen to him!" Lenore's voice was harsh and strident. "He's got some underhand motive. He's telling these lies to split our protest movement."

Paco smiled mirthlessly. "You're wrong, Miss Hitchcock. You're the one who's splitting the movement. You're being paid by Southwestern to do that, just the way you used to be paid by Olympia Tires."

Lenore's face went pale. Her eyes flicked nervously around the room. She opened her mouth to shout another protest, but Paco forestalled her, his resonant voice expanding into an angry roar. "And don't you dare deny that! I've got the proof of it here, the photostats of those checks from Olympia." He stepped up to the council table and flung a pile of documents on it. "There's a copy there for each of you honorable council members. Take a look, and then tell me who's doing the lying."

"Don't let his so-called evidence fool you," Lenore cried, an edge of hysteria creeping into her voice. "What he's showing you now are blatant forgeries. But I'm going to tell you the truth he's afraid to reveal. I'm going to tell you the name of this mysterious benefactor. He's a man by the name of Neil Brewster, an outsider who came here a few months ago and forced his way into your town by buying out one of your fine old families. He got into some legal trouble with Terry Morrison, and then when he found he couldn't buy off your honest judges, he bought off Terry instead, by offering to finance her housing project. So think again, fellow Taoseños. Who are you going to trust? Honest businessmen like the men from Southwestern Towers, or this arrogant millionaire with his dubious motives?"

"Lenore made quite a slip that time," David said sotto voce, "coming out with a plug for Southwestern Towers!"

Paco had evidently come to the same conclusion—that Lenore would expose herself more with each word she uttered. He didn't respond to her tirade, simply gave a contemptuous shrug. The gesture seemed to exacerbate Lenore's frenzy.

"I'm sorry to do this," she shouted, "but Paco has forced me to it. I'm going to show you another plan of Neil Brewster's. If you let him get his foot in the door, the next thing you know he'll be doing *this* to your plaza!"

She strode briskly up to the slide projector, removed Paco's slide and dropped in another. A concerted gasp went up from the crowd as the forged composite drawing flashed on the screen.

"Look at that," she declared. "A fourteen-story apartment building right in the midst of your historic plaza. Can all of you read the signature in the right-hand corner? If not, I'll read it for you: Teresa Morrison, that brilliant young architect Paco was praising so highly. What I choose to call her is Neil Brewster's partner in crime."

Paco's lips curved into a grin of pleasure. He looked like a cat about to pounce on a mouse. "I'm glad we've finally got this thing out in the open." He turned toward the council. "In case you don't know this young woman, I'd like to tell you about her. She came here three weeks ago and immediately joined our protest movement. From almost the first day, she's been stirring up dissension among us, making all kinds of rash proposals, turning our supporters against each other. Her crowning touch was this forged drawing she's showing you now."

He paused for a minute, surveying the council members through narrowed eyes. "But this isn't the first time you've seen this drawing, is it? I'm sure each of you has already received a copy. Well, now you know where that copy came from—this paid employee of Southwestern Towers's parent company.''

"You're lying!" Lenore denied hotly. "You can't tell us that signature is a forgery. I can bring a hand-writing expert to prove this is Terry's drawing.''

"I'm not denying that Terry designed that build-ing," Paco said matter-of-factly. "It won first prize in a student contest—six years ago, out in California. A copy of it was kept in the university library—the copy you found and xeroxed, Miss Hitchcock, the copy that served as a basis for some other draftsman to draw in the plaza buildings around it.''

"That's lies, all lies! You can't possibly prove it.''

"Oh, yes, we can!" Paco nodded toward the first row of seats. "Miss Turner, please come up and stand beside me.'' The gray-haired woman who had been sitting beside him promptly got to her feet and joined him at the council table. "Now, will you please tell our council members where you're em-ployed?''

"Certainly, Mr. Reyes. My name is Elizabeth Turner. I'm a librarian at the UCLA library—specifically, in the architecture department.''

"Thank you, Miss Turner. Now suppose you show the council that book you brought with you.''

"Let me describe it first. Then the council mem-bers can examine it for themselves.'' She held up the large black ledger she was carrying. "We keep a register of all withdrawals from our department's ar-chives.'' She opened the book to a page where she'd placed a marker. "This is the page for June 6th of this year. The fourth signature from the top is that of Lenore Hitchcock.''

Terry followed Paco's gaze back toward Lenore. The dark-haired woman had sunk back down into her chair, white faced and shaken. "Just to anticipate any objection," he purred smoothly, turning back toward the council, "we have had this signature checked by a handwriting expert. The signature in this book matches that in Miss Hitchcock's local bank-account file. It also matches the endorsements on those checks from Olympia Tires.

"So I say what I said when we started this campaign. We aren't going to fall for these underhanded tactics. We're going to stick together, we Taoseños, and show Southwestern Towers they can't destroy the town we love."

The crowded room broke out into noisy cheers. The chairman pounded his gavel, trying vainly to make himself heard above the uproar. Terry, cheering along with the rest, felt Cecilia suddenly clutch her arm. "Look, sweetie, look! Two rows behind you!"

Her heart leaped as she stared where Cecilia was pointing. There was no mistaking that leonine figure. Ben Montoya was on his feet, waiting calmly to get the chairman's attention. She felt herself going rigid with apprehension. What was the powerful old man about to say? Had this new evidence convinced him of her good faith? Or would he try to tilt the scales against Paco?

She didn't have long to wait. As soon as the audience noticed Montoya standing, the cheers gave way to a rapt attentive silence. At the chairman's respectful signal, Montoya's voice boomed out into the room. "I want to thank Paco Reyes for performing a public service. He has opened all our eyes to Southwestern's deceptive tactics. I owe an apology to my fellow townsmen for the statement I made in support of that gang of schemers. In my considered opinion, these Texans have forfeited any right to a hearing. The only good thing about this distasteful business is the new opportunity it has brought to our county. I am greatly impressed by Miss Morrison's professional skill. I've been advised by people within my own family of her sympathy for the needs of our young married couples. I hope she'll be given the chance to extend her good work through this new housing project."

The old man nodded and returned to his seat, apparently oblivious to the clamor rising around him. Cecilia was gleefully shaking her arm. "You've done it, Terry, you've done it. After that testimonial, no one will vote against you."

Terry's eyes were fixed on the council table. The members were conferring together in hurried whispers. Then Chairman Abeyta stood up and rapped his gavel. A hush fell over the crowded room.

"The chairman will entertain a motion to table Southwestern's proposal until the next meeting. In the meantime, I suggest we form a committee with members drawn from both our council and the county commission to consider the merits of the project in Llano Quemado. I sincerely hope that Mr. Ben Montoya will accept the job of chairing this committee."

Terry swiveled to look at Montoya. The stern old face had relaxed in a dignified smile. "I accept with the greatest pleasure.'' Another cheer went up from the crowd around her, but Terry herself was rendered speechless by the hectic pace of events. The motion to table was then passed by a unanimous vote of the council members.

As the chairman adjourned the meeting, a final triumphant shout rose from the campaign supporters, who then broke up into little clusters, excitedly discussing the events of the evening. A knot of beaming well-wishers formed around Terry, congratulating her on her victory. Over their shoulders, she caught a brief glimpse of Lenore pushing her way toward the exit, her face a stony mask.

Ward McKevitt's round rosy face loomed up beside her. He reached for her hand, pumping it up and down heartily. ''Congratulations, Terry.'' His voice dropped to a low confidential note. ''Sorry about our little misunderstanding. I wanted to call you last night and let you know it was all a mistake, but our mutual friend, Mr. Brewster, put his foot down— said he wanted to wait till tonight and surprise you.'' Observing her confusion, he added, ''Looks like he succeeded in doing that.''

''Tonight has been full of surprises,'' Terry said meaningfully. ''Like gaining you as a convert to low-cost housing. If we do get to work together on building my project, I'm sure you'll find it a very rewarding experience.''

McKevitt blinked confusedly, then turned away without answering. Terry's moment of triumph quickly gave way to dejection. So Neil had been here in Taos last night. He'd brought the librarian with him, had made his deal with McKevitt. Where was he now, then? Why hadn't he come to the meeting? With Southwestern's defeat assured, had he already carried through on that threat to leave Taos forever?

She started pushing her way toward the exit, feeling exhausted and empty, not elated, as she knew she should be. "The impossible dream," she'd called it. Thanks to Neil, that dream was about to come true. But now he wasn't here to share it with her.

"It isn't fair. It isn't fair at all." Terry wasn't aware that she'd spoken aloud until she saw the strange look Cecilia gave her.

"What's the matter, Terry? Don't you feel well? You look like death warmed over."

"It's all this excitement, I guess—makes me feel kind of dizzy. I'd better get home now, Cecilia. Tell everyone I'll see them tomorrow."

"But, sweetie, you've got to talk to Ben Montoya. After that great testimonial—"

But Terry had already left her behind in the milling crowd. Just as she reached the rear exit, she felt a hand on her shoulder. She looked up into Skeeter's mournful face. "I want to apologize, Terry." The boyish eyes were dark with pain. "I've been such a stupid cluck, letting Lenore fool me like that."

"Don't blame yourself too much, Skeeter. Remember, she fooled me, too. We were both taken in by an expert con job."

Skeeter nodded grimly. "There's someone else I ought to apologize to. I really lighted into Neil Brewster that night at Lenore's house—called him a playboy, a dabbler, a rich dilettante. But after that offer of his, I've got to admit he really cares about Taos." His face softened into a wistful smile. "Will you tell him that, Terry, the next time you see him? I think it's the time to tell you, too, that you were right to hesitate about us. But something tells me you and Neil could make it."

Terry stared at him for a moment in stricken silence. *It's too late now, Skeeter.* The words were pounding somewhere deep in her brain. *I'm never going to see Neil, never again in my long lonely life.*

Blindly she turned away and plunged through the doorway. By the time the tears broke through her steely control, she was safe in the Jeep she'd borrowed from Gus Pickett, heading down toward her house in Talpa.

CHAPTER TWENTY-THREE

As she eased the Jeep into her driveway, she blinked in dismay. Why had she left all the lights on in her living room? Her frazzled emotional state must be making her absentminded.

Jumping out of the Jeep, she walked quickly toward the house. The lighted windows seemed like an invitation, welcoming her to a comforting world of warmth and brightness. But they brought no comfort to Terry. She knew the aching emptiness that lay behind them. In her mind's eye, she saw Neil's rugged features lighted by the glowing embers. Again she heard him say, "When I came through that door tonight, I felt I was coming home...." Impatiently she brushed the memory away. It was time to get rid of all those useless daydreams, too—to get on with her life.

She opened the door and stepped across the threshold. A tall lithe figure rose from the sofa. "Hello, Terry," Neil said. "You really should learn to lock your doors. You could let in all sorts of undesirable strangers."

Terry's mouth was dry, her jaw stiff. "Undesirable?" she finally managed to murmur. "That's not exactly the way I'd put it."

She stared at him tremulously for a moment, not knowing whether to laugh or cry. Then his arms were around her, holding her close, the warmth of his body healing the aching void within her, his hands moving over her flesh, reacquainting themselves with all her most secret places, his lips on hers, urgent, compelling. There was no need for words.

Clinging together, they sank down onto the sofa. She reveled in the feel of his heavy torso pressing down on her tingling breasts, his thrusting knee parting her long slender legs. Hungry to touch his bare flesh, her frantic hands tore at his clothing. She could feel the tide of desire pounding within her as he helped to strip the last garments from both of their bodies. Then her hands were moving over his muscular shoulders, caressing the planes of his back, trailing down across his buttocks, squeezing the hard backs of his thighs. Raising his torso a little, he cupped her aching breasts in firm sure hands, kneading them softly, then lowering his mouth to her hardened nipples. Convulsively her body arched up to meet his, her head thrown back, her mouth opening in a moan of agonized pleasure.

The sound seemed to spur Neil on to new levels of frenzy. He pulled her close again, wrapping his arms around her, his hips pressing down on hers in sinuous motion. Searing heat inflamed her loins as she writhed against him. A fierce uncontrollable hunger clamored inside her, blotting out the past, obliterating the future, leaving only this one burning moment of utter sureness. This time no force on earth could stop them from merging completely with each other.

With a little gasp, she lifted her legs apart to welcome him and felt the unutterable joy of his loving warmth deep within her. They lay quietly for an instant, each savoring this long-awaited moment of coming together. Then, slowly, he began moving again, each deliberate thrust adding strength to the wave that was cresting in Terry's body. Her own hips picked up his rhythm, rising to meet him, urging him on to a faster and faster pace. Her nails digging into his back, his hands cupping her buttocks, they raced together through endless timeless space, swept along on wave after wave of inexorable passion.

Suddenly Neil moaned and clutched her tight against his shuddering body. At that instant, the wave within her finally crested, crested and broke, dashing her into a thousand fragments of ecstatic sensation, then ebbing slowly away, leaving her glowing softly, secure at last on the peaceful shore.

When she came back to earth, she found she was lying next to him on the sofa as he tenderly stroked her hair, watching the firelight flicker across her face. When he saw her looking at him, his face crumpled into a rueful grin. "That's not in the script, you know. You shouldn't be smiling. You should be denouncing me in a series of stinging incandescent phrases."

"Denouncing you?" Terry sighed. "Why on earth would I want to denounce you?"

"I can think of all sorts of reasons. For my general arrogance, my cavalier use of money to get what I want, for stealing the plans of your housing project and presenting them to the public without even asking your permission. You could have the law on me, you know. Burglary's still a crime, even here in hospitable Taos.''

She smiled impishly. ''That's a pretty dangerous suggestion. The last time I took you to court, you didn't do well at all.''

''That was three long weeks ago, when I was a stranger in town. Since then, I've become a genuine Taoseño.''

''Oh, yes, Neil, you have!'' Terry raised herself on one elbow and gazed down at him in earnest entreaty. ''You can't give up on this place just because some people acted a little unfriendly. People turned cold on me, too, but deep down we were friends all the time. Isn't that one of the marks of genuine friendship? You can weather periods of anger, differences of opinion—''

''Terry, my sweet, you're preaching to the converted.'' Neil's eyes were lit with tender amusement. ''Nothing on earth could drag me away from Taos.''

''You're not going away? But you said—that morning at Midnight?''

Neil tensed at the reminder. ''I said a lot of stupid things that morning. But that was before I almost lost you. When I saw you there on that ledge, with only a few crumbling rocks between you and destruction, I suddenly knew I couldn't go on living without you.''

The tense serious look gave way to a teasing smile. ''Besides, you know what an old-fashioned person I am. I still think husbands and wives should live together. And since you've been so unwise as to saddle yourself with a job that will keep you here for the next two years—"

"Me saddle myself!" She lifted her chin in mock anger. "There you go with your usual arrogant statements. Maybe I ought to take you to court after all."

"There's only one answer to that. We'd better get married fast, so you won't be allowed to testify against me. I wish your old southern colonel were here right this minute." His arms closed around her, drawing her against him. She felt his lips moving over her neck, across her cheekbone. A wave of exhilaration flooded through her. Once more she felt the sense of peace and safety she'd felt in Neil's little bedroom.

"So do I," she said in a dreamy voice. "But poor refugees like us have to put up with a lot of makeshifts. I'm sure we'll manage to find a good substitute."

"Refugees no longer." Neil's hands were stroking her softly, sending a new flood of warmth through her limbs. "We've found a home for the rest of our lives."

"Yes, Neil," Terry murmured. "After all those false starts and disappointments, we've found the perfect home—our love for each other."

SUPERROMANCE

Longer, exciting, sensuous and dramatic!

Fascinating love stories that will hold
you in their magical spell till the last page
is turned!

Now's your chance to discover the earlier
books in this exciting series. Choose from
the great selection on the following page!

Now's your chance to discover the earlier
books in this exciting series.

Choose from this list of great

SUPERROMANCES!

SUPERROMANCE

Complete and mail this coupon today!

- -

Worldwide Reader Service

In the U.S.A.
1440 South Priest Drive
Tempe, AZ 85281

In Canada
649 Ontario Street
Stratford, Ontario N5A 6W2

Please send me the following SUPERROMANCES. I am enclosing my check or money order for $2.50 for each copy ordered, plus 75¢ to cover postage and handling.

☐ # 26	☐ # 32	☐ # 38
☐ # 27	☐ # 33	☐ # 39
☐ # 28	☐ # 34	☐ # 40
☐ # 29	☐ # 35	☐ # 41
☐ # 30	☐ # 36	
☐ # 31	☐ # 37	

Number of copies checked @ $2.50 each = $_____
N.Y. and Ariz. residents add appropriate sales tax $_____
Postage and handling $_____.75
                                              TOTAL $_____

I enclose _____
(Please send check or money order. We cannot be responsible for cash sent through the mail.)
Prices subject to change without notice. Offer expires November 30, 1983

NAME_____
                         (Please Print)
ADDRESS_____APT. NO._____
CITY_____
STATE/PROV._____
ZIP/POSTAL CODE_____

305560000C

Share the joys and sorrows
of real-life love in the new
Harlequin American Romances! ®T.M.

GET THIS BOOK
FREE as your introduction to
Harlequin American Romances —
an exciting new series of
romance novels written
especially for the North American
woman of today.

Mail to:
Harlequin Reader Service

In the U.S.
1440 South Priest Drive
Tempe, AZ 85281

In Canada
649 Ontario Street
Stratford, Ontario N5A 6W2

YES! I want to be one of the first to discover the new
Harlequin American Romances. Send me FREE and without
obligation *Twice in a Lifetime.* If you do not hear from me after I
have examined my FREE book, please send me the 4 new
Harlequin American Romances each month as soon as they
come off the presses. I understand that I will be billed only $2.25
for each book (total $9.00). There are no shipping or handling
charges. There is no minimum number of books that I have to
purchase. In fact, I may cancel this arrangement at any time.
Twice in a Lifetime is mine to keep as a FREE gift, even if I do not
buy any additional books.

Name _____ (please print)

Address _____ Apt. no. _____

City _____ State/Prov. _____ Zip/Postal Code _____

Signature (If under 18, parent or guardian must sign.)